Death on the High Route

Death on the High Route

A Novel

Ken Stichter

iUniverse, Inc.
New York Lincoln Shanghai

Death on the High Route
A Novel

iUniverse books may be ordered through booksellers or by contacting:

iUniverse
2021 Pine Lake Road, Suite 100
Lincoln, NE 68512
www.iuniverse.com
1-800-Authors (1-800-288-4677)

ISBN: 978-0-595-42874-8 (pbk)
ISBN: 978-0-595-87213-8 (ebk)

Printed in the United States of America

For Julie Ann—wife, best friend, and partner in many wanderings.

Acknowledgements

The results of a labor of love come not without sacrifices and support. On both accounts, *Death on the High Route* is no exception. It could not have been written without the encouragement of others.

My good fortune has been a wealth of outdoor experience which began early in my life as a result of my father's interests. My childhood was filled with fishing, camping and backpacking adventures in the Eastern Sierra. As an adult I have continued this adventure with my wife and kids and friends.

I am indebted to the many historians and writers whose work has focused on the Eastern Sierra. Also, I found local Owens Valley sources such as the Paiute Shoshone Indian Cultural Center, Eastern California Museum, Manzanar National Historic Site, and the Inyo Register to be helpful.

Thanks also go to my many backpacking friends, especially James, and to Ron, Phil, and all members of my family who wandered with me on many a trek into the Sierra Nevada over a period of fifty years.

Reading and feedback on the many iterations of the manuscript were provided by several people—Todd, James, Christy, Phil, Nancy, Greg, and Julie. Todd's editing, suggestions, and assistance with graphics were most useful. Thanks to all.

Finally, thank you to my wife Julie Ann and our three kids—Mark, Todd and Jennifer. Without your, love, confidence, and interest I would not have been inclined to write.

Eastern Sierra and the Owens Valley

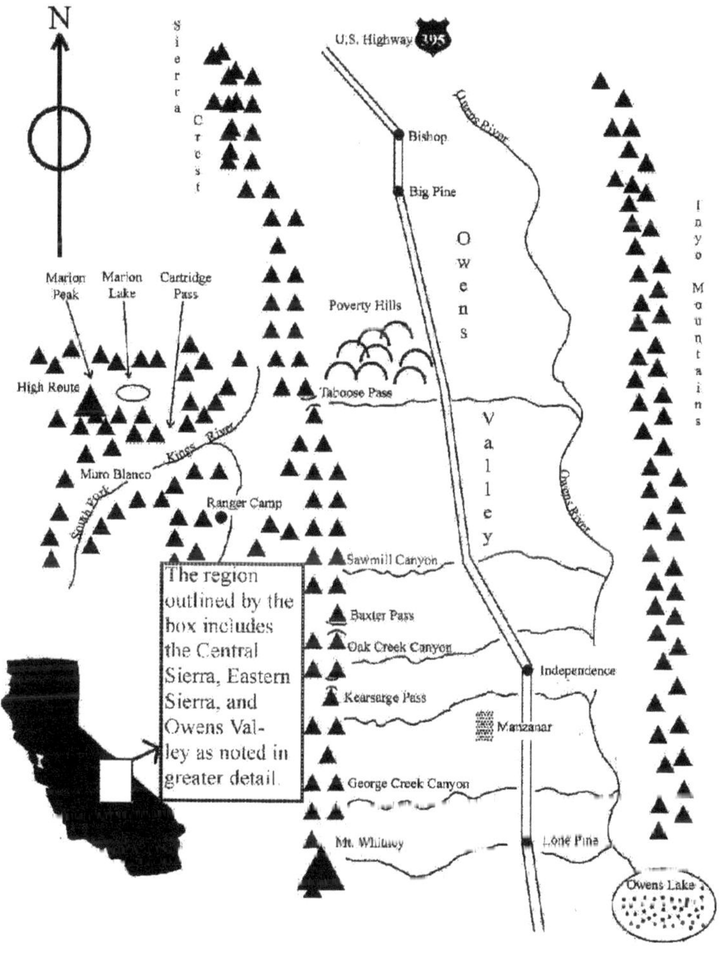

Chapter 1

Finding the Remains

At a point near the southern end of the High Route, in the heart of the Sierra Nevada,
at 11,400 feet on the North Slope of Marion Peak in August

Rob just stood there staring. Relieving himself and staring at the skull. He had seen dead bodies before, but this was different. It was a skeleton, or what seemed to be most of a human skeleton. There were remnants of clothing. The boots were very weathered, the bones protruding from what was left of the gaiters, and there appeared to be a belt. Everything else was shredded. Shredded and faded bits of clothing altered but recognizable; suggested the outfit worn at the time of death. But it was the shoulder blade that drew his stare. An ice axe, the old wooden shaft variety, with the 'pick' of the axe slanting into the body cavity, was resting against the shoulder blade. The stark reality on first glance was that this pick could have once penetrated the flesh of the victim's back.

Several feet down slope Sti was oblivious to the find. He was studying the shafts of sunlight that drilled through the dark clouds of the impending storm. The rays struck the terrain randomly to create a checkerboard of dark and light granite across the landscape. A windy, cold, and wet conclusion to this day of hiking would soon be at hand. Sti knew they would need to find a suitable camp site soon.

Rob wanted to call out to his hiking partner, but decided to say nothing until he finished. Then, zipping his pants, and turning, he summoned Sti. "Take a look at this."

"Whad ya find?" was Sti's response as he turned from photographing the view across the valley and moved towards Rob who was standing amidst a group of waist high boulders some twenty feet up slope.

Rob was again staring. "It's a human skeleton. You won't believe it." At 11,000 feet, one does not move quickly up hill with a full backpack, and Rob continued to describe what he was looking at while he waited. "There is an ice axe beneath the right shoulder blade. This guy had some kind of accident." He stood aside as Sti approached.

"Whoa!" Sti's reaction was all surprise. Then there was silence as they both studied the skeletal remains that lay on the bed of broken rocks, gravel, and decomposed granite a couple of feet up slope from them.

The two hikers knew each other well. They had spent many days each summer hiking together in the Sierra Nevada Mountains of California. Over the years they had encountered many unique experiences in the backcountry. On several occasions they had endured significant hardships on a hike. A couple of times, they confronted serious danger. But, always, they kept their wits about them. This occasion was no different. They were both content to study the find for many seconds before discussing their observations.

Sti broke the silence. "A she!"

"What's that?" Rob responded without looking up.

"I think it was a female ranger." Sti was probing what appeared to be the sleeve of a shirt with the point of a hiking stick. "This looks like the remains of a U.S. National Park Service patch." Indeed, as Sti reached down and cleaned the dirt away from the patch, the owner's profession was clearly identified.

Removing packs some ten feet away, they returned for a closer look. The reference to "she" was a historical recollection. She had been a National Park Service ranger, and with Sti's comment they both knew who the victim was.

Rob remembered the name first. "You think this was Harris? Wasn't her name Harris, something like June or Jennifer Harris?"

"Yeah," Sti responded, "I think it was June. Disappeared a couple of summers ago, I think. There was a write up in the L. A. Times. She was on patrol and never returned. If I am not mistaken, when she was discovered missing, one of those summer storms hampered search operations for several days. Didn't we see a poster alerting hikers to her disappearance at the Taboose Creek trail head a couple of months later."

Rob's comments added more history. "And when we ran across the back country ranger station along the creek coming down from Lake Marjorie, Harris's replacement had been there only a few weeks and said they had no idea of her whereabouts. She just disappeared. Strange! You'd think it would be standard operating procedure for rangers to log something like a flight plan before heading out on a long day hike or at least on an over night patrol."

"This is a long ways from her backcountry station" was Sti's response. "Even without a pack, it is a good two days of hiking to the back country ranger station in bad weather." Silence again, and then, "But, you and I both know this was a strange accident. She, if it was Harris, was either killed by someone, or she killed herself accidentally." There was a lull in the conversation. "Exposure, severe sprain, sickness, or some other calamity perhaps." Another long pause. "You think she could have fallen on that ice axe?"

Rob questioned. "In her back? There is no way you can drive an ice axe through the flesh of your back unless you have a very unconventional fall, and I do not see anything that she could have fallen from. The only other way is for someone to drive it into you from behind. Gee! How brutal can you get? Somebody killing you with an ice axe."

Studying the body and the ice axe, Sti commented on the assumption. "We're assuming it was her ice axe."

Rob was squatting now, taking a closer look. Pieces of weathered cloth, leather, and undistinguishable artifacts were scattered about. "You know, we have seen many pieces of cloth, canvas, and nylon that have weathered exposure in the Sierra for several years, but some of this material looks like it has been here for much more than a couple of years. Some of it looks like it is leather and heavy canvas that has been here for a long time. It doesn't fit. Or am I wrong? Look at this," he held up a piece of what looked like leather, and Sti took it from his hand.

"Yeah, looks more than two years old to me." It was hard to tell just what it was that they were looking at. They were also reluctant to touch or move many objects. Sti laid the piece back where Rob had picked it up, and was now down on all fours, as if a closer look would tell him more. But his close inspection was short lived, and he stood up and took a step or two to the side to survey the scene from a wider perspective. And then he noticed that there were bits and pieces of cloth or what ever they were, scattered about in a wide area some distance from the human remains. Some pieces were ten or more feet away. He pointed this out to Rob and the two retraced their steps backward to look around.

The strange leather and old oil canvas pieces had to have been in the possession of the ranger at her death. That these items should be here for any other reason was just not probable. This was a conclusion reached independently by the two hikers. So alike were they in their thinking that verbalization of this reality was not necessary.

Finding weathered odds and ends in the Sierra backcountry is common along established trails and at traditional camp sites. Despite efforts to encourage low impact use of the backcountry, day hikers, fishermen, backpackers, and packers with stock have steadily contributed to a growing presence of "trail trash." In some areas, where early miners probed the earth for gold, silver, or tungsten, more prominent artifacts can be found. And on rare occasions, vary rare occasions, Native American artifacts have been found. But the latter are usually arrow and spear heads found in the valleys where game were hunted. However, the idea of finding artifacts of any kind at 11,000 feet in an area with no trail within miles was alien to the two experienced hikers.

Several minutes later, after they had exchanged information about how widely scattered things were, Sti sat down on a rock, and sized up the situation. "Well, this sort of changes everything. I guess we had better decide what's next. Can't go ahead with our original plans, can we?" They both knew the answer.

Time passed. Both backpackers were immersed in their own thoughts.

Chapter 2

The Quake of 1872

Owens Valley, California, March 2

At 2:30 AM, on Tuesday, the second day of March, a large earthquake shook the young pioneer town of Lone Pine, California. Located on the East Side of the Sierra, the community of Lone Pine then, as now, sits on the western edge of the Owens Valley, and in the evening shadow of the continental United States' tallest mountain. At 14,495 feet, Mt. Whitney is some 10,000 feet above the town and a few miles west. The Owens Valley and surrounding countryside has a long geological history of volcanic and earthquake activity. The quake was just one of the innumerable natural calamities that have beset the area since long before humans were on the scene. No quake since 1872 has been as strong or as damaging in this region.

What made the March 2, 1872 quake significant was that it leveled much of the town and took the lives of 27 people. When the shaking stopped, Mt. Whitney was twelve feet higher above the valley floor and a new 20-foot escarpment just west and north of the town was lasting testimony to the power of Nature. The escarpment that this quake made is visible today to travelers along U.S. Highway 395.

* * * *

On Sunday, five days after the earthquake, while many of the surviving residents of Lone Pine and surrounding communities paid tribute to 16 of their citizens recently laid to rest in a mass grave on a small hillside just north of what was left of the town, a lone Paiute Indian woman wandered into the community. Quiet, but visibly weathered and near exhaustion, the woman was in search of food supplies. The quake had taken its toll up and down the valley and no one expected the local Indians were immune to its ravages. The fact that it was still winter in the valley made survival amidst the destruction, even more difficult.

If the Indian woman was not alone in her needs, she was alone in her method of payment. Many people from the nearby mining communities of Cerro Gordo, Darwin, Candelaria, and Montgomery were in need of food and Lone Pine was a small trade center where local farmers could sell their goods through one of the several merchants. Quietly, without drawing attention to herself or her plight, she approached a merchant known to be kind to the local Indians. She wanted flour and corn meal, and she paid with gold—small pieces of solid gold. And then, with sacks of flour and meal resting in her conical shaped "burden basket" strapped to her back, she disappeared, walking north and west as quietly and unnoticed as she had entered the town.

But her gold payment did not go unnoticed. She had insisted the merchant accept more in gold than her purchase was worth. She gave him the nuggets and left, never to be seen again.

Within a week of the quake, similar transactions took place in small towns, crossroads and farms up and down the Owens Valley. Places such as Independence, Big Pine, Laws, and Bishop were visited. In each instance, the merchant was known to be friendly to Indians and was paid with gold nuggets worth many times more than the value of the flour, corn meal, and other stores purchased. Again, in each instance, the Paiute Indian was a female who departed quickly and was never seen again.

Within days, the news of the Indians trading with gold nuggets was known to all those who lived in and about the valley. There was great speculation, and rumors of course, about the origin of the gold, but even the knowledgeable miners could not begin to answer the questions. For weeks, every Indian in the valley was suspect, and it was thought that by closely monitoring them, the whereabouts of the source of the nuggets could be discovered. Some Indians, especially the women, were followed and spied on, but to no avail. In time, the residents of the Owens Valley realized that even many of the local Indians that were known to residents did not know anything about the origins of the nuggets. They appeared to not even know the Indian women who traded with the nuggets. It was as if the gold nugget trading Indians were of another, unknown Paiute tribe within the valley who needed emergency supplies at any price, skillfully sought out and acquired what they needed, and then just disappeared. No one ever saw any of them again.

That the Indians had traded with gold nuggets was strange enough. Gold nuggets were not something one expected to see in the Owens Valley. Mining on the south-east side of the Sierra had never produced the treasure trove of gold nuggets found in many of the streams and mines of the west side of the mountains. But more importantly, the nuggets were not typical. Most valley residents considered typical nuggets to be worn smooth in streams and with no jagged edges. These nuggets were different; they did not come from streams. A local prospector living near Aberdeen described them more aptly as "chunks of gold."

CHAPTER 3

LATER ON DISCOVERY DAY

A flat spot amidst a sea of boulders, gravel, and tundra

They set up camp a couple hundred yards from the ranger's remains. It was the only decent spot around. The chosen site featured a bed of decomposed granite—a sandy gravel-like material that results when granite weathers and breaks down. A storm was coming and the site would drain the rainwater well. It was a site just big enough for their tent. Boulders, smaller rocks, and tufts of grass surrounded this small platform on the northwestern slopes of Cirque Crest. Were it sunny, Marion Peak would have dominated the skyline, but its 12,719-foot summit disappeared into the clouds at about the 11,600-foot level. It had been raining on and off all day. In fact, it had been raining on and off for the last four days, and it was about to rain again. At the five thousand-foot trailhead where this trip had started four days ago, the rain was of little consequence, a nuisance really. Today, at eleven thousand feet, it was cold. To the rain and the dropping temperature at night would be added the wind that would move up and down the canyon as nature sought to find equilibrium between thermal layers.

The environment here was classic Sierra alpine. No trees! Just granite! Everywhere, granite, interspersed with hardy alpine grasses and an occasional patch of snow tucked into the shade of large granite boulders or hugging the north-facing slopes of ridges or peaks. With the continuous rain over several days, small rills of runoff were everywhere, adding to the small perennial alpine creeks that were numerous and swollen at the lower elevations. The water seemed to saturate every depression or flat spot before moving on. This was a cold, damp, barren and spectacular environment. Its ruggedness was visible in every direction. This was the heart of what cross-country backpackers in the Sierra called the High Route.

To those who visited these alpine environments, the beauty was unmatched. But the beauty belied the potential for disaster. This was not a place to be caught unprepared when the weather changed for the worse. Without the proper equipment and knowledge regarding survival, even in the middle of the summer, death stalks the weary and uninitiated. Here, at eleven thousand feet in the middle of the Sierra Nevada, one was exposed and vulnerable to the effects of simple mistakes. It was only three in the afternoon, but the cloud cover made it seem much later. It would be a long wet and cold evening before nightfall, and now was the time to prepare. What would be rain at lower elevations could turn to snow at this altitude, even in July. And then there was always the possibility of electrical storms. Exposed on this granite slope, a lightening storm could spell disaster for even the most experienced hiker or climber. Traveling through this region during daylight hours in rainy and cold weather is challenging enough. Ensuring a comfortable night during which the rain could fall continuously and the temperature could drop to freezing, required attention to detail. This was not an environment for the casual backpacker with limited knowledge. Conditions here required experience and good judgment.

* * * *

Sti and Rob went about setting up camp with a routine that reflected their experience. The selection of the site, positioning of the expedition type dome tent, and the storage of gear was testimony to their philosophy of planning for the worst. Their conversation was sparse. They each knew what needed to be done. They also knew that adequate preparation required teamwork. Backpackers of their experience usually harbor a strong self esteem, and a belief that they can survive anything Nature can throw at them, but not without preparation. And yet, they silently welcomed the occasional comment or recommendation of the other. This trust and respect for the opinion of each other was important in times where judgment left little room for error. This give and take relationship was one reason Sti and Rob were good friends and why they had shared many successful backpack trips in even the most miserable of conditions.

The tent was a Northface VE-25, more than enough tent for these conditions. It had a lot of miles on it and had served them well Sti thought as he stored his gear inside. They had been at a much lower elevation and in a much more protected area last night when the rain was steady for about eight hours. Tonight would be different, but they were prepared. Then, he turned his attention to setting up a place for the small, but efficient, MSR stove. The wind was already making its presence known and the rain would not be far behind. Somewhere among the boulders, where the stove would be sheltered from the wind, was preferable.

Rob was off pumping some water from a small rivulet that had, over many years, cut a channel through some soft grass impacted alpine tuft. They had not always used a pump to obtain water in the Sierra. However, the alternative to pumping was to gamble that one would not get *giardia*, microscopic protozoa that did not originate in the Sierra, but was probably introduced by cattle or other animals. Nevertheless, these small protozoa could make your life miserable if you were foolish enough to drink water contaminated by its presence. Both Sti and Rob knew other backpackers who thought drinking from an alpine cascade was safe, only to contract the intestinal effects of *giardia* six weeks later. It was easy to be safe, and Rob, by default, had become the keeper of the pump.

Although a necessity, pumping water was tedious, and Rob reflected back over the day's events. They had been on the trail for four wet and cold days, and their plan called for four more days of mostly fun and down hill hiking that would take them to the Copper Creek trail head in Kings Canyon National Park. The weather had been unexpected. Rob had begun to reason that it was not likely to last four more days, and he had expected the trip would end with at least some sun. Both he and Sti were hoping that the weather would let up when they got to the Horseshoe Lakes. There was good fishing in the larger lake. They had looked forward to replicating the success they had at Horseshoe Lake on previous occasions. But today's discovery had changed things.

Rob knew that later they would discuss the alternatives. They had to contact the National Park Service. The logical and probably quickest way to do so would be to return to the backcountry ranger camp where the John Muir Trail and the

Bench Lake Trail intersect. The ranger there had the communication equipment needed to contact the officials at Kings Canyon and send the necessary personnel to retrieve the remains. If the weather stabilized, or better yet, if the rain stopped, they could probably make it in one long day. Logic with this option depended on one unknown. Would the backcountry ranger be at the station? Such rangers were often on the trail all day and sometimes an extended patrol took them out overnight. If it was the ranger's day off, who knows where he or she might be. When they had stopped by the station two days ago, the ranger was nowhere to be found. If they opted for this choice and the ranger was not there, they would either wait, or hike on out to the Taboose Pass trail head and drive to Aberdeen and call the Forest Service. The latter would require an additional long and arduous day of hiking.

If the decision was to hike to Kings Canyon, it could be done in two very demanding days of hiking. Either way it was at least two days to get out. In the rain the hiking would be slow. It would grind them down. It would be exhausting. Without the rain, it would be little better. The first day in both cases would be hiking without a trail. If the decision was to retrace their route, the unimproved trail on the south-facing slope below Cartridge Pass would run more like a creek than a path for hikers. Add the fifty-pound pack each was carrying into the picture and you have the recipe for a physical meltdown for a sixty year old backpacker regardless of experience and conditioning. These were Rob's thoughts as he returned to camp. Sti was already heating the last of their bottled water, and Rob's acquisition would replenish the supply.

Sti spoke first. "What was she doing up here Rob? I keep wondering. Why would she have ventured this far from her station? It does not make sense when you consider that the weather had been very bad for several days before and during the time she disappeared. Surely there were hikers in the immediate vicinity of the backcountry station or at Bench Lake who needed monitoring. In view of the weather, she had good reason to stay put and lend assistance if needed." Although these questions were being analyzed and processed over and over in Sti's mind for the last hour, he was also not without some humor when thinking and talking out loud to Rob. "Ah well, who knows what lurks in the mind of a back country ranger. Maybe she had a secret rendezvous up here with some mountaineering lover."

"Or, maybe, like you, she just liked to wander," was Rob's offhanded remark.

"Give me a break." It was a stock response from Sti.

"No, no! Think about it, you have done that. We both have done it."

"Done what?"

"Wandered off and lost track of time. Found ourselves somewhere else because we were so absorbed in wandering and looking that we did not realize how far we had come. Remember that time in the Anza Borego desert back in the seventies when we left the wives and the kids about mid day and went off for what we assured them was just a short hike. Every time we thought about returning we determined that we would go just a little further. After about six miles we decided to not turn around but to detour over to that rock house and return by another route. It was dark before we returned, we had lost track of time."

"Yea, I remember. Our wives were pissed."

"You do it all the time when you are fishing a stream. I have seen it. You are lost in thought. You have said it yourself; you get 'mesmerized' by the activity and all that is going on around you. I have been on the receiving end, waiting for hours for you to return. When you finally return, you make some comment like 'Oh, I didn't realize how late it was.' You would say this even though you had a watch on. Our ranger friend over there could easily have wandered up here from Marion Lake, lost track of time, had an accident, and died because she was trapped by the injury, failure to file a route plan, and the weather. Probably happens all the time in this type of environment."

Sti was thinking while he prepared the dinner. Well, preparing really made it sound like sophisticated work. It really amounted to boiling water, pouring a measured amount into a heavy plastic bag with freeze dried food, mixing the contents, and then waiting for several minutes. With the remaining hot water, they usually had Cup-O-Soup or a hot drink. Dinner at this altitude required patience, and with patience came the time to reflect, relax, and discuss the issues at hand.

"Right!" Sti shrugged. "And how do you account for the fact that we found no backpack or signs of a camp?" Sti knew Rob had a point about wandering and losing track of time, but there were too many odd things about this situation. "You know, there could be a lot of reasons for her to be up here. There could have been a problem she was looking into. Maybe she just wanted to see the area. Maybe she wanted to see the plaque commemorating Joseph LeConte's wife Marion." Sti and Rob knew that the plaque was located in one of the most remote corners of the backcountry and few knew of its existence. However, those who tramped the High Route would go out of their way to see it. "I don't know, but it just does not make sense that she would be up here at that time, in the midst of a storm, without appropriate gear. There is no way she was here without a pack. No way!"

Sti had a point, but Rob was not ready to concede. "It does look strange. But if she was injured, it could have been so severe that she could not carry a pack, and so she went on without one. The pack could be anywhere in this area. We could look for years and not find it. It was just by chance that we found her. Had I not stopped to take a leak, we would have walked within a few feet and never have seen her. It is conceivable that she would never have been found."

"I guess so. It could have been just plain bad luck for her. I can't help wondering anyway." Sti was serving the food. Ha! Serving was a glamorous term for spooning the Turkey Tetrazzini into a bowl for Rob and eating his own share directly from the packet. Well, that is how you cut down on the mess to be cleaned up.

It was starting to rain. Experience dictated that it would be raining much harder in a few moments. "Let's get moving. Everything in the tent we need?" asked Rob.

"Hope so," was Sti's reply. "Let's move the stove over to the vestibule. It's early and we will probably want something hot to drink later. By the way, I threw the maps in there. We need to decide what we're going to do tomorrow. Everything else is covered. Whoa! It is starting to come down."

Rob was sitting at the mouth of the tent, removing his boots as Sti crawled in.

For a while they just listened to the rain. It is an odd characteristic of backpackers. They like to just listen to the rain on the tent. The wind was not real active yet, and Sti and Rob just sat staring out the door of the tent at the rain and the dark, damp, softening affect it had on their vision of the granite basin that stretched out before them.

This was what backpacking was all about. Traveling by your own accord into the remote wilderness and experiencing the full force of Nature. Some would look on such an experience as ridiculous, dirty, uncomfortable and with a 'Why would anyone do this?' attitude. To Sti and Rob, this was a reward. Of course there was objective danger. But it could be managed. It was just a matter of what one liked in life. Every day in the backcountry had its rewards. Whether it was bright sun and puffy white clouds or rain in the midst of thunder and lightning, they would take it. It just didn't get any better than this. They sat in silence and took it all in. Conversation was not needed. But Ranger Harris, or whoever she was, was not far from their individual thoughts.

Later, as the wind came up and the full force of the storm was unleashed, they zipped up the entrance and began the long task of deciding what to do the next day.

Chapter 4

The High Route

It is aptly named the High Route. It is not a trail. It is a route. By comparison with traditional Sierra trails, the High Route pushes the higher elevations of the Sierra Nevada. Hovering at an altitude that averages above 10,000 feet the route winds its way from Kings Canyon in the South-central Sierra to Mono Village in the Twin Lakes region of the North-eastern Sierra. In total, the High Route covers about 200 miles. Unmarked by a trail, the route moves cross-country through canyons and across numerous plateaus and high basins, over and along ridges, and through notches between peaks. For most of the distance, the High Route parallels and crisscrosses the more famous John Muir Trail. But unlike this neighboring, famous, and well traveled trail, the High Route is not well known and tends towards the more inaccessible terrain of the central Sierra. Much of it is unknown except to the most adventurous of backpackers. For that reason, the more remote portions of the High Route are sometimes referred to as *terra incognita.*

Except when it descends quickly to a canyon floor and rises abruptly on the other side, the High Route is at or above the tree line. The landscape experienced by the backpacker is dominated by metamorphic rock. It is an alpine environment of granite, slabs of exfoliated granite, decomposed granite, large and small blocks of granite and peaks and pinnacles of granite. Everywhere there is granite. Ridges, pinnacles, peaks, buttresses, and domes of rock abound. Broken sheets of glacially polished granite look slippery even after thousands of years of weathering and attest to the geologic history of the region. Large and small boulders called 'erratics', some worn from years of glacier grind, stand alone on smooth, sometimes reflective surfaces polished by glaciers. The glaciers may have receded and eventually disappeared thousands of years ago, but their impact on the Sierra is evident wherever one looks. You can not travel the High Route without sensing the magnitude and power of these ancient sculptors of the Earth.

Because everywhere the granite is exposed much of the scenery can appear opaque and redundant at first glance. But to the backpacker who spends considerable time in the Sierra, every view offers up new images of the beauty and power of the rock. And no experience in the Sierra provides more proof of this beauty than on those rare twilight evenings when the light is just right and the rock takes on a radiant personality in shades of gold. This is *alpenglow*, and it overwhelms the hiker camped in an alpine basin surrounded by these golden peaks of rock jutting into the sky. Such an experience packs an emotional punch not soon forgotten.

Having paid such tribute, it would be misleading to suggest that the scenery is inanimate. It would be equally misleading to suggest that the lack of plant life in the region is obvious. For the most part, the organic portions of this environment are small, unassuming, and all but ignored in favor of the more massive and dominant quality of the rock. But a closer look reveals hearty and well-entrenched grasses, flowers, shrubs and scraggly pines.

Where there is moisture, the plants grow and seem at times to survive in the most unlikely places. Regardless of the winter, spring and summer find a wide variety of plants thriving and flowering. To the passing hiker, the seepage and rivulets of water from a higher snowfield can create a ribbon of foliage that hugs the ground as it makes its way down slope. Whether it is a rainy and overcast morning or a sunny and warm afternoon, the small alpine flowers present themselves as a welcome relief to the granite features. If it is windy, the grasses and flowers dance and ripple with the gusts that sweep across the slopes and through the large and small canyons at the higher elevations.

Depending on the conditions, there may be a few trees, such as they are. The White Pine and Foxtail Pine may be found in small clumps at the higher elevations. The weather having taken its toll, the White Pine may look more dead than alive. Sometimes, even at 12,000 feet, the Foxtail Pine can be found twisted, deformed and growing close to the ground. At these higher elevations, the regular winds of both summer and winter give definition to the development of these pines. The result is a stunted pine that is both beautiful and grotesque. It is little wonder that the pine trees at the upper elevations of the Sierra are scattered and thriving only where the conditions are suitable for survival.

So too, the Sierra Juniper can be found clinging to life at the higher elevations. It is not uncommon to find a short and stout Sierra Juniper growing on a rocky summit exposed to the full force of winter storms and summer winds. These junipers may look bleached and scarred by the effects of lightening strikes. They look twisted, distorted, and wind blown. They appear to be just hanging on to life. But these qualities are the Sierra Juniper's strength. She survives because she has adapted to the land of rock. For that, she holds a special place on the slopes and ridges of the High Route. She also attracts the attention of the traveler who recognizes the juxtaposition of this tree against the surrounding environment. The lone Sierra Juniper, clinging to life on a remote ridge, is often the subject of many photographs.

Where once there were glaciers, there are now remnant moraines. Crushed and ground up rock deposited thousands of years ago provide ridges and mounds. Behind some are small lakes and tarns that hold the water of snow melt. From these waters there is seepage that slowly feeds the slopes and canyons below. Others are the source of creeks and streams that rush and tumble their way toward larger streams and rivers. The lakes and creeks have names that, along with the peaks and canyons, which are also named, define the geography of a topographical map.

Animal life at these altitudes remains sparse, and is seldom seen. The big exception is the Yellow-Bellied Marmot. Resembling an oversized squirrel with an extra long coat of fur, the marmot is the most common resident in these environments. Often encountered as he basks in the sun atop a rock, the marmot misses little. For the occasional backpacker, the marmot observes from a distance. But he is brave and will, with craft, invade a campsite or pack in search of food. Not a few backpackers have found a hole eaten in a tent or pack where a marmot has been in search of a cheap meal. However, regardless of whether backpackers have been in the area, the marmot always looks healthy with a body that is plump and a coat of fur that is golden and shines in the sun.

So prevalent are the signs of granite that the High Sierra seems synonymous with granite. However, the reality is that the Sierra granite shares the stage with other types of rock. Of course, as one would expect, there is considerable evidence of volcanic rock and its presence is seen in regions throughout the Sierra. There are also slate and schist, very grainy rock, but most of this is in the areas north of Yosemite National Park. Quartzite and sandstone are also evident outside the central parts of the Sierra. But, for those who hike the central Sierra, the rock that always comes to mind is granite.

Some mountain ranges where the dominant building blocks include large amounts of calcareous rock such as limestone, dolomite, or marble are home to many natural caves. Although calcareous rock is metamorphic, it is much softer than the metamorphic granite of the Sierra, which provides few opportunities for natural caves. But, there are caves. These can be found in those areas where there is calcareous rock in significant amounts. Boyden Cave, Crystal Cave, Clough Cave, and some lesser-known caves in the Kaweah River drainage and other areas, are examples. Although tourists can visit Boyden Cave, caving interests have not been significant in the Sierra and it is speculated that there are probably many caves as yet undiscovered. No doubt there is some truth to this hypothesis, but one would suspect that the Native American Indians who traveled the Sierra long before the arrival of Europeans were probably aware of many caves that have been long since lost from the world of contemporary knowledge. These native inhabitants of the Sierra regions, unlike their modern counterparts, were not just passing through. They depended on their knowledge of the landscape, plants, and animals to survive. Caves would have been an important part of their knowledge.

Finally, there is the lichen. Resistant to heat, cold, drought, and strong sunlight, the lichen grows everywhere. A type of fungus, the lichen absorbs moisture from the air and mineral salts from the surface of the rock on which it grows. So much a part of the rock at first glance, lichen is often mistaken for rock by the novice and ignored. But these gray, brown, black, dark-green, and sometimes white plants are a primary wrecking crew of nature. Lichen produce strong acids that decompose rocks to obtain the needed minerals.

These qualities of the Sierra high country draw the backpackers and climbers. Perhaps it is the durable nature of both that makes the relationship rewarding. Perhaps it is the desire to find and share the experience of remote ruggedness.

Perhaps it is the reward for successfully negotiating a difficult climb or enduring an arduous hike. Whatever the reasons, an extended trip to the alpine regions of the Sierra provides an environment quite unlike that experienced by those who travel the more popular trails of the Sierra. Two things are certain for those who travel the High Route. First, you are not likely to see many other people. Second, you will have to work hard to have this luxury.

* * * *

Sti and Rob visit the High Route region for the same reasons most others avoid such areas. There is no trail. The area is remote and demanding. There are no people there. Every view is unspoiled. Every experience is new. The backpacker to the High Route can take some incredible photographs, collect some great memories, and find fodder for some wonderful backpacking stories. You just never know what you will find.

CHAPTER 5

THE HIKE OUT

Marion Lake, Lake Basin and the Cartridge Pass trail
East of Marion Peak

For Rob and Sti, the hike to the Bench Lake ranger station to report the discovery of the remains was delayed because of weather. The day after the discovery, it was very windy, rainy and cold. The rain was heavy at times. Thunder rolled across the basin, and lightening danced across the surrounding peaks. It was not a day to travel. And, really, there was no need. Sti and Rob had, over the years, sat out many a storm. They were perfectly comfortable in their tent—spending the time reading, studying topographic maps, talking, and listening to the storm. Both knew that unless they had to travel in such inclement conditions, it was better to wait. Sierra storms often come and go quickly in the summer. If the storm abated later in the day, they could always high tail it to a lower elevation.

Where some may have felt an urgency to report the find, Sti and Rob were patient. The remains had been there for some time. They were going nowhere. For their part, neither were Sti and Rob. So they waited.

The previous day, before searching for a campsite, Sti and Rob had taken action to assure that they could lead authorities back to the remains. They had stacked a collection of rocks on a large boulder so it could be easily seen from a distance. A red handkerchief was also anchored on the same boulder. It all looked the same around here. Without a marker, they might not find the spot easily. They knew the rangers were likely to retrieve the remains by helicopter and they wanted the spot to be visible from the air. Meticulous in their planning, they also triangulated their position with features on the Marion Peak Quadrangle 7.5 Minute Series topographical map. They capped off their efforts by taking several readings on Rob's GPS unit.

The second day after their discovery, the storm was slow in coming. It was an opportunity to seek a lower elevation. Having ensured that they could find their way back to the location of the body Sti and Rob struck camp quickly and set a fast pace for Marion Lake. Before they got far, the rain started again, but there was no lightening. Pouring rain compounded the rigor of cross-country hiking. After two hours of hiking into a frontal assault of sheets of rain, even the appropriate protective gear could not keep them from getting soaked. Once at Marion Lake, they quickly set up camp and retreated into the tent to brew some hot soup. They would go no further on this day. The only benefit of their move was that now they were more sheltered from lightening, and they were three hours closer to their destination. They could only hope the weather would improve before they had to cross Cartridge Pass, which was very exposed at 11,800 feet.

* * * *

The hike to the backcountry ranger station the next day was slow and tedious. It was all there—rain, wind, and cold. Under other circumstances, Sti and Rob would probably not have left the lake. But, if people think they get cabin fever in a cabin, they ought to try a 35 square foot, three and one-half foot high, backpacking tent. After a while, you will suffer any inclemency just to get out. It is easy to let such discomfort affect reason. So, they seized on a break in the thunder and lightening to make a dash up and over Cartridge Pass.

They hiked in silence. The John Muir Trail ran through this area before it was abandoned when the official trail was rerouted in 1938. Although not maintained and little better than hiking without a trail, the Cartridge Pass Trail was better than cross-country hiking under these conditions. They set a quick pace, with the miles passing in silence. The fact that they did not talk much was not unusual. The fact that they did not stop often to observe or point something out to the other was unusual. Usually they stopped frequently to observe surroundings. So many hikers never take a deliberative approach to observing the environment through which they pass. Sti and Rob were the exception. However, today was different. The hike on this day was very focused. It did not leave time for a casual approach. There was no time for taking in the sights. Each hiked alone with his thoughts.

For Sti, hiking was an inward experience. It was the act, not the destination, which counted. However, this did not mean a slow pace. On the contrary, Sti was a fast hiker, but always keenly aware of all that was going on around him. It had always been this way. It was what he loved. But on this day it was otherwise. The destination was the point. Accordingly, Sti just hiked, and spent the time in thought. The miles gave way to reflection.

Sti was sixty, and it seemed he had spent a lifetime hiking and camping. His father had introduced him to backpacking at a very early age, and Sti never looked back. This was what he loved to do—backpack, fly fish, and study the Sierra. When asked what he liked to do most, Sti's response was always one word, '*wander*.' What a life! As a high school and college student he had also been involved heavily in rock climbing and remembered with fondness his years of climbing at Joshua Tree, in Yosemite Valley, and in the back country of the Sierra. Climbing was a great sport. Nothing in life matched the thrill of a big wall. But it was a sport Sti had to set aside when his kids began to need more of his time. Backpacking, on the other hand, was something the family could do, and they did. One of the great advantages to being a teacher was the fact that he was free when his kids were free. Free to wander with his family.

Sti thought about the countless backpacking trips he and Rob had taken together. Theirs was an easy friendship and the backpacking relationship was made simpler by the fact that their wives were childhood friends. The two families had raised their kids together—camping, backpacking, and skiing trips were common. Over the thirty plus years of their friendship, Sti and Rob had a lot of unique experiences and stories to go with their shared interests. No doubt, this story would top the list. Well, perhaps not. Who knew where this story would lead? They had found the skeletal remains of a ranger who had been missing for a few years. At the time she was first missed, a massive manhunt over several weeks sought to find her. The results turned up nothing. June Harris had just disappeared. No one had any idea where she might have gone. Remembering the newspaper reports, Sti knew that June was alleged to have gone out on an extended patrol. Reportedly, she had taken a backpack with several days' rations.

However, the direction and purpose, if there was a purpose other than a simple patrol, remained a mystery. Given her vast experience, territory of responsibility, and the usual patrol routes, the search for June was widespread. But it turned up no information. Backpackers in the area who were interviewed did not recall seeing her. There was no shred of evidence as to her whereabouts. Strange!

For Sti, the location where Rob found Harris only intensified the mystery. The area was not heavily traveled country. The only backpackers likely to be there would be very experienced and would leave behind only the occasional footprint in soft soil. There was something about June Harris's death that bothered Sti. The location, the ice axe position, the lack of a backpack, and those small pieces of leather and canvas were puzzling. Too many unanswered questions and Sti felt uneasy about what was to happen once they made their report. He was not certain why, but he had doubt that their role in this would end after filing the report.

For his part, Rob was hiking with his own thoughts. For the last two days they had discussed June Harris from every angle. Like Sti, Rob kept rehashing all the details. In addition to debating the best course of action for notifying the Park Service, they had also speculated on how the remains would be retrieved. Or would it be the Sheriff who had jurisdiction. Perhaps it would be both agencies. In any event, he had suggested, and Sti concurred, that they would try to encourage the idea that if a helicopter were used, they would need the two of them to help spot the site. After all, they could not guarantee that their marker would be easily seen.

Rob also wondered about June Harris. As he recalled the newspaper articles, she was young and had worked this area for several years as a backcountry ranger. Clearly, she knew the area. He could not imagine that she was unfamiliar with the terrain along the High Route. There was plenty written about it, and although it was remote and exposed, there was nothing really dangerous about it unless one just ignored standard backcountry procedures. Of course, the weather at the time of her disappearance was a severe anomaly. But, a ranger with Harris' credentials was not likely to expose herself to unnecessary danger. So, why was she up there? This question and all the related questions dominated his thoughts as he put one foot in front of the other.

Chapter 6

Taboose Creek Canyon—1863

Along the rugged slope, well above the creek, in the upper reaches of the canyon, April

The food and provisions were heavy, but the culture had developed ways to transport these items. But it was not so for the rifles, pistols, powder, and cartridges. These were heavy and awkward. So too were the shovels and picks—implements only recently introduced to the Owens Valley Paiute. The weapons and tools did not fit easily into the conical shaped burden baskets. If anyone was suffering from the burden, it did not show. Most certainly no one would complain.

As they had so many times in the last year, they continued on in silence. They had a job to do, and time was important. This the young Paiute woman knew as she put one step in front of the other. The time had come for the young in the tribe to take action and she thought about all that had happened.

Only a few days earlier, the young and fleet of the tribe had attacked a group of soldiers near Camp Independence, and then quickly retreated. It was a temporary effort. If the soldiers felt threatened, they would likely stay close to the camp and not venture far in pursuit of the tribe. This delay provided the time they needed to enter the canyon and gain enough altitude to avoid the soldiers and their horses.

For the past couple of years, her people had fought several times with the settlers and the soldiers. Both sides had lost people. And although they outnumbered the whites, the Paiute experienced only temporary victories. The settlers and soldiers kept coming and the people of the Paiute were forced to seek refuge in the remote corners of the valley.

Now, while many of her conquered brothers and sisters were being escorted southward and out of the valley by the soldiers, those who remained had come together. Theirs was now a desperate effort to prepare for a different future.

The long line of her people, men and women, young and old, each following the other, made its way up the steep canyon of the *taboose*. Their destination was the inner world at the center of the mountains. There, under the leadership of their acknowledged leader, Joaquin Jim, they would spend the summer months preparing for a future when they would join their people from the north, the Mono, and drive the white man from the valley.

In the meantime, they must stock their small camps and hiding places in the canyons. They must transport the goods and weapons needed to secure the great camp inside the mountain. That was the purpose of this journey. Where once they traveled these canyons to hunt and to trade with their brothers west of the great range now their knowledge of these mountains must rescue them from the menace of the white man and his soldiers. This she knew.

* * * *

Taboose Creek cascades down the canyon that bares its name. Taboose is the Paiute name for a plant that can be found along many of the creeks in the canyons of the Sierra eastern slope. The plant was a food source for the Paiute. Drawing water from the melting snows of the surrounding peaks which are between 12,000 and 13,000 feet in elevation, the creek begins as a small rivulet and quickly builds to a rushing torrent of water. It plummets some 6,000 feet over five miles before it meets the Owens Valley floor at about 5,000 feet. From there it moves across an alluvial fan to meet the Owens River at 4,000 feet.

The walls of Taboose Canyon are a steep terrain of sand-like decomposed granite, talus, and large boulders and broken slabs of granite that slope quickly upwards to meet walls of vertical granite that jut into the sky. Shrubs and trees hide the creek from view most of the time, but the cascading water makes its presence known through sound. The creek is a constant companion to anyone traveling through the canyon.

Travel through Taboose Canyon is not easy. With its exposure to the Owens Valley, the heat is intense. Add to this the steep slopes, the broken talus, distance, and difficult route finding, and one finds travel very demanding.

* * * *

For the Paiute making their way up the canyon without the benefit of a modern hiking trail, the task was arduous. In fact, it would not have been easy even if they had not been carrying burden baskets. Clearly, the purpose of their endeavor spoke to a level of commitment that was driving them on despite the rigor.

The 1860's were not good times for the Paiute. But if the people of the valley were to have a future, it would happen because they joined together. Perhaps Joaquin Jim was right; they must prepare for the future and then wait for the right moment to return. This the young Paiute woman knew as she wondered about her future and the future of her people.

CHAPTER 7

THE TELEPHONE CALL

Education Building, California State University, Fullerton

As he entered his office at the university, the phone was ringing. He groaned to himself. Sti hated the phone. If he were at home, he would not have answered it. The call would usually be for his wife. So he would let her answer it, or he would let the message machine take down the necessary information for a return call. Here at the university, the calls were always for him.

"Sti here."

"Dr. Sti William Pierce?" The pronunciation was slow and deliberate. The speaker either was not sure of the proper pronunciation of 'Sti' or had never addressed Sti before.

"Yes."

"My name is Harris, Matthew Harris. My granddaughter was June Harris." He had Sti's attention. There was no immediate response from Sti, and the pause lingered. "Dr. Pierce....?"

"Sti is fine, Mr. Harris. "Just call me Sti."

"Yes, well, Mr. Pierce, or, Sti, I want to thank you for finding my granddaughter's remains." There was another pause. Matthew Harris was collecting himself.

Sti sensed that it was difficult for Mr. Harris to say his granddaughter's name.

"June was very special to me, and although it is difficult to acknowledge her death, I do appreciate that you and your friend found her and notified the authorities."

"Thank you," was Sti's response, but his effort to comment further was cut short by Harris, who seemed in a hurry.

"I know you are probably wondering why I am calling you several months later. You are probably also wondering how I was able to find your telephone number. Those questions can be answered, but I prefer to do so in person. I need to talk with you and your friend Rob in person."

Ever cautious, Sti's intrigue was not without questions. How could he be sure this was June's grandfather? How did Harris locate him? Why the personal meeting? But, he continued to listen. Heck, he had to admit that he just did not like talking on the phone, but this call intrigued him.

"I assure you, Dr. Pierce, I do appreciate what you have done for my family, but I must meet with you."

"Well Mr. Harris, ah …" Sti was never comfortable on the phone. Talking on the phone did not allow one to observe the other person in the conversation, and he felt at a disadvantage if he could not read the other party. He was also off guard, another quality of the call Sti did not like. There was nothing worse than feeling uneasy in a conversation—not knowing how best to respond. "Ah, I do appreciate your call. I am sorry you had to experience such an unfortunate ending to your granddaughter's life. My friend Rob and I were just….," can't say *lucky* here, "… we just happened across her remains and knew that we had to report our finding. But, really, we can talk about it over the phone. You do not need to make a special trip."

"Not at all, Dr. Pierce, I have some pictures and things I would like to share with you. Also, it is important to me that I get as much detail about the area in which you found June as I can. It is important to me. It is important to my family. My son and his wife, June's parents, were killed many years ago. My own wife died many years ago. June was all I had left. We had a special bond, and I would like to share it with you and your backpacking colleague. I would also like to bring closure to this tragedy by talking with you and Rob."

Sti acquiesced. After all, there was no harm in talking in person, at least it would allow him to see June's grandfather. Better yet, if Rob was in on the conversation, Sti could take his time sizing up Matthew Harris, and take his time responding to questions. Rob was the talker. He could talk with anyone, anywhere, anytime. But, Sti still felt a need to control the situation. "Tell you what, Mr. Harris, where are you coming from?"

"Oakland."

"Do you plan to fly or drive?"

"I will be driving into Orange County. Actually, I will probably come into your area on what looks like the 57 Freeway. I can come anytime, weekday or weekend. Just name the day and time."

Sti was still cautious. "Why don't we do this: I will contact Rob and find out when he is free. Maybe we can set up sometime during next couple of weeks, say a late afternoon or evening on Tuesday, Wednesday or Thursday. Then I can call you and confirm the time. I will make arrangements for a conference room here at the University for our meeting."

They concluded the arrangements. Sti would call to confirm.

* * * *

"I told you that you would not believe it. He sounded straight, but I still have questions. After all, it was a year and a half ago that we found the body. Why would he be calling now?"

Rob was intrigued, but not so guarded. "Sounds to me like he just wants to share some things about June, and find out where and how we found her. Can't be any harm in a friendly conversation. He probably just wants closure."

"Well, can you make it next Wednesday at about 6:00 PM, after my class?"

"Yeah, I can be there. I'll bring the pictures we took and a topo map so we can show him our route and where we found his granddaughter. You know, if he was her grandfather, he must be retired. I can not see how he would be a problem. He probably wants some memories. Sounds like she was the only one left in the family. He's alone now."

"Ok! Let's meet here at my office after my class. I'll call and tell him where to park and to meet us at the entrance to the library. Some good conference rooms there."

"Yeah, well you had best give him clear instructions on parking. That university is a disaster when it comes to parking. Harder to find a spot to park than it is finding a place to park at the Mammoth Mountain main lodge during the Presidents birthday weekend in February. By the way, will this old parking permit of yours still work?"

"You bet. I'll see you Wednesday."

Chapter 8

The First Meeting

In a conference room,
California State University, Fullerton, Pollak Library

During the initial introductions Sti was thinking. Matthew Harris is an elderly man with a ruddy complexion, whose age is difficult to determine. Otherwise, there was nothing remarkable on the surface. He was wondering if Harris's granddaughter had any of his features. How strange it is to try and put a face on a skeleton.

The pleasantries of introductions were over as they entered the conference room and took seats

Not waiting for Rob or Sti to take the initiative, Matthew Harris began the conversation. "I know that you both are probably wondering why I insisted on this meeting. I assure you …"

Rob inserted, "Well, we are intrigued …"

"Yes, well, as I was saying, I want to assure you that I am very grateful. But I have some things I want to share and show you, and it could not be done over the phone. To do this, I needed to see you in person. I guess my many years of teaching have led me to the conclusion that much is gained by reading the audience when talking."

Not waiting for further comment, Sti noted lightheartedly, "Well, I certainly understand your philosophy. As for the phone, it never appealed to me anyway, so a meeting is my preference as well. Besides Rob is a talker, so I don't think there will be any lack of verbal exchange." It was an attempt to lighten things up, but it struck no humorous note in Harris.

Sometimes, when strangers meet, caution is the order of business. But Rob and Sti were not likely to put anyone off, and Matthew Harris sensed their friendly nature. Harris was not surprised. After all, he had checked both men out through an acquaintance. By all accounts, they could be trusted, and what he was about to share with them was the first step in what could be a risky venture. So, caution prevailed.

"I needed to meet with you, to know who it is I am sharing this information with."

Despite the secretive and intriguing air that pervaded Harris's comments, Sti and Rob did not need to look at each other. Over the years of rambling through the mountains, hitchhiking along U.S. 395, bumming rides to and from trail heads, and striking up conversations with complete strangers, they knew how the other was reacting. They also knew that the other was patient and would give Matthew Harris as much time as he needed to say his piece. They also sensed Matthew Harris's loss, and they were not the type to cut him off or show signs of rudeness. If there was any lull or awkward time in the conversation, Rob would speak up with some kind words that would give Mr. Harris time to collect his thoughts before going on.

Sti, by contrast, was the listener. Not necessarily quiet, but not much for small talk, especially with someone he did not know. Sti was an introvert. For this type of encounter, Sti preferred to be analytical. He might take a note or two, think out loud, or ask a question. Or, he might clarify a point made by Rob. Both Rob and Sti knew that this was likely to be his part in the initial conversation. Later, he might have more to say, but only if words were needed. On the other hand, if Sti's comfort level increased during the evening of conversation, he would reflect this by engaging more openly in conversation. For now, Rob would take the lead.

"Mr. Harris, Sti and I are ordinary people who just happened to find your granddaughter. We did not go looking for her. Backpacking is a hobby, although sometimes our wives see it as an avocation, and we were just in the right place at the right time to find her. I guess we take some comfort in being able to help you bring closure to your loss, but except for the three pictures we took of the remains and the description about the discovery that we gave to the NPS investigators and the Fresno County Sheriff, there is not much more to tell."

"Oh, but there may be more," interjected Harris.

Sti quietly followed up on Rob's qualified remarks about the discovery. "Mr. Harris, we could probably give you an endless list of minutia about the discovery, but I do not think it would be of any value. You lost a granddaughter. From what Rob and I have heard from other National Park Service rangers, she was a first class ranger and a good person. We tried to be very thorough in our account of what we found. We also did not tamper with the remains. In the end, the investigation, as we understand, concluded that June had an unfortunate accident in a very remote area of the Sierra during very stormy weather, and died."

Matthew Harris quickly responded. "But, I am not sure it was an accident."

This time Sti and Rob did glance at each other. Now the conversation took on a different tone. Matthew Harris had touched on something that they did not expect. Except for their initial observations on the day that they found June Harris's remains, and later private discussions between themselves after the investigation suggested an accident, the idea that June had died by any other means than an accident, was not something they pursued in conversation with those who were not family. The suggestion of foul play in June's death was not something they wanted to discuss with Harris. After all, their opinion was strictly conjecture, and had no basis in fact. Not to mention, neither of the two was in any way knowledgeable about forensics. They were content with the findings of officialdom. So, the suggestion by Mr. Harris piqued their interest.

"I know, I know." Matthew Harris continued. "Let me back up. We are not off to a good start here. I want you two to know why I have come to see you, and I hope that you will be able to help me. So, please, tolerate the thoughts of an old man for a few minutes. Then we can discuss your questions and my desire for some answers to my questions."

Matthew Harris, seventy some years of age, resident of the Berkeley hills, and retired professor of geology at U.C. Berkeley, opened a small manila folder and removed what looked to be several pages of typed material. Occasionally glancing some notes, he proceeded to give Sti and Rob a chronology of events about the lives of three generations of the Harris family. Sti and Rob settled into the role of listeners.

"For forty-one years I was a geology professor at U. C. Berkeley, and much of my research focused on the Sierra Nevada and surrounding foothills and valleys. Unfortunately, I have always had high blood pressure and my doctors always cautioned me about hiking to the higher elevations. Not a good malady for a field geologist interested in a fourteen thousand foot mountain range. So, I spent much of my time on the lower western and eastern slopes of the Sierra. I loved fieldwork, and my wife enjoyed a supportive role. So, naturally, when we had children, we took them into the field with us. We had two children, Megan June and Matthew—we called him Matt. They were three years apart in age, and they loved the field work activities.

"During the early 1950's much of my field work was focused on the eastern side of the Sierra, in Mono and Inyo Counties. Megan June and Matt were youngsters then, and places like the Owens Valley, and the cities of Lone Pine, Bishop, Mammoth, and Lee Vining were like home to them. They especially liked studying the culture and history of the Native American's living in this region, the Paiute and Shoshone. In time, they developed a great expertise. Then tragedy struck. At eighteen, just before she was to go off to college, Megan was diagnosed with Leukemia. She fought hard for a couple of years, but medicine then was not what it is today and before she was twenty, she passed away. We were devastated, but not more so than Matt. Megan and Matt were more than siblings. They were best of friends. A year after Megan's death, Matt entered college. But Matt had changed. He somehow felt guilty about Megan's death. It was the old 'Why her and why not me?' question over and over. In college, Matt pursued his studies in anthropology with dedication that bordered on obsessive. Before her death he had vowed to Megan that he would continue their studies of the Indians of the Eastern Sierra.

"By the time Matt was twenty-four he had a MS in anthropology and was working on his Ph.D. at Stanford. Whenever possible, he spent as much time in the field as he could. If he was not in the halls of Stanford, he was tramping up and down the Eastern Sierra studying, taking pictures, cataloging artifacts, and tracking down evidence. There was no story, rumor, tradition, belief, or theory about the Indians of the Eastern Sierra that Matt did not try to track down. He was relentless, obsessed. It was as if he was on a mission. But he was not reckless. He knew that results gleaned from fieldwork often depended on process. I guess through his experience with my wife and me he developed the habit of meticulous recording and cataloguing of artifacts, information, and observations. In time, he had mounds of information, much of which was of no use to his dissertation, but which he somehow believed would be of value to him in the future. From our conversations at the time, I knew the Ph.D. was just a point on a continuum of research that extended into issues well beyond the parameters of a dissertation.

"I apologize if this story sounds tedious, but I have given it much thought, and I feel it is important background information for the questions I will raise later."

Simultaneously: Rob: "Not at all, go on." Sti: "Sure, continue."

"About two years into his studies at Stanford, Matt met a young geology research assistant. The geology connection was a natural, and we noticed that Kathryn began spending more and more time in the field with Matt. They made a great pair; each person's knowledge complemented the other's interest. Needless to say, my wife Eaddie and I were very pleased for Matt. Kathryn seemed to bring out the qualities of the old Matt that we had known before Megan's death. A two year courtship was followed by Matt earning his Ph.D. and soon there after, by a wedding.

"Matt's work regarding the Shoshone, or more specifically the Owens Valley Paiute Indian, was original and attracted the interest of several research institutions. But Matt took a post graduate position with Stanford so that he could continue his research with the assistance of a very lucrative grant from the Alfred Kroeber Institute for Native American Studies. For the next several years Matt focused more and more on fieldwork that found him traipsing up and down canyons along the eastern escarpment of the Sierra. I do not need to tell you, some of those canyons are very rugged. But Kathryn and Matt were right at home searching out and investigating sites where the Paiutes had lived and traveled during their history. Operating on the theory that the Paiutes had traversed the Sierra for purposes of trading, they crisscrossed the Sierra on backpacking trips, in search of evidence.

"Then, June was born and named after Megan. Eaddie and I were both delighted and concerned. Kathryn and Matt spent so much time in the field, how could they raise June? But our worry was without cause. June was the focus of their life, and she went where they went.

"Soon after, Matt began to draw the attention of critics with his articles hypothesizing that the Paiute Indians had developed an elaborate trading route across the Sierra. Matt's work suggested that the Paiutes were acting almost as brokers for an extensive trading system that ran goods between the Pacific coast and the mountains and deserts of the Great Basin. Some critics were not very kind, but this did not deter Matt. According to Matt, he had found evidence to support his theory and he was confident that additional evidence would vindicate his controversial views.

"By the time June was ten, Matt was a professor of some note at Stanford. But to Eaddie and me, and to some other close friends, he was changing again. In June of 1978, he and Kathryn uncovered a small cache of relics. Among the relics were several finely woven baskets containing items that implicated the Paiutes in contact with several different tribes west of the Sierra and east into the Great Basin. These items included stones of unique quality, hunting implements, and other items that reflected a variety of tribes and geographies.

"Also, among the items, were several small pieces of gold. Matt called them 'chunks of gold.' Characteristically, Matt was very thorough and compelling in his cataloguing, study, and evaluation of the items in this find. The discovery was a significant contribution to the knowledge concerning the Paiutes and other tribes east and west of the Sierra. Museums were clamoring for a piece of the action. Uncharacteristically, on this occasion, Matt also made one exception to his research protocols. He took one of the small gold chunks and had it put on a necklace for June. When I questioned him about the ethics of this action, he commented, 'Dad, it is important now that I give something to June that will ensure that she is linked forever to the work that Kathryn and I are committed to.' It was a strange comment. I did not know what to think. We never spoke of it again. As you shall see, his comment was prophetic. As for the necklace, it became one of June's prize possessions, so special and prized that she wore it only on special occasions. The rest of the time it was under lock and key. Because several other chunks of gold had been found and were noted in Matt's research, the entire family knew the necklace could not be worn in public."

Rob and Sti were rapt in their attention. This was fascinating.

"Matt's publication of his discovery attracted the usual critics and doubters. But the recognition was confined to the world of anthropologists, their publications, and special interest stories buried in small columns in the local Inyo newspapers. Nevertheless, the discovery solidified Matt's position at Stanford, and he, along with the department of anthropology, looked forward to a long tenure of Native American Indian studies in the Eastern Sierra.

"The next Christmas was very wet and cold in the Owens Valley, and not conducive to fieldwork. So, for one of the few times, Eaddie and I hosted Matt, Kathryn, and June for a long holiday. It was a good time, and we all had fun. We were June's only grandparents and she loved to spend time with us. Matt seemed happy as well, despite the fact that Eaddie and I sensed an edgy and impatient quality in his actions and comments. On New Years day, after we were sick of watching football games, Matt and I took a long walk through the Berkeley Hills. We talked about his work and analysis of his previous summer's findings. I tried to probe his thoughts and his future intentions. Finally, sensing that I was concerned and genuinely interested in his work, Matt stopped me. He said 'Dad, that find last June was the tip of the iceberg. There are more caches, bigger and better caches to be found, and I will find them. I fear, however, that I may not be the first to have discovered them.' I commented that it may not be all bad. The discoveries of others would only confirm his hypothesis about the Paiute trading habits. 'No Dad' was his response. 'I fear some sites may have already been discovered and the items have escaped the scrutiny of study for ever.' I was puzzled, and then Matt just laughed. 'You know me Dad, I always have these crazy ideas. Let's just wait and see what the future brings.' Matt also wanted to know if I was aware of any out of the ordinary inquiries about his research. Did I know of any others who were studying the Owens Valley Paiute? I answered 'no' to both questions. That was the last good conversation we ever had about his work. Kathryn, Matt, and June left the next day for Palo Alto.

"In early spring of that year Matt was back at work in the field. We had a few telephone conversations, usually from a pay phone on their end when Matt or Kathryn would call from somewhere in the Owens Valley. Usually they would call seeking some specialized piece of geological or anthropological information not easily available in the field. Knowing they could reach me and quickly access my resources at Berkeley, they would call, exchange a few pleasantries, and then ask if I would track down some information for them. Then the conversation would end. At the time, their phone requests or questions seemed appropriate, and I did not suspect otherwise. Looking back now, I see some problems with some of their requests. But at the time, I was busy and did not take notice. Anyway, in September, just after June went back to school, both Kathryn and Matt were killed in an auto accident on U.S. 395 just south of Big Pine. At least, the Highway Patrol said it was an accident, and we accepted it as such." There was a long pause as Harris breathed deeply to control his feelings. "Well, I am getting ahead of myself."

Again, Rob and Sti glanced at each other.

"Eaddie and I were devastated. June, who lived with school friends in Palo Alto when her parents were in the field during school months, tried hard not to believe the truth of her parents' death. Because she had no other family, she came to live with us, and in time she grew more accepting of reality. It was a struggle for all three of us. I doubt any one of us could have managed alone. We were able to lean on each other during those times of depression and despair; we all survived and grew closer together. But our lives never seemed to become more normal. I don't think any of us ever really got back to a normal life after Matt and Kathryn's deaths."

Harris glanced at his notes, flipped the page, and seemed to collect his thoughts and a deep breath, before returning to his biography.

For their part, Sti and Rob sat with respectful intent.

"June was a good student in school, and following graduation from high school she enrolled in U.C. Davis to study forestry. In the summer, she worked for the National Forest Service. My contacts, as well as the reputation of her parents, opened some doors. June was a natural in the backcountry. Between her junior and senior year, she took a backcountry ranger position with the National

Park Service and worked the trails of Sequoia and Kings Canyon National Parks. She loved being a backcountry ranger. It is all she talked about.

"But like her father, events changed her. In 1991, the out of control fire in the Berkeley and Oakland hills severely damaged our home. June rushed home to help us straighten things out. In the process of cleaning up, June began to go through the stacks of old files, journals, and artifacts collected by Matt and Kathryn. Day after day, she methodically perused these items. Finally, she had to go back to school, and asked if she could use my university copier to make copies of some of the journal entries and records. She said she found some interesting information about the Paiute and wanted to take it back with her so that she could read it more carefully when she had some time. Eaddie and I also noticed that for the first time in many years, she started wearing the gold chunk necklace that Matt had made for her. It was no longer kept locked away; she wore it 24 hours a day. But she was discrete and kept it under her blouse. In the coming months leading up to June's graduation, her interest in Matt's work seemed to increase. When we inquired about what she would do after graduation, June only commented that she intended to continue working for the Park Service or the Forest Service. She also made it clear that she intended to work somewhere on the eastern side of the Sierra where she could readily follow up on her renewed interest in her parents' work.

"A few weeks after June's graduation, Eaddie, whose health had not been good for several years, suffered a stroke. Four weeks later she was dead. June was home for a week after the initial stroke and then returned to her backcountry assignment when doctors indicated a somewhat positive prognosis. Three weeks later she was home for the internment. Throughout the ordeal, June was dutiful and compassionate. But it was obvious that her mind and soul were back in the mountains. A few days after the services, June departed. I did not see her again for some time.

"For the next two years I did not see much of June. I did, however, hear from her on a regular basis. Off-season she seemed to have employment working for the Inyo region of the U. S. Forest Service. When summer rolled around, she worked at the backcountry ranger station near Bench Lake for the Park Service. That was the station she was working out of when she disappeared.

"Then she called me on the phone one day and said that she was sending me some packages. She asked that I not open them, but that I just hold on to them for her. She said they were some things she had acquired and needed a safe place to send them since she had no permanent residence. For the next year, an occasional package would arrive self-addressed to June. All were mailed from the small towns in the Owens Valley. I did not open them. I just stored them and thought nothing of it. Being alone, I had directed my attention to assisting some former colleagues on small geology research projects and did not have time to worry about the packages. I tried not to worry about June, but it was never easy.

"Several months after the phone call about the packages, June was in town for several days. We were able to catch up on each other's activities. She seemed so happy with her life. Her interest in Matt's work, she said, had given her a new purpose in life. June was especially interested in his theory that other caches of Paiute artifacts existed and she was trying to decipher where they would be located. June used the word 'decipher' because, according to her evaluation of Matt's work, his notes regarding cache locations were cryptic. But she laughed, 'Well I'm a Harris and if anyone can break Dad's code, it would be someone related.' I asked June if Matt's notes mentioned anything about other people discovering some of the caches. Her response was one of surprise, and she asked what prompted the question. I shared Matt's New Years day comment of many years previous. Clearly, this information piqued June's interest. Almost instantly, she seemed distant, lost in thought. She was quiet for the remainder of the day. When she departed that evening, she apologized, declaring that I must have misinterpreted what Matt had said. According to June, the alleged comment from Matt did not fit with what she knew to be true. I know now that she behaved just the opposite. Her response was to direct my attention away from concern for her safety. At the time she was successful.

"Four years ago last August I received a phone call late one night from June. In fact it was about one or two in the morning and startled me. June said that she had a couple of days off and had hiked out and hitched a ride to Independence to call me. She said she was going into Lone Pine the next day to file some reports and get some supplies. She advised me further that a package would arrive in a couple of days and that I was to open it and read the letter. She did not have the time to go over everything with me on the phone. The letter would explain everything. June always called me 'Pops' and she concluded the conversation by saying 'Pops,' you are the greatest. You, Grandma, and Mom and Dad are the greatest people I have ever known. I don't know what I would have done without you. I love you. I will see you soon.' It was the last time I ever heard her voice. I have played that conversation over in my head a hundred times. I can still hear her voice. It ..."

Matthew Harris seemed lost in sadness. He bit his quivering lip, seeking to control his emotions. Silence dominated. He was alone.

Rob sensed what was next in the conversation and picked up Harris's thoughts with the hope of leading him back into the story. "I am sure there was a special bond between you and June. Did you ever get the package and letter she said was being sent?"

Matthew Harris looked up, there was sorrow in his eyes and he waited a second. His voice quivering, Harris went on. "Yes, it arrived a week after the call. In it was one of Matt's journals, a couple of well used topographic maps, three or four aerial photographs, photocopies of articles, and a book on Native Americans of California, Marry Hill's book *Geology of the Sierra Nevada*, and a book on the history of mining in the Sierra Nevada. There was also an enlargement of a picture of what looked to be a chunk of gold similar to the one on June's necklace, and a journal in June's handwriting. The most intriguing item in the package was Junes' gold necklace. I wondered why she had sent it. I opened the letter in search of some explanation. What I found raised more questions than it provided answers. It was also a letter written in confidence. I have made a couple of photocopies of the letter so that you can read it."

Harris handed Sti and Rob each a photocopy of the letter. The text was neatly handwritten. They read in silence.

> August 5
>
> Dear Pops,
>
> Each of us is all that the other has left. You mean a lot to me. You're my best friend. That is why I know that in sending you this letter, you will respect its confidentiality.
>
> I am writing this letter to you from the backcountry. The weather has been cold and miserable for several days. I am restless. There are not many hikers on the trail with this constant rain. There is snow at the higher elevations.

Most of my time is spent checking on how the few hikers at Bench Lake and the lakes just south of me are holding up under this unusual weather. Some are well prepared; others are miserable and I try to boost their spirits and give some advice that may make their life in a tent more bearable. I have an extended patrol planned in a couple of days and I hope that the weather improves. But if it does not, well, I intend to go on the patrol anyway. I need to get out and move. I get restless sitting around.

Tomorrow I am going to make a quick trip out to the valley to call you and mail this package. I think I will take a good hot shower and eat a good meal as well. Then I will return to my station and go on an extended patrol.

But let me get to the real reason for this letter and package.

Since those days in 1991, when I helped you and grandmother clean up after the fire, I have been studying Dad's work and probing some of the issues he wrestled with. I have read his articles, journals, and field notes. I have also visited most of the field sites. I even read what his critics said. Sometimes that hurt, but it was valuable. I realize now that Dad faced major professional obstacles and it must have been difficult for Dad and Mom to have to put up with some of that criticism.

I also realize that Dad became obsessed with the need to prove his critics wrong. So determined was Dad that he may not have kept an open mind about his studies. I am not sure that he was willing to accept the fact that some of his harshest critics had ideas that, had Dad been willing to listen, could have eventually provided valuable support for some aspects of Dad's research. Dad seemed to personalize criticism and it may have blinded his ability to be objective.

In any event, I think Dad was right in stating that there had to be more and bigger caches to be found. His findings over a period of time suggested that there was a chain of caches. Had he lived, I have no doubt that he and Mom would have found them.

However, two things trouble me. First, my own studies do not support Dad's theory regarding an elaborate trade system, which put the Paiutes in the position of brokers. Second, your comment last year that Dad believed others had found some of the caches and was hoarding them or using them for profit continues to haunt me.

There may be another reason for the existence of the caches, and it has nothing to do with an extended trade route. I think I know the reason and if I am able to substantiate the reason, Dad's hypothesis about the existence of other caches will be vindicated. However, his critics will be proven correct regarding the idea of the Paiutes as trade merchants.

I am also troubled that Dad's belief about others discovering and misusing the other chases was, and is, probably correct.

I have discovered two caches my father did not know about. I think I know where one or two additional caches are located. But I also fear that there are others looking for them as well in the same area.

I have sent you the enclosed items because I no longer need them. More importantly, I fear they could be a liability. It is hard to have any privacy here. I also suspect others may be interested in some of these. I have some research to do in the few remaining weeks of this season, and I can not afford to leave these things in my tent while I am on the trail. I know you will keep these items, and the other packages I have sent, safe.

I love you Pops. Throughout the many difficult times of my life, you have always been there for me. Well, I need your help one more time. Please keep these items safe and share them with no one. When next we talk, the season will be over and I will be on my way to see you. If all goes as I intend, Dad's reputation will once again be at the forefront in the minds of western American anthropologists. Several wrongs will be righted, and I shall be free of a nagging problem.

Love ya Pops,

June

The letter compounded the mystery of June's death. It also substantiated the value of Harris's biographical background information. Matt Harris had opened Pandora's Box. Sti and Rob now knew why Harris had been so adamant about a personal visit, and why he believed June's death may not have been an accident.

Sti sat up and looked directly at Harris. "This is heavy information. Clearly, what is being suggested here is that June was on to something that could have lead to her death; a death at the hands of one or more persons. Mr. Harris, I do not know what other evidence you have, but I do know that if you suspect foul play, then you must go to the appropriate authorities. I do not know what Rob and I can do to help. We did not see anything that would suggest support for your theory. At least, I do not think we did, did we Rob?"

"You're right. We reported everything verbally and in writing. We even suggested to the NPS people that it looked like the ice axe might have been related to the cause of death. Obviously the experts did not reach the same conclusion. How can we argue with their findings when we did not find anything that would prove otherwise?" This was a bit of an inaccurate statement since it was not a matter of proving. What Sti and Rob found was no different from what the NPS people found. They saw the ice axe position. But the lab apparently found no indication that the ice axe was used as a weapon. It was also true that neither Sti nor Rob had seen the final cause of death report. "Mr. Harris, do you have a copy of the final report about the cause of June's death?"

"Yes, the indications are that since the body and clothing had decomposed and only the skeletal remains were left, there was no way to determine any cause of death other than an accident. According to the report, a body exposed on a slope at 11,000 feet in the Sierra is likely to be moved over time by snow, ice, rain, wind and animals. The bones did not show any injury that would suggest the ice axe or anything else had caused the death. Since the region was remote and no other people were known to be in the area, the only conclusion was that June had some kind of accident and died from wounds and/or exposure before she could get help." All of this was stated matter-of-factly and reflected the scientific mind of Harris.

This was an awkward situation for Rob and Sti. They wanted to be sympathetic, but they were cautious about anything that would suggest the results of official investigations might be inaccurate. In fact, they agreed with the report speculation that the body remains could hardly expected to remain static over time. It was not that they were unwilling to consider the possibility of death at the hands of some other person. It was that they were realistic. They were not experts. They had no basis, other than their initial observation, on which to form a conclusion.

Sti carefully chose his words as he raised a point. It was directed at Rob, but Sti intended Harris to hear. "You know, we did find, and report, that there were strange pieces of canvas and leather present at the scene and that they looked out of place. Remember? We thought they were old and not something one would find around today."

Rob was about to respond to Sti when Harris cut him off. "What kind of things were they?"

Rob redirected his intended response to Harris. "Oh, they were not things, just pieces. We told the rangers about them. But they dismissed the significance since it is common practice for rangers in the field to pick up and carry out trash. You know, old rope, string, cloth, leather, canvas, nylon and other items left behind by thoughtless backpackers. On an extended patrol, they said, rangers often return with a knapsack full of junk."

"But they never found a pack or any overnight gear," replied Harris.

Rob and Sti had discussed this fact several times. Yes, there was no sign of a camp or any overnight gear. However, they, along with the rangers had concluded that June had either set up camp elsewhere and was on a short hike or she was injured and wandered away from her backpack. It was very common for an injured person to abandon gear and try to seek help in a desperate situation

"That is right Mr. Harris. Rob and I looked around and found no pack or gear of any kind. But the small amount of old leather and canvas could have been carried in a pocket. All we can do is speculate, and our speculations are weak testimony at best."

"That may be, but I think there is something else you need to know. Among the items in one of the packages June sent to me the previous summer was a plastic bag full of old pieces of canvas, leather, and various kinds of cloth in various stages of deterioration. Each had an identification number and catalog code affixed to it. In another package there was what looked to be a piece of an old hiking boot from before the 1950's as well as a couple pieces of leather attached together in a way that would indicate it they may have been part of a moccasin or some earlier form of footwear. It also had an ID number and catalog code. However, the package did not contain any catalog journal so I was not able to place the significance of the artifacts."

This was too much. Sti and Rob felt like they were playing one of those 'who done it?' games, and Mr. Harris was dolling out the evidence very cautiously.

"Mr. Harris, something is happening here." Rob was cautious. "You have come to us because you believe your granddaughter was the victim of a crime. What you have told us, shown us, and suggested makes it clear that you have given considerable thought to this evening's meeting. But still, what we have heard and seen is not compelling enough for us to abandon the findings of the authorities in this situation. I suspect you know this as well." Rob was operating on his senses here. "I would guess, by your credentials and by the way you carefully articulated your thoughts, that you would not have approached us unless you did have compelling data...."

It was Sti's turn. "I suspect also Dr. Harris that the decision to come and talk to us was not made hastily. You are a very careful man. I think you know more about us than we know about you. I also think that you came prepared to share additional evidence because you knrw that we would ask for it. Are we correct on these assumptions?"

"Yes, I am afraid so," answered Harris. "I must be honest here. I owe a great deal to the two of you. In finding June's remains, you brought some closure to the mystery of her disappearance. However, the discovery of her remains also raised new questions.

"Let me be more specific. A couple of months after June's disappearance, I began to look through some of the packages June had sent to me. But as I looked, the issues June raised in her last letter kept haunting me. The more I looked, the more questions I had. When I finished looking through all the packages, I began to look through Matt's logs, journals, and records. Again, the more I looked, the more questions I had. About a year and a half ago I approached the Park Service with my suspicion that June may have been the victim of violence. But I had no hard evidence, and they were not really willing to consider that my ideas had any merit. I think they were just humoring an old man by listening. Even I had to admit the evidence of the Park Service suggested that indeed June had gone on a patrol and must have had an accident. But I just could not accept that. I talked with the rangers and the Fresno Sheriff several times. They always listened and expressed appreciation for my thoughts. To this day, I don't think they lifted a finger to follow up on my ideas. From time to time I was tempted to share the contents of the packages and June's letters with the Park Service or the Fresno County Sheriff, but I did not. Guilt, and a great loyalty to her spirit, steered me away from doing so. And yet, intense feeling tells me there is more involved in

June's death than meets the eye. With the passing of time, I am more and more convinced that there is a mystery here. I needed to follow up on the information I have, but I have to be careful about who I share the information with"

"So, why now Dr. Harris? Why us?" were Rob's questions. "We have a lot less authority and ability to pursue your suggestions and evidence than does the Sheriff or the Park Service."

Sti added, "We have no expertise, just our observations. There must be private sector investigators much more qualified than us to assist you."

"I know. But you have something no other people have. You have your initial observations and suspicions. I know you both shared the notion with the Sheriff that June's death may not have been an accident. I reasoned that you would be inclined to consider my interpretation. Regardless of the evidence I have, no one else is likely to give it the objective consideration that the two of you can provide. That is why I come to you. I come to you at this point in time because I have done as much with the evidence on my own as I can. Someone else will have to help me from this point on. You are the only ones I can trust to help."

The hidden message being delivered carefully by Harris did not go unnoticed. "So you do know more about us than you have shared," was Sti's response.

"Yes I do. As a geologist at Berkeley, I worked on some projects for several state and federal agencies. These experiences gave me contacts. I have never used these contacts until now. I learned from experience many years ago that one must check out credentials in advance of doing business with strangers. So I decided to see what I could find out about the two of you before approaching. Before I called Sti, I knew enough to conclude that whether or not you would decide to help me, I could trust you not to violate the confidence I brought to this conversation. It was never my intention to know more about you than I needed. You are both honest, have good families, have no need to expand your egos by seeking attention, and will likely respond to new ideas with an open mind. I also know you are good and trusting friends, something of a rarity in the professional world these days. You also know the Sierra better than most. Other than these qualities, I did not need to know anything else."

There was a silence. But it was not for a lack of interest on part of Sti or Rob.

"I know that it may seem like I have violated your privacy. I assure you, that was not my intent. I felt awkward doing a background check. But it was something I believed to be necessary. I have endured my fair share of tragedy in this world. I think I have earned the right to be cautious. If my actions suggest otherwise, I apologize."

Sti tried to give some direction to what was turning out to be a protracted discussion. "Dr. Harris, you have given us much to think about tonight. It is also getting late. I think I can speak for the both of us that we are not pleased with any background check you may have done on us, but I think we understand why. Assuming you have no intentions of violating the confidentiality of anything you may have learned, we will pursue the matter no further. However, Rob and I need to talk. I suspect that you are seeking some commitment from Rob and me that we will help you conduct some sort of investigation into your granddaughter's death and into some other questions which have developed out of your own investigations. Before we can go any further, Rob and I need to talk. Is that a fair assessment of the situation Rob?"

"I think so," was Rob's initial comment. "We need to reflect on what you have told us and consider its implications. I think Sti used the word commitment. If we decide to help you, it probably involves a significant commitment of time. It would also require that we have access to all the evidence you may have. Sti and I need to, as I said, review and consider what we have heard here."

Matthew Harris seemed satisfied with this response. "That is OK with me. I know it is asking a lot. If you decide to help, I will gladly let you see any evidence you need."

"You will also have to be 100 percent honest with us in responding to any and all questions we may have, regardless of how sensitive they may be," was an added condition presented by Sti.

Harris nodded.

Rob again, "I think that once we have had several days to review tonight's discussion we will be able to give you an answer. If the answer is yes, well, we can plan to meet again. If not, I trust you will respect our decision. Agreed?"

"Yes, yes! That is very fair. I am pleased." Harris was obviously relieved. He knew it would not be an easy sell. Sti and Rob were not the type to be lead where they did not want to go. If they decided to be involved, it would be because they deemed it a worthy venture. Money and other offers would not persuade them.

Again, Sti added a condition. "One other thing, Dr. Harris. If Rob and I agree to assist, it must be understood that we will call our own shots. Your granddaughter's death is old history. There is no need to rush into things. If we are assisting, it will be at our pace. We do, after all, have other lives to live. I am sure you understand."

"Oh yes, I would be very grateful. I am not the young man you fellows are; I am limited in what I can do. I just think some questions need to be answered before my tenure on this Earth is concluded. You fellows are my only hope. I would not interfere."

"Good, Dr. Harris, then you will give Sti and me several days to discuss this matter? Here is my card." Rob, quickly wrote out additional phone numbers and gave the card to Harris. "If you need to contact us, this is more than enough information. Could you give us your address and phone number?"

Harris's card was interesting. It was Matthew M. Harris, Ph.D., Department of Geological Research, University of California, Berkeley. There were three phone numbers, a fax number, and E-mail number. On the backside Harris had already written his home address and appropriate communication numbers. Harris had anticipated this exchange.

The three men exchanged pleasantries again, and Dr. Matthew M. Harris departed. It was late; Sti and Rob talked as they walked to their cars. They agreed to get together over the weekend to discuss this situation. They were both intrigued, but rushing to judgment was not their style. Reflection was the next order of business.

Chapter 9

Poverty Hills Survey Camp—1908

Poverty Hills and Goodale Creek, Owens Valley, October

Although late October, it was unseasonably warm for the Owens Valley, and George Kennicott relaxed. Most of the survey crew had departed, leaving only George and the camp maintenance crew. George was not due in Independence for three days. He would have time to follow up on his discovery.

For several weeks George's crew had been surveying the area between Big Pine and Sawmill Creek, a distance of about 20 miles. Their task was twofold. First, they were gathering data that would make it possible to confirm the best route for the aqueduct once it departed the Owens River and began its long journey towards Los Angeles. Second, they were gathering data about the best way to channel water from Birch, Red Mountain, Tinemaha, Taboose, Goodale, Davidson, Sawmill, and several smaller creeks into the proposed aqueduct.

Unlike most of his crew, George liked the time away from home. He did not mind the isolation of long days traipsing across this desert-like landscape. In fact, he preferred it to the small towns and larger construction camps. As a result, George often took long hikes or horseback rides after hours and on days off. He found exploration of the valley and adjacent canyons to be of greater interest than socializing. The canyons that collected water from the Sierra peaks and underground springs and then delivered it to the Owens Valley provided ample opportunity to explore the unknown and the beautiful.

Each creek had a personality. The terrain of each was different. Access to the canyons varied according to the way the water had cut through the terrain. Although all the canyons traced their origins to the same geological timeline, each canyon held its own geological mystery.

In every instance the creeks originated along the ridges and peaks of the Eastern Sierra escarpment. In this region of the Sierra, the escarpment elevations are between 10,000 and 12,000 feet. The creeks have cut canyons that run roughly from west to east. The descent from these elevations to the valley floor at 4,000 feet is rapid. As a result, the canyons are usually rugged and navigation is a challenge to any hiker or horseback rider.

So when George Kennicott took his solo outings, there was no interest from others. Most of his coworkers did not share any interest in exploring the canyons. They had done enough walking and hiking during the day.

But George had another reason for not departing with the rest of the crew. It was a selfish reason. Two weeks earlier, while conducting a routine survey of the slope of Goodale Creek from where the water exited the Sierra canyon that bares its name to where it flows into the Owens River three miles down slope, two of the crew reported that they had found the remnants of an old Indian camp. That evening, George rode over on horseback and checked out the report. Sure enough, it was an old campsite. But more importantly, it revealed more than a few pottery shards and stone tools. A faint and small path, almost undetectable except for the packed condition of the soil, led up stream for about a half mile to a large granite bench that was recessed into the rocks and surrounded by small pines and overlooked the mouth of the canyon. The view down the canyon was exceptional. There, secluded beneath a lean-to that was not visible from anywhere below, George had found several clay pots and baskets. All the pots were severely damaged, but not completely destroyed. The baskets showed signs of being well used and in a state of decay and were probably in no condition to serve the needs for which they were originally intended. George spent the night at the site and his obsessive interest in the artifacts resulted in a most unexpected find.

While clearing a spot to sleep, George found a long leather strap. When he picked it up it lifted out of the granular soil to reveal that it was attached to something wedged between two large slabs of granite. Had not the leather strap been found, George would never have noticed the find that intrigued him the most.

Tightly wrapped in a large piece of leather was a small pouch. The leather wrapping and the leather pouch were very weathered and so hardened that both cracked as George first unwrapped the outer leather, and then opened the pouch. Inside, he found four pieces of gold. They were not the usual placer nuggets, which would have been smoothed and rounded by the flow of water. These were pieces that looked to have been chipped or gouged out of rock. George was amazed at his luck, but he was not stupid. No one was to hear about this. He wondered. What were the chances that there were similar sites elsewhere in the valley? These four pieces were worth about a total of $300.00. Many pieces could be worth a small fortune. Find the source of this gold, and one could be rich.

With the days he had before his presence in Independence was required, George continued to check out the site and surrounding area. George was a wanderer and searching for similar sites and artifacts was a pastime that fit well with his personality. His wandering qualities were accepted by others, and his absence for a day or two never raised concern among workers or superiors. Perhaps, once he concluded his survey obligations, he would have more time to spend exploring the Eastern Sierra canyons. The Goodale Creek camp could not be the only such camp. His conversations with the Paiute Indians on the survey crew suggested that canyons in the area had long been used by Paiute hunters of deer and mountain sheep. No doubt, reasoned Kennicott, similar camps were probably located up and down the Owens Valley. The key for Kennicott was to continue his hunting without betraying his finds.

Chapter 10

After the First Visit to the Harris Residence

Sti's home in Orange County, California

They were comparing notes. Together, they had spent three days at Matthew Harris's residence in Berkeley reviewing the Harris archives. It was the only way one could describe the collected notebooks, artifacts, articles, and personal possessions of three generations of the Harris family.

When they had entered the Harris household, it took Rob and Sti all of a second to realize that they were in one family's museum. Everywhere, there were remnants of a lifetime of collecting and studying rocks, manuscripts, books, artifacts, and a variety of other items, some of which could not be distinguished from the more general term, 'junk.' Sti would have described much of what was exhibited as 'dust collectors,' but on close examination, the house was very well maintained and there was no dust.

Harris had everything organized for easy reference. A remarkable feat, given all that was stored there. But, as his two guests discovered, it was not surprising given the Harris penchant for meticulous record keeping. In one room Matt's notebooks, field journals, collection of artifacts, professional journal articles and papers, photographs, audiotapes, and books were neatly ordered in shelves and cabinets. The room was referred to as Matt's study. But this room had the quality of a museum and not that of a typical study. Items were not formally indexed, but they were easy to find. Everything was meant to be visible, accessible and studied. According to Dr. Harris, Matt had never really used the room as a study since he and Kathryn lived in Palo Alto. After their death, Matt's things were collected from his home and the university and consolidated in this room.

June's packages, personal belongings, photographs, maps, books, logs, and personal journals occupied a corner of another room. The remainder of the room was shelf after shelf of geology books, rock displays, geology journals and papers, and carousel slide trays of geology related photos. The room was also both a museum and a study. It was designed to facilitate study and research. Equipment included a slide projector, two computers, large roll-down maps of California, fax and copy machines, microfilm and fiche readers, and a device that transformed aerial photographs into three-dimensional images. A desk and appropriate shelves and cabinets had been set aside for June's items, but the remainder of the room was for Matthew Harris Senior. Sti and Rob were struck by the similarity between the two rooms, or studies. The two rooms transcended three Harris generations, but the common qualities suggested grandfather, son, and granddaughter approached research with the same frame of reference.

The living room, family room, and two bedrooms featured numerous book shelves and display cabinets packed with all manner of books, rocks and fossils, Native American artifacts, and a wonderful collection of antique science laboratory and field equipment.

A small dining area was the exception. Here there was a fine collection of photographs of the Sierra, the Owens Valley, Death Valley and numerous desert areas of southeastern California. Matthew Harris had known Ansel Adams, and the famous photographer's work was displayed throughout the house. But the highlight of the dining room was the family portrait gallery. Everyone was pictured, and if the viewer was not aware that all but one member of the family was deceased, it could only be concluded that this was a thriving all-American family. Both Sti and Rob noticed the sadness in Harris's voice and demeanor when he concluded the household tour with the dining room. Curiously, during their stay, Matthew Harris spent most of his time in this dining area where he read, conducted phone conversations, made notes, typed on his early model laptop, and ate his meals. Noticeable also was the fact that whenever Harris was in this room, he was seated facing the wall of family photographs. Harris did not seem to be alone in this room.

Harris's organization of things made the review of Matt's work and June's materials easy.

Initially, Sti and Rob were wary of taking Matthew Harris up on his request for assistance in looking into the death of his granddaughter. The clincher was Harris's offer to pay all expenses and to gain them access to restricted materials concerning Sierra Nevada and Owens Valley histories in the Bancroft Library at U.C. Berkeley as well as the Eastern California Museum in the town of Independence. Harris would also provide them with complete access to Matt's work and June's writings, collections, photos and maps. If necessary, Harris would finance a return trip to the High Route area of his granddaughter's death, as well as an airplane flight over the area for photography and sightseeing purposes. These were tempting offers. But the task requested by Harris required time.

Although semi-retired, Sti and Rob really did not have time to follow-up on Harris's offer. Sti had recently retired after thirty-three years as a high school teacher and administrator. He was now a professor with more time under his control than previously. But, he did not have a lot of unstructured time. Retirement only meant that he would have more time to chase the numerous ideas and plans that he had been pursuing part-time while fully employed. He had thought that retirement would mean he would not burn the candle at both ends. However, always impatient, lest idle time be wasted time, Sti quickly filled retirement with a long list of self imposed goals, responsibilities, and commitments that ranged from teaching at the university, to research, writing, consulting, and volunteer service. To meet one of his priority goals, spending more time hiking, fly fishing, and skiing, or most importantly just wandering, Sti had to work hard to see to it that other commitments did not interfere.

Rob was self-employed, and, like Sti, had to exercise discipline to insure time for non-commercial endeavors, namely backpacking, day hiking, cycling, and skiing. For many years he had worked out of his home on numerous projects related to his design expertise in optics, optical instruments, cataract surgery instruments, and corneal transplants. Rob was extremely successful in these ventures, but sharing his friend's wanderlust, he had numerous other interests. Not the least among these was his interest in wandering and studying the Sierra and the valleys and deserts that comprised the Great Basin to the east. Rob liked nothing better than exploring some little known corner of the Great Basin—wandering, taking photographs, and investigating intriguing qualities. Together with Sti, he worked hard to control his professional activities so that he could spend the kind of time needed to follow outdoor interests and dreams. Responding to Harris meant another encroachment into the time factor, but Rob reasoned that the purpose was aligned with backpacking in the Sierra and that was reason enough to take Harris up on his offer.

At Dr. Harris's request, Rob and Sti had agreed to drive up to Berkeley and to inspect the evidence at the Harris house. It was several weeks since their return, and they were finally able to get together to shoot some hoops, drink some beer and compare notes.

"I couldn't believe it. We could of stayed there a week," lamented Sti. "Harris had it all—great study facilities, a wraparound deck that overlooked the bay, great wines and beers, and some of the best photographs of the Sierra I have ever seen. Gee, it was great!"

"I got to wondering though," said Rob, "It was almost too perfect."

"Meaning?"

"Have you ever felt things were organized to direct attention away from other issues?"

"Give me a break, Rob."

"No, think about it. Harris invites us up there. Everything was taken care of. All we had to do was read, study, sleep and eat. What kind of person does that, puts out a welcome mat like that? I mean, I almost felt guilty. And Harris, he hardly stepped out of that dining room. If he wanted a book or something, he went to another part of the house, retrieved what he needed, and took it back to the dining room. He didn't use his own study. In fact, when I think back on it, the place had the appearance of making everything accessible, without making it possible to know whether we really had access to everything. Strange!"

"Yeah, well, it was different. So, what do you think about what we did see and study?"

"I think we have a lot of unanswered questions," Rob responded.

Sti was on the same wavelength. "I don't know about you, but my take on this whole affair is that there is more here than just a question of how June Harris died. She was a very interesting young lady, almost a precocious adult. Her family was of a different sort. The history of that family is one of mysteries."

"It seems to run in the family. Her father and her mother were mysterious people. I'd say, Matt and June were chips off the old man's block." Rob was trying to characterize the family. "They were different. I know we talked about this on the drive home, but somehow Matt's work is connected with June's obsession with the High Route area. But deciphering both Matt and June's coded notes. How we do that, I do not know."

"I don't know either. I am not sure I have the time this whole thing will take," was Sti's observation. Both of them knew that their preliminary work at the Harris house had opened more doors than they liked to think they had time to explore. June's death was probably accidental, but there was just enough perplexing information in the things they reviewed in Berkeley to raise questions and encourage pursuit of answers. Neither wanted to admit that although they did not really want to take the leap of commitment that following up on these questions would require, they were very interested in many of the other things they had uncovered, which may or may not be connected with June's death.

"OK!" Sti unfolded what looked to be a flowchart. "I tried to create the comparison chart that we discussed. I took all of the things highlighted in your notes and my notes and created some categories of comparison. So! I have headings that reference High Route, Paiute Indians, caches, geology, gold chunks, and unknowns. The unknowns are the cryptic notes that we could not understand." Sti handed Rob a photocopy. "I have two columns under each heading, one for your notes and one for mine. In some cases there are sub-headings, like under Indians there are tribe, history, trade, artifacts, and Sierra crossing headings. I also separated references to Matt and June. What do you think?"

Rob studied Sti's comparative information before responding. "I think what we have here is a good summation of the things that struck each of us as interesting, intriguing, or somehow related to June's death, or at least her presence in the High Route area. But, the questions are more so than ever."

Sti continued. "So, we could abridge all these data to say, what? That June had studied Matt's work and found references in his notes about interviews with some old Paiutes? His notes focused on several routes traveled by the Paiutes in crossing the Sierra for trade. Located strategically along the routes were caches of food, supplies, and trade items. Matt used a cryptic code in his journal to identify what looks to be the location of several caches and other information that remains completely unknown to us. Why the code?"

Rob interrupted. "We are just guessing about the contents of the encrypted information. It will take a lot of our time, or someone else, to decode the journal entries."

"Matt also had some hand drawn maps with coded place names. June may have broken this code and knew where some of the caches should be. We also know from Matt's self drawn maps that he had an interest in the High Route area between Cartridge Creek and Muro Blanco."

Rob added, "But, given what we were able to understand, there were references to the possibility of several other caches located in Sierra regions. Some areas are much more accessible than the High Route. Why choose to search in the High Route area where it would be more difficult to find the cache? And what has this got to do with her death?"

Sti knew where Rob was going with this last question. "You may be right. Perhaps we need to focus on the issue of the cause of death first and then see where that evidence, if there is any, takes us. I think calls to the Sheriff and the Park Service officials to see if there is anything in their findings that suggests a cause other than an accident is a good idea at this point. Based on what comes out of that, perhaps we can return to the question of why June was on the High Route."

CHAPTER 11

MANZANAR WAR RELOCATION CENTER—1944

A mile west of the Manzanar War Relocation Center, Owens Valley, August

Behind him the full moon was bright, lighting the desert floor like a quilt of sage, shadows, rocks, and sand that sloped upwards and westward to the Sierra. Highlighted peaks stood out against the night. An apron of alternating ridges and shadowed canyons flowed down from the peaks to the desert floor of the Owens Valley.

There was no trail, but Henry Kubota knew exactly where he was. He had done this many nights, even when there was no moon.

Scanning the view ahead, Henry marveled at the scene. Born and raised in Garden Grove, California, he had only the distant mountains surrounding the Los Angeles basin as a reference before coming to Manzanar. For many years he dreamed of visiting the San Gabriel Mountains. But his loyalty was with his parents who worked in their fields daily. Dream as he might, this loyalty meant that he never visited the San Gabriel. Now, as an internee at the Manzanar War Relocation Center for the past two years with his family and most of his relatives, he discovered another mountain range, the Sierra Nevada. He had the 'bug' to hike and could not get enough of the Sierra. The Sierra dominated the Owens Valley and Henry could not venture outside his family's tarpaper house in Manzanar without gazing and finding himself mesmerized by the Sierra.

Tonight, as he had done so often, Henry walked away from Manzanar and towards the mountains. It was warm, clear and quiet—perfect conditions for a two-day journey. Henry could see his first destination about a mile away, the mouth of George Creek canyon where it opened onto the valley floor. The trees and shrubs that lined the creek as it flowed steadily downward and across the desert towards the Owens River painted a snaking dark line shadow against the bright Moon-lit sand. The creek was to his left and about a quarter mile away. When he reached the mouth of the canyon, he would intersect with the creek.

Just inside the canyon and about fifty feet above the creek was a cave. Not a big one, but room enough for two people. Here he would pick up his pack and some supplies for the two day hike ahead. If Tom had been to the cave since Henry visited it last week, he might find a note. Last time they talked, Henry inquired about more information regarding Oak Creek. He was hoping that Tom had left some details that would make the exploration purpose of this trip rewarding.

Almost a year ago, while on one of his outings along George Creek, Henry encountered Tom Littlebear hunting near the entrance to George Creek canyon. Henry found himself apologizing profusely for unwittingly scaring off a nice Mule deer that Tom was stalking. Henry expected Tom, whom he did not know at the time, to be upset. Instead, Tom acted as though it was not important and that he was very glad to make Henry's acquaintance. In fact, Tom was well acquainted with Henry. Not by name, but by Henry's habits. Tom had long observed Henry during Henry's forays away from Manzanar. He knew Henry as the 'Little Wanderer'.

Tom's family and ancestors as far back as stories go lived in the Bishop area. Like Henry, Tom too was a wanderer. He was also a bit of a loner, which was reflected in the many days and nights he spent alone wandering. Over the years he had become familiar with all the canyons that opened into the Owens Valley.

Tom's wandering endeavors also fit well with his employment. For several years he had worked for the Los Angeles Department of Water and Power. During the summer he patrolled the canyons to monitor the flow of the creeks that fed water into the aqueduct. During the winter he had the job of measuring the depth of snow in the canyons and Sierra backcountry. Both summer and winter tasks were demanding because travel up and down many canyons was strenuous. However, it was his work in the winter that had made Tom a valuable asset to the LADWP. It was the kind of work that required days of plodding through deep snow, taking periodic measurements, and spending time alone. Tom was ideally suited for this task.

The two became good friends. Henry, from the beginning, felt like someone who was being welcomed back to a family after many years of absence. In time, Henry realized that their friendship was due, in part, to many similarities between the two. Tom liked to compare the experiences of the two. They both liked to wander. Each was drawn to the mountains. And, interestingly, Tom liked to point out that they had something very important in common. Henry's people were like Tom's people. Both cultures found their freedom restricted by the white man. And both were constantly running away to find freedom while wandering the valley and the hills.

Leaving the cave, Henry intended to hike north all night until he came to Oak Creek Canyon. There he would take a nap for a couple of hours before hiking up the canyon. Several weeks ago, following sketchy information provided by Tom, he had found an old Paiute Indian camp on the south side of Oak Creek Canyon. According to Tom, there was also a cave farther up the canyon on the south side.

This would be a long hike. He had planned for two days and two nights. Henry's objective was to make the return to Manzanar by night. His brothers and cousins would easily cover for him for two days. After all, Henry had something else in common with Tom, the Anglo-American soldiers who guarded the camp could not tell the difference between people of other races. For Anglo-Americans, most Native Americans looked alike and most Japanese Americans looked alike.

Henry was especially excited about this trip. He had explored only one other cave that Tom had directed him to. There was little to see. Others had violated the cave and the only artifacts were broken pottery shards, some very old flour sacks, arrowheads, and various other pieces of broken artifacts. During the past two years he had discovered many Indian artifacts intact as well as items left by the early white settlers in the Owens Valley. In most instances, such as old Paiute campsites, Henry left the artifacts in place. Artifacts found elsewhere, he often took back to the George Creek cave for Tom to identify. Then, he or Tom would return them to their place of origin.

He never ceased to be amazed at Tom's description of the Indian artifacts. Often, the description included a story. Every artifact seemed to have its place in Paiute history, and Tom Littlebear was compelled to recount every piece of the history known to him. He was a living history of his people. Sometimes Tom told Henry the artifacts were of little significance. Other times he would launch into a story only to get so deep into the historical culture of his people that he would forget the artifact and wander through a series of tales that seemed to be linked together in ways that were not clear to Henry. On occasion Tom seemed to talk himself into a trance. It was as if his mind was somewhere else. Suddenly, he would return to consciousness, stare at Henry as his mind came back to reality, and then he would make some comment like "Oh well, you don't want to listen me ramble on." Henry would then have to beg Tom to return his focus to the artifact and continue his story.

Some Paiute artifacts were stored in the George Creek cave along with many items of Anglo origin from the early days of the white settlers. Occasionally, Tom would suggest that an artifact was of such importance that it needed to be protected from 'would be' scavengers. He would give the artifact to Henry with the request that Henry hold on to it until he could give it to a museum for safe keeping. Tom repeatedly lamented the demise of the Paiute culture and the lack of interest in cultural heritage among the younger tribal generation. He seemed to feel that one of the few good institutions of the white man was the museum. At least future generations of his people could go there to see their ancestors' work. Henry tried to get Tom to give the items to the museum himself. Tom would shake his head, saying that he had once tried that and the people at the museum accused him of stealing the items and trying to make money off of them. It would be better coming from Henry.

As a result of all of this, Henry had a fine collection of Paiute artifacts stored in a small repository beneath the floorboards of his parents place in Manzanar. He would have to keep them there until the war was over. If he tried to give them to someone now, people would know that he had been leaving the camp often.

Along with the artifacts, Henry kept notes indicating where the items were found. He would decide what to do with the artifacts at a later date.

Most of the time Henry was confined to camp; attending school, participating in activities, and acquiescing to his parent's wishes. In exchange for attention to responsibility, Henry's parents tolerated his outings. They also knew that Henry would often return with a variety of sundries or hard to get meats, nuts, and fruits. These were complements of Tom. What his family did not know was that Henry also returned with artifacts which were added to a growing collection of items that would peak the interest of any archeologist, anthropologist, historian, or museum curator.

Someday, when all of this was over and Henry's family returned to the freedom they enjoyed before Manzanar, he would share these items with family, friends, and museums.

But tonight, his mind was set on Oak Creek canyon and what may be found there.

CHAPTER 12

WHAT DO WE DO NOW?

A telephone conversation

The question was simple. "What do we do now?" Sti spoke for both when he vocalized what appeared to be a rhetorical question.

The call to the Fresno County Sheriff had proved futile. Their offices were content to leave the matter in the hands of the National Park Service. Yes, the county coroner had issued the certification of accidental death. But, any investigation would have to be done by the feds if there was to be any additional follow-up.

So, Rob called in a chip. A distant cousin worked for the National Park Service in the Southwest. Rob telephoned and inquired about how best to probe the issue of what was being done to investigate June's death. The cousin got back to Rob with both a list of people in the Park Service to contact as well as some 'I have it on good authority' information regarding June's death. Apparently the Park Service has a division which is dispatched when a death or other mishap warrants a special investigation. Rob's cousin had talked several times with members of this team and was able to get information not generally available. The team that looked into June's death was indeed very thorough. Supervisors and fellow rangers were interviewed, as were several backpackers and packers who had seen and visited with June during the days and weeks prior to her death. There was also information gathered from interviews conducted at the time search parties were looking for June.

According to Rob's cousin, the NPS investigators reached a conclusion that the death was an accident. But the conclusion was a consensus, not a finding of fact. Several of the investigators were puzzled, but they had no evidence to suggest anything other than an accident.

Some of those interviewed as part of the investigation suggested that June, although she was diligent in meeting her responsibilities, seemed distant and often preoccupied during the weeks leading up to her disappearance. During her free time she was usually studying aerial photographs of the Sierra, studying geological and topographic maps of the Sierra, and studying historical documents and articles about the Owens Valley pioneers and Indians. Interestingly, a search of June's backcountry house-tent did not reveal much that would be considered documents or articles of this type. Allegedly, June kept a journal, but the investigation turned up nothing of this sort.

This last piece of information piqued the interest of Sti and Rob. They knew that some of the information the Park Service investigators had not seen was in the possession of Matthew Harris because June had sent him a package before she disappeared.

Also, the investigators discovered from interviews that on days off June often hiked north to wander in the Muro Blanco canyon, Cartridge Pass region, or the slopes bordering the east and west banks of the headwaters of the South Fork of the Kings River. It was a curious fact that June often inquired if cross-country backpackers, especially those traveling the High Route, Muro Blanco canyon, and Arrow Creek region had come across any artifacts or seen anything strange. When those questioned inquired as to her interest, she was evasive and non-committal in her response. It was clear to others that she had a special interest in these areas, but had no intention of sharing her interest with others.

Several Forest Service and Park Service rangers noted that when June had consecutive several days off, she seldom used them for R&R in the Owens Valley. Usually she backpacked selected canyons and passes on the eastern slope such as Shingle Mill Bench, Goodale, Division, Sawmill and Oak Creeks, Armstrong Canyon, and Baxter and Sawmill Passes. The common comment of those who observed her on her return from such outings was that she seemed distant and always seemed to be searching.

As for the days just prior to her disappearance, those interviewed indicated that June seemed anxious for any information regarding the upper Cartridge Creek and Lake Basin. She monitored closely anyone who was coming from or heading towards the High Route between Horseshoe Lakes and Marion Lake. However, investigators found nothing unusual that happened in that area or surrounding areas, except the unusually harsh weather. In fact, the thing that intrigued them was that June departed from her usually sound judgment and ignored the weather to go out on a patrol without noting her route and timeline. By all accounts, June's decision went contrary to her usual adherence to regulations, common sense, and attention to detail. At least that was the perception of her colleagues.

One other curious fact emerged from the inquiries of Rob's cousin. The NPS and Fresno Sheriff's Department officers, although they found the body with ease and as described by Sti and Rob, they did not find anything to suggest the ice axe could have been involved in June's death. The ice axe was indeed behind the shoulder, but it was on its side, angled up, but not so as to suggest clearly that it had protruded into the body cavity. It did not appear to be in a position that would suggest an ice axe had severely wounded the victim. Had the ice axe pick penetrated June's back, there should have been damage to surrounding bone tissue. There was none. The investigators reviewed the statements of Sti and Rob and chalked their suggestions up to a sense of imagination. From the point of view of the investigators, Sti and Rob probably overstated what they saw because they wanted to believe that the ice axe had been the cause of death. Also, there was no damage to surrounding bones to suggest a blow from the axe.

Sti and Rob now knew that there was more to the death of June Harris. They knew what they had seen, and they had a picture to prove it. An ice axe does not find its way behind a body unless there are very extenuating circumstances. Certainly, a peculiar accident could have resulted in the body collapsing backward onto the axe, but such circumstances would have to have been very strange. June's body was not at the bottom of a slope where one could conjecture that she had fallen and eventually rolled on top of the axe. So, Sti's question, 'What do we do now?' was not really rhetorical. They both now realized that Dr. Matthew Harris had good reason to be suspicious of his granddaughter's death. But what to do about such thoughts was not a question easily answered. Again it required reflection, a task Sti and Rob would probably not have spent much time on when they were young. However, with age comes patience and the situation involving June Harris and her death was no longer a simple matter of humoring her grandfather's suspicions.

Rob spoke first. "I think we need to have another visit with the good Dr. Harris. Didn't he say he had read the investigative report? If he did, he must have seen that the ice axe was reported to be on its side rather than penetrating into the body of June."

It was Sti's turn. "I think we go back to the Harris residence, talk to the old man, review the archives, and look for some other ways to investigate this whole affair." After a few seconds, "We need to spend some time formulating some questions. There are others out there with more knowledge about what this is all about than us. We need to be careful."

"We also need to go back to where we found June's body and take a look around. We may need to wander that whole area," was Rob's thought. "The ante has just been upped, and we are holding few cards of any note. We need to learn some things real fast if we want to play this game."

Rob and Sti both knew that understanding the cause of June's death required that they get inside June's head. It is not likely that a murder on the High Route would be just another random act of violence. Obviously, if she was killed it was because she saw or knew something or was about to know something that others did not want her to know. Someone was willing to kill her to prevent her from knowing. Maybe they were even willing, after the fact, to destroy evidence that would suggest anything but an accident led to June's death. Some answers had to be in the Harris archives. If not there, the answers had to be somewhere in the Eastern Sierra. Either way, their work was cut out for them, and neither Sti nor Rob was certain they wanted into this game.

It was early spring, so a trip to the High Route would have to wait. In the mean time, what they had to do now was walk in June's shoes by learning what she had learned before she went into the mountains during that fateful summer.

CHAPTER 13

SIERRA CLUB BASE CAMP—1935

Upper Horseshoe Lake, Kings Canyon National Park, summer

Lillian Hamner had been on several Sierra Club outings. This one was different. It was much more rugged. After this trip, she could attest that any previous outing paled in comparison. For days they had traveled steadily up hill from Kings Canyon to Horseshoe Lakes. From there it was one ridge after another. Granite and more granite were crossed as they made their way to Marion Lake and Lake Basin. The beauty of it all was unrivaled, but it could only be described as rugged. You had to hike it to understand. How the mules and horses negotiated this terrain was a mystery. That they repeated the effort on their return trip just made it even more unbelievable.

The sun was warm against her skin. But the late afternoon breeze and cool surface of the rock tempered the sun's effect. Laps of water, pushed by the wind across the surface of Upper Horseshoe Lake, provided a constant slapping sound as each little ripple struck the face of the granite rock that jutted out into the lake. Journal in hand, Lillian reflected. Tomorrow they would begin the descent back to Kings Canyon. If she did not record her thoughts of the past couple of days, they would begin to fade. On previous trips she had failed to bring closure to her trip journal until the trip was over. She found that once removed from the backcountry, the little things important to the time and place of events lost their significance.

Thoughts and visual impressions of what Lillian saw up higher began to surface. What should she say? There was no obvious answer. Lillian just started writing.

TWO DAYS AGO WE LEFT OUR CAMP AT MARION LAKE. THE HOUR WAS VERY EARLY. SOME OF THE PACKERS HAD ALREADY DEPARTED. WITH ANY LUCK, WE SHOULD HAVE MADE HORSESHOE LAKES BY LATE AFTERNOON. AFTER ALL, WE WERE SIMPLY RETRACING OUR ROUTE OF FIVE DAYS EARLIER.

THE TRIP WENT SMOOTHLY EARLY ON. HOWEVER, IN EARLY AFTERNOON, AS WE WORKED OUR WAY PAST SEVERAL SMALL TARNS AT ABOUT 11,000 FEET, SOMETHING SPOOKED THE MULES AND HORSES. ONE MULE BOLTED DOWN SLOPE TOWARD THE SOUTH FORK OF CARTRIDGE CREEK. SEVERAL OTHER MULES JUMPED AND STUMBLED. IT WAS AN AWFUL SCENE. THE PACKS OF SEVERAL BROKE OPEN AND GOODS AND SUPPLIES WERE THROWN ABOUT. THE ROCKY TERRAIN WAS VERY UNSTABLE AND I WAS SURE ONE OF THE MULES OR HORSES WOULD BREAK A LEG. EVEN THE PACKERS SEEMED TO BE CAUGHT OFF GUARD.

WHEN THE ANIMALS CALMED DOWN, THE PACKERS BEGAN THE PROCESS OF GATHERING GEAR AND RELOADING THE PACKS. AT THE SAME TIME, ONE PACKER AND THREE MEN WENT AFTER THE MULE THAT HAD RUN AWAY. THE MULE, THE PACKERS CALLED HER MADGE, WAS QUITE FAR AWAY BY NOW. AT TIMES WE COULD SEE ONLY PART OF HER FAR DOWN SLOPE AMONG SOME LARGE BOULDERS. IT WAS AGREED THAT ONCE THE REMAINING ANIMALS WERE RELOADED, WE WOULD GO AHEAD TO HORSESHOE LAKES.

AS WE WENT AHEAD TO WINDY RIDGE WE LOST SIGHT OF THE OTHER FOUR AND DID NOT SEE THEM UNTIL LATE EVENING WHEN THEY SHOWED UP WITHOUT THE MULE. IT WAS A STRANGE SITE. ALL FOUR MEN WANTED TO TALK AT ONCE. THEY DID. THAT WAS YESTERDAY. SINCE THEN I HAVE HEARD THE STORIES TOLD SEVERAL TIMES.

APPARENTLY THE FOUR GOT WITHIN ABOUT A QUARTER MILE OF THE MULE WHEN SHE DISAPPEARED BEHIND A SMALL RIDGE. THEY LOST SIGHT OF HER FOR ABOUT TEN MINUTES. THE GOING CONSISTED OF VERY ROCKY FOOTING AND IT TOOK CONSIDERABLE TIME TO MAKE PROGRESS. THEY WERE AMAZED THAT THE MULE WAS EVEN WALKING. WHEN THE FOUR

GOT TO THE TOP OF THE RIDGE, THE ERRANT MULE WAS NOWHERE TO BE FOUND. THEY SPLIT UP AND LOOKED FOR HER. HER PACK HAD BEGUN TO COME APART AND THERE WAS A TRAIL OF PACK ITEMS THAT SUGGESTED THE MULE HAD MOVED FARTHER DOWN SLOPE. THEN, THEY COMPLETELY LOST HER TRAIL. THEY SEARCHED FOR TWO HOURS AND FOUND NO SIGN OF THE MULE.

LOSING THE MULE MEANT THAT OUR REMAINING FOOD SUPPLY WAS CUT IN HALF SINCE SHE HAD SOME OF THE FOOD SUPPLIES. BUT IF LOSING HER WAS BAD, HER COMPLETE DISAPPEARANCE WAS A MYSTERY. MORE OF A MYSTERY, HOWEVER, WAS THAT THE PACKER AND ONE OF THE MEN CLAIM TO HAVE SEEN WHAT LOOKED LIKE TWO PEOPLE. MORE SPECIFICALLY, THEY SAID THE UNKNOWN PEOPLE LOOKED LIKE INDIANS.

THE TWO INDIANS WERE QUITE A DISTANCE AWAY AND SEEMED TO BE PREOCCUPIED. THEY YELLED AT THE INDIANS WHO TOOK NOTE OF OUR PEOPLE AND THEN, AS IF THERE WAS A DOOR INTO THE MOUNTAIN, DISAPPEARED. WHEN THE MEN WENT UP TO WHERE THEY THOUGHT THE INDIANS HAD BEEN, THEY FOUND NOTHING. THE AREA WAS VERY MUCH BROKEN UP BY LARGE ROCKS AND SHALLOW LITTLE CANYONS. A PERSON, OR A MULE FOR THAT MATTER, COULD EASILY AVOID DETECTION IN SUCH AN AREA. THAT WAS THE CASE. THERE WAS NOT A TRACE OF MULE OR INDIANS. WHEN THE FOUR WERE BACK TOGETHER, THEY AGAIN TRIED TO SEARCH THE AREA WHERE THE INDIANS WERE LAST SEEN. NOTHING OF THEIR PRESENCE WAS FOUND. NO FURTHER EVIDENCE OF THE MULE WAS FOUND. SO, THE FOUR BEGAN THE LONG HIKE TO WINDY RIDGE.

SO, OUR LITTLE OUTING HAS ITS MYSTERY. EVERYONE HAS BEEN SPECULATING ABOUT WHAT REALLY HAPPENED TO THE MULE. I HAVE EVEN HEARD SOME COMMENTS THAT MAYBE THE FOUR MEN MADE UP THE STORY BECAUSE THEY WERE NOT ABLE TO FIND AND BRING BACK THE MULE. I DO NOT KNOW. BUT I THINK I BELIEVE THE MEN.

Lillian found the environment to be very peaceful. This was a place you could visit many times and never get enough. Time seemed to stand still. There was no hurry. Laying journal and pen aside, she reclined on the rock and stared up at Windy Ridge. She thought: 'What beauty these mountains show. What secretes they hide. I wonder if the men really saw Indians? Maybe the Indians were up here for the same reasons we are? Maybe they have other reasons. I wonder?'

So, here she was. Finishing up another backcountry trip; this was the worst part. Waiting to go down the hill, to the car, and back to civilization. Lillian worked hard to preserve her thoughts. She wanted to hold onto a moving image of every day of this trip. She tried, but she knew it was only temporary. That is why she wrote.

CHAPTER 14

SECOND VISIT TO THE HARRIS RESIDENCE

Matthew Harris residence,
Berkeley, California

The second visit to the home of Dr. Harris was not unexpected, according to the professor. Harris acknowledged as much when Rob called and made arrangements. Harris indicated that he knew that the two friends would find the search for June's killers compelling once they began to see the inconsistencies in the evidence. As far as Harris was concerned, Sti and Rob were always welcome. For his part, Rob was cautious. He acknowledged that there were some peculiar takes on some of the evidence, but he did not express any verbal support for the Harris theory regarding June's death. Rob simply inquired if a visit two weeks hence would be acceptable. When Harris indicated the timing was no problem, Rob brought the discussion to a close. It was not that Rob did not wish to talk, that is seldom the case. However, Rob and Sti had agreed that any discussion with Harris should be listened to by both so that there could be no misconstruing what Harris said. The two hikers were already of the opinion that Harris had not shared everything with them and they were not going to leave anything to chance.

The Harris home was just as they had left it—very neat, organized and clearly the residence of someone, or a family, that thrived on research. Again, while they worked, Matthew Harris spent most of his time in the dining room. During the two days, Harris did go to the Berkeley campus for a couple of hours to participate in a meeting. However, Harris indicated that he seldom had to go to the campus because he no longer taught and any communication necessary could be handled by computer, phone, e-mail or fax.

The focus of this second visit was on the packages that June had sent to Matthew Harris in the months prior to her disappearance. Of special interest was June's journal and how her coding methods compared with those of her father and grandfather.

The packages had been opened, but Harris had stored the contents of each package in the original box and packaging material so the postmarks and order they were received could be confirmed. Ever the field scientist, Matthew was meticulous in his storage of all manner of things.

Sti and Rob were not long into their review of the packages before they realized that June Harris had probably sent home most of the artifacts, articles, books, notes, and journals related to her studies of her father's work. June Harris had amassed a sizeable collection of primary and secondary material regarding the work of Matt Harris. If these were the objects that dominated her time and attention during the weeks and months prior to her disappearance, why had she sent them home? Was she anticipating problems? No wonder investigators found nothing of note at her backcountry residence.

Equally important, June had an intriguing collection of artifacts including a wide assortment of Paiute Indian relics, old horseshoes, pieces of leather and canvas, and some old baskets of exceptional quality. A collection of amateurish photographs showed some old miners picks, petroglyphs, and what appeared to be scenes in the Sierra back country. Sti and Rob recognized some of the pictured Sierra scenes. They also recognized the similarity between some of the items in June's collection and the items scattered about her body when Sti and Rob found it.

What was most fascinating about all of the items was that June Harris had given each a reference number, which corresponded to a listing of items in her journals. All anyone had to do was find the corresponding reference number to find out about the item. Or so it seemed. Reading the documented information was not easy. June had the information in a coded form. What made the code unusual was the fact that it was both unique to the Harris family and much more complex than the codes of her father and grandfather. It matched, in many ways, the code Sti and Rob had encountered on their previous trip when they reviewed Matt's journals. But the task of deciphering both codes would not be an easy task.

Rob remembered the first conversation with Harris. "Didn't Harris tell us that his son had adopted the good Dr.'s field coding system when Megan and Matt were very young and accompanied Harris and his wife on their field outings?" Not waiting for an answer, Rob continued. "It seems to me that Harris could probably tell us how to read this code." This one-sided discussion was more a matter of thinking out loud. Rob was wondering why Matthew Harris did not tell them that they would find journals with coded information and that they need only talk to him to get them translated.

* * * *

Later, Matthew Harris was overly apologetic. "I knew you would both eventually confront the need to translate the coded information. I had no intentions of keeping the information from you. It's just that what appears to be a code on my part is nothing more than an elaborate cataloguing technique, developed by Eaddie and I when we were collecting samples in the field. The code uses numbers in place of letters, and letters in place of numbers. When I realized that there were colleagues who would steal my ideas and finds to benefit their own futures, I expanded the technique to include other information that only Eaddie or I could understand. The expanded code used abbreviations, some of them peculiar to my use, in place of traditional wording."

"But did you not tell us earlier that Megan, Matt and Kathryn adopted your coding methods?" asked Sti.

"Yes, but later Matt and Kathryn modified it to be much more difficult to understand. Even I do not have the capability to read it without considerable work. I knew that you would eventually realize that June's code takes the family code in new directions." The two friends were aware that June's code was not simple. It was not easily decoded even with the help of their knowledge about

Matt's coding system. In fact, at this point, Sti and Rob were not confident they could translate June's code accurately. They also knew that much of the difficulty in translating June's code was because Matt had also expanded the family code into a much more sophisticated code than the one used by his father.

"So, why not tell us all of this up front?" was Rob's question.

"I suppose I could have. My intent was not one of deception. My intent was to be cautious. I was not sure how the two of you would take this whole thing. If you decided not to pursue it, then you did not need to know more than I told you. If you went forth with the investigation, well, my intent was to then give you more information as needed. However, Matt's code and June's code are much more complex than the one I used, and I am not confident I can do both justice in translation. That is where we are now."

"Not quite Mr. Harris! Sti and I have looked into this matter with some degree of interest, albeit with amateurish methods, but with the growing certainty that there is more to your granddaughter's death than meets the eye. You came across sincere in our first meeting. Since then, we have begun to doubt your sincerity."

"I am not sure that I understand what you mean."

"What Rob is saying, is that we have come to believe that you are actually doing more than not telling us information that we should know. You are purposefully withholding information that we cannot do without if we are to pursue your original request." Sti paused. The intent was to let his comments sink in.

Two could play this game. Sti and Rob were not about to tell Harris that they had contacts within the NPS. They preferred to appear to be as amateurish as possible. For both Harris and anyone else that they would come into contact with, the more they looked like a couple of rookies checking out a hunch, the better.

Always the tactful and friendly communicator, except when he was negotiating a car or truck deal, Rob laid out the line of thinking. "Dr. Harris, you came to us with the belief that June's death was something more than an accident. You already knew that the NPS and the Fresno Sheriff and Coroner's Office had ruled it an accidental death. No doubt you had already pushed the issue with these two agencies and did not get the satisfaction you wanted, is that not true?" Rob was speculating, but it was a reasonable assumption. Why else would Harris have gone to all the trouble to contact Sti and set up a meeting?

Harris was caught off guard. But he had learned long ago that when you are in such a situation, you collect your thoughts before responding. "Yes. I have long been convinced that June's death was not accidental. I made repeated inquiries as to why the Park Service and Sheriff's officers would not pursue my convictions."

"But, you did not give them enough compelling evidence to make your suspicions reasonable. You gave them no evidence other than the information they already had, correct?" Sti was demanding a response.

"I tried to show them that June would not do something that would result in her death. I could not believe she would go off so unprepared as to die of exposure. I pointed out that her daypack, which would have contained the necessary items for survival, was nowhere to be found. But they would not listen. Oh, they were kind, but I knew they did not care."

"I think you are missing the point here, Mr. Harris." Sti gauged his words. He did not want to reveal that the pictures that he and Rob took seemed to show the ice axe in a position that may have seriously wounded, if not killed, June. "You were convinced it was not an accident because you have evidence which you were unwilling to share with the authorities. You did not even share the letters and packages June had sent you. Why?"

The two friends were watching Harris closely. But he just stared at them. He knew that more was to come.

"Remember when you mentioned your son's death in an automobile accident to us? At the time you told us that was the conclusion of the Highway Patrol. You also indicated that you were getting ahead of yourself. The implication was that you would come back to that point. You never did. Dr. Harris, an automobile accident is usually a matter for which the Highway Patrol has considerable expertise. Do you have concrete evidence to suggest otherwise? You suggest you have evidence that June's death was not accidental, but you have not shared it with us." Rob stopped and turned to Sti.

Sti stared long and hard into the professor's eyes as he spoke. "Mr. Harris, if you want us to look further into this matter, then you had best come clean with the truth. Otherwise, we go home."

This was the old 'good cop, bad cop' game. At least it was the novice version. Rob added, "This is not a threat Dr. Harris, it is a matter of integrity. My friend here would say it is a matter of 'efficacy.' You want us to search for the truth regarding June's death, but you do not want to empower us to do a thorough job. You want us to make a difference without having access to all the evidence." Rob was leading Harris. "June's death may not be an isolated incident. We would agree that everything we have looked at suggests that June, Matt, and you are tied together in the truth. You may not know who is responsible for her death, but you do know that you probably share in the guilt." There, it was out. The finger of guilt was pointing at the Harris family.

Matthew Harris now knew that the two friends were well aware that June's death, if not an accident, was possibly part of a large picture of intrigue and wrongdoing that maligned the entire Harris family.

The pause was interminable. Four eyes were focused on Harris and awaiting his response. The two friends knew Harris was not one to just start talking. His scientific nature required deliberate reflection before launching into explanatory comments.

Slowly and thoughtfully Harris began to respond. "You are right, of course. And again, I apologize. As you will see, I have good reason to believe my granddaughter's death was not accidental. But I too am an amateur when it comes to dealing with an investigation of this sort. All my life I have been investigating, comparing pieces of evidence, drawing conclusions, placing blame if you will. I am accustomed to looking for 'cause and effect' relationships. Always testing and searching for empirical evidence that provides proof to support or reject hypotheses—my own as well as those of others. But on this matter, I needed help. I cannot go to the site of the incident. I do not have the capacity to follow up on every detail. But I could not let just anybody investigate with my support. That is why I chose the two of you. You are all I have."

With that preface, Harris backed his mind's chronological clock up, and started the story.

"In the late fall of 1948 Eaddie and I were studying the rock formations on the south side of Sawmill Creek. You have probably been there."

Sti saw the statement as a question. "Yes we have, several times." Sti remembered all too well the approach to the canyon. "It is very rugged where the creek exits into the valley. The old sawmill makes it an even more interesting canyon." The comment was also more than a polite response. It was also a way of letting Harris know that his two guests were very familiar with the valley and the Sierra's eastern slope.

Harris continued. "That is why we were investigating the area. The construction of the old sawmill and flume resulted in exposure of several layers of rock. It was an excellent area for collecting and study.

"One day, while probing the slopes on the south side of Sawmill Meadow, Eaddie came across the narrow entrance to what looked to be a cave. But Eaddie was not fond of caves and brought it to my attention later in the afternoon. I told her we would check it out before we exited the canyon, which would not be for a few days. Small caves are not uncommon, and seldom yield any valuable geological information in this part of the Sierra. In fact, from a geological point of view, most are not true caves. They are often little more than a random arrangement of very large boulders and granite slabs that give the appearance of a small cave.

"Two days later, I was working the steep slopes above Mule Lake on the same side of the creek, when I came across an area with smoke scarred rock. From experience, I knew that a fire had once burned next to the rock. However, because of the sawmill business, which had taken place in the canyon, my interest was not immediately aroused. Then, as if it was put there to draw my attention, I saw some evidence that a large flat rock had been used to grind grain or pine nuts. This surprised me. On closer investigation of the area, I uncovered marginal, but proof nonetheless, that Indians had once used the area. Looking down the slope, I realized that the location was well suited to scan the entire canyon. No one could go up or down this canyon without being seen from this location. I was intrigued, and later mentioned the find to my wife. Her comment surprised me.

According to her observations, the cave she found showed signs of smoke soot on one of the rocks on the slope above the cave.

"The next day Eaddie took me to the site of the cave. As it turned out, it had all the qualities of a small cave, but it was not a true cave. It consisted of one large and several small blocks of granite resting across several other slabs. Once you negotiated the very narrow and hidden entrance, it opened into a chamber about twenty feet deep and twelve feet wide. But what we found inside was not typical of small caves. It had been lived in. There were rock and wood benches. On the benches were pottery items, baskets, wood and stone implements, and what looked to be the remains of leather goods. On a sloping rock shelf at the rear of the cave, there were the remains of what appeared to be cloth sacks that once held flour or some kind of grain. To one side there was a fireplace and one could see where the smoke exited circuitously through a crack in the ceiling. It was the rock where the smoke exited into the sky that was charred with smoke and was visible to Eaddie outside several days before.

"But it was not the Native American artifacts that surprised us. Off to one side of the cave was a rock shelf with the dust coated remains of several well-crafted arrows. We blew the dust off. There were no bows, but there were three rifles and a pistol. A leather pouch held several rounds of ammunition. Eaddie and I had heard from time to time that people uncovered Indian artifacts. We had once met a fellow that worked on the LA Aqueduct project in the Owens Valley, and he described how one of his field superintendents had decades earlier found a small cave with several very valuable artifacts in it. These items were now on display in the Eastern California Museum in the town of Independence. At the time we had never heard of such finds including rifles and guns.

"Eaddie and I made meticulous notes regarding the location and contents of the cave. We did not remove any item. I modified my geological specimen cataloging code to record each item we found in the cave. Our intent was to, in time, inform those who knew more about such artifacts so that a proper investigation could be conducted. That is not to say I was not interested in the find, but my fellowship at that time did not afford time to be spent in other endeavors. I would have liked to study the artifacts, but I was not an expert. I did not have time, and I could not afford it. I would take care of it at a later date.

"A week later, we were out of the canyon, just ahead of a heavy snow storm. All of our gear and specimens were on two donkeys and we had to make our way over to Aberdeen where a colleague was to pick us up in two days. Our two young children were not with us on this trip. They were already in school in Berkeley and staying with friends. There was no time to stop in Independence and inquire at the museum. Eaddie and I reasoned that the items in the cave had survived many years and another winter of time would make no difference. With the early snow, no one was going to go up there before next May or June anyway.

"During the winter, I talked with a couple of the university anthropology studies department members with whom I had casual contact. I mentioned that I had found several Indian objects in the Sierra. I did not reveal the location. My inquiry sought to identify who was doing research on the local Sierra Indians and how best to bring this to their attention while at the same time insuring that the area in question would not be overrun with anthropologists and their graduate students. One of my colleagues put me in touch with a professor from Stanford who had worked with A.L. Krober when he was at Berkeley."

Sti was familiar with Krober. He had read Krober's exhaustive study of California Indians, *Handbook Of The Indians Of California*, as well as *Ishi In Two Worlds*, Krober's most successful work. Sti commented so as to note for Harris that he was aware of Krober's work.

Unimpressed, Harris continued. "Anyway, in late winter 1949, I got a call from a professor, a Dr. Freeman, who indicated that he did not have the time to put into such an investigation but would have a Dr. Allison, a Native American anthropologist living in the Owens Valley contact me. Sure enough, a few days later Dr. Allison called me. He said he was going to be in the Bay area for a few days and could we get together. I invited him to meet me at the University, but he declined saying that he was on a tight schedule but would be able to meet with me in downtown San Francisco. A week later, I met him at the old Sir Francis Drake Hotel.

"Dr. Allison knew the Owens Valley and the Eastern Sierra very well. He spoke openly of its great history, his concern for the impact of the L.A. Aqueduct and water pumping on the Valley's future, and the need to preserve the rich culture of the valley Indians and pioneers. He was very supportive of the efforts to develop the fledgling museum in Independence. He indicated that he had heard from Dr. Freeman that I had discovered some artifacts. I acknowledged as much, and indicated that I was cautious about revealing the contents and whereabouts to just anyone for fear that the artifacts would not be handled properly. I also indicated concern for the integrity of the area of the find, not wanting it overrun with archeologists and anthropologists. Dr. Allison, if that was his name, agreed and assured me that it was a relief to find someone not in it for money. He went on to indicate that such a find would be very valuable for the Eastern California Museum, just what it needed to solidify its place as a legitimate museum. If it was all right with me, he would have a representative of the museum contact me. That would give me time to think about how best to reveal the details. At the time, I thought this was a very considerate approach and agreed to await contact.

"Within days, I was contacted again by Dr. Allison who informed me that one of the founding board members of the museum would be attending a family wedding in San Jose during what would be the university spring break. Dr. Allison said he too would be at the wedding and wondered if Eaddie and I could join them in San Jose for dinner and a discussion. Usually I would be in the field during spring break, but this was an especially severe winter and fieldwork was out of the question. So I agreed to the meeting.

"The meeting took place in a very nice old hotel in downtown San Jose. The hotel has long since been razed. Dr. Allison and a Mr. Garsuch hosted us for a wonderful evening. They had a private room with dinner catered to the room. Both Allison's and Garsuch's credentials appeared impeccable. They were not pushy. They seemed to be willing to accommodate any suspicions and concerns that I had. They indicated that they were not in a hurry.

"Unfortunately, I was not equal to their game. Although not pushy, they did make some minor inquiries as to the general vicinity and elevation of the find. They indicated that some of the local Paiute and Shoshone Indians seemed to have a history of isolation and some of them even lived in very small bands with little or no contact with others. It would help them to be able to do some advanced research before working with the actual artifacts if I could give them the general vicinity, especially the elevation, of the find. I saw no harm in this since they did not know where on the eastern side the find was located. I indicated further that the Indians were clearly willing to endure difficult travel to reach and live at the location of the find, which was right at 8,800 feet. They appeared delighted and suggested that such remoteness indicated a very small band of

Paiute Indians known for living at the higher elevations, even in the winter. They commented that such Indians usually lived in a cave and Allison inquired if that was the case here. I was impressed and said yes, indicating that I had found another site, but it was not a cave and did not have any artifacts. Then, after additional conversation of no consequence, the evening ended and I agreed to look Mr. Garsuch up in Bishop when I went into the valley for my fieldwork immediately following the end of the semester in May 1949. I left impressed; they were willing to wait until the summer. They must be reputable. I could also check Mr. Garsuch out in greater detail at the Eastern California Museum next time I went through Independence.

"It was not until the month of June that Eaddie and I were able to get away for my fieldwork. We took the kids with us and headed for the Owens Valley with a long list of places to study. World War II had stimulated some interest in mining at various locations on the eastern slope. Study of the tailings at places such as the Union Carbide tungsten mine at Rovana, the mines in the Armstrong Canyon area, and the large mining activity in the Poverty Hills area could reveal some valuable information. We had managed to purchase an old truck and trailer, and planned to spend most of the summer in the field. Since we did not want to push the old truck too hard, we went south through the Central Valley to Bakersfield and then crossed over to the east through Tehachapi before turning north and entering the Owens Valley from the South. We set up our base near Aberdeen for the first part of the summer. A week later, I drove alone to Bishop to look up Mr. Garsuch. When my knocks on the door were answered, I knew I had been had. This was not the man with whom I talked in San Jose. When I described the Mr. Garsuch I had met, the real Mr. Garsuch had no idea who I was talking about. Embarrassed, and unwilling to go into more detail regarding my visit, I apologized, excused myself, and drove back to Eaddie and the kids. To say I was shocked would be an understatement. To say I feared the worst regarding the disposition of the Sawmill Creek Cave site was well short of my real feelings. I was angry. But it would be two weeks before I could check out the site and confirm my fears.

"When I did make it to the cave, it was empty. The only implements inside were the old flour or grain sacks. I was devastated. I returned to the truck and drove to Independence where I tried to locate the whereabouts of Dr. Allison. When I found no information indicating he lived in the Valley, I called Stanford University seeking to talk to Dr. Freeman. Again, I had been duped. Dr. Freeman had indeed received a call from my friend at Berkeley, but he apologized for treating it in a cavalier fashion and tossing it on the desk of his secretary and asking her to find someone who might be interested as he did not have time to pursue this. That did not surprise me. I have done the same thing. You get caught up in your research. Despite the finds of others, all you can think about is your project and you do not let any other evidence interfere with your work. The whole thing runs counter to what most people would think is quality research. The world of university research is not what most people think. Anyway, Freeman apologized and indicated he would try to find out what happened. I knew there was no chance of this. It was a dead issue, or so I thought.

"A couple of weeks later, Eaddie and I took the kids to Bishop for the weekend. You can conduct only so much fieldwork with your kids and wife along, and then you have to find civilization for a while. When we returned, the trailer had been broken into. Everything in the trailer had been turned inside out. It took us a good two days to put everything back in order. It was not until we had finished that I noticed that my file on the Sawmill Creek cave site was gone. At that point I knew that whoever was interested in the site would go to any lengths to get information, no doubt for big profits. I was not scared, but I was concerned for the family. I did not tell Eaddie about the stolen file. Instead, I feigned concern about some of the local miners and ranchers who probably did not want us in the area and suggested we move the trailer north to work the area in and around Bishop.

"The remainder of the summer went by without incident. However, during that summer and for many summers after, I always had the feeling that from time to time someone had been watching my work. Several times I could have sworn that someone had wandered through our camp and entered our trailer when we were gone. No single piece of proof, mind you, just several little things out of place that said someone had been tampering where they should not have been. I never said anything to Eaddie. I did not want to upset her. I was afraid she would want to take the kids home and I would have to work alone in the field. Yet, I always suspected she knew something was up.

"It is a funny thing about marriage. Eaddie and I were devoted to each other, and never held secrets until then. Out of fear or selfishness, I purposefully kept a secret. But something inside me said that she could read my emotions. You don't have the kind of relationship we had without knowing when something is not right. Eaddie never let on.

"Nothing much happened for several years, and I found myself thinking less and less often about the Indian artifacts. Then Matt began to develop a strong interest in the Paiute and Shoshone cultures. I could not interfere; it was a healthy interest. You do not deny your kids the opportunity to develop such academic interests and corresponding skills. But Eaddie and I were concerned about a future we could not control. When Matt became engrossed with his work following Megan's death, our concern increased significantly. It was not a stretch to reason that the so-called Dr. Allison and Mr. Garsuch were watching, waiting. Would our Matt be the next victim? When Matt's work became very visible and stimulated considerable debate, our concern grew even greater.

"It all came to a head that last Christmas holiday I told you about at the first meeting. When Matt indicated someone had already found and ransacked some cache sites, I knew who he was talking about. Eaddie and I had never told him about the Sawmill Creek Cave Site, we were embarrassed and only wanted to put that horrible experience behind us. When Matt said he was on to something big and that he would find out who was stealing these artifacts, I feared the worst, and again did not say anything to Eaddie.

"After Matt and Kathryn's deaths that September, Eaddie and I drove to Big Pine to claim their belongings that had been found in the wreckage. We then drove to Bishop, to claim the items they had in storage in a small garage rented from a local couple. We brought back many boxes of materials; they are all in there in the study organized and catalogued. We also brought back a strong feeling that Matt and Kathryn did not die by accident.

"Matt's car allegedly went off Highway 395 and rolled over twice. There were no witnesses. There were no seat belts. Kathryn was thrown and died instantly. Matt was taken to Northern Inyo Hospital where he died shortly after emergency surgery. As one would expect, the car was demolished. Likewise, any gear they had was scattered inside and outside the car. The local towing and storage company collected as much as possible and had it available when we arrived. Conspicuous in its absence was Matt's current journal. It had to have been in the car. Matt would not have gone anywhere without it. Eaddie and I searched the car and spent hours searching the area of the accident. We never found it.

"In Bishop, the young couple who had rented a one room guest house and garage to Matt and Kathryn went out of their way to assist us. They had not touched anything in the guesthouse or garage. Both were kept locked. But when we entered the guest house with the key they provided it was clearly evident that someone had methodically gone through Matt's files. Whoever entered the house through the bathroom window had been thorough in their search without knowing that most of Matt's research materials were located in a portable storage box in the garage. It had not been tampered with. The couple was very sorry and apologized profusely. Bishop was not a town where this type of crime was common and they could not understand who would do such a thing. I knew who did it. I also knew that they probably did not find the journal in the car and that is why they broke into the house.

"What concerned me most was that none of Matt's journals were to be found in the house or garage. Eaddie and I feared that the culprits had found and taken them. The only consolation was my knowledge that if someone had illegally taken the journal they probably could not easily decipher Matt's coded portions of the journal.

"Driving home, Eaddie and I went over everything. We knew it was the same people who had broken into our trailer and who had duped us many years ago. But why? We argued that question from every angle. But we both knew the answer. Matt was on to some big finds and those who had raided the Sawmill Creek Cave Site would do anything to get their hands on Indian artifacts.

"Later, after we had recovered Matt's belongings from his Stanford Office and storage facility, the situation became clearer. Apparently Matt's last journal was started at the beginning of his last summer of fieldwork. All previous journals and notes were locked in this office. September was the end of the field season and the beginning of classes and Matt and Kathryn had made a Labor Day weekend trip to Stanford to deposit much of their summer work. They had gone back to Bishop to retrieve what they needed and to prepare to store nonessentials for the winter.

"Once I had all of Matt's retrievable work and collections back at our home it sat untouched until the following summer. Having lost both of our children was devastating to Eaddie and me. I had my own classes and work to occupy my time for several months. Eaddie had to look after June, which she did with a passion. Eventually, I began to sort through the files, documents, notes, articles, photos and journals. Because I was somewhat familiar with Matt's coding, cataloguing and abbreviation system, it was possible to translate some of his notes and journals. With time, I began to realize how prophetic Matt's comments had been two and a half years earlier during the Christmas holidays. He had uncovered four cache sites. Two had been ransacked, nothing of consequence remained. One site had been severely damaged by flooding and cave-ins and most of the contents were demolished and rendered worthless. The fourth site was a treasure trove of pots, baskets, weapons, containers of food, and a small pot with chunks of gold. I could only guess what valuable information was in his last journal."

"The source of the gold for June's necklace?" was Rob's question. They had been listening for some time, and compassion seemed appropriate. "It sounds like your son was on the verge of a great breakthrough in his research."

"He was past the verge. He had discovered that one of the baskets had been woven into a pattern what appeared to be a very subtle map. On investigation, Matt realized that the map identified the location of other sites. Deciphering the information was not easy. It was not possible to decode the entire map. One had to focus on finding one site which would make it possible to then find other sites. Methodically, Matt tracked down three sites. One was a site located near a DWP powerhouse built in 1931. Workers had discovered the site; the contents ransacked. Nothing remained. The second site was the Sawmill Creek cave site, and you know what happened there. A third site above Sawmill Lake was located. It was untouched and contained only potsherds and several old flour sacks."

Sti asked a question. "All of this explains your reasons for being suspicious regarding Matt's death. However, it is not conclusive evidence. Did you do anything to pursue your hunches? Did you inquire with the Highway patrol? Did you interview those who were at the accident site? Do anything else?"

"We visited the Highway Patrol office in Bishop, hoping they might have found his journal. They did not. But we did talk with the officer who responded to the initial call. He said the accident was reported by an anonymous phone call. However, the CHP was not concerned. Then as now, there are many such accidents along 395 and passers by who do not want to get involved report the accidents anonymously.

"It took several months to go through Matt's things and I knew that Eaddie would not want to suffer through protracted efforts to prove Matt's death was not an accident. She was just beginning to adjust to being a mother again. I could not bear to see her suffer more. So I continued to study Matt's research without saying anything to Eaddie. If she knew I was secretly studying Matt's interests, she did not let on."

Sti sought to move things along. "And the more you studied, the more convinced you became regarding the cause of Matt's death. I suspect you also continued to uncover more information regarding Matt's findings and plans?"

"Yes and no," Harris responded.

Sti and Rob recognized a reflective, almost distant look in Harris. They had seen this look in Harris before. They knew more was to come.

"I began to realize that Matt's theories were both truth and fiction. He was right about the caches. They existed and there were probably more to be discovered. But he appeared to be wrong about the elaborate trading system. Interestingly, I sensed Matt too had come to realize that this part of his theory was inaccurate. I found no evidence of an alternative hypothesis. However, since he had no research competition on the matter, time was on his side. He was more concerned about someone else finding and ransacking the sites. He suspected those responsible were watching him. Matt believed they were using his research, plus the monitoring of Matt's fieldwork, to help them locate the sites. Then they could step in and take the contents. Matt sensed that they had already gone through this camp in search of information. He became cautious, and, no doubt, those watching him became aware that he was being cautious and would not reveal any information easily. So, he began to expand the complexity of his coding and to send things back to Stanford as a way of maintaining security. Hence, the Labor Day trip."

Rob was curious. "Did Matt actually identify the location of other sites? Did his journals or notes have specific information regarding locations?"

"Yes and no! Mind you, my decoding of his work is weak. However, it appears that Matt pieced disparate information together to form theories, or more appropriately, to speculate about the location of several other sites. Most sites were in eastern slope canyons north and south of Sawmill Creek. He even noted some probable site locations with some degree of specifics. However, and curiously I might say, Matt spent a lot of time investigating the possibility of a site or sites located in the backcountry, in the area of the headwaters of the Kings River and surrounding areas. The Muro Blanco appeared to be of special interest to Matt. My initial take on this was that these areas in the central Sierra backcountry have long been considered as possible locations for summer hunting by the Paiute. They are strategically located along travel routes and these routes are also used by migrating animals."

"Muro Blanco?" was Sti's reaction. "That is a very rugged area and in a very remote region. A site in that location seems out of character with the other eastern slope sites."

"It would appear so. I have reviewed the notes thoroughly. The information is sketchy. Nonetheless, I am convinced it was the focus of Matt's work just prior to his death. Also, although the evidence is not clear, Matt and Kathryn apparently spent some time hiking up and down the Muro Blanco. This is apparently not an easy task."

Sti and Rob smiled.

"I think Matt's final journal contained additional information. I have never found that journal."

"You did not follow up on these leads? I mean, you did not go to some of these sites?" Rob's questions were as much statements as questions. They needed no answer. Harris responded anyway.

"No, I have not. My work and especially my health precluded dedicating such time. Also, I go back to my concerns for Eaddie. It was not something she would have supported. It seemed such a shame. Matt was on to something big, but those who would have taken what he had without working for it, as Matt did, cut his life short. Worse, there was nothing I could do."

Sti and Rob had the picture. Matthew Harris had continued to study Matt's work and to organize it into the archives now found in the Harris study.

Such irony thought Rob. "Over time you came to know enough about Matt's work that you could have pursued his leads. However, you were trapped by your marriage, your work and your health."

A quiet response came from Harris. "Yes, I guess that was it."

Rob continued. "You were also trapped by the knowledge that those who were willing to kill Matt for information were also willing to kill you, your wife, and June to get what they wanted. Any effort on your part to follow up on Matt's work would have revealed the information in your possession and would have brought their wrath down on you and the family. It was a risk you could not afford to take."

This elicited a soft nod from Harris.

It was Sti's turn. "At least not until we came along. Our finding June's remains opened the old wound. The sense that her death was attributable to those who had both duped you and killed Matt was strong. Strong enough that you were willing to take a chance that Rob and I could be your last hope of revenge. There was only you now. Nobody left to get hurt but you."

"I was grasping at straws. With June's death, I had to do something. I was not sure what I would do if the two of you found the killers. I only knew that someone had destroyed my world with greedy interests. If the two of you were successful, I could perhaps do something."

A lot of ideas and emotions had been laid on the table in the last hour or so. Rob knew, as did Sri, that there was much more to the death of June Harris than they originally bargained for. Time was needed to review Matthew Harris's story. Perhaps more time would be needed reviewing the contents of the Harris archives, but that could wait.

"One more thing Dr. Harris. You told us that June helped you sort through things after the fire. Did June have an opportunity to see the information regarding the possible location of additional caches?"

"I believe so."

"Could June have somehow found the final journal of Matt's?"

"I don't know. I doubt it. She was so young when all of that happened. I don't know how she would have found it."

It was time to bring this interview to a close. No doubt it would be necessary to talk with Matthew Harris again, and quite possibly spend more time in the study. For now, Sti and Rob needed time to reflect. They thanked Matthew Harris for the time and support. The two had a much better handle on the magnitude of this venture. Before they could continue they needed to take stock of this new information.

For Sti and Rob, the reality was that they were hooked on the intrigue of this amateur adventure into solving a mystery. Nevertheless, they remained cautious, if only to control their eagerness and to protect themselves from the mistakes novices are inclined to make. They took their leave. The drive south would provide time for discussion and reflection.

CHAPTER 15

THE QUESTIONS

Southbound and somewhere on Interstate 5,
an hour outside of the Bay area.

They did not drive home immediately. One of the luxuries of semi-retirement is that one can live more spontaneously. Sti, who liked to play with words, called it 'senior efficacy'. The difference between working full time and retirement was a matter of controlling one's time. The retired person, conscious of opportunities, could find value in life without actually seeking something. This was the serendipitous side of senior efficacy.

The day and a half at the Harris residence had provided the two with new information that challenged their sense of involvement in the matter regarding June Harris. Before the visit, they had doubts about the belief that June's death was accidental, but Sti and Rob could accept the conclusions of the experts because they really had little else to suggest otherwise. There was the photo of her body that the two had taken, but it was inconclusive. The photo, in reality, only showed the location of the ice axe relative to June's body. It proved nothing. Now they had difficulty justifying any conclusion. They could argue both accident and murder. The new information provided new opportunities to reconsider the level of their involvement with Matthew Harris, and his effort to find the cause of June's death.

After leaving the Harris residence in the afternoon, they had driven to San Francisco, rented a room at one of the big hotels downtown, and went out for a meal at a small, quaint restaurant known to Rob. Throughout the evening they compared notes and tried to match the information gleaned from Harris with their own take on the events and facts. Their caution continued to filter the facts and observations. Their perspective was changing. They had gone from believing in an accident to believing that June's death could possibly have been the result of foul play. Sti and Rob struggled to keep perspective focused on maintaining an open mind on the matter. They struggled to not let their imagination lead them to conclusions for which there was no clear evidence.

Now, on the drive home, with Rob at the wheel as usual, they sought to synthesize everything into a manageable picture. They were an hour into the drive south on Interstate 5, and they had boiled everything down into two categories—known information and questions/issues.

Sti reviewed his handwritten notes. They had confidence in this list of known information. It was information that fell into several bulleted subheadings.

- The discovery of the body of June Harris. She had died under unusual circumstances. Although deemed an accident by authorities, the observations and photograph taken by Sti and Rob suggested there was a possibility that the cause was otherwise. A complicating factor here was that the helicopter sent to retrieve June's body was delayed three days because of bad weather. Was it possible that the time delay could have changed the visible facts? However, the body had been exposed for some time; what difference could another few days make?
- Substantial and valuable information about the Harris family and their endeavors could be found in the journals, articles, notes, photographs, and artifacts at the Harris residence. The information was interesting; but it did not provide any clear answers to the questions surrounding June's death. Although, the information was sufficiently intriguing as to raise other questions, which may or may not be related in some way to events surrounding her death.
- Information provided by Rob's cousin suggested that the Park Service officials were not unanimous in their determination that June's death was accidental. However, here again, there was no evidence to the contrary.

- Information provided by Matthew Harris could, for the most part, be easily substantiated and Harris knew they would check the necessary verification sources. On the other hand, Matthew Harris was an impassioned piece of the puzzle and his judgment could easily be biased by his desire to want to believe that June's death was a murder.
- Finally, all Rob and Sti really knew about June and the rest of the Harris family was reflective of what the good Dr. Harris told them and let them see. 'Let them see' was the part that bothered the two.

This last group of information, that which was based on input from Harris, was accepted with reluctance for the time being. They had to start somewhere, and even though they were not altogether confident that Harris had told them everything, or that he had given them the information with complete accuracy, they had to acknowledge that much of it must be the truth. If it was not beyond verification, they accepted it, at least for now.

What puzzled Sti and Rob most were the questions and concerns they had. Their discussions the previous evening kept raising questions. What started as a reflective inquiry, ended up as a list of doubts. 'Doubts' was the best description because the two kept coming back to gut level feelings that Harris was keeping information from them. These doubts gave way to 'what if' questions and the reality that there was probably too much faith being placed in reliance on the so called list of known information.

It was evident to the two that they needed to pursue some answers on their own. If they could check out some of their questions without relying on Harris perhaps their doubts would give way to a more reasoned approach to finding out what happened to June Harris. The more they talked their way south on the Interstate, the list of questions gave way to a short list of 'things we need to do'. Sitting in the passenger seat, Sti scanned the list of agreed to concerns and possible courses of action. They had typed and printed the list the previous evening. The list was not long, but it was complex.

1. Contact the Eastern California Museum in Independence. According to Matt Harris's records, the museum was supportive of his work and he sent a goodly number of artifacts in the museum's direction. In addition to expanding their knowledge about Matt's work in the Valley, they

might also learn more about the Paiute Indians who may or may not be an important part of the puzzle.

2. Review more closely Matt's research and published articles. Of special interest was Matt's cache findings and his hypothesis about the possible locations of other caches.

3. Follow up on three items they found in June's packages. There was a very poor photocopy of several pages of a journal kept by a member of the Sierra Club High Country Outing of 1935. Clearly, June had studied the journal entries and had made copious notes, which suggested that she may have had a reason for spending considerable time in the High Route section between Horseshoe Lakes and Marion Lake. There were also several notes and a reference to the existence of Paiute-Shoshone artifacts donated to Eastern California Museum by persons other than Matt Harris. Who made the donations? Was or were these persons alive? Last, there were three very old flour sacks. Had June also visited the Sawmill Creek cave site? Where did these sacks come from? What did they mean?

4. Visit the Sawmill Creek site, as well as the other three sites known to Matt. Matthew Harris was only too willing to share the locations with them; apparently there was nothing to hide there. They would find out.

5. Decode and track down information regarding several other entries found in June's journals and notes. Some were minor items. Others were more important. Entries included reference to studies of the Owens Valley Paiute by Liljeblad and Fowler; work by the principal ethnographer of the Owens Valley Paiute, Julian Steward; and studies on trans-sierra trade routes of the Paiute and other tribes. They needed also to hike and investigate some of the backpacking routes June had outlined on several 7.5 and 15 Minute Series topographic maps that covered the eastern crest of the Sierra between the towns of Big Pine and Independence. These appeared to be off-trail excursions to some of the most remote canyons on the eastern slope.

6. Investigate the Owens Valley Indian wars of 1861–1865. June's journal also had several entries regarding a renegade Indian named Joaquin Jim who plied the slopes of the Eastern Sierra while carrying on a war with the local settlers in the 1860's. Joaquin Jim's importance was questionable, but interesting. They would check it out.

7. They needed to go back to the High Route area and also explore the very rugged Muro Blanco area. This was something, for the time being, that they would delay. There was no sense in returning to the High Route until they had exhausted their investigation. Then perhaps what they may find would have more meaning.

There was one more need. It was a delicate one. Sti and Rob needed to know more about Matthew Harris. It was not on the list, but they had discussed its importance. They needed to talk with those who had known Matthew, his wife, and the family for some time. So far, Harris was an enigma. He may be well known in certain circles, but to Sti and Rob he was the mystery. They felt that the more they talked with Harris, the more distant he seemed. They needed to know about him from another source.

Completing these tasks would take time. This was a problem. It meant they had to abandon their somewhat unstructured approach to things.

As Sti looked up from his study of the lists he stared out across the San Joaquin Valley and commented reflectively; "We need to resurrect our old selves, dust off the calendar books, and get our act together, just like we used to have to do when we were models of gainful employment."

Sti's comment was humor on the surface, but its meaning was not lost to Rob. "I am not sure our wives can handle it," responded Rob. His comment was more a reality check than a conclusion. "They would probably prefer more predictability in our behavior. During the past several months they have not been too keen about our spontaneous lifestyles and the matter of Matthew Harris." If they were going to continue with this investigatory escapade, they needed the support of their wives. It could be a hard sell.

Each thought about the implications of continuing to pursue the question of June's death. They had questions. They both knew that they could walk away at this point. Nevertheless, they also knew, without comment between them, that they were in the hunt for now. Where it would lead? They could only guess.

Chapter 16

Eastern California Museum

Independence, California

Independence is a classic small town in the Owens Valley. Its Main Street is just another name for U.S. Highway 395. It is peaceful and quaint. Town history extends back to the middle 1800s. To travelers heading north, the destiny is usually skiing, fishing, or hiking. For those headed south it is Los Angeles or the various suburbs of the L.A. Basin. For these travelers Independence is little more than rest stop for food or fuel, a short stretch along the highway where one must quickly slow from 65 plus miles per hour to 35 mph before one just as quickly accelerates back to cruising speed.

However, to residents of Inyo County, Independence is the County Seat. The town boasts an historic courthouse built in the Greek revival tradition. It has served as a backdrop for movies and commercials. The Winnedumah Hotel is equally historic along with the former home of Mary Austin, one-time valley resident in the Nineteenth Century and author of *The Land of Little Rain* which recounts her experiences in the rain shadow environment of the Owens Valley and points east.

Independence enjoys a rich history that is closely linked to the early settlers of the valley. Usually a sedate community, it receives little attention except to meet the needs of travelers or to conduct the business of county government in a laid-back style. Like the town, the population is small and the side streets serve old but practical homes that are shaded by a variety of trees that line the streets.

To Independence and Owens Valley residents, and a few travelers from L.A., Independence is also known for its old jail that played host to Charles Manson and his followers after their arrest by the County Sheriff. But that was many years ago, and the County is now served by a new jail facility on the southeast edge of town.

To the town's quaintness, history, tourist services, and civic center qualities is added the Eastern California Museum, which sits on the northwest edge of town on Grant Street, only three blocks from the highway. The museum is a gem. It is a repository for just about any type of artifact, document, or photograph that testifies to the history of the Owens Valley and the Native American, pioneer, and mining history of its surrounding Great Basin environments. For the visitor, there is a new indoor facility that provides rich displays of documents, photographs of the valley's history, Native American artifacts, mining industry artifacts, and many other items of local interest. The outdoor portion of the museum is an acre collection of old buildings, farming and mining equipment, and outdoor collectibles. The museum is ideally suited to those who like to wander through history.

* * * *

The Eastern California Museum is also a wonderful place to do research. Sti loved the type of research associated with museums and libraries. The quiet collection of artifacts, monographs, data and memorabilia are like the untraveled world of a mysterious land. One can easily ply these shores in search of clues about the unique history of the valley. Experience had taught Sti that research was much like wandering. One could set out in a specific direction, cognizant of research questions and purpose, and soon one could find oneself wandering into unknown territory and stumbling across new information that opened doors to new questions. Such probes required the wanderer to remain focused on the questions at hand. And yet, there was value in not being so overly focused as to prevent the wanderer from recognizing hidden values in seemingly unimportant information. This is the kind of experience gained from small, very local, museums in remote corners of the American West.

Another quality that made the Eastern California Museum especially appealing was the casual accessibility of things. Just about everything in the museum was of primary quality. This museum is the repository for the actual past, no reproductions here. For the Owens Valley, the Eastern California Museum is the rendezvous for the history of the Eastern Sierra. History could literally be placed in ones hands. For those wandering the outdoor grounds, the touch and feel of the past could consume hours.

The museum is also appealing because its contents have remained uncensored by a highly credentialed curator or someone with overly formal training. There is innocence to this museum. No attempt is made to determine what the public should or should not see. This is a take it as it is museum. The informal atmosphere gives the museum a quality of quiet and personal authenticity not available in the larger, more organized facilities of the cities.

Getting entrance for the purposes of research was easy. Harris had contacts and they were only too eager to facilitate Sti's access on the pretense that he was doing some research for a U.C. Berkeley professor. The stated purpose was to review the collection of Native American Artifacts. The real purpose was to identify the sources of artifact donations. Who found them? Who donated them? When and where were they found? Where did Matt Harris fit into these finds and donations? In addition, Sti was looking for any information, which would help him understand the Paiute and Shoshone Indians studied by Matt, Kathryn, and June.

* * * *

Although small and largely funded by donations, the museum is remarkably efficient and the mostly volunteer staff has kept meticulous records. All of this, plus the friendly and helpful volunteers and employees, made Sti's work much easier than anticipated.

A good collection of Paiute and Shoshone baskets, pottery, clothing, weapons and miscellaneous artifacts reflected a wide range of sources. Among the donors were Matt and Kathryn Harris, and several other scholars who have worked the area. This was expected. What was not expected were the several items donated by 'Dr. and Mrs. Matthew Harris.' Harris had not mentioned these donations. How had he obtained them? Interestingly, they were donated at intervals extending back to the 1940s, and through the 1950's, 60' and 70's. Was Matt aware of these artifacts? Were they logged in Matt's journals? Why were the place of origin and the date of find not noted for many of these items? Was this further confirmation that Matthew Harris did not intend to be completely honest with Sti and Rob?

Also, among the museum's possessions was an odd collection of Native American weapons and pioneer firearms and knives along with some Paiute pottery and basketry that did not look similar to the mainstream Paiute items. Various people had donated these over a period of many years. In many cases the donating party was unknown. In the early years of the museum, detailed records of an artifact's origin were not kept. Sti observed that some donations were from individuals whose family name was prominent in the history of the valley. Several artifacts were donated in the name of former Los Angeles Department of Water and Power employee, George Kennicott, soon after the museum first opened. Another interesting donor was Henry Kubota. Henry had apparently collected the items while he was a teenage internee at the Manzanar War Relocation Center during World War II. The donations were made in 1948. When Sti inquired about who Henry Kubota was, he got no answers. It seemed that after the donations were made, the museum had no further contact with Henry Kubota.

Information regarding Joaquin Jim was not plentiful, but what was available was none the less valuable because it provided enough background to suggest that he was not someone a pioneer settler would want to anger. He was a rebel. He had been active in the wars of the 1860's, and then just disappeared. Sti knew he would have to do more research.

Finally, and perplexingly, there were several very fine baskets and intact pottery items that were on loan from the Los Angeles Department of Water and Power, or the DWP as it was called in the valley. According to the staff, the items were uncovered by DWP employees during survey outings and DWP work projects in the late 1940's and the 1950's. What made the donations perplexing was the fact that they were not donated until 1993 and there was no record as to their whereabouts prior to the donation. Interestingly, there was no information about where each item was discovered and who discovered them. Where had these items been all these years? Who had found them? Where were they found? Was a scholar such as Matt or other anthropologists ever made aware of these items? Did June see these items? Was there a connection between these items and those donated by George Kennicott?

Sti, using his laptop computer, made copious notes about Paiute history, artifacts, culture and personalities. He paid particular attention to the artifacts such as baskets and pottery. He recorded as much information as was available regarding not only the donors of these items but also those who may have been involved in conducting anthropological studies in the valley.

Because he was not sure what it was he was looking for, Sti found it difficult to give order to the information recorded. However, he knew that down the road there could be questions related to some of what he saw at the museum. As a result, Sti sought to record information that could be easily followed up on. Where possible, he took or purchased photographs of artifacts. He purchased museum literature related to both the valley history and the Paiute-Shoshone culture. Names of experts or knowledgeable people were especially important since future questions could best be pursued if one could connect questions with a possible source for answers. In addition to the names and background information of donors and researchers Sti noted the names, phone numbers and areas of interest of those that worked or volunteered at the museum. He may have questions for them at a later date.

When finished, many of Sti's notes were lists of bulleted information. At a later date these items could be organized.

Sti had no doubt that he would be following up on threads of information gleaned from his visit. He was also certain that he would be contacting Florence Chadwick and Francis Martin again. These two part-time volunteer curators, long associated with the museum, seemed to have an ability to find answers to questions related to just about any of the museum possessions. However, what made them most valuable was the fact that their lives seemed steeped in the valley history and culture. Each was an encyclopedia of knowledge regarding the Owens Valley and its surroundings. If need be, they could provide the name of someone Sti would want to talk with regarding some unique piece of information.

Florence and Francis did not skip a beat in sharing their knowledge about Matthew and Eaddie Harris. Both remembered the early years when Matthew would bring his family to the valley for summer fieldwork. For both curators, talking about Matthew and Eaddie brought back fond memories. However, they remembered Matt Harris as very intense and not at all like his mother and father. Oh, Matt could be friendly, but he was always focused on the task at hand and had little time to talk. But, as the two curators noted, Matt was also very thorough and had an expertise regarding the Native Americans of the Owens Valley that was unrivaled by any anthropologist since. Both agreed; it was a very sad day when Matt and Kathryn died. Their loss was a major loss for the research community in the valley.

They also knew June Harris as an impetuous young lady who did not accept superficial answers. Everyone at the museum had encountered June many times. She was well liked, but all the employees agreed that they did not see June using the scientific approach so evident in the work of her parents and grandparents. June's approach was unorthodox. She was also secretive, and provided little background information to her questions.

Sti also came away from the museum with the names of others that had or were currently conducting research regarding the Paiute. He knew none of these, and Florence and Francis suggested none could hold a candle to Matt Harris. Whether any of these other researchers was linked to the task facing Sti and Rob would remain to be seen.

Chapter 17

June is Being Watched

The upper reaches of Goodale Creek Canyon
a couple years before June's death

June sensed she was being watched. No, she knew she was being watched. At first she had the feeling that her outings and interests were being observed by others. That was a couple of years ago. With time and evidence, she concluded that her interests in Matt's work, her inquiries at Stanford and at the Eastern California Museum, requests for information from various sources such as local newspapers and libraries, and general questioning of citizens and experts familiar with the Eastern Sierra history were drawing attention. Someone, or some group of people, was interested in her extracurricular interests and activities. In recent months she had become convinced.

As she leaned against a rock and absorbed the rays of the rising sun that had just topped the peaks of the Inyo Mountains on the eastern side of the Owens Valley, June thought back over the past couple of years. She thought about how she came to the realization that there were others competing with Matt to find the caches. When first she visited this spot, it was after painstaking study of Matt's logs and many days of following dead-end leads. She had explored Goodale Creek Canyon several times before she found the site. When she finally found the site, she was not surprised at the location. Like the Sawmill Canyon site, it was located by its creators so as to provide a view up and down the canyon.

Most importantly, it commanded a view that allowed one to observe any who might enter the canyon from down stream. But it also allowed the observer to go undetected. The latter point was critical. June remembered exploring within 25 yards this site on a previous occasion without even noticing the site.

On discovery several months previous, June had been initially thrilled. Pottery shards, bits and pieces of leather and broken hand implements left no doubt that this site served the Indians well for some time. However, on closer inspection there was little doubt that others had been here and were not Paiutes. The distinct grouping of gravel sizes provided the evidence. Someone had sifted the site. With screen in hand, they had sifted through the soil in search of artifacts. The fine sand and dust in one location contrasted with the larger gravel a few yards away.

Whoever was responsible had not destroyed the site. There remained sufficient evidence to indicate that this site and the smaller site a quarter mile down canyon had been used, probably before the 20th Century. The educated eye saw this. It also saw that the site had been thoroughly studied. Someone had spent considerable time here. Whoever it was made certain that they were careful not to damage the site except to remove whatever valuable and moveable artifacts could be salvaged. But this had occurred some time ago, probably decades ago, because the time and weather since had erased most of the evidence of intrusion except what the educated eye could see. Because she had spent so much time at this and other sites, June knew well the effects of those whose interests were other than anthropology or the heritage of the Paiute. She could tell when outsiders, non-Paiutes, had been to a site.

After spending two days at the site and taking copious notes during her first visit, June left. She had other leads to follow during the winter months. She would visit the site again later.

Now, here she was on her return visit after several months. It was clear; someone had spent time at the site in her absence. Whoever it was had been careful to make their intrusion not obvious. However, to June's skilled eye their visit was evident. While they left many artifacts in place, it was clear that they had probed the nooks and crannies of the site. They had removed dust in many places in their search. A couple artifacts were missing. Jill knew this because she had studied the site carefully on her first visit.

It was a distressing situation. How was it that in such a short time since her first visit the site had been tampered with? It could not have been discovered accidentally. Who had been here? Why? Did June's discovery encourage someone else? Had someone followed her? June had the sinking feeling that someone must have known of her interest in the site. In all probability, the person was not a Paiute and had little interest in the Paiute heritage. Whoever it was, they were seeking to benefit from their finds.

On the current occasion, June had not intended to visit the site. Her goal was really Taboose Creek Canyon and she had only intended to spend an hour or so here to check a hunch. The hunch checked out. June had recently begun to suspect that others were following her. This visit seemed to confirm that hunch. Others were aware of this site and were probably pursuing efforts that paralleled her own. June Harris was not the only one on the trail to discover other Paiute Indian caches. Who were these others? They were very careful to not do more damage to a site than necessary. But where there is a desire to obtain artifacts, it is difficult to avoid damage. The best efforts to cover the damage could not fool one attuned to studying anthropological evidence. June believed that there were at least one and probably two people who had been here since her previous visit.

June was anxious and worried. Who were they? What was their motive? Was it to find and sell the artifacts? Surely they were not Indians? These were interesting questions. But they were not the most intriguing. The real questions focused on how they found the site. What did they know of June's efforts? Had they followed here to other sites? Were these same people aware of the possibility of additional sites unknown to her and to them? There were many more questions. June had the feeling she would eventually find the answers. She was also beginning to feel scared. She now knew what she had previously only suspected. She was being followed.

The effect of this visit to the Goodale Creek Canyon site was that June decided that she would continue her work on two fronts. First, she would continue to search for, identify, and study other caches that her father had alleged existed in the canyons of the Eastern Sierra. Second, she would try to develop evidence that would help her identify the competition. Neither task would be easy. However, June sensed that wherever she was in her efforts, others would be watching. Perhaps in their efforts to find the caches they have left some evidence of their work behind. Probably in the same places June had been investigating.

June was confident she would find additional sites. Her father's theories would be vindicated. Unfortunately, June feared that others would benefit from her work and their cause was not as noble. She was not confident that she could successfully deal with the competition.

CHAPTER 18

JOAQUIN JIM

Owens Valley, 1860s

Joaquin Jim was one of those characters in history whose factual biography can not be clearly separated from fiction. An enigmatic character, the truth of his exploits and ultimate demise has been shrouded in mystery. In retrospect, his life in history may be larger than in reality.

By birth, Joaquin was born and raised in the Fresno area of California's Central Valley. Also called the San Joaquin Valley, the valley was the source of Joaquin's name. Though little is known about his childhood and family, it is evident that he developed a hatred of the white settlers and was, during the 1850's and 60's, actively involved in armed uprisings against his self-proclaimed enemy. So outspoken and active was he in this endeavor that he was allegedly outlawed by his own people and became the renegade for which he is known in history.

The 1860's found Joaquin Jim actively involved as a leader of Indian uprisings in the Owens Valley.

Relationships between the early settlers in the Owens Valley and the Paiute Indians were initially congenial. There was land and game for both. The crop-oriented activities of the settlers were not overly extensive and the Paiutes could tolerate the settlers. However, as the cattle business began to take hold in the valley the encroachment on the culture of the Paiute was significant. Grazing cattle was an endeavor that knew few boundaries. Unlike the small farm settlers, the stockmen never seemed to have enough land. Also, they were intent on killing off animals that competed with the cattle—deer, elk and of course the predators such as the mountain lion, bear and other flesh-eating animals. With this change the Piute soon found that they were increasingly disinherited from their ancestral lands.

Conflict between the Paiute and the white men came to a head with the Indian War of 1861 and 1862. Although hostilities appeared to be ended with a successful conference in January 1862, a large number of Paiute under the leadership of Joaquin Jim did not participate in the conference and had no intention of abiding by any agreement.

Typically the Paiutes were not inclined to resort to violence to settle an issue. However, life for the Paiute was challenging even before the white settlers. The more the white man settled land and converted it into farming, the more the Paiute were forced to look elsewhere for game. When the cattlemen began to graze their herds anywhere there was no fence the Paiute soon found that they did not have access to vast areas of the valley. These areas were increasingly claimed for their exclusive use by the cattlemen. For Joaquin Jim the Paiute were a people open to leadership that pledged to revenge the encroachment of the white man. Through out the winter and early spring of 1862 the conflict resulted in several skirmishes and small battles. The culmination was the Paiute victory in the Battle of Bishop Creek in early April. According to some accounts, the Paiutes seemed to be in control of most of the Owens Valley by May. As for the actual number of Indians in arms, the estimates ranged between 1000 and 1200.

Residents of the valley appealed to Governor Leland Stanford for assistance. A company of about 157 men was dispatched from Los Angeles and they took up residence at a site named Camp Independence about 18 miles north of the community of Lone Pine. By this time it was July 1862. For the next several months efforts to bring an end to the hostilities in the valley were hampered by the fact that Indians in tribes to the north and south of the Owens Valley continued to assault travelers and small settlements. In November additional troops were sent to Camp Independence.

In April of 1863 the well armed soldiers, there were about 120 of them along with about 35 citizens, took up the task of actively pursuing the Paiute under Joaquin Jim's leadership. The campaign lasted throughout the Spring of 1863 and involved activities in the Owens Valley and north into Long Valley and the Mono basin. Joaquin Jim was especially effective in his leadership among the Mono Paiutes to the north of the Owens Valley. However, according to W. A. Chalfant, early historian of the Owens Valley, Joaquin Jim was an acknowledged leader among rebellious Paiutes in the northern and central part of the Owens Valley.

With the increasing number of settlers and the presence of the military the future of the Paiute in the valley was a forgone conclusion. During 1863 and 1864, there were small incidents of violence where white man and Paiute alike lost lives. In each instance the soldiers and/or self appointed vigilantes took up the task of retribution. Again, according to Chalfant, neither Joaquin Jim nor any other Indian chief or leader was ever subjugated.

What little is known about Joaquin Jim suggests that he preferred a form of what today would be called guerrilla warfare tactics. He would attack and withdraw as soon as the effect of surprise was over. In most instances his retreat was into the canyons of the Eastern Sierra. He was reportedly very organized and had established hidden sites throughout the valley where his warriors had access to supplies and weapons. They could go to a site, prepare to attack, carry out their assault and withdraw to hide in this or another site. Some who tried to track Joaquin Jim or his warriors also believed that he actually had hiding places or redoubts that required one to cross over the eastern crest of the Sierra and venture into the canyons and valleys of the interior range. Such speculation was apparently common in the 1860's 70's and 80's. However, no evidence was ever provided as proof. With time conjecture was mixed with fantasy and any facts that could provide a starting point for field research were lost.

But, along with the passing of time was the increasing chance that one of these hidden sites would be discovered. First, the attractiveness of the Owens Valley as an agricultural haven brought farmers and cattlemen. In time, this alone would have led to discovery as more and more land was cultivated and the headwaters of streams were investigated and tapped for irrigation purposes. As cattlemen on foot and horse tracked down wandering heads of cattle, they had to invade some of the most remote canyons. Second, mining has long been a part of the valley's history and miners, in search of gold, silver, and especially tungsten, roamed over the most inaccessible areas of the valley for almost a hundred years. Third, building of the Los Angeles aqueduct increased the chances of discovery. When the City of Los Angeles tapped the streams that fed the Owens River, which drains the Mono Basin and the Owens Valley, the engineers and surveyors building the aqueduct appear to have investigated the upper and lower portions of every Eastern Sierra canyon between Le Vining in the North and Tehapachapi in the South. And finally, the Twentieth Century found the Owens Valley increasingly attractive to tourists, especially backpackers, mule and horse packers, and fishermen. The latter loved to wander and investigate streams in their effort to catch fish. It seems that discovery was just a matter of time. And yet, recorded discoveries were few. What is not known is the possibility that there were discoveries that were not made known to authorities or those who specialized in researching Indian history. No doubt some discoveries remained unreported as the discoverers pilfered the sites of artifacts and either saved the findings for personal use or sold them for profit.

As for Joaquin Jim, his presence in the Owens Valley came to an end. He simply disappeared. The leader of a recalcitrant group of Paiutes who had created the cache sites, he led many successful attacks on the settlers and soldiers. And then in the early 1870's he ceased to be in existence in the valley and the attacks stopped forever. His whereabouts after that is unknown.

CHAPTER 19

THE OWENS VALLEY AND THE PAIUTE

Owens Valley, 1860's

The more they investigated the matter of June's death, the more Rob and Sti were drawn into a study of the Paiute Indians and the early history of the Owens Valley. It was easy to see why Mathew Harris, and subsequently his son Matt, developed a keen interest in the region. The environment and the early Paiute inhabitants of the valley had lived in harmony. But the dominant factor for both was the Sierra Nevada, the snowy range of mountains named by the early Spanish explorers. The rock of choice in the Sierra is granite, and it is evident everywhere—the peaks and valleys are monuments to the combined qualities of ruggedness and beauty. The fault line that separates the valley from the eastern slope of the Sierra is responsible for the almost shear face of granite that rises from the valley floor of 4000 feet to a ridge line of peaks that jut into the sky at altitudes of 12000, 13000 and 14000 feet. Little wonder the Owens Valley is called the 'Deepest Valley'.

But the Sierra is much more. It dictates the weather and habitat of the valley and much of the great basin region to the east. The snow and rain runoff from the peaks has cut hundreds of canyons that descend from the high peaks to the valley below. In fact, the traveler on U.S. 395 cannot but be fascinated by the innumerable canyons that pour their alluvial fans onto the valley floor at regular intervals throughout the length of the valley. Water makes its way down these canyons to feed the Owens River, which at the time of the early settlers, and up until the Los Angeles aqueduct diverted the water, fostered a valley water table that was only a few feet below the surface. This provided an ideal environment for wildlife as well as for agriculture purposes. The Paiute Indians were all too well aware of this environment and their knowledge served them well. As for the white settlers of the 1800's, they too soon learned of the agricultural benefits of a shallow water table. It did not take the settlers long to tap into the resource. In doing so, the stage was set for conflict with the Paiute residents of the valley.

The Owens Valley is, as Mary Austin described it in her 1903 classic, *The Land of Little Rain.* The Sierra forces storms from the Pacific to dump most of their precipitation in snow and rain before the storms reach the valleys to the east. But the Owens Valley is a beneficiary of this activity as much of the runoff from snow melt and summer rains finds its way into the valley.

The archeological studies of the Paiute suggest that they were a people well adapted to the environment dictated by the Sierra. Their life included fishing, hunting, gathering, and cultivating. But to suggest that the Owens Valley was a paradise belies reality. At the western edge of the Great Basin, the valley is very much a desert environment. In the summer it is extremely hot and in the winter temperatures are consistently below freezing at night. Life for the Paiute in the Owens Valley was demanding, and survival was tied to their knowledge of both the desert and the Sierra Nevada.

* * * *

Technically, the Paiute are part of the Shoshone Indians whose presence is evident throughout the Great Basin regions of the West and the deserts of Southern California. The Shoshone live just east of the Cascade Mountains in Washington and Oregon and the Sierra in California. Their languages and culture tie them to the many Indian groups of the Great Basin. The Owens Valley was home to the southernmost branch of the Northern Paiute. The Paiute in the Owens Valley, like those to the north lived not so much in tribes as in communities that were loosely organized. Unlike the image and reality of many Native Americans who migrated with the seasons each year, the valley was a permanent home for the Paiute. The Paiute did not migrate; but they did eke out a living from among many resources found in the wide range of climates, flora and fauna governed by the Sierra Nevada.

The volcanic activity of the region provided ample supplies of obsidian to make all manner of implements for hunting, working tools, and weapons. The grasses and willow reeds along the rivers and lakeshores fostered weaving skills that produced a wide range of useful products. Basket weaving was an art form that served practical purposes. Pine nuts and a variety of seeds provided a food staple that depended on the harshness of winter. Fish could be found in streams and the streams could also be diverted to irrigate land for cultivating purposes. Wood was available in the valley and on the slopes at the higher elevations. Fur was available from a wide range of animals that inhabited the valley and canyons and the interior of the Sierra.

* * * *

What struck Sti and Rob as most interesting was the growing evidence that the Paiute had considerable contact with Indians from west of the Sierra Nevada. Trails over the Sierra Crest were many and they were the keys to trade with Indians from the Central Valley. These same trails provided access to the Sierra backcountry where wildlife were abundant during the summer months. Evidence of backcountry activity and possible trading routes are found in Oak Creek canyon near Independence, Taboose Creek and Pass, Big Pine Creek, and the upper Bishop Creek basin. In essence, much of the early work of Matt Harris was being vindicated by more recent field research. Just how much the Paiute played the role of trading broker between Indians west of the Sierra and the Shoshone tribes of the Great Basin remains debatable, but the fact of trade routes has been confirmed. June had to know this and when she coupled this information with her knowledge of Matt's work, she was well positioned to pursue some of his theories regarding routes and possible locations for Paiute camps in the canyons and backcountry of the eastern Sierra. With this information at hand, conjecture about the location of possible caches was very possible.

Fieldwork at Paiute sites provides evidence of shells and implements that could only have come from trade with western tribes. Likewise, artifacts crafted from Owens Valley obsidian have been found in field studies of Central Valley Indians such as the Yokuts and the Miwok. Digs at campsites in the interior of the Sierra Nevada in places such as the upper reaches of the San Joaquin River drainage, and the Middle and South Fork of the Kings River, including the Muro Blanco area, have revealed Paiute pottery shards and obsidian arrowheads.

And yet, in spite of this wealth of knowledge, Sti and Rob found there were several obvious questions unanswered. The fact that there were Paiute camps did not explain the existence of caches that included significant stockpiles of supplies, baskets and pottery, weapons (including rifles) and gold. These did not sound like they served a trading purpose. Did they serve hunting purposes? Also, the caches discovered to date did not implicate the presence of a camp in the traditional sense that the Paiute had camps in almost all of the canyons on the east side of the Sierra. These caches appeared to be deliberately hidden to all but those who knew of their existence. What purposes did these sites serve? Also, all the caches discovered to date were in the canyons. Were there others in the interior of the Sierra, west of the Sierra Crest? These questions were important to Sti and Rob; but the answers were not easily found.

However, not initially obvious to the two were questions about more clandestine purposes that the caches might have served. For Rob and Sti these questions only came about after considerable reflection and pondering over the disparate bits of information uncovered during their probing of the Harris archives, the museum in Independence and other sources. Did the weapons, especially the rifles implicate less obvious purposes? Why the chunks of gold? Gold was much more prevalent in the Northern Sierra and the western slope of the Sierra. Why would gold be traded? The Paiute were very practical people and there was no real place in their culture for gold, unless it served non traditional purposes. Did Matt have some idea regarding answers to these questions? If so, were his ideas such that his life was jeopardized? Did June's investigations lead her to knowledge that placed her in harm's way as well?

Clearly, this was not a job for amateurs. But what else could Rob and Sti do? They were intrigued enough, and just stubborn enough, to see the whole thing as a worthy challenge. After all, if there was something to all of this, someone other than the authorities had to take the initiative. The Sheriff and NPS had no interest. This left only Rob, Sti, and Dr. Harris.

Investigating and finding some answers only lead to more questions. It also led to a growing concern that they too might come under the scrutiny of that someone or persons who were perhaps responsible for the death of Matt and his daughter. Where was all of this going, and what would they find at the end? Perhaps their naiveté was their best friend in this instance. While they were definitely out of their league, they were not inhibited by the cynicism that comes with a life of investigating crime. To Sti and Rob it had an element of fun, and they did not sense any potential for harm. Their minds were open to any ideas and they entertained a laundry list of thoughts regarding what could have caused June's death and why. In a way, it was a game and the thought of losing did not really occur to them.

Chapter 20

The Sierra and the Owens Valley

A relationship

Wanderings among the nooks and crannies of the floor of the Owens Valley as well as the canyons that pour out into the valley at regular intervals provide hints into the life of the Paiute and the settlers of the 1800's. On the one hand, the valley is isolated and protected with barriers on either side. On the other hand, the valley was not easy to live in and those who did had to be equal to the challenges.

The Owens Valley provides an environment that is caught between the alpine peaks to the west and the rugged desert-like Great Basin to the east. Even today, despite the Los Angeles Aqueduct and the valley's evolvement into an agricultural and recreation center, much of it remains as it was when the first settlers arrived in the middle of the Nineteenth Century. Because of the demand for water for those living there and those in Los Angeles, the valley is more arid. But it still posses the rugged qualities that made it the ideal habitat for the Paiute. The geology, the plant and animal life, the weather and the isolation that accompanied the Paiute are much in evidence today.

The floor of the valley, that part which is relatively flat, has benefited from the water that most of the canyons have provided for millions of years. Although the general width of the valley averages about four miles, only the area along the Owens River is relatively flat. Here the Owens River meanders southward and the vegetation along the banks can be thick and almost impenetrable. For the Paiute and the early settlers, the river was the lifeblood of the valley and was complemented by a very shallow water table below the surface of the valley floor. Springs rising to the surface today and in the past paint patches of green in places surrounded by an arid and sage dominated landscape.

For the Paiute, the valley floor along the river and its environs must have been lush and filled with game. Certainly the reeds and grasses here were a source of effective basketry material and resources for constructing clothing and housing. Then, as now, one only has to go a short distance, perhaps a quarter mile, on either side of the river and the land begins to slope up towards the Sierra on the West and the Inyo Mountains on the East. Here the landscape turns dry and takes on the characteristics of the desert.

For the valley traveler, the line of demarcation between the greenbelt of the valley floor and the desert of the gentle slopes is clearly evident. As one moves up the slopes the plant life in the valley reflects the sandy nature of the soil and the weather influence of the Sierra. The valley is in a rain shadow and annual precipitation is low. The valley floor has the creek, stream and river water in captivity. But on the slopes the rain shadow dominates and it is a desert. Scientists suggest there are over 2000 species of plant life in the valley. In the transition between the valley floor and the canyons the dominate plant life are sagebrush and scattered pinion pines at the upper levels.

Moving from the valley floor, up into the canyons, and then to the higher elevations of the Sierra one passes through several plant communities. One noticeable change is the increasing numbers of Pinion Pines at elevations between 5,000 and 7,000 feet. The latter was a major food staple of the Paiute. The nuts could be easily ground into a flower and used for all manner of cooking purposes. The first significant forest is found at about 7,500 feet where the Lodgepole Pine, Jeffrey Pine, Junipers and White Fir are present. Above, at about the 9,500-foot level are the Whitebark and Foxtail Pines. Timberline is at about 11000 feet where the only shrub of note is the Alpine Willow. Passing through each of these zones one encounters a wide variety of plants, each specific to a particular altitude range, soil or exposure. Many of these were used by the Paiute as sources of food and medicine.

No one knew these canyons like the Paiute. This became very evident when the white man began to have conflicts with the Paiute. The canyon refuges allowed the Paiute to have a protection zone.

Geologically, the relationship between the Owens Valley and the flanking mountains has been, in the past few million years, an inverse relationship. While the White-Inyo Mountains and the Sierra Nevada have been increasing in altitude, the valley has dropped. The reason, geological faults lie at the junction of the valley and each mountain range. Compounding this periodic movement has been extensive volcanic activity along the whole length of the valley.

Though not visible to the untrained eye, fault activity is clearly evident in the valley. The quake of 1872 was just one of many significant quakes that have taken place in recent centuries. However, anyone who spends time in the valley grows accustomed to lesser quakes that occur on a regular basis. To the Paiute, there was most certainly an explanation for these events. Today we know the fault movements are to be expected. The reason for this can be found in plate tectonics. With minimal training, one can spot the results of activity along numerous faults as one drives along U.S. 395. The most notable evidence is the 1872 fault escarpment visible north and west of Lone Pine.

Although both the Sierra Nevada and the White-Inyo Mountains reach considerable heights, they are in fact very different ranges. While the Sierra and foundation rock of the valley floor are predominately granite, the White-Inyo are primarily sedimentary rock. This sediment has been metamorphosed; it does not take long to see the differences between the two ranges. For obvious reasons, the valley floor appears sandy because it is essentially alluvial fill from eons of erosion from both ranges.

Volcanic rock is evident as one is approaching the valley from the north and south along U.S. 395. To see this one must be accustomed to looking at the variations in the landscape. The steep decent down the Sherwin grade into Round Valley and the City of Bishop is really a decent that takes place on top of an ancient lava flow that extends down from the Long Valley caldera some 30 miles north of Bishop. From the South, as one approaches and enters the Owens Valley at Little Lake, the evidence of volcanic activity is everywhere and can not be missed. Lava flows, cinder cones, and volcanic rock are in residence on both sides of U.S. 395. Once aware of the volcanic history, the traveler can not but notice the evidence at various points in the valley proper. Although inactive in recent history, there is other evidence of the volcanic underpinnings of the valley. Hot springs at Coso, Keough, and other locations provide testimony that volcanic activity is not far from the surface of the valley floor.

The volcanic rock was of great value to the Paiute. The obsidian was an endless source of material to craft tools and weapons. It was also in demand elsewhere, and became an effective trade resource. The volcanic rock that did not have the obsidian qualities, but which is also present in great abundance throughout the valley, is excellent habitat for small animals, rodents and certain bird species. This rugged rock, with its pockets and numerous hiding places, allows game that live there to be more protected than otherwise would be the case. Animal life here prospers and thereby provided the Paiute with an excellent source of food, hides and feathers.

As for the granite, it has dominion over much of the valley; the soil, the water resources and the weather are all products of its influence. Stand anywhere in the valley and look west. The view is that of an escarpment of granite. In some places this wall of granite is nothing less than over powering as it rises almost vertically for several thousand feet. But regardless of this barrier, the water flowing from its slopes has cut deep and rugged canyons over eons of time.

The canyons are not hospitable environments. Only through arduous walking can one penetrate the canyons. In some instances progress requires hand over hand climbing. In other places the stream flowing at the canyon floor has cut a deep trough leaving vertical walls as insurmountable obstacles to movement up the canyon. In a few canyons the stream is hidden by extremely dense tree and shrub growth that is almost impenetrable. Quite often, the rock talus has formed fields of giant granite rocks that provide an imposing presence to any passer by. Some of these slabs of granite form small caves and hiding places. Yet, these rugged canyons, and the ones more easily accessed, were valuable to the Paiute. The canyons provided a habitat for mountain sheep, mule deer, bobcat, badger, black bear, raccoon and other important animals.

The canyons were also important because they were the routes to the higher elevations and passes that lead into the backcountry. Through these canyons the Paiute established routes that lead to valuable hunting grounds in the Sierra.

They also lead to contact with Indians who lived on the Western slope of the Sierra. Over time the Paiute became very familiar with each canyon and its environs.

Even with a maintained trail, movement up many of the canyons is not easy. Every step is up and elevation gain is quick. For the Paiute, there might only have been a rudimentary path and in some cases no visible route at all. When one considers that the modern hiker with specially designed boots and other gear must struggle to negotiate these canyons, the ability of the Paiute to maneuver is in deed amazing.

But the canyons were more than just a route. They were an escape hatch. Those unfamiliar with the valley could not know how the canyons benefited the Paiute as a refuge. As visible as the canyons are from the valley floor, the distance and size of the canyons hide the fact that they are complex environments that contain many places to hide, including small caves and secluded spots among rocks and trees that are not visible to the visitor or uninitiated. But to the Paiute, who knew these places in great detail, the canyons were a safe haven when escape was necessary. It is little wonder that the canyons contain significant evidence of Paiute passage. It is also little wonder that several canyons have Paiute names.

Today, in many canyons there is a maintained trail that departs the valley floor at about 5,000 feet and winds upward mile after mile towards a pass that leads into the Sierra interior. At between 11,000 and 12,000 feet, each pass is attained after thousands of feet elevation gain within a distance of about 6 miles. Moving upward at a rate of about 1,000 feet per mile, the hiker, even without a pack, works hard. Carry a modern pack and the task is daunting. It does not take much imagination to see how skilled and strong the Paiute must have been when negotiating these canyons.

The Owens Valley and surrounding environments provided a rugged homeland for the Paiute Indians. There was water, game, plant food, and soil good for cultivation. But it was far from an easy place to live. Nothing was in such abundance that it could always be relied on as fallback resource. The summers could be very hot and the winters very cold. It was not an easy place to live. For their part, survival required significant adaptation by the Paiute to Nature's demands. The Paiute had to be equal to this challenge by becoming equally rugged, skilled and opportunistic. The Paiute could not take life-sustaining qualities for granted, and it would not take much to upset the balance between their culture and the environment they lived in.

The Owens Valley is a paradox. It was and is a hard, rugged, and unforgiving paradise.

Chapter 21

The E-mail

At respective homes in California and Colorado

The e-mail message arrived at both homes simultaneously. It was not read until the next day, first by Rob, and then by Sti after Rob had alerted him.

Strange, this was another twist in the ongoing saga of Matthew Harris. It seemed that the more they investigated the death of June, the more they found out about Matthew. Who was the mystery here? It seemed the entire family history was a series of strange circumstances. Sti and Rob were constantly amused by the turn of events. At their age they had experienced many of life's ups and downs. Sometimes it was difficult to take things seriously. It might be better to describe their reaction to this new piece of the puzzle as verisimilitude. Absurdity often wore a face of humor rather than one of seriousness. It was not that they found June's death and the surrounding events to be humorous; no, it was more like a "well, what's next" response or a "well, you have got to admit, it is different" response.

Regardless, they were intrigued. The message for both was the same. Susan Renaldo sent it.

> Dear Mr. James and Dr. Pierce;
>
> Please excuse me for contacting you. For several weeks now I have struggled with whether or not to write. I don't even know you. For all I know, contacting you might not be a good idea. But, my intuition tells me that it is the best thing to do. For me there are too many unanswered questions to the events of the last 40 years. If you are doing what I think, then this information may be of use to you.
>
> My story is not short, and perhaps somewhat convoluted. I fully expect that after reading this you will quickly see the similarity between my brother and me. Neither of us ever seems to have a simple explanation for anything. This is one of our few common characteristics. Time and distance has eroded most other brother and sister commonalities.

This of course piqued the interest of both Rob and Sti. Without reading any more, they were well aware that the message referenced Matthew Harris and that they were about to be provided with another piece of the puzzle surrounding Matthew, June and the Harris mystery.

> Many months ago, it was well over a year ago, a friend shared with me an already dated article about the finding of June's body. My friend did not know that June was my niece. She shared it with me because I am a long time backpacker. My married name is Renaldo and I do not use my maiden name of Harris. For months I gave thought to contacting my brother with whom I had not had contact for some 40 years. It was only when I was in San Francisco sometime later that I decided to go across the bay and pay my brother Matthew a visit unannounced.
>
> When I got there, he was not home. Since I had by this time decided to face my brother, I did not immediately go back to the hotel. I sat on the porch for awhile, reviewing what I would say when my brother came home. It did not occur to me that he might be away and would not come home that day. I began to reflect back to visits many years ago. The fire had drastically altered the look of the landscape and surrounding neighborhood, but the house really looked the same. At some point it occurred to me to look in the flowerpot where my brother and wife had always kept a key. Sure enough, there was one, some things do not change. I let myself into the house to await Matthew.
>
> As you can see, on my curious side I am a bit venturous, so once inside I looked around. Not much had changed. There were more collections. I should have expected that with the 40-year hiatus. But, I was especially intrigued by the photos in the dining room. They brought back many memo-

> ries. I remembered young Matt and Megan, the unbounded inquisitiveness of their lives. They seemed to be following in their Dad's scientific footsteps at a very early age. I remembered too the tragedy of Megan's death. It broke the heart of everyone in the family. I do not think things were ever happy again in Matthew and Eaddie's life. The pictures were almost too much, and I considered leaving at that point.
>
> I wandered into the study, a room that I had always found fascinating. I am not the scientific type, but the study was like a museum. For some reason, I have always loved museums. While wandering in the study I came across a stack of notes that looked to be written by Matthew. Lists would be a better explanation. They were lists of items on post-it notes, with dates and comments to be given to Rob and Sti. Attached were the business cards for each of you. I recognized the names immediately. You were the two people listed in the article about the discovery of June's body. It did not take long to realize that my brother had been in contact with you on the matter of June's death. At the time I was somewhat confused about why. Now I think I know. My brother must have asked or paid you to investigate her death.
>
> What was interesting is that your business cards suggest you are anything but investigators or detectives. This was confusing in the beginning. Sometime later I began to see that there was a reason why you were involved. This is where my story really begins.

For Rob and Sti, this was like listening to Matthew. Whether she knew it or not, Mrs. Renaldo was telling a story much like her brother would. She provided extensive background information and followed a communication style that is long, detailed and conversational.

> In many ways I have always been my brother's estranged sister. He is 13 years older than I am, and the distance meant that we were never the typical brother and sister. Nevertheless, for the first 20 years of my life we had as good a relationship as the age difference would tolerate. It was more like very good friends than brother and sister. When dad died, Matthew became even more important to me. And out of an effort to make our relationship work, I tried to take an interest in the work he and Eaddie were doing in the Sierra. I read his articles and related books, and visited them in the field when possible.
>
> My brother was a hard worker. He was meticulous, and would not publish until he completed a study. I think this was a problem, because he was always under pressure to publish. But he seemed to be more in love with the process of study than with the publish or perish philosophy of the university. I think if he had spent more time writing, lecturing, and publishing, things would have

turned out different, but it was not to be. Subsequent events ruined our relationship.

One summer I visited my brother and aunt Eaddie (I know it sounds strange, but from my youngest years I always called her 'aunt Eaddie' because she was so much older than me and I never referred to her as 'sister-in-law.' I did not see her as a sister.). It was early June, I think, and they were finishing up working in the field before the heat of summer made such work very hard. I took the bus north from Los Angeles and Eaddie picked me up in Big Pine. Our initial contact was very warm, but on the drive out to their site, Eaddie warned me that Matthew was under a lot of pressure and seemed to be distracted. I was an optimistic college student and paid little heed to her warning. However, I too was well aware of his mood only a short time after arriving at their camp in the Poverty Hills. Although we were never real close, I sensed that something was distracting my brother.

The first real evidence was that much of his time that week was spent in the field alone. This was very unusual, the previous times I had been with them in the field, my brother and his wife always worked together. Their day was always a routine that you could count on. Their relationship was also very close, and to that point in time I never thought of them as doing anything apart. It was also evident that my presence did not make my brother comfortable. He was distant and hardly acknowledged me except to ask me to stay out of the way. My aunt just shrugged her shoulders.

The second piece of evidence was that Matt and Megan were not with them. I had expected them to be there. My aunt indicated that some scheduling problems made it difficult and that Matt and Megan went back to the Bay area earlier than expected.

But what ended our relationship started with a conversation that I was not supposed to hear. Late one evening after my aunt and I had gone to bed early because we were tired from an all day hike, my aunt's snoring woke me up. I laid there awake for some time. But I had to go to the bathroom. It was probably 11 PM or later, and my brother was sitting outside working by lantern light. It was a warm evening, and he often stayed up late.

Not wanting him to know I was up, I sneaked out of the trailer through the door left open to vent the heat inside. I walked up the road a little ways and went into the small outhouse my brother had built for use that season. While there, I heard a vehicle coming up the road. I glanced up, but it did not have lights on. My brother walked to meet it about 75 yards from the trailer. In the partial moonlight, I could see my brother approach the car. The engine was then turned off. I could have sneaked back to the trailer at that point, but I was frozen, curious.

The conversation is one I thought I had washed from memory. But events of late brought it back. I did not hear all that was said by my brother. He appeared to work hard to be quiet for fear it would wake my aunt and me. I did hear very clearly the voice of the man inside the car. From the start it was threatening. He told my brother that if he valued his career and family, my brother was to follow through with the deal. My brother's comments must have suggested his intention to not do something, because the man indicated that if my brother did not change his mind now he would find out what is was like to be arrested for stealing artifacts and selling them. My brother's response was again very quiet and unintelligible. The man in the car raised his voice and said something to the effect that he expected to receive the agreed upon items before the week was out or there would be hell to pay. My brother backed away from the car. The car started and I heard the man inside say loudly and laughingly as he put the car in gear, "After all Dr. Harris, you are going to get another $5,000 out of this deal." He then slowly backed the car up. My brother just stood there and watched the car go away. Scared, I made my way quickly back to the trailer. I do not think I slept at all that night. The more I thought about it the more convinced I was that something was wrong. My brother was in trouble.

I did not say anything the next day, and my aunt sensed something was wrong. I played coy. I was troubled, but not certain what to do. Also, unfortunately, I was just old enough to successfully talk myself into believing that I was equal to whatever the challenge was in this matter. After all, I had just completed my first year of college. I had taken a class in geology, despite being an English major, and certainly this issue with my brother could not be so big that I could not help resolve it. It was just a matter of finding the right way to approach the issue.

A day later, while my brother was away in Bishop to pick up some things and allegedly send some specimens back to U.C. Berkeley, I decided to talk with my aunt. Clearly, I was young and impetuous. I asked her what it was my brother was selling for $5,000. Her response was one of initial surprise, and then the look of someone whose worst fears had just been realized. She became stern and just stared at me. I remember thinking that she was trying to decide how to answer. In fact, I was shocked by her response. Just as quickly her demeanor changed, her face softened, she smiled a forced smile, and said, "Oh, what makes you think your brother is selling something for that kind of money?" I told her about overhearing the conversation two days before. She was silent, and then in a disciplined and noncommittal way suggested that it was probably a matter best left alone. In her words, I was certainly nosy for someone who was a guest. She suggested that we drop the subject and leave the task of dealing with the matter to my brother. I got the message loud and clear—no more discussion!

The next morning was like the weather had suddenly changed to winter. My aunt was extremely quiet. But my brother was angry. I have no doubt that my Aunt had shared my comments with my brother. "You will be leaving today," my brother said in passing. I reminded him that my bus was not for another 3 days. His comment was unequivocal, "You have put your nose into matters that do not concern you and it is time you left. I will take you into Bishop and get you a bus ride for this afternoon." I spoke up in resistance. I reminded him that I was an adult, and should be treated as one. He exploded, threw his coffee cup against the trailer, and shouted that I was a "pain in the ass," and had worn out my welcome. "Why," I asked; "because I accidentally overheard you in a conversation and simply inquired as to what you were selling for $5,000?"

At this point my brother tried to collect his composure. He stared at my aunt. He asked my aunt, what else I knew about this. My aunt, also trying to control her emotions, indicated that I had only inquired about what was being sold.

As if I was not standing there my brother turned his full attention to my aunt. What followed was something like "I told you this was not a good time for her to come here. Everything I have worked for hangs in the balance. I have never turned my back on you or the kids. But my line of work takes money and the University does not pay enough to have both a home and to be able to work in the field with my family. Everything I have done is for you and the kids, and now this. Well, we won't have her around here again."

The next line was uttered as he walked away towards the mountains. "I wish I had never found that Indian stuff. It will haunt me to my grave."

I have thought about that comment many times. But it was only years later, when I went to hear Matt lecture at UCLA, that I began to see a clear picture. I just happened to see an announcement in a school events calendar and went. Matt was very cordial, and asked why I had not kept in touch with the family. Why had I not come to Megan's funeral? I told him I was not aware of Megan's illness and death until well after the funeral. I thought Matt's comments were interesting, since it was his father that made contact and knowledge about Matt's family impossible. But, I pressed the issue and inquired about Matthew's interest in Matt's work with Paiute anthropology and archeology. Matt said his father had his own work and did not have time to take much interest in his work.

But it was Matt's lecture comments about his fieldwork that interested me most. According to Matt, there were Indian camps and hideouts that were being pilfered by people and the things they found were not being placed in museums but were being sold for profit to private interests. This had been going on for many years, and no one had been caught. Matt's comments came across prophetically when he stated that those who were stealing these irreplaceable items had to be spending a lot of time in the field and had to have a great knowledge of the geology and geography of the region as well as the habits of the Owens Valley Paiute.

As I reflected back on what I saw and heard during those days in the Poverty Hills, the picture became clear. I came to believe that Matthew Harris had found some of these artifacts and was selling them. They had to be very valuable to bring the kind of money it appeared he was being paid at that time. Matt did not know it, but his own father was one of the culprits.

All of that was many years ago. But I have come to believe that there was something very wrong going on with my brother. The fact that he cut off relations I took to be a blessing. That way I would not be involved in whatever problem he was caught up in.

So, you are probably wondering what happened a few weeks ago when I went to my brother's house. Well, brazen as I can be, I chickened out. I went back outside and put the key in the planter. I sat on the porch for a couple of hours. Matthew did not return, so late in the afternoon, I left. I do not know what would have happened if we had made contact. However, once I saw your names and began to realize that June's death, and perhaps Matt's as well, were possibly not accidents, I knew that I could not stay quiet forever. I wrote down your names and contact information before I left.

I do not know your involvement, but I suspect the information I have just shared with you is not information that my brother has shared with you. That is, unless he is different than I have known him to be these past 40 years.

You have my e-mail address. If what I have just shared is useful, good. If you need to speak with me more on the matter, you can reach me by e-mail. I have thought about whether you would share my conversation with Matthew. At first, I did not want you to do so. However, after long thought, I realize it makes no difference. Forty years is a long time. As much as I would like to renew a relationship with my brother, it means nothing unless he has the same feeling. Do as you wish.

By e-mail and phone Sti and Rob discussed Susan's information. Assuming what she had shared was accurate, the issue of June's death remained even more arcane. What did become clearer was their ongoing suspicion that Matthew Harris was not giving them the whole story. The more one looked at the big picture of this situation, the more evident it became that June's death was caught up in motives and actions far more complex than surface evidence suggested.

The reality of this life-size conundrum was very disconcerting. The two friends had the feeling that they had waded into a mess that was on the brink of overwhelming them. They were not professional investigators, and really had no interest in being amateur detectives and crime solvers. What to do was their dilemma. Paralleling any thoughts they had about the significance of Mrs. Renaldo's revelations, was the reality that they should consider backing out of this whole affair before it was too late. Also, and this was expressed by Rob, there was an issue of liability. Rob's business sense told him that the increasing involvement carried with it the potential for a variety of negative outcomes for the two of them. On the one hand they were messing around in the affairs of others. This recent e-mail only confirmed that there was more here than expected and the players in this whole affair might include some high stakes players who could cause Sti and Rob problems. A second issue was that all of this could place the two, and their families, in harms way. Both knew that these concerns alone were reason enough to withdraw.

For the time being, Sti and Rob elected to make no decision. They were due to be together for several days of skiing in Colorado and would review things at that time.

* * * *

The day of skiing was good. But there had been no talk of the Harris situation. Instinctively, both knew that such a discussion needed to be focused and uninterrupted. It could take place at Rob's house in the evening. There was plenty of time.

Now, with a couple of glasses of good Cabernet Sauvignon, snacks, and Sierra Nevada Chileno Peppers, they turned their attention to the matter of the Harris family.

The discussion quickly focused on what Susan's e-mail added to their knowledge and their projections. Carefully, Sti and Rob stepped through what they knew and tried to stick to the facts. But try as they might, conjecture kept coming to the front of their thoughts and communication.

Wandering with his thoughts, Rob began to speculate. "All of this just looks to be tied together. But I cannot help but think that if there is a central piece, it must start with Matthew Harris. Renaldo's information keeps reminding me of the number of times we have talked about the fact that Matthew does not seem to be telling us everything. It seems that something, a chain of events, started with Matthew and ended with June's death."

"Or, perhaps it has not yet ended," reflected Sti.

"Yeah, maybe it is continuing and we are in the middle of it. That's what scares me. We keep getting deeper and deeper into all of this. Where's it going?"

"Who knows, but we need to decide where we are going in this."

Rob acknowledged the task at hand and began the long night of review. "Well, let's go back and try to put this all in some kind of order of events. Maybe we can then get a better handle on what we need to do."

"Alright, ah …" Sti was searching for a starting point. "Let's say for the moment that it all begins with Matthew Harris who is doing field work in the valley. We know from reviewing his notes that in the years between the late 1940's and through the 1950's he was traipsing around the base of the Sierra escarpment. He and his wife were studying the canyon wall rock exposed by the streams that cut the canyons. They collected a lot of samples, which they shipped back to the university. They also had field camps all along the east side from Round Valley to Lone Pine. They spent twelve to fourteen hours a day in the field, poking and probing and collecting. So, now this info from Renaldo suggests that he may have found more than just rocks."

"They?"

"I know, I know. But we do not know what Faddie's knowledge was."

"Oh, I think we do," was Rob's response. "Those two were too close for her not to know. I tell you what, for the sake of argument, keep it fluid. We can discuss this as if one or both were involved in some kind of selling of Indian artifacts." Rob paused, he was arranging thoughts.

Sti knew enough to let him continue.

"I am going out there with this. I am guessing that one or both of them were on to some special or unique artifacts. They found them in their work in the field. Now you are really going to like this next piece." Another protracted pause followed. "This stuff they find is valuable, so they or he tries to sell it. And this is where it really gets interesting. Renaldo said that her brother was under pressure to publish. You know, you publish, make a name for yourself, and you move up in the academic ranks. Remember, Renaldo indicated Harris spent too much time on process—the fieldwork. But fieldwork is not cheap. Matthew Harris needed money."

"We both know where you are going with this." Sti ventured. "He needed money. So they sell some items. You can't sell to just anybody. These are Paiute artifacts and to knowingly sell them would invite real trouble. I think the Federal Antiquities Act is clear on that matter. So, you sell the stuff under the table. But once you do it, you are in the hooks of those who would buy. Especially if you are not really comfortable selling in the first place."

Rob chimed in, "Yeah, the seller has some feelings of guilt, but the buyer has none. Harris was trapped."

Sti again, "So Renaldo wanders into this mess and creates a real problem that gets her excommunicated from the family. She sits on this for 40 years. But Harris had to know that his sister knew something wrong was going on. She has always been there with the information, or part of the facts, at least."

"But she was family, even if she was cut off. Family seldom squeals. Maybe he was just holding on to that piece."

"Could be. But I am banking, and I know you are aware of this also, that there is a connection between the incident that Susan witnessed and the problems that later plague young Matt Harris. It could be that the same people who were buying and putting the heat on his dad were also the ones who were putting the heat on Matt."

"The sad thing," observed Rob, "Is that Matt may not have known that sequence of events, but his father must have seen some connection. Remember, Matt told Matthew that someone was invading the caches and making off with artifacts that would not be studied by Matt, another researcher, or a museum."

It was like a shot. Rob's reference to a museum struck a memory. Sti immediately reflected. He was searching for a more concrete connection with Rob's ideas. In an effort to bring it to the surface Sti just started talking. "Ok, stop there. When I was at the museum in Independence I came across some baskets and pottery that had been on loan to the museum from the LADWP. Allegedly they had been discovered by DWP employees in the 1940's and 1950's but were not made available to the museum until the 1990's sometime. At the time I thought it funny that no one had known about the discoveries and there was no record about the origin of their discovery."

"I could see where some worker would find some items and turn them into the company. The stuff gets lost in the system and turns up later. The DWP is trying to establish better relationships with the valley people so they do a good deed and turn the items over to the museum. No big deal."

Sti responded quickly. "I know, but there was a strange connection to all of this. I tried contacting the DWP and got nowhere. In fact, no one in the DWP seemed to know anything about the on-loan items. The community relations department was, I was assured, the department that would have handled this. No one there had the slightest idea about all of these baskets and pottery items. At the time I was not surprised because I know how large and cavernous bureaucracies work. Internal communication often falls far short of efficient."

There was a long and searching pause before Sti spoke again. "And now that I think about it there was another peculiarity. As I recall, a Manzanar internee had found some items which were turned over to the Eastern California Museum after the war."

"A who?" Rob was perplexed. "Where does Manzanar come into this?"

"Wait now. There was this young guy, a Japanese-American who was in Manzanar. It seems he donated a number of Paiute items to the museum in the late 1940's or early 1950's. His name, well, I need to go over my notes again to find it. No one at the museum had any current information about him. They did not know if he was even alive. It seems that after the donations they never again heard from him."

Rob, "I think we are getting bogged down. There quite possibly is a connection between Matthew selling artifacts and his future problems, and maybe even the death of Matt. If that is true, then I am more likely to say there may also be a connection that involves June's death. In which case, we are playing with fire. These people, whoever they are, do not take prisoners."

"Hmm, you are probably right."

"Even if we do not want to follow up on all of this, we need to confront Harris. I am ticked. He has given us the run around. He thinks he can play games with us."

"I say we have another very frank discussion with Harris. I say we put all the cards on the table and see what happens. Then we decide what to do." Sti knew that what he was suggesting was that they stay with the case a little longer. But what he was suggesting was clear to both. They could not just let go. The more involved they were becoming, the more intriguing it all was. Also, something inside said that there was evil out there and they were not comfortable letting evil win this game.

So, they made plans.

Chapter 22

The Third Visit to the Harris Home

The dining room

The scene was very emotional. Harris was clearly startled when confronted with the fact that his two investigators had come across information involving Susan Renaldo and the events of some 40 years earlier. He read the email sent by his sister. It took him time to collect his thoughts. He wandered into the dining room and sat down, motioning but not asking Sti and Rob to sit down. He was silent. And yet, as he sat, there seemed in his expression a sense of relief. When he did speak his comments were as much an expression of 'at last it is out' as an explanation.

"I knew I could not keep it a secret forever. Oh …, these many years Susan has been on my mind. With the loss of everyone else in my family, I have thought of her often. She is all that is left of family—my own sister. You'd think that…. Ah, well, I am the one in the wrong here. My actions and pride for these many years has been the undoing of a relationship with my own sister."

Rob's response was pointed. "Dr. Harris, perhaps you can give us some insight into what Susan is talking about. Quite frankly, we are frustrated with this whole affair."

"I know. I know...." Harris was quick to respond, but Sti was not about to let the elderly Ph.D. go on and he cut Harris off.

"No, No! Now just wait a minute." Sti was in his lecture mode, a result of his trade. Once in this mode, as his students, wife and kids knew so well, there was no interrupting him. "We came here as much to find out what happened as we came to let you know in no uncertain terms that we have just about had it with your problems. From the beginning we made it clear that you had to be up front and honest with us. Twice we have had to follow up with you on an issue because you were not telling us all that we needed to know. This time we want to make our position as clear as possible. Whether we decide to continue on your behalf depends here and now on whether you give us everything we need to know.... Let me phrase that another way, we want to know everything—what you know and what you suspect. We want names."

Even Rob was impressed. Sti was on a roll. If this did not bring it all out of Harris, nothing would.

Sti continued. "We want dates. We want places. We want events. We want to know everything you know and think you know about what is happening."

Rob's look at Sti was a reminder of one other matter. "Oh yes, we also want access to everything you have on all of this. Your stuff, all of Matt's records and journals, and anything June had or wrote. Now, is that clear?" Sti was not done. "Then we will decide whether to continue."

Rob did not wait for Harris. "What Sti says is critical Dr. Harris. Sti and I suspect that the stakes may be very high in this game, and we are not professionals. We can not afford to be involved in something that could bring harm to us or our families. In fact, we can't be involved in something that would bring harm to anyone, including you. You are smart enough to know that at some point, if we feel there is reason to believe illegal activity is involved anywhere in all of this, we will go to the authorities. You know that don't you?"

Matthew Harris just looked at them. Then he looked away. He got up and walked over to face the family pictures on the wall. After a few moments, he walked into the living room and stared out the window that looked towards the bay and the city of San Francisco. He breathed deeply, organized his thoughts, and began his response.

"Everything in Susan's e-mail is accurate. But it is only the tip of the iceberg." Harris paused. It was normal for him. Sti and Rob had seen this several times before. The scientist in him was weighing thoughts and looking for the best way to express them. "I am solely responsible for the estranged relationship with my sister. But, if you can believe this, I always thought it was for the best. It was my foolish way of protecting her from a situation that she was closer to than she knew." Still facing the window and talking, "If you look at the picture with several people standing on a rock with Mount Whitney in the background, Susan is the one in the front on the far right. That was a family picture taken when Matt, Megan, Eaddie and I hosted other members of our two families on an outing in the Alabama Hills many years ago when all were much younger. She was very young then."

Sti and Rob got up to look. But it was an inconsequential observation since the picture was taken from a distance and faces were not really clear. It provided little information about someone who was now much older.

"Come in here and sit" suggested Matthew. "This discussion could take some time. Also, I have coffee, beer and wine if you want any." Sti and Rob declined the beverage offer. They were content for the moment to listen to Harris.

"Probably the best place to start is with Susan. We can work back from the present." Harris was now sitting across from his two guests. "Susan's husband Richard is several years younger than her. It is her second marriage and his first. They have been married about twenty-five years now, give or take. Susan's first husband died of a heart attack after about ten years of marriage. They had two kids who are grown now and I have no idea of their whereabouts.

"The reason I am telling you this is that Susan's husband's family was involved in the incident she observed 40 years ago. She does not know this, and I doubt very much that her husband knows anything about it. But, I do."

Looking quizzical, Rob asked the obvious. "If you were estranged from Susan all these years, how do you know all of this?"

"For many years I did not. However, it seems that my wife and Susan kept in periodic contact by mail for many years, from the time of Megan's death to Eaddie's death. I was not aware. Eaddie was a prolific letter writer. I was never home when the mail was delivered and paid no attention when I was. Eaddie ran the show in the house. After her death, I found all of the letters and read them. It was only then that I realized how foolish I had been. But it was also … at least this was my thinking, necessary to not have any contact with Susan.

"Let me explain. Susan's husband is a very successful mining engineer, like his father. He is also an avid backpacker, photographer and environmentalist. He and Susan met on a Sierra Club outing and their common interests led to marriage."

Sti and Rob looked questioningly at Harris.

"I know, you are wondering what all of this has to do with the story. Well, believe me it is a complex web of circumstances. Richard Renaldo's father was also a mining engineer. Pablo was his name. He made a name for himself in the 1930's when his work at the tungsten mine at Pine Creek resulted in major cost and labor savings for the company. As a result, he came to the attention of Mulholland and his engineers who were upgrading the aqueduct and related facilities. It seems that Pablo became a major figure in the work of the DWP.

"But, Pablo had another connection, other than mining and the aqueduct, with the Owens Valley. It seems he was born near Mojave. His mother was Owens Valley Paiute and his father a Spaniard whose wealthy family had lost its fortune and had fallen from grace in the homeland. He had come to America with little more than a background in engineering, and ended up wandering the minefields where he made a name for himself and was considered successful."

Rob spoke for the two, "Dr. Harris, certainly you did not learn all of this through the letters between Susan and your wife."

"No. I did not. Remember how I told you two early on that I had done some investigating before coming to you." Seeing their nod Harris continued. "Well, it is the researcher in me. When I discovered in the letters that Susan had married someone named Renaldo, I recognized the name. Renaldo was the name of the individual in the car to whom I was speaking on the night that Susan overheard the conversation. His first name I did not know at the time. He simply went by Renaldo. It is later that I found that his first name was Vincent. Vincent Renaldo was the younger cousin of Pablo Renaldo. Only his real name was Vincent George Littlebear Renaldo. 'George' referenced the great Paiute chief of the 1860's who had a dwelling along what is now George Creek. 'Littlebear' was a name often used by Pablo Renaldo's wife's side of the family. This was the Bowers family, which was well known in the valley because one of the Paiute chieftains in the 1860s and 1870s had adopted the name Joe Bowers. Vincent was cleaver, and rode his cousin's coat tails to become an employee of the LADWP.

"Anyway, I need to get to the part that I am most ashamed of. It is something I shall carry as guilt to the grave.

"As I told you earlier, Eaddie and I had found a Paiute camp site and cave in Sawmill Canyon. Our experience there was not a good one as we were taken advantage of by someone who represented themselves as interested in the artifacts for purpose of study. We had been burned."

The two guests nodded. They knew this part of the story.

"Life can be cruel, and Susan was right. I spent more time studying in the field when I should have been publishing. Grants were scarce in the 1950's and a professor's pay was not that great. We also had two young kids and this house to pay for. Money was tight. But as luck or lack of luck would have it, I was paid a visit by Vincent Renaldo. He was well aware of our Sawmill findings and I suspect was also aware that we were financially in bad shape. He said he had a patron that would pay good money for artifacts if we found any.

"My initial response was outrage. But the need for money was significant. I broached the subject with Eaddie. She was firm in her response of 'no!' For a year this issue hung over our head and grated on our marriage. Then in the spring of the next year I found another cache. It was a very small site in Taboose Creek Canyon. But it had a number of well preserved pots, baskets, weapons, and some pieces of gold in one of the pots. I was startled. And I soon started thinking about Renaldo. Eaddie told me not to contact him, and I indicated I would not. But, greed and the desperate need for money worked on me for weeks. I called him. And that was the beginning of a period of my life that I will forever regret. My life and the life of my family changed forever after that."

Harris was struggling. He wanted to continue, but it was difficult to talk about this next phase of his life. For their part, Sti and Rob, as much as they tried to put on a face that said we are not going to succumb to sympathy this time, they could see what was happening. All too often people make decisions they think will help the family, only to start down a path that they can not retrace. Once Harris made the decision to sell some artifacts, no matter how good a person he was, the reality of what he had done would affect him forever.

Harris got up and wandered into the kitchen. Without saying anything, Rob and Sti followed. Harris and Rob filled cups with coffee. Sti rummaged around in the refrigerator for something and settled for ice water. Each knew that this informal activity would help Harris save some face as he continued to explain what happened.

Talk in the kitchen was small talk and the three soon reconvened in the living room. "Renaldo gave me several thousand in cash for the materials I delivered to him. The goods included several pots, baskets, arrowhead weapons, and some smaller things. I did not give him the gold nuggets. Since I did not know what to do with the nuggets, I left them in the small cave. I told no one where it was or that it even existed."

Sti interrupted Harris with a question he knew Rob shared. "Did you ever find out who Renaldo was working with? After all, he does not seem like someone who would have that kind of cash."

"No. But my conversations with him indicated that either he or some other persons with whom he was working had a great deal of knowledge about the Owens Valley. But, what I am about to tell you will give you some idea of the magnitude of all of this. Needless to say, I felt a great deal of guilt for some time. The season ended, I paid off some big debts, and we went back to the University for the fall term. It was sort of an out of site, out of mind situation. I repressed my guilt. Eaddie and I did not talk about it. I know that she was aware of more than she let on.

"Then, soon before the end of the spring term of the following year, as we were preparing to go back to the valley, I got a call from someone who said he was working with Renaldo. He indicated that Renaldo would be contacting me and that I would be well advised to keep the contact secret and to not make things difficult. I recognized the voice, I had heard it before. It was the person who called himself Dr. Freeman. Thus, before that season in the field even took place, I was confronted with what I had suspected all along. I was in over my head. So, you can see that when Susan came to visit us my mind was not fully on my work. I knew there was trouble."

"You mean to tell me that you went into the field knowing that the people you had dealt with years earlier were involved with Renaldo?" was the question put to Harris by Rob.

"Yes, I knew there was a connection, but I could not tell Eaddie. Our relationship was already strained. To protect the kids, Eaddie had made arrangements for them to go to a summer camp for several weeks after their school year ended in June. However, she insisted that Susan be allowed to visit. Susan was, after all both my sister and an adult. Well, you know what happened while she visited."

"Dr. Harris, what came of your contact with Renaldo? Did you sell him more items?"

"It was an old gambit. They had me in a corner. If I did not cooperate, they would let key people at the University and other places know that I was stealing and selling treasured items. I was well aware of what was happening. I was looking for a way out of the bind. Then they hit me with the heavy blow.

"I agreed to meet Renaldo in Bishop when I was getting supplies. In those days I usually went into Bishop even though it was a longer drive because there were more options to purchase needed items. While there it was my intent to probe Renaldo and find out who was behind all of this. But my intent was met with a different Renaldo. Renaldo was all business. He was not the easygoing person I had dealt with before. He was not the person Susan had heard several days before. He was on a mission. From the start, he made it clear that my resistance to sell more items did not please those he represented."

"Did he give you names?" Sti said while thinking out loud.

"I'll get to that. The blow came when Renaldo said, and I do not think I shall ever forget his phrase, 'Dr., one of the baskets you gave us had traces of gold in it!

My client insists that you sell him everything you recovered from the site. My client also knows that this is not the first site you have uncovered. If you value your reputation, you had best deal honestly with us. Otherwise, you will have dealings that you will regret.' I was on the verge of exploding. But I was determined to maintain my composure. I tried to talk with Renaldo while I thought of something more concrete to say. I could only think of my reputation and family. I had to do something quickly.

"Renaldo kept pressing me, and I kept trying to buy time. So, I put all the cards on the table. I told him that I had no desire to withhold anything that was a Paiute artifact. I told him I did not want any money and I would not accept any money. All I wanted was out of this. In exchange, I would tell whomever he was working with where the site was located. I knew the gold was still there as were several other items. I was gambling that if I met the other person then I would know who was behind all of this. So, I told Renaldo that he was to go back to his associate or associates and tell them that I would only talk with those who also called themselves Dr. Freeman, Dr. Allison and Mr. Garsuch. If they wanted to know the location of the site, they could meet with me.

"I could tell Renaldo was caught off guard."

The two listeners were entranced. This story was right out of Indiana Jones. They were also dumbfounded. If what Harris was telling them was true, he had found some moxie when he was dealing with Renaldo. He had played Renaldo's game. It is a wonder he was still alive.

"I was so scared, but the more I talked the more it became clear to me that I could not just go along with Renaldo. My life and those of my family were at stake. This I sensed. So, I fabricated a situation."

"Gee Harris, you were playing a cat and mouse game with a lion" was Sti's comment.

"I know, and afterwards I was shaking. But Renaldo's surprise bought me time. At the time it is all that I could think of. Anyway, I told Renaldo that I recognized the caller who contacted me before I left to come to the Valley. I told him that after the phone call I sat down and wrote out everything that had happened in our earlier contacts. I told him I even included descriptions of those with whom I had met. I told him that my wife and I worked on it together to make sure that we did not miss any details. I also told him that we did the same thing in describing what had taken place the previous year when we sold Renaldo and his friends the Paiute artifacts. I explained that all of this information had been notarized and given to my attorney to be opened and provided to authorities in the event of my death.

"I went out on a limb. I wanted him to tell his associates that I had some trump cards and they were positioned to be played if they did not cooperate. After all, I was not asking for anything except to be left alone. In exchange, I would say nothing to anyone because it would in turn ruin not only them but me. Also, if I was killed, it would only hurt them because I would be out of the picture."

"Incredible" one of his listeners responded.

"I thought so too. After it was all over, and for many years, I kept saying to myself that it was almost like a mystery novel. I could not believe that I had said it. For a long time after, I would get the chills just thinking about that encounter."

Rob inquired, "But did it work?"

Sti asked, "How did Renaldo respond? Did you meet with them?"

"Renaldo seemed shocked. It was as if he did not think I had it in me to say those things. It was clear that he was not prepared to deal with my response. He seemed to fumble around for a response. I thought at the time that the shoe was now on the other foot. Anyway, he said that he would have to get back to me. He was unsure and he was angry; but I sensed he could not act alone.

"I made another quick decision. I told him he had best do it soon because I was ending my fieldwork early that season. I told him they would never find the site unless I either showed them or drew a map, and that I might not be back in the field for two or three years. I told him that I clearly remembered the people I had dealings with in 1949 and would not accept any excuses. I would meet with them. When he got back to me there would be no negotiations. It would be my way or else."

"But you did not really hold that many cards. You had no certainty that the items in the site, even the gold, were worth that much. Certainly not enough to lose your life over," was Sti's reaction.

"That was my initial response to my own ideas. However, as I became more and more bold in my dealings with Renaldo, I remembered that the person who passed himself off as Dr. Allison, an anthropologist and associate with the Eastern Sierra Museum, had once commented that they suspected many sites were in the valley and that they were linked together. He commented that he would not be surprised that one site could provide sufficient information to help in discovering the other sites. The more I talked the more convinced I was that there was more to Renaldo's associates than even he realized. So, I upped the ante, bluffed, and he went for it."

Sti and Rob asked questions. Did he meet with Renaldo's friends? If so, when and where? How did it go? Did they leave you alone?

"Oh they met with me. It was a Sunday afternoon at the Park at the North end of Lone Pine. We were on our way out of the Valley for the season. I had already determined that we could leave early and would not come back the next season."

"Did they all show?"

Harris responded almost humorously. "Funny you should ask. Renaldo was there. The individual I knew as Dr. Allison was there, but he was very aged since I had last seen him. I thought at the time that he looked like he was dying. The Mr. Garsuch, who had previously been the perfect host, was there, but this time he was very quiet, almost recluse and he stood off with his head down. I thought later that he had the look of someone who was doing everything to avoid being photographed."

"So they thought you might be having them photographed? Great, what a dangerous game you played." Rob's comment was more in the line of congratulations than anything else.

"I wish I had thought to do so. But looking back on it, I am sure they thought they might be photographed. In retrospect, that thought must have been to my benefit because I never saw or heard of them again. Anyway, I was scared, but I was also determined to make this work. I stared at each of them long and hard as we talked. As I did so I realized that the fourth person was the voice I had heard in 1949 when he represented himself as Dr. Freeman. He was also the voice I had heard back in April. But more importantly, he looked very much like someone I had seen somewhere else. At the time I could not place his face."

Sti and Rob inquired almost simultaneously about whether Harris ever was able to identify the person.

Harris nodded. "I could not place him at the time. His face had distinctive features. I knew that I had seen the face before, but not this man. He had to be related to someone whose face I had seen. It was many months later that I was able to put a name to the face. He was related to George Kennicott. Reviewing old photos of the construction of the L.A. Aqueduct, I found a picture of Kennicott, the man I met was a spitting image of Kennicott."

Sti and Rob looked puzzled.

"Who is Kennicott you ask? George Kennicott was one of the field supervisors for Mulholland. He was Mulholland's eyes and ears as well as the man overseeing much of the survey and construction of the aqueduct."

Sti's mind was racing. He could not help but want to see a connection between all of this and the fact that considerable donations of Paiute artifacts had been donated to the Eastern California Museum by the LADWP. He elected to not say anything. He would talk again with Rob about this later.

"I never met Kennicott, but he is legend in the valley. He is reputed to have walked every inch of the aqueduct many times over. It has been said that Kennicott knew every slope above and below the aqueduct. But what I did find out later was that one of his close companions during the 1920's and 1930's had been Pablo Renaldo, Vincent's cousin. Vincent, for whatever reason, had adopted this cousin's sir name. The Kennicott I met had to be an elderly George Kennicott or descendent."

"So you now knew Vincent Renaldo's connection with the Owens Valley. But this must have happened long before Susan was married to Richard Renaldo. You only found that out later, right?" asked Sti.

"Yes, much later. I did not know Susan had even married the first time. I avoided knowing anything about my sister. I only found out about her two marriages when I read Eaddie's collection of letters. When I saw the name Renaldo, I knew there was a high probability of connection. When I found out that Susan's husband's family had ties with the valley, I knew the connection was solid. However, again, following some investigation in the mid 1980's, I concluded that Richard was in no way connected with any of this. It was purely a coincidence. So, I made sure there was no contact between Susan and me. I did not want to open up a can of worms. The way to protect her was to keep me out of the picture."

Harris knew what his two guests were thinking. They were thinking ahead and making connections between what he had just told them and the situation with Matt. "Now you have some idea why I have always suspected that Matt's death was not accidental. You also know why my field trailer had been broken into."

The discussion went on for some time. Harris indicated that when his children developed their interest in the Paiute and Shoshone Indians of the Eastern Sierra, he and Eaddie were caught between two conflicting values. On the one hand they knew that their children's interest could come into conflict with the same people that had caused problems with Matthew. They also knew that you did not discourage your children from healthy and constructive interests. So, they supported their children. They also avoided doing fieldwork in the regions around Sawmill and Taboose Creek when their children were in the field with them. They stayed well to the South and the North. It was not surprising to Eaddie and Matthew when Matt expanded his professional interests to focus on these areas. They also knew that in time Matt would probably find new sites and the sites they had found.

They discussed the fact that Matt's findings included the two sites previously discovered by his parents. When Matt indicated that he had sites that had been pilfered, he was completely unaware that it was his father who had done some of the pilfering. But the fact that Matt had also discovered other sites, some with gold pieces in them, was testimony to Matt's talents in the field. Matt was very bright and that he suspected that he was being watched did not surprise Matthew. Matthew knew it was just a matter of time before Matt came under the focus and possible influence of Renaldo and friends.

Harris openly admitted that he blamed himself for Matt's death. Had he never got tangled up with the Renaldo bunch, it is likely that Matt would still be alive.

However, the more the three discussed the situation the more Rob and Sti began to suspect that there could have been several other people involved in addition to those Matthew Harris had met. How did Vincent Renaldo get involved? Was there a connection with the pilfering of the sites and with George Kennicott? Where did Pablo fit into the picture? Where did Susan's husband, Richard Renaldo, fit into the picture?

As the evening wound down, Rob asked if Harris was ever aware of the whereabouts of Vincent Renaldo and the other three following the Lone Pine meeting. Harris said he only knew about Renaldo. It seems that in the 1960's Renaldo was accidentally shot and killed by his brother while deer hunting near the Alabama Hills. How did he know this? Matthew indicated that he had long subscribed to the Inyo Register, a biweekly newspaper out of Bishop. He remembered seeing an article about the accident. The name of the victim was Vincent Littlebear Renaldo. The article indicated that Vincent was survived by, among others, his elderly cousin Pablo Renaldo. To Harris, the connection was clear. As for the other three, only the Kennicott character was still vivid in his mind. But he did not know what had happened to any of them. Harris surmised that they could be dead since they appeared at the time of their encounters in the 1950s to be considerably older than him.

He knew he had to ask the question. "Are you going to stay with me on this?" asked Harris. "I have told you everything I know. But we have not talked tonight about June and I am certain there is a connection there. We need to discuss this. Will you come back?"

Sti and Rob thanked Harris. They indicated that they would return the next day if Harris would be available. They wanted to talk more with him and to access some of Matt's records, June's journals, and Matthew's records.

* * * *

Later that evening over dinner and a bottle of wine the two reviewed the discussion with Harris. Both had information they wanted to connect with Harris's comments. Now was a better time to do so than it would have been while at the Harris residence. Both realized that the Harris theory that his granddaughter was the victim of violence may be closer to the truth than either of them was willing to admit before this afternoon.

The discussion focused on tying together pieces that Sti and Rob had come across. Only now they saw the meaning. First, they discussed the possible George Kennicott connection with the LADWP donations of 1993. It was too coincidental. This issue required more inquiry. Could it be that George Kennicott had found some Paiute artifacts? A second issue concerned the connection of Renaldo, or Vincent, with Pablo and Kennicott. Some research was needed here as well. If there was a connection, it could be that things started with Kennicott and Pablo Renaldo, and were extended by Vincent. A third discussion point was the Harris donations of artifacts at the museum in Independence. Sti and Rob had forgotten to pursue this issue with Harris. If memory served them right, these donations had been made by Matthew at the time that Matt was doing some of his best work in the Sierra. Did Harris Senior find additional artifacts or were these left over from earlier finds? And then there was the gold. Chunks or nuggets, whatever they were, they were an important piece. The Paiute artifacts were obviously worth something. But the gold was another matter. If gold was found at multiple sites, then there is reason to believe that there was a source. If they were chunks, and not just nuggets, then that source could have been close to the Eastern Sierra. Whoever found the source was potentially rich beyond reason. Sti and Rob knew all to well that this latter matter was a major issue. People kill for gold.

There was another matter. This involved the Paiute artifacts collected by Henry Kubota, the name Sti had run across in the Eastern California Museum. Henry's finds were excellent pieces. But how had he come by them? There were quite a few pots, baskets, pouches, and other items. Did Henry find gold also? Did he save all that he found or did he hide or dispose of other items? This latter question arose because it is hard to believe that he could have hidden a large quantity of items at the relocation camp. How did all of these items survive after the war? Who was Henry Kubota and what was his role in all of this?

Finally, there was the discussion that evolved into conjecture regarding possible connections between the Paiute artifacts plundering and June's death. Sti and Rob both now saw a possible connection. The credibility of Dr. Harris was of much greater concern in this discussion than it had been before, but one could not ignore the fact that Harris may be correct in suggesting June was murdered. Perhaps there is a connection. But who? Vincent was apparently dead. His three cohorts in crime were, if not dead, very old. Certainly they could not make trips into the off-trail backcountry to carry out a murder. Even if they could, why would they? Was June on to something? Had June followed her father's leads into a danger zone? Did her actions just prior to her death suggest she had a premonition? Was she being followed? Had she stumbled, like her grandfather, and perhaps father, onto something bigger than her?

Sti and Rob would have to renew their discussions with Harris. And, they would have to spend more time searching through the Harris archives. They also would have to look into the matter of Kennicott, the DWP and Henry Kubota.

This was hardly what they had in mind for retirement life. They had to admit that while their amateur investigative activities may be keeping them off the streets, they were not necessarily keeping them out of trouble. In fact, it could be leading them directly into trouble.

CHAPTER 23

SIERRA CLUB HEADQUARTERS

San Francisco

As its name suggests, the Sierra Club is a product of interest in the mountain range. Created by John Muir, sometimes called the father of the environmental movement, the club focused most of its attention on the Sierra Nevada for the first 75 years of the club's history. Since World War II the club has been a leader in environmental and ecology issues worldwide. Today, the club exists amidst a love—hate relationship with those who know of the Sierra Club's activities. You either love the club or you hate it.

For those who love the club and are active participants, the Sierra Club provides a wide range of activities. Foremost among those activities are the club sponsored outings that afford opportunities to visit and explore local as well as remote regions of the world. Among the many outings, the oldest are those conducted in the Sierra Nevada. Since the 1920's the club has sponsored annual trips into the heart of the Sierra. For many years the extended annual outing into the Sierra was called the Sierra Club Base Camp. People who participated in these trips hiked and or rode stock into some remote area of the Sierra and over a period of weeks explored this region. A common practice was to follow up the trip with an annual Base Camp publication that recorded the culture and events unique to each year's outing. This scrap book of extensive narrative covering everything from meal menus to camp fire songs included photos, rosters of all participants, and notes on all activities and events of the annual trip. It was an amateur publication, but it documented well each year's trip.

Rob had made many phone calls to the Sierra Club headquarters in San Francisco. Finally he made contact with Duane Edwards—the so-called curator of the Club archives. Through this contact Rob was able to follow up on photocopies of the Journal kept by Lillian Hamner. Responding to Rob's inquiry, "yes, the club has records regarding the 1935 Base Camp trip." Over an extended phone conversation Rob was able to ascertain that the Club had copies of the annual Base Camp publication for that year, a collection of photos taken by various people on the trip, and a small number of items collected during the trip. Edwards also indicated to him that it was curious that Rob was calling about the 1935 trip and asking questions about what the Club had regarding the trip. It seems that a young female, the curator remembered her as a field ranger for the National Park Service, had contacted him a couple of times several years earlier. She was interested in anything the Club had available on the trip. She was especially interested in the names of those who participated. The curator indicated that it was very apparent that the young lady, he could not remember her name, already knew a lot about the trip. She was, however, very curious about the artifacts from the trip.

According to Edwards, about two months after contacting him she made a visit to check out the artifacts. No one had looked at the artifacts for years. Everything had to be pretty much as it was when first collected in 1935. She looked through the items thoroughly. Apparently there was nothing of interest to her. At least that was the curator's initial impression. She asked if the Club had information about anyone else who might have mementos from the trip, especially items related to the "runaway mule incident" that took place on the trip. Edwards indicated he did not know what she was talking about but he did not have any other items and he was not in a position to refer her to anyone else. She was very appreciative, and that is the last he heard from her.

Reviewing Rob's findings afterwards, Rob and Sti knew that there was a good reason why June's photocopy of Lillian's journal was so worn. The High Route held significant meaning to June. She went out of her way to investigate the area, collect information on the region above and west of Marion Lake, and visit this portion of the High Route. She also died there. Or, if Harris was right, she was murdered there.

But what was the connection? "We can't ignore the significance of the High Route," said Rob. "It's significant and she went there without telling anyone. We also know that when we found her skeleton we also found old leather and canvas artifacts…."

"That probably came from the '35 Sierra Club trip," interjected Sti.

"More importantly, they probably came from the runaway mule incident June referred to when she talked to Edwards," was Rob's conjecture.

Sti restated the obvious. "We need to revisit the High Route. No doubt, some of the old artifacts that were there when we found her are still there. We also need to look around. Maybe just looking around will give us some insight into why she was so obsessed with the place."

"Yes," said Rob. "I cannot help but think that some how all of this obsession with the High Route would have to be connected with Matt and Matthew Harris if someone was out to kill her. I cannot believe that this was someone trying to kill her, if indeed she was murdered, for reasons that had nothing to do with her father and grandfather. It's just too much coincidence. You agree?"

"If it doesn't have any connection, then this rivals any TV soap. If there is a connection, then this whole thing just keeps getting more mysterious," was Sti's response.

Rob continued the thought. "But if there is a connection it also suggests that the stakes are very high. The issue has to be more than just some Paiute artifacts. It has to be the gold."

CHAPTER 24

JILL KUBOTA

Residence of Jill Kubota, Newport Beach, California

Jill Kubota was very friendly. She was not in the least apprehensive about discussing her father's experience at Manzanar and his subsequent and long-time interest in the Owens Valley. When Sti and Rob arrived at her door she ushered them in as if she were welcoming a long lost relative. The home was in an upper income neighborhood in Newport Beach, California. The homes in the area were custom built, many from decades earlier. Although the neighborhood suggested elegance, the Kubota home was modestly decorated and featured a blend of Japanese collectibles in a traditional American interior. The most notable feature was the family room view of a beautiful and meticulously maintained rear yard landscape that clearly reflected the Japanese heritage of the home's inhabitant.

Finding Jill Kubota was no easy task. Kubota is a common Japanese name in America. However, at the suggestion of a friend, contact was made with the Manzanar Survivors association. This contact led to several possible phone numbers. Bingo! The first call resulted in reaching Jill, Henry Kubota's only offspring. Talking with Jill Kubota was very refreshing. Unlike talking with Harris, the National Park people, the Sheriff's office personnel, and many other sources, Ms. Kubota was most eager to give the two any information she had. You had the sense she was not hiding anything. Sti and Rob would soon find out why she was so receptive to their inquiry.

Jill explained that before World War II her father's family owned land in Garden Grove, Westminster and Anaheim, California where the family grew vegetables. Theirs was a very successful business because they sold to markets as well as marketing directly to the public themselves. But under the provisions of Executive Order 9066, signed by President Roosevelt in February, 1942, the family was uprooted and sent to the Manzanar War Relocation Center. It happened very quickly and there was no time to make appropriate arrangements regarding the homes, land, and businesses left behind. Like all relocated Japanese Americans, there was the potential that the Kubota family could lose their land in their absence. However, a longtime friend of the family, Juan Batista, whose family had long resided in Orange County, told Henry's father that he would look out for the land until the Kubota's came back. When the war was over the Kubota family found that Juan had been true to his word. Juan became a partner in the farming business. The primary crop soon became strawberries, and they were successful beyond expectation. Later the land was more valuable for housing than crops. However, unlike many who sold to developers, the Kubota family became developers themselves in the 1960's and 1970's. They developed housing and commercial uses on their own land.

Henry's parents died in the 1960's. Henry then became the head of the family business. Trained as an attorney, Henry was a workaholic. He made the Kubota family even more successful. But through it all he never lost his passion for the Owens Valley. With the backing of Henry and many other former internees, Manzanar was designated as a California Registered Historical Landmark in 1972. In 1992, Congress designated Manzanar as a National Historic Site under the jurisdiction of the National Park Service. Unfortunately, Henry's health, long a problem following a bout with rheumatic fever soon after the war, began to fail in the late 1980s and he died in 1999. For the family it was a great loss, for Jill personally, it was devastating. Henry had not only been a successful businessman and father; he had also been Jill's greatest teacher and a model of integrity. The latter quality was evident in the Henry Kubota that Jill shared with her two guests.

Jill Kubota hosted her guests in the large and very comfortable family room and offered them tea. Sti and Rob sensed that Jill was comfortable hosting visitors and was skilled at making them comfortable. "Before the war began my father was a high school student in Garden Grove. He was the oldest child in the family, and was both liked and looked up to by his siblings. He was one of those children that all parents want. He was likeable, responsible, handsome and intelligent. There was no doubt that he would bring honor to the family. At school he was much respected and was an honor student. But things changed after December 7, 1941. The family soon found itself as residents at Manzanar.

"You would think that such an experience for someone like my father would cause him to be angry and hostile. But he always said it made him stronger. At some point in the many, many times I discussed the Manzanar experience with my father he would remind me that 'Life's experiences are not matters to be judged for their fairness. They are really opportunities to learn, and to make ourselves and those we know into better persons because of the experience.' As far back as I can remember I have always admired the forgiving and reflective quality of my father. Whenever a relative or another person would launch into critical commentary about what happened to Japanese Americans during World War II, my father would wait for an opportune time to turn the discussion into consideration about what was being done to learn from that experience and make the world better because of it. There are not many people like my father. I count my blessings that he was indeed my father. I was so lucky.

"But you did not come here to listen to my melancholy reflections. Dr. Pierce indicated that you wanted to talk about my father's interest in Indian artifacts."

"Yes, Ms. Kubota. And by the way, your insights into your father's character, while not directly related to the topic of Native American Indian artifacts are probably the best way to start this discussion. You see, we know little or nothing about him. All we know is that he donated some items to the Eastern California Museum after the war." Sti was speaking carefully; trying to choose words that were friendly.

Sti continued. "I have had an opportunity to observe the baskets and pots you father donated to the museum. They are of the highest quality, and the museum curators told me they are among the finest in their collection. However, they also pointed out that following the initial donation the museum lost contact with your father and never heard from him again."

"Oh, he did more than just donate items to the museum. Ever year he made an anonymous donation to the museum. He did that from the time he left Manzanar to the year of his death. I have continued to make the donations. I have honored his request that his name not be associated with the donations."

Sti and Rob looked at each other. Henry Kubota was much more than just a former detainee at Manzanar.

Rob asked a question. "Why the anonymity? And why are you telling us?"

"Well, while it seems strange to you, it is consistent with my father's actions on many things. He always said that it is important in a democratic society to share ourselves with society. It is not important that others should give recognition to those who fulfill this responsibility. My father used to say, jokingly, 'I pay taxes, but when the government uses my tax dollars I do not expect them to thank me for the money. I was merely fulfilling my responsibility.' I always liked that comment and I have tried to live by it as well."

Sti and Rob smiled.

"As for why I would tell you two about the anonymous donations, well let us just say for now that I trust you with the information. Before this visit is over, you will better understand my trust."

This was indeed an odd way to start a discussion with a stranger. However, Sti and Rob were on the receiving end of the information stream and did not question or take issue with Jill's comments.

Rob tried to give some direction to the conversation. "You know that we are interested in the artifacts your father donated. We are most interested in how he came by them." Rob stopped; he needed to rephrase his comment. "We have been studying the Indian artifacts of the Owens Valley for several months. During the course of our investigations we came across many interesting artifacts in the Eastern California Museum that are attributed to Henry Kubota as the donor. The original location of these items would be important to our investigation. That is why I say that we are interested in how he came by them?"

Sti now, "Please understand that we are not sure exactly what we are looking for, but we thought you could help us understand the origins of the artifacts donated by your father."

"I think I can help you," was her response. Jill Kubota got up and walked over to a small cabinet and picked up a small framed photograph. She walked back to her guests. "This is a photo of my father several years before his passing. You will recognize where it was taken." Sti and Rob nodded. Jill's father was standing next to the Manzanar Memorial, or Cemetery Tower as it is sometimes called, which sits just outside the western edge of original camp. In the background was the crest of the Sierra against a deep blue sky.

"And the man next to your father—your husband?" asked Sti.

"No, sadly that was my fiancé, Jason Tanaka. We were scheduled to be married about a year after that photo was taken. Jason was an environmental engineer. He was killed when his plane went down while studying the effects of the Alaska oil pipeline on behalf of the U.S. Department of the Interior. Dad was devastated. Somehow, marriage never appealed to me after Jason's death."

Rob and Sti were quiet. A response was not needed.

Jill pointed out several other photos of her father; but she indicated she liked the one taken at Manzanar because it was informal and because it was his last visit to the Owens Valley.

"My father loved to have conversations with me and to tell me stories. After my mother died when I was in high school we became very close. He was very diligent about spending time with me. As a successful attorney he worked long hours. But I always knew that when he did not have to be at work he would spend his time with me. Over the years I heard much about his experience at Manzanar and his interest in the valley."

"Could you take us back to those conversations?" There was a pause. "Of course we do not want to invade your privacy and we understand if you are not comfortable discussing some things. However, as Rob said, we are very much interested in his experiences in the valley."

"Yes, and some of this is based on comments from other family members who were at Manzanar. It seems that everyone in the family, as well as some friends, knew of my father's interest in the Indians." Jill's comments were always articulated well and with a smile.

"When my father went to the camp he was determined to make it a positive experience. To do that, he needed one thing that was not readily available—solitude from time to time. It was always a characteristic of him. He needed time alone to think and reflect. It is something my grandmother told me started when he was very young. He would go on walks in the fields and think. She said he could see the mountains surrounding the L.A. basin and always dreamed of going there. When he got to Manzanar he saw the open space and the mountains. He needed to see it all up close. He needed to investigate. He also needed to get away from the lack of privacy the camp imposed. So, after several months he began his forays at night. I think it is the only time he ever broke a rule."

"Forays is an interesting way to describe his activities," commented Sti.

"As I understand it, one day he encountered a Paiute Indian by the name of Tom Littlebear Bowers."

Sti and Rob both reacted. They said nothing, but Jill observed their reaction.

"Did I say something wrong?"

"Oh, no," said Rob. "We just recognized the name. We have run across the name ourselves. We were just struck by the coincidence. Please go on."

"Well, it seems the two of them struck up a good friendship. Tom knew the area well and gave my father information on things to see, how to navigate the valley, and information on distances. After awhile the friendship became such that they recognized each other's needs. The two also knew that they had something in common. They were both on the receiving end of prejudice. But neither bore any malice. They were both aware that their intellect, their beliefs, and their values, could rise above any prejudice or injustice. In time, because there was no way they could always set a meeting time and be sure that both were able to be there, they selected a meeting place. As my father described it, it was a small cave just inside the entrance to George Creek. Apparently it had once been a meeting place or camp for the Paiute Indians. My father said there were pots, baskets, and other items in there. Tom gave him lessons on the Indian artifacts including how they were made, their purpose, and how to read the drawings on the baskets and pots."

One of the two guests asked if her father had kept any of the items from this cave. "Oh no, the cave was a meeting place. They would leave notes for each other there. After awhile their notes began to reflect the fact that my father taught Tom some Japanese characters. In turn, Tom taught my father some Paiute words."

"So, how did Henry come by the many items he collected?" was Sti's question.

"One night my father, made a trip to Oak Creek Canyon."

"Oak Creek?" asked Sti. "That is many miles, fifteen or so, from Manzanar. That is where the trail to Baxter Pass starts. How could he do it without being missed?"

"At first my father's journeys were just during the night. But as time went on the camp security loosened. After all, the guards never had any problems with the Japanese Americans and even if someone left, they could not go far because there was no where to go. So, my father extended his trips to a day or two. His parents and family did not like it, but they could easily cover for him. Also, my father would sometimes bring back items that were not available in the camp, some canned goods and fresh food. Sometimes he brought back deer meat. 'Venison,' my father called it. When my father told me about this he commented that Tom claimed that he had a reputation as a bad hunter and a poor shot. But he managed to provide venison for his family as needed.

"My father also arranged a special signal that was a flag. He had a pair of binoculars given to him by Tom. He could see the flag from many miles. If he saw it, he knew to return immediately."

"But ten, or fifteen or even twenty miles? There is just no way to get there easily, unless…."

"You are thinking unless he had a ride, say a horse or a ride in a car, aren't you?" was her comment.

"Exactly," was Sti's response.

"My father said that he learned to ride a horse, a horse Tom would provide, without a saddle. On a couple of occasions he was given a ride in an old truck driven by Tom. On the trip to Oak Creek, he rode a horse alongside Tom. It was a two-day trip. But it was a very important trip. Tom left my father to roam the canyon and came back the next day to guide my father back to the camp. He had to search for my father and when he found him my father was very excited because he had found a cave where there were many Paiute artifacts. According to my father, Tom was very surprised. My father asked Tom if he could take some of the items back to the George Creek meeting cave because the baskets and pottery had designs on them. My father wanted Tom to help him identify what the drawings or design patterns meant. Reluctantly Tom agreed."

"Together they studied the artifacts. Several months later Tom went with my father to see where the Oak Creek site was located. Together they studied the remaining artifacts. My father was apparently very interested in these artifacts. So that he could spend more time with the items, Tom allowed him to take a few at a time to Manzanar. The agreement was that no one else was to see them. My father hid them below the floor boards of their tarpaper house in Manzanar."

"According to my father, Tom was very concerned about what was happening to the Paiute culture and history. He believed that as the Owens Valley population grew the demand for land and resources would push the Paiute out of the picture. The only real connections with the past were the artifacts."

"If you do not mind my asking," said Rob. "How do you remember all these details? Are they written down somewhere?"

"No, Mr. James. My father told me this information many times. I will never forget these and many other stories. It is why he was so committed to supporting the museum."

"How's that Mrs. Kubota?"

"Well, it seems that early in the last year of my father's stay at Manzanar, Tom told my father that he had reason to believe that there were many other sites in other canyons where Paiute artifacts were located. He, Tom, did not know where they were, but he did know that someone had stolen the artifacts from a couple of sites and may have sold them. Tom's fear and the fear of many of Tom's friends was that if this continued much of his people's history in the valley would be lost forever. He was especially concerned because legend had it that the drawings on the pottery and baskets and other implements told secrets about the canyons and the Sierra Nevada. If lost, those secrets would never be known to the only people who mattered, the Paiute.

"The two of them discussed several options. Finally they decided on two courses of action. The first was that they would take the Oak Creek items, especially those that were important, and store them in their secret George Creek cave until something could be done to protect them. The second decision was one that my father had to talk Tom into. My father suggested that since the war looked like it would be over in a year or two, things would change for him. After the war he would have a person of good reputation donate the items to the Eastern California Museum. There they would be preserved and studied."

Rob was concerned. "Weren't they concerned that someone would discover their cave? Didn't you say it had once been a Paiute camp?"

"You are a good listener Mr. James. Yes, that was a question my father put to Tom. But Tom said that the cave would only be used for a short time. As soon as they found another place, they could move the items."

Sti asked, "Did they move them later? Where?"

"To the safest place in the valley at the time. They buried them at Manzanar."

"Weren't they afraid that they would be dug up by large equipment when the camp was closed?"

"Not really, they buried them in the cemetery." All three chuckled.

"So, what happened then?"

"My father and Tom continued their explorations. They found other items in Oak Creek Canyon and later in Shepherd Creek Canyon. Always, they took just the important items, and left enough that someone would think that no one had been there."

"After the war my father returned home to the land my grandparents owned in Garden Grove. But he kept in touch with Tom. Tom did not trust that his mail would not be read. He said there were no secrets in small towns. So, they had a code that allowed them to communicate."

Again, Rob and Sti looked at each other.

"Something else I said has prompted a reaction?"

Rob: "Well, yes. You could say that. It is just that our investigation has turned up the use of codes by others."

Jill went on. "Sometimes they talked by phone. Once, Tom made a trip to Los Angeles and they got together for several hours. On other occasions, they were able to meet in the Owens Valley. However, these meetings were never in public."

"A couple of years after the war, my father went to UCLA as an undergraduate. Later he went to law school. Initially his practice did quite well and he also helped manage his parent's lands. Then in 1953, he made a trip to the Owens Valley. He and Tom dug up the artifacts."

"But how did he donate them without raising concerns," asked Sti.

"Oh, that is one of the best stories of my father. It appears that there were quite a few artifacts so my father initially donated several in his name. This was four years after the war. The rest were buried for safe keeping and then dug up in 1953. However, in 1953 he was concerned that if he donated all of the items at one time, people would begin to question how he came to have the items. So he set them aside to be donated anonymously over time. That is why today you see several items with my father noted as the donor. A few were done right after the war. Most donations were done in about 1948 and 1949. However, many of the other items on display do not have the donor noted, and most of those where the donor is not noted were given to the museum anonymously by my father over a period of years after 1953

"Separate from the anonymous donations of artifacts, my father began to make anonymous donations of funds to the museum. By 1958, he was giving considerable funding to the museum annually. You will remember that he never let on about who the donor was. But by that time the museum must have believed that this donor who wished to remain unknown was someone of note. My father liked to believe that they probably thought that the donor was a wealthy Anglo who lived in the valley. They would never suspect a Japanese American and former resident at Manzanar. Nevertheless, through an attorney friend, who was by birth a Mono Paiute and graduate of UCLA, the artifacts were donated to the museum. Along with the donation of the artifacts was a considerable sum of money with the stipulation that the items be preserved in a particular way and that study of them be limited to someone who was a specialist on Paiute anthropology. That person would be named later. Well, it seems the whole thing was too good to resist and the museum agreed. After all, the funding would not only guarantee the security of the artifacts; it also provided a sizeable amount of funding that could be used as the museum saw fit. Finally, there was a guarantee that as long as the museum agreed to these stipulations, funding would continue to be donated annually. A great story don't you think?"

"Great is not the word. It is fantastic," said Sti. "You were right; your father was a man of great integrity. Tom could not have known that your father would follow through in that manner. Did their friendship continue until your father's death?"

"Oh yes. They kept in touch up to the time that Tom Littlebear died. My father went to the funeral, but stayed very much out of the way. The next night, he visited the gravesite and paid his personal final respects. My dad loved Tom. He liked to say that Tom helped him to see the importance and value of preserving the little things in a culture. He and Tom only met a few times after those years at Manzanar, but they were like brothers. They even had a special strategy to inform each other when one died. I do not know what the method was, but it worked. My father used to say, 'little things matter in big ways.' I have learned to respect that value."

"Yes Mrs. Kubota, I can see it here in your home. The value is now yours," commented Rob.

Sti had been thinking. No doubt Rob was also curious. Displays and information at the museum clearly indicated that the Paiute artifacts had been the subjects of an organized study over several years. But the real question for Sti and Rob was 'who conducted the studies?' "Do you remember Mrs. Kubota if your father ever told you who was given authorization to study the artifacts? I ask the question because all or most have been labeled and studied by now."

"Indeed, I even met the person once. Although, he did not know me and he certainly did not know who my father was. We saw him speak at a conference on California Indian artifacts at UCI back in the 1970's"

"Oh, who was it?"

"His name was Matt Harris, a.…" Jill observed the reaction. "The two of you know this person?" Although stated as a question, Jill already knew the answer.

Rob now, "Yes, we do. We never met him, but we are aware of his work. You are correct, he was an expert."

"Yes, well, he did conduct studies. In fact, my father, unbeknownst to Mr. Harris, provided funding, through a grant, to support Matt Harris's work."

"Mrs. Kubota, did your father ever learn about the findings or results of Matt Harris's study of the artifacts donated by your father?"

"That is an interesting question Dr. Pierce. Yes, my father was adamant about his anonymity, but he wanted to make sure that he was supporting a study that was of value to the Paiute and not just some university professor. So, through the attorney I mentioned earlier, he set up at least two phone call conversations with Matt Harris. There may have been others, but I know of only two. My father told me later that it was refreshing to talk with someone who was genuinely concerned about the destiny of the artifacts. He also told me that Matt Harris had learned a lot, but the more he learned the more he was convinced that the artifacts my father and Tom had collected were the tip of the iceberg. The information Matt Harris had gleaned from his study was that there were other sites. Also, some of the sites were located over the mountains.…"

"What do you mean, over the mountains?" Sti asked.

"You know, some of the sites were on the western side of the Sierra crest. If you went up Oak Creek and over Baxter Pass and some of the other passes, there were supposed to be other places with baskets, pots, and other things."

Rob this time, "You speak like you are familiar with Baxter Pass. Have you been there?"

"When I was in college my father encouraged me to travel. I asked him if he would mind if I visited the Owens Valley. He encouraged me to do so. He even encouraged me to visit some of the places he explored. So, I hiked many of the trails over a period of years. Beautiful country! But I never visited any sites. My father said it was for my own good that he would not tell me where the sites were located."

"Why do you think he was concerned?" asked Sti.

"Because my father was concerned about things that Matt Harris had told him. After one of his phone conversations with Matt Harris, my father became very concerned. It seems that Matt Harris was convinced that Paiute sites were being looted. Matt indicated to my father that he had a good idea where other sites were located. He only hoped that they had not been looted. It seems that Mr. Harris believed that the looting not only removed important pieces of the Paiute history but also removed valuable information about the reasons for the sites."

"Reasons? Did your father explain what the reasons might be?"

"My father did not really know. However, Matt Harris apparently had begun to believe that the routes up these canyons and over the passes were for more than just hunting and trading purposes. Harris seemed to think these sites, my father called them 'caches,' were only weigh stations along routes that led to much bigger sites on the other side of the passes."

Sti and Rob were dumbfounded. They could hardly believe what they were hearing. Jill Kubota had just filled in several blank spots on their agenda of need to know information.

"Did your father ever indicate any knowledge about why he used the word cache?"

"No."

"Did he ever say what else was found at the caches besides pots and baskets?"

"Oh, yes. He said that Harris had also found Paiute weapons and old rifles from the mid 1860's and 70's."

"Fascinating," reflected Rob. "Baskets, pots and weapons, white man's weapons. No wonder there was real interest in these caches." But Rob was really hoping for more information. "But why would anyone want to steal these items. They could not have been worth that much money. Besides, someone could trace where these items came from. No good public collection would feature stolen items."

"But you know the other reason," said Ms. Kubota. "Otherwise you would not spend so much of your time investigating this matter, correct?" She waited for a response.

Sti knew that Jill Kubota was well aware of why they were here. "You mean the gold that could be found in some of these sites." It was not a question.

"That is correct, the chunks of gold."

"Ms. Kubota, how did you know about the gold?"

"How do you think my father, in his early years after the war was able to make sizeable donations to the museum?" She paused long to let them see the significance. "My father and Tom agreed that the gold would be needed to pull the whole thing off. It was enough in the early years, after that it was donations from my father's wealth."

"Did Matt Harris know your father's connection with all of this?"

"Not really. However, he trusted my father and I suspect that the trust came about as Matt Harris put the pieces together and realized that my father was one of the few people genuinely interested in preserving the Paiute legacy in the valley by making sure that the pilfering was stopped. You see, my father had a way of talking that was gentle and reassuring. His humanness and kindness were always evident. If you met my father and exchanged words for even the shortest period of time, your first impression would be that you liked him. So, even though they did not meet formally, they became friends. Matt and my father both knew that the artifacts were very important and valuable. In the wrong hands they would be lost forever. However, they also knew that the gold and the desire to find the source was motive enough to drive those competing with Matt to go to great lengths to get information. The more my father communicated with Matt, the more he realized that Matt was very aware of being in harms way."

Rob took a chance. "And Matt's death?"

"Not an accident," Jill responded quickly. Rob and Sti realized that she was well aware of what was going on.

"Mr. Pierce and Mr. James, I support what you are doing. I do not know all the details, but I suspect you know more than you have shared with me. That is OK. But like you, I want to see justice here."

"So, if your father, and later you, suspected foul play in Matt's death, why did you not contact the authorities?"

"You know why. My father had more power in all of this as an anonymous donor. He was able to guarantee the security of the artifacts in the museum. That security remains today. The museum does not know that my father is dead. As long as they think he is alive, they can not afford to tamper with the agreement."

Sti: "Are you telling us that there are artifacts in the museum that Matt Harris never saw?"

"Oh, no! He saw everything. His journal contains that information."

"His journal," Sti blurted out. "What journal? The one that has been missing since his death?" He was thinking fast and talking fast. "You know where that journal is?"

"I do. Matt Harris realized his life was in danger. Should someone get a hold of his journal, they would eventually break his code and find out what he had learned. That would be devastating for the history of the Owens Valley Paiute."

"You have it here?"

"No, No! I know where it is buried.

The reaction from Sti and Rob was obvious astonishment.

"Like I said, Matt Harris trusted my father. But the two could not meet. Matt believed that his every move was being watched. So, my father told Matt to leave it at a particular place during the night. He told Matt that a most trusted friend would retrieve it and bring it to my father for safe keeping. Matt did as my father requested, and Tom retrieved the journal."

Rob: "And then Matt was killed?"

"Exactly, and when Tom found out he called my father. The original agreement with Matt was that the journal would be in safe keeping with my father; but when Matt and Kathryn were killed, it was necessary to change the plans. Tom and my father agreed, bury the journal in the same spot that the artifacts had been buried. That is where it is today."

"Very clever and ingenious," responded Sti. "Your father was true to your early comments about him. He was a man of integrity. But, in turn your father needed to make sure that should anything happen to him, the secret would be protected. So, he told you. And then three of you knew what was up."

"Actually there might have been four," said Jill. "Apparently Tom's brother was not an honest man, in fact he was deceitful and a criminal, and was on to the idea that Tom was hiding something. He was apparently involved with those trying to find out what Matt knew. Unfortunately, Tom's brother was killed in a hunting accident …"

"By Tom!" said Rob.

"Unfortunately!" replied Jill.

"And your father approved of this?" asked Sti.

"No! My father was very upset. But, it happened because of a decision made by Tom. My father was also practical. He trusted Tom, and although he disagreed with what Tom did, he never said anything to Tom. I remember my father saying that sometimes it is a blessing to be known as a bad shot. But, I think my father also understood the effect of Tom's decision."

"Ms. Kubota," asked Sti. "Do you know why we are really here."

"I think so. June Harris was Matt's daughter. You are looking into her death. You suspect it was not an accident. You suspect it may be connected with the events we have just discussed, am I right?" She did not wait for an answer. "I really do not know much more than I have told you. I have been sitting for some time on all that I had told you. My intention has been to continue making donations to the museum to hold off any fallout that would come from opening up the artifacts to anybody. It has also been my intent to find someone to turn the artifacts and journal over to. However, I have struggled with what to do with the journal. Now you come along, and I have some new options."

"But you could not know that June's death was not an accident. Also, you could not know someone would investigate all of this."

"You are right. But, I did suspect there could be a link between June and all of this. You are also right that I had no Idea that someone was investigating. I got lucky. You contacted me. And you two are definitely not professional investigators or detectives. You are not even amateurs. You are, however, concerned humans. Your actions today tell me that I have nothing to fear from you. In fact, you can help me as much as I can help you."

"How is that," asked Sti.

"Working together, you can help Matthew Harris resolve the questions he has about his granddaughter's death. You can also help me put the journal in the right hands."

Sti and Rob looked at each other.

"You are surprised I know about Matthew Harris? You should not be. My father was a man of many interests. When he learned about Matt Harris, he had Matt's credentials investigated. His father, Matthew Harris, was and continues to be a renowned geologist of the Eastern Sierra. My father knew a great deal about father and son Harris. We went to hear Matt speak three times over the years. My father's conclusion, Matt Harris was a 'chip off the old block.'"

"When you called me, I simply put two and two together. So, now, where do we go with all of this?"

Rob responded for both guests. "Much of this is very new to us. Yet, I still come back to a question I raised earlier. Why would you share all of this information with us? It can not be based just on your impressions of us today. You began sharing before we really got to know you. Are we missing something here? Or, did you know in advance that we did not pose a threat?"

"Yes to the last question."

"Then you knew who we were before we came here today?"

"Indeed. Oh, do not get me wrong. I could not have shared with you about my father if I could not be certain that sharing would lead to positive effects."

"De ja vouz! First Harris and now you." Rob was chuckling as he talked.

"Your father's attorney?" Sti questioned.

"Yes. Let me explain. You see, I know now that my father had shared details with me because he knew that someday I would have to take his place. Someday I would have to carry the burden of determining how best to deal with several key issues in all of this." Jill counted them on her hand as she shared with Sti and Rob. "First, there are the deaths of Matt, Kathryn and June. The Harris deaths were probably not accidental but rather the result of foul play. Second, the Paiute artifacts as yet undiscovered face a grim future if something is not done to guarantee their preservation and study. Third, Matt's final journal contains valuable information that cannot come to light until the issues of three deaths and the future of undiscovered artifacts is certain. Finally, the motive behind the uncertainty in this whole matter is the potential that somewhere there is a large quantity of gold. Those motivated to get this gold have the potential to do so at any cost. My father entrusted me with these dilemmas. I gladly accept the challenge, but I cannot do it alone. I have waited a long time to find the best way to address these four issues. When the two of you came along, and after some background checking, I knew that the time was right and that you share a desire to resolve these issues to the satisfaction of all concerned except those who would do harm."

Sti and Rob were quiet. There was silence, the silence that comes with understanding, even in the face of more questions.

"So, I go back to my earlier question. Where do we go from here?"

CHAPTER 25

FOURTH VISIT TO THE HARRIS RESIDENCE

Once again in the Berkeley Hills

Jill Kubota's description of the location of Matt Harris's last journal presented problems. It could not be easily retrieved. No doubt, it contained information valuable to their inquiry. But for the time being, Sti and Rob would have to continue their investigation without it. Of course, this was not altogether a problem. The other information shared with them by Jill was not only valuable but it suggested that a closer look at Jill's journal and collections could be fruitful.

So, here they were again; back at the Harris residence for a fourth time. Matthew Harris was pleased to see them. He had feared they would not go forward with their investigation after the last meeting. Now he sensed that Sti and Rob were much more upbeat and encouraged. He did not know why.

In fact, the two friends were very encouraged. They had a renewed enthusiasm for their adventure. Ms. Kubota gave them much to think about. After a long discussion following their visit with her, they had decided to return to the Harris residence. They had also had some follow-up phone conversations with Jill as they sought to sort things out. Ultimately, they had come to an agreement with Jill. They would continue their investigation. They would not, under any circumstance, compromise her wish to maintain her father's anonymity, or hers for that matter. Nor would they dig up the journal at this time. And, at this point in time, they would not tell Matthew Harris about the existence or location of his son's journal. However, Jill, Sti and Rob agreed that something had to be done about Matt's journal. It could not be lost forever. The contents quite possibly contained information of such value to the Paiute culture and history that if it fell into the wrong hands it could do great damage. They agreed that the issue of Matt's Journal would be decided at a later date. It would have to be dealt with, but there was no rush.

Unlike their previous study of the Harris archives, Sti and Rob were now beginning to focus in on specific questions. To facilitate this effort, they rented a portable photocopy machine and a computer scanner to be used at the Harris residence. If at all possible, they did not want to have to return to the Harris residence. With this preparation and their list of questions, they began what turned out to be three days of reviewing records. Of course, the two did not deviate from many of their habits of friendship. They took interludes of time to take exercise hikes in the Berkeley Hills and to eat at some fine restaurants in the bay area. For the latter, as always, Rob was the expert on the names and locations of these establishments. Matthew Harris was not invited to these evening culinary escapes. However, for breakfast and lunch, which was ordered in, he was included. Harris understood the need of the two to be alone to talk at dinner. He was pleased that they included him in the meals. He had become fond of the two, and he had come to respect them for their honesty, if not strange way of mixing business and pleasure.

For their part, Sti and Rob sincerely believed that they had gotten past the Harris reluctance to tell them everything. Matthew Harris was now well aware that they had a better handle than he did on the events leading up to June's death. Matthew Harris was also cognizant that after this visit the two would have everything they needed to either continue the search for June's killers or abandon the effort all together. Sti and Rob would not need to return to the Harris residence after they finished their work on this visit. The two friends also knew that they, not Matthew Harris, were in the driver's seat. For their visit on this occasion they needed Harris as a reference to find information, answer questions, clarify confusing information, and to do their bidding. Whether or not Matthew Harris ever saw or heard from his two friends after this visit depended not upon Harris but upon what was found at the Harris home over the three days.

When you are onto something, there is an excitement. Sti and Rob sensed that they were just a step away from blowing this whole issue of June's death out of the water. What they would find was unknown. They could not even speculate as to the potentials. But they did sense that Matthew Harris had been right all along. June's death was not an accident. Jill Kubota, that woman of impeccable integrity and insight, was also convinced that there was a connection between June's death and events in the lives of Matthew and Matt Harris over many decades. These events were wrapped up in the Paiute artifacts located in what must be many cache sites in the canyons of the Eastern Sierra. These sites were not just sites created along trade routes that extended over the passes of the Eastern Sierra. No doubt, Matt's communication with Henry Kubota was the prophetic component in this mystery. The caches served purposes more related to the gold that was found in them than to the pottery and basket artifacts. But the pots and baskets held the key to understanding this relationship. They provided the key to finding the ultimate location of caches in the higher elevations of the Sierra Nevada. There was little doubt that whoever was competing with Matt, and later June, to find the caches sensed this also. No doubt the scientific and cultural interests of Matt did not drive these competitors. They were driven by the potential for locating the source of the gold that was found in the caches.

All of this directed the focus of Sti's and Rob's visit. How much did June know about her father's findings and his hypotheses? Did she build on her father's work and thereby put herself in harms way? If so, there must be answers in her journals, letters, collections, and personal effects. The two friends knew that the keys to their success in answering these questions rested with their ability to meet three challenges. First, they had to break through the many barriers created by June's system of coding valuable information. There was much in her journal that was not coded, but there were key pieces of information such as cache locations and contents that were coded. As yet, Rob and Sti had been unsuccessful in decoding these key pieces. Second, they needed to look at the evidence in totality and not as individual pieces. The skill would be to see the facts not as they stood alone but as they connected to other evidence and thereby painted a larger picture. Third, they had to see what evidence was missing. Sometimes it is as important to identify what the evidence was not saying as much as it is important to note what conclusions could be drawn from the evidence.

Probably, if professional investigators or detectives were involved in this search for answers, they would have gone about it very differently. Like so many television newscasts portray, they would have invaded the Harris residence and hauled out everything to some storage facility. There they would have applied their trained and experienced skills to the search for motive and supporting evidence.

But the two longtime friends and hikers were not fettered by convention. They were amateurs, and perhaps this was to their benefit. They really did not know how one was supposed to do this investigation stuff. On the other hand, what they did know was the Sierra backcountry, and especially the Eastern Sierra. They had, over decades, hiked up every major canyon on the East Side several times. They also knew the Owens Valley. In fact, their strong suit in this hunt was both their knowledge of the Sierra and their lack of formal training on how to conduct an investigation. To them, there were no stupid questions, and there were no limits to their imagination about what could have happened.

To someone who might have observed their methods it might have been called 'plodding'. Others would have said their approach was distended and not organized. To Sti and Rob, it was, however, simple. You wandered through the information looking for connections to a list of questions that just kept growing. You also looked for anything that caught your attention and met the test of curiosity. When you found something, no matter what tradition said about evidence value, you stopped and talked about it. To them it was like finding a good campsite or the best route over rough terrain. Every location is different, so what makes for a good campsite or a good route is not always describable in generic terms. However, for those with experience in finding good campsites or routes, you know a good site or route when you see it. So, that was their approach as they sifted through pages, artifacts, boxes, books, and personal items.

* * * *

For the two friends, experience on the trail had taught them patience. Sometimes the journey was far more important than the destination. Moreover, they had learned to accept the serendipitous. Always, their planned route was only tentative. Along the way they let Nature, their interests, intuition, and events dictate the actual route. When asked how they planned trips, Sti and Rob would often indicate that their planning ended with a decision of where to start an outing. After that, the trip 'evolved.'

So, it was no surprise that Sti and Rob followed an investigation strategy similar to their backpack trip planning. They let the evidence take them in unplanned directions. Like hiking cross-country without a trail, decisions regarding direction are made reflective of both experience and circumstances. The case of June Harris had taken them in many directions, but patience had allowed understanding to evolve.

* * * *

A three-piece map of the Eastern Sierra was taped to the wall. Published by the U.S. Forest Service in 1983, the map showed the John Muir Wilderness Area as well as Kings Canyon and Sequoia National Parks between Mammoth Lakes in the North and Mount Whitney in the South. It was a topographic map that featured details of all trails, lakes, passes, and terrain. The eastern border of the map was U.S. 395 in the Owens Valley. Each of the canyons on the eastern escarpment of the Sierra was detailed topographically. Laid out in sequence, all three pieces connected together provided a view that was four feet wide and nine feet tall. As they needed to have more detailed renderings of the area surrounding the location of June's death, they also posted 7.5 minute topographic maps.

On the maps Sti and Rob had put small colored Post-its to identify a list of things—known Paiute cache sites, information on who discovered them and when, places were Matthew and Matt had conducted field studies, and places visited by June. Also, the hiking routes and paths connecting these pins were highlighted with various colors. Additional odds and ends were also noted on the maps, anything that was connected with the investigation. The more they read or studied, the more they added pins and notations to the maps.

In addition, they kept a timeline. Everything on the maps was also added to the timeline of events. Every time either of them thought something was curious, they added it to the timeline. Every time questions arose, they were added to the time line. The questions were very important because they suggested need to know information where there were gaps in the timeline. The timeline consisted of several sheets of 8.5 by 11 inch paper taped end to end with a long line running from left to right—resulting in a timeline that was about four feet long. The line started with the date of 1860 on the far left and ended with the most recent date on the far right. There was ample room for notations that were done in pencil so that corrections could be easily made.

A running list of questions was also maintained. Initially they tried to categorize the items on the list. Finally, as the list seemed to grow faster than the categories, they just kept adding to the list. Later they could categorize. One of the tasks they gave Matthew Harris was to look at the list and identify where information or answers regarding the questions could be found. When Harris could not answer, a companion list of people to contact was attached. These could be followed-up on later.

Rob started a 'connection list'. In the beginning the idea was to show connections between some of the questions and issues they were considering. Eventually this list became a combination of cause and effect list and a way to link things on their timeline. When the task became too complex, the list was abandoned.

* * * *

Although he was included as much as possible over the three days of work, Matthew Harris was not included in everything. At dinner and back at their hotel in the evening, Sti and Rob would review their findings and questions.

The first day was spent more on organizing things than discovering information. However, by the end of the second day a clearer picture of June and her activities was emerging. That evening, in their hotel, the two self-anointed novitiate detectives reviewed their findings.

June was a prolific journal keeper. There were few days in the field for which she did not provide entries. For her, the field was anytime and any place where she was on adventures, outings, backpacking or explorations away from home. She was meticulous in her record keeping, but like her father and grandfather before her, she used cryptic notes when she was recording sensitive information or anything she did not want others to understand. However, unlike their earlier reviews of June's materials as well as those of her father, Sti and Rob had by now created a way to provide some translation of June's writings. The journal codes were similar to those of her father and grandfather. The more they reviewed of June's journals, maps, and records, the more they began to piece together a picture of what June was up to during the last several years of her life. June had been doing what Sti and Rob found themselves doing. She was investigating events in the lives of her father and mother. Although it was not written in a single clear statement, anyone studying June's writings and work would sense over time that she believed her parents were killed for reasons related to their study of Paiute artifacts and the location of sites where the artifacts were found.

The take on this by Rob and Sti was that June's work was based on a set of assumptions regarding the deaths of her parents. At the heart of these assumptions was a belief that they had been killed by rivals whose interests were not motivated by research but greed. The fact that June never openly stated this belief, but rather operated on it as an assumption, was probably her way of avoiding the emotional stress that comes with thoughts of murder of loved ones.

Initially it looked like June was merely interested in the work of her parents. She had clearly read and studied her father's publications and many of the books in his library. But what started as an interest in her parents increasingly became an obsession with their work. Sti and Rob found that in time June's journal began to reflect not just what she had read but the results of independent investigations and research related to the Paiute culture and history, artifacts from their past, and the locations of Paiute sites in the Eastern Sierra. June had clearly probed and studied the work of many authorities in these areas.

In addition, especially during the years that June worked for the National Park Service, she used personal and company time to seek out and study the very field work sites of her parents. She also spent countless days probing the various canyons on the eastern slope of the Sierra in the region of the Owens Valley. According to her records she wandered in these canyons for days. Sometimes she visited certain locations multiple times. Her maps were filled with coded margin notes, circles, lines, and routes traced with pencil, pen or a highlighter. Over a period of years June had logged an incredible number of days and miles conducting her investigations. She was clearly not interested in established routes, trails, or abandoned trails. If a place was obvious, she was not interested in a close look. If it was not obvious or if it had a strategic position in a canyon, she would look at it closely.

June was the consummate wanderer. She was always probing. Her notes indicated that even after exhaustingly wandering a canyon or area she would write in her journal that she must have missed something. But, often as not, June's outings would turn up something. An arrowhead, a pouch, piece of leather, potsherds, and an array of implements were collected on these outings. Often she went to sites studied by her father and mother. Other times it was evident that she was acting on a hunch. Occasionally she would discover a former Paiute campsite not previously noted in her father's studies.

When new sites were discovered, June's journal was replete with both elation and what appeared to be coded details about her finds. For several days following such finds, her journal reflected a desire to provide analysis that appeared to be a combination of realistic inquiry and uninhibited inference regarding possible meanings. Extrapolation of evidence found was not governed by a school of theory or philosophy. June was a free thinker in her efforts to find meaning. The lack of orthodoxy may have been unique to June, but it was acceptable to Rob and Sti because it was similar to their approach to the unknown.

As Sti and Rob began to develop a timeline of June's activities at home and in the field, it began to become evident that June had bought into much of her father's interpretation of the significance of the Paiute caches. She became convinced that the caches were used to support larger numbers of Paiutes trekking into the heart of the Sierra. In an effort to explain the caches, it was also evident that June had begun to develop some original interpretations of the evidence uncovered by her parents as well as the evidence uncovered by June herself.

Apparently June's work at the higher elevations of the Eastern Sierra began to result in a growing belief that the Paiute campsites and caches at these elevations were part of a larger endeavor. To this end, June began to focus more and more attention on the activities of the Paiute in the Sierra backcountry.

If the second day had suggested that June Harris was beginning to formulate theories based on her own discoveries as well as those of her parents, the third day provided an explosion of new information.

At the end of the third day the two amateur investigators let Matthew Harris know that they would come back the next day to pick up all the items they needed to take with them. They could say their goodbye then.

That evening and late into the night they discussed what they had found. What they had discovered that day was eye opening. But for every improvement in their understanding of what June was doing, there was the emergence of new questions and baffling circumstances. But when all was summed up, Sti and Rob could not avoid the conclusion that June, during the months preceding her death, was growing concerned that she was being watched. She began to see herself threatened and she understood the danger her parents had faced. She was being watched, perhaps followed, because of what she now knew. June must have known that if she continued to pursue her obsession she stood a good chance of facing the same fate of her parents. This was not mere conjecture; it was evident in June's words and actions.

As they discussed these matters, Sti and Rob were all too aware that although they now believed June could have been the victim of foul play at the hands of someone or others because of what she had found, there were clearly some missing pieces. These missing pieces were somehow tied to four new issues gleaned from their three days of study.

"As I see it," Rob began, "we need to try and understand the connection between the following three items:" Rob listed them on his fingers.

"First, June, just before her death, began to focus on the High Route area covered by the Sierra Club outing of 1935. Although we do not have the evidence, she seemed to believe that there was evidence brought back by the packers that suggested they found Indian artifacts.

"Second, June kept going back to the Muro Blanco, and her maps suggest she was looking at some kind of relationship between the canyon and the High Route area. Her exploration of the canyon was almost exclusively on the northern slope."

Sti: "curious."

"Third, and this is the new piece that we must follow-up on, June had somewhere uncovered information that Joaquin Jim was somehow connected with some of the cache sites that she, her parents, Matthew Harris, and some unknown persons had discovered."

"Luck would have it. We could easily have missed Joaquin Jim's name in all of this," Sti commented reflectively.

Rob summed up. "These three are connected. We have some ideas, but we need more concrete information about each before we can connect them together or with June's death."

Sti nodded, but he and Rob both knew that there was a fourth issue. Potentially, the issue of the gold chunks, the amount and source, was probably the key to all of this. "Yes, yes, I agree, we need to follow up on these. But, the gold. There's the matter of the chunks or nuggets? From my perspective, the ultimate motive for killing Matt and his wife had to be the gold. If June was murdered, gold would also be a significant motive, especially if she knew what her father knew."

"I could not agree more," was Rob's response.

Sti went on. "But this issue of the gold is perplexing in another way. When June discovered new sites, her reaction was elation and she developed a detailed list of items found. There is great detail to description. But, there is no mention of the gold. Why?"

"She chose not to mention that the chunks were there?" posited Rob. "If I knew that I was being followed I would not want my journal in the hands of those who would care only about the gold. Details about the site and artifacts would be important to research but not to those who cared only about the gold. Besides, the only detail about the gold that would be important would be the number of chunks and the total weight of these."

"Yeah. June was a Harris. So, hide that part of the truth."

"Don't get sarcastic!"

"I know, I know."

"Keep your mind focused."

"Yes master Yoda. So, let me ask you, do you suppose that the gold is somehow connected to the High Route, Muro Blanco and Joaquin Jim?" Sti asked.

After a pause Rob responded. "Don't know. I'm sure there is a connection, but I don't have any idea what it is."

"You know," said Sti, "maybe this is like a long hike up to a trail pass you have never been to before. Every time you crest a ridge you think you are about there, only to find that there is another ridge ahead. In the end you are better off if you do not try to guess what is around the next bend in the trail or over the next rise. The secret is to just keep moving ahead. Look at what you can see, take it all in, don't try to speculate on what you can not see." Again, experience was their teacher.

After chuckling, Rob cast doubts on Sti's assertion. "We want to see a connection. You are suggesting that there may not be one? I don't know. I am not ready to believe there is no connection. There is something that brings these four things together."

Sti took issue with Rob's conclusion. "Oh, I am not saying there is no connection. I am really saying …" He thought for a moment. "I am saying that perhaps the connection is there but the fact that we want so to see it is possibly clouding our ability to see it."

"Like not seeing the forest through the trees?"

"Could be." Sti was trying to grasp onto a thought. "It's more like, the connection is there but it is not anything like what we expect."

It was Rob's turn now. "It is like the expectation leading up to your first view of something you have never seen, right? All the things you have seen in the past and what you have heard create an image of what it is you will see. But when you get there it is nothing like what you expected."

"Something like that."

"But there is another angle on this," said Rob. "When you anticipate what you will see, it influences how you see your final destination. However, if you had avoided supposition on what you would see, you would be neither disappointed nor happy at the final outcome. You would see it for what it was, not what you anticipated."

"Whoa," Sti reacted. "This is getting heavy. But, it may not be off the mark. The connection may be much different than what we suspect. While we must look closely for a connection, we must not let our scrutiny of the details distort our ability to look at the big picture."

All of this exchange was not unusual, at least not to Sti and Rob. For years they have played this game of erudite jousting. The idea is to pull from disparate disciplines when advancing or challenging ideas. Backpacking sometimes brings with it the need to kill time. Waiting out a storm in your tent or killing time in the evening because you do not want to go to bed at 7:00 PM can lead to diversions. So, Sti and Rob had long ago, and unintentionally, developed a form of intellectual bantering as a way to pass the time. Interestingly, they sometimes found it served as a way to approach and discuss issues, especially issues for which there was no easy resolution. They also found that humor can sometimes serve as a refreshing pause, a sort of clearing of the mind, before returning to necessary matters.

Rob advanced the definition more. "We can't let the details and search for a connection inhibit our consideration of the absurd. Like Chaos Theory, somewhere at the heart of the turbulence, at a remote but fundamental level, there is a pattern, an explanation."

"I love it. Another case of verisimilitude! The absurdity of reality. The mix of seriousness and humor. Everything in it proper perspective. And so our hunt for the great connection goes on." The language of the absurd. This was the way of Sti's thoughts when he practiced the art of not taking the world too serious. In this sense he was a true child of M*A*S*H.

Rob was ever more practical than Sti when it came to keeping everything in its proper perspective. He suggested where they should leave this philosophical exercise and refocus on the task at hand. "It seems that a call to the spirited Ms. Kubota could be one of the next steps. She seems to have an uncanny ability to remain aloof from extraneous evidence. Perhaps she has a different take on what we have found. Should we call her?"

"Yes," Sti said passively. He conceded Rob's point and was thinking ahead. "How do you want to go about gathering more information on Joaquin Jim, the High Route and Muro Blanco, divide it up?"

"I think you look into Joaquin Jim. You have the best line on where to go to get information on him. I will try to find out what I can about the mining of gold in the area accessed by the Paiute. Also, I will try to find out if any other Indians of the Sierra region were trading in gold. As for the High Route, Muro Blanco and the 1935 artifacts, I think we both know what we have to do."

"Go there! That is my thinking as well. I think we will need to wait until August. We want to go to the High Route area when the snow has melted from the upper altitudes. Also, the South Fork of the Kings will be lower and will make exploring the Muro Blanco much easier."

"Agreed!" Rob was thinking of another objective. "I also think we need to spend some time in the canyons. Why don't we visit the Sawmill cave site? Maybe by looking at one or more of the cache sites we will get a feeling about all of this. Come to think of it, maybe we should visit the Poverty Hills were Matthew was in the late 1940's and the 1950's and '60's. Maybe we should wander around in some of the other canyons."

On Rob's suggestion they agreed. They could do this in the late spring.

They now had some directions to follow in the immediate future. However, the ultimate goal was the High Route. They could not avoid going back. For both the idea of going back to where they found June's body was greeted with mixed reactions. On the one hand they both had known almost from the beginning of their investigation that they would eventually have to revisit the region. On the other hand, the more they had investigated June's death, the more they had come to realize that the location of her death had a certain foreboding. What was it about the area? By its very nature—high, remote and rugged—the portion of the High Route just north of Marion Peak was mysterious. Sti and Rob could not help but believe that the beauty of this area hid not only secrets to June's death but secrets about the Paiute. Did they really want to know both sets of secrets? It seemed there was no choice. You could not have one without the other.

CHAPTER 26

ANTONIO JUAN BATISTA, ATTORNEY

The offices of Batista and Associates,
Newport Beach, California

Sti and Rob were greeted with the institutional script of "Oh, Mr. James and Dr. Pierce, it is so nice to meet you both. Mr. Batista is most eager to meet you and asked that I show you in immediately upon your arrival. Please, this way." However, it was clear that Julia Rodriguez was much more than just an executive secretary. It was evident from the moment that Sti and Rob entered the spacious and conservatively decorated and refined atmosphere of the offices of Batista and Associates that Ms. Rodriguez commanded the respect of the receptionist and the several other secretaries and clerks who inhabited the visible work space. One also had the feeling that she was accorded much more responsibility than just serving as the executive secretary for the firm's namesake. Sti and Rob had considerable experience with office atmospheres and it was evident from a short exposure that Ms. Rodriguez had been considerably empowered by her boss. To complement her status, her demeanor and actions were genuine, and she was greeting the two with a mix of friendship and efficiency. Sti and Rob were not just ushered into the office of Juan Antonio Batista; they were escorted and welcomed.

Juan Batista met them at the door of his office and welcomed them as if they were entering his home. His comments, smile and outstretched hands reflected a personality that was sincere and never patronizing. With Juan Antonio Batista, the world was about respect, integrity, and friendship. There was nothing phony here.

"How good of both of you to take time out of your busy schedules," was Juan's comment as he directed their attention to a corner of the office where Jill Kubota was sitting. Though momentarily caught off guard, on reflection, neither Sti nor Rob was surprised to see Jill present. After all, Mr. Batista had a long association with the Kubota family. It had been Juan Batista senior who took care of the Kubota land while the entire family was in residence at Manzanar during the war. Also, for many years, apparently, Juan Antonio Batista had served as Henry Kubota's personal attorney as well as confidant in the matter of donations to the California Eastern Sierra Museum. "You know, of course, Ms. Kubota, the daughter of Henry Kubota." Sti and Rob acknowledged their acquaintance as they both shook Jill's hand and extended a slight bow. Odd to many who might happen upon such circumstances, the formality of greeting among all four seemed both appropriate and honest. There was friendship here, as if four friends, long separated, had come together in deference to the need of another not in attendance. Such feeling was in fact, as it turns out, not far from reality.

The office was spacious. A deep, rich and shiny wood paneling with fine finish work enclosed a comfortable setting that was handsomely, and no doubt professionally, decorated. The bookshelves that housed both legal references and other types of books consumed an entire wall.

Following pleasantries, Juan familiarized the two guests with the contents of the office.

On the walls were several fine paintings. To one familiar with the area, they were paintings of prominent features of Orange County before the vast developments of the post World War II era. There was a modest collection of awards acknowledging the civic contributions of the Batista Family over many decades. There were also the obligatory diplomas that included both UCLA, a degree in Political Science, and Harvard Law School. Accompanying photos and documents highlighted a career that included the Harvard Law Review and a clerkship with a federal judge in Washington, D.C.

Several other items reflected the inhabitant's interest in both environmental issues and archeology. In several photos Juan was in the company of noted environmentalists such as David Brower, William O. Douglas, Diane Fosse, and others. Coffee table books and some spectacular photos and magazines suggested Juan had a substantial interest in archeological sites of early man in North America.

In an alcove, where most similar offices might have a wet bar, there was a collection of old photos highlighted by special lighting. Although an initial glance might result in a conclusion that these were just old family photos, a closer look revealed much more. These were pictures of both the Batista and Kubota families. They seemed to reflect a history of family ties extending from the 1990's back to the 1930's. Individuals, groups with members of both families, farm land, and Manzanar. And, a photo easily overlooked that included Juan, Henry, and a third individual who was clearly of Native American origin. Could this be Tom Littlebear?

It was both an office and a museum. But it was also comfortable and far from the opulent excess associated with offices of many very successful attorneys in the Newport area. This office was both functional and a reminder to guests that Juan Antonio Batista was much more than just another exceedingly successful attorney.

Juan's genuine greeting was followed up by a seating arrangement that was not across a large desk but in a comfortable section of the office where all could be both personable and relaxed. It was as if they were being hosted in the living room of one of those present. No sooner did they sit than Ms. Rodriguez ushered in one of the clerks who provided tea or coffee and small scones. "As much as I love my mother's cooking, I must admit that I have developed a great fondness for that English treat, the scone," was Juan's comment. "But I must thank Ms. Rodriguez for this because she had the foresight to hire one of our office staff who is both highly qualified in the necessary skills and as a cook, Cynthia Kotley." All four laughed as they accepted the refreshments and thanked Cynthia, the clerk who was obviously pleased with the compliment that was paid her.

Some people leave first impressions that urge caution. Not so with Juan Antonio Batista; what you saw is what you got. No pretenses. No pedantic rhetoric.

No attorney superiority. It was easy to see that much of his success was due to his personable behavior, friendly and honest mannerisms, and Ivy League dress attire. Not too formal and not too casual. Probably in his sixties, Juan was in excellent physical condition and had what some would call 'command presence'. He exuded confidence in himself, but not at the expense of others. If first impressions were valuable, Juan Batista was a rich man in more ways than just financial assets.

It soon became evident that Juan was also articulate. His vocabulary, although not overly intellectual, reflected one who was well-educated. Thoughts were expressed logically and simply. Metaphors and similes served to provide appropriate illustrations. For those who knew him well, he was also a great story teller.

The refreshments and formalities of open-ended conversation consumed considerable time. Juan was an excellent host, and the exchanges worked to build a comfortable, if not friendly atmosphere. The host knew how to create the necessary atmosphere for a frank and serious conversation.

Eventually, Juan brought their attention to the matter at hand. "It is very special for me to host this gathering. The Kubota and Batista families have a long-standing relationship. For me, I have known Jill since her birth. Her father was my dearest friend, and her family made it possible for my family to achieve great successes. I would not be in this office if it had not been for the assistance that Jill's grandfather and father extended to me."

Jill responded without hesitation, "The thankfulness goes both ways. Juan Batista senior's integrity, loyalty, and skill made it possible for my grandfather and grandmother to return to their home following the war. I know that all Kubota family members hold the Batista family in the highest regard."

"But of course the two of you have already been introduced to this remarkable relationship." Juan went on. "So, as a prelude to this discussion, I want you to know that I have set aside the afternoon for our discussion and I want to take whatever time is necessary to work our way through several issues that are of interest to all of us. I believe I shared as much in my letter to all three of you."

Sti responded with several nods.

Rob, as always, was compelled to speak. "Yes, we found your letter both intriguing and surprising."

"I can well imagine. I debated on whether I should contact you by phone or by letter. I opted for the letter, because, in part, I find it much easier to write communications than to catch people off guard on the phone."

Jill smiled and nodded. Elegant, but simple in her attire, Jill was the dignified and gregarious person Sti and Rob had met several weeks earlier.

"I can attest to the impact of your letter," was Rob's response. "It served its purpose well. I think the letter provided sufficient information and expressed a level of sincerity that suggested that this was of great import to you as well as to us."

"Jill and I discussed how best to broach the subject. Having met with you, Jill was adamant that a meeting would be the best way to expand on the information that I provided. Mr. James and Dr. Pierce, I hope that this meets with your expectations."

"Please, Sti and Rob will do," was Sti's response. "I think that we all share the same interest in the matter of Henry, the Harris family, and the Paiute antiquities. As you know, we have been looking into the death of June Harris. But, and here I think I am speaking for both Rob and me, we are not professional investigators. We are just a couple of backpackers who stumbled on something unique. We tried to distance ourselves from it, but curiosity has gotten the best of us and we just keep probing a little deeper into the matter of June's death."

Rob added, "Yes, it seems that every time we have tried to opt out of this matter, we sense an injustice is being perpetrated at one or more levels and we can not leave it alone."

Jill interjected. "For my part, I was most pleased that the two of you contacted me. For some time I had harbored both facts and thoughts regarding the endeavors of my father. I do not know if June's death was an accident. But whether it was or was not, does not diminish the importance of her work, her fathers work, and the role my father played in both of their lives."

Sti and Rob looked at each other, accentuating a unified question. "Your father's role in June's life?"

"Perhaps this is a good place to start our discussion," was Juan Batista's response. "To begin with, my role in this is more than that of an attorney who continues to serve the needs of the closest of friends. I do hope that we can participate in this discussion as equals, and I insist that you refer to me as Juan." The attention of all was upon Juan. There was no doubt in the minds of Sti and Rob that he was about to take their interest in the Harris family in new directions. There was also no doubt that he and Jill had choreographed today's meeting. The latter assumption was not a negative. On the contrary, it was evidence of the seriousness of their approach to this meeting.

"Let me back up and set the stage for what I am about to share with you." There was a pause as Juan looked at his typed notes. This was another sign of the importance of the meeting. These were not the typical yellow legal pad notes. "Several weeks ago, when Rob contacted Jill, she gave me a call and inquired about how best to respond to your request to meet. I know Jill well and was comfortable with her assessment of your intentions. Both of us agreed that, based on initial inquiries and discussion, Jill was at liberty to share whatever she deemed necessary. I was, as you would expect, concerned about the matter of anonymity regarding Henry. But following her conversation with you Jill assured me that the two of you were both honest and sincere in your interest in the calamities that have befallen the Harris family."

"We are pleased that we passed the litmus test," responded Sti.

"And we suspect that prior to our meeting with Jill, and as a prelude to today's meeting, you have done more than just leave assessment of our intentions and veracity in the hands of conversation based feelings on Jill's part." Rob was choosing his words carefully. "Somehow we get the sense that there was some investigation of our credentials and other sources. Is that not true?" Rob was friendly in tone and smiling.

Jill interjected before Juan could respond. "You are certainly correct. Both Juan and I agreed that he would do some background checking discretely before I met with you. We were aware of June's death and the fact that the two of you had found her body. But I could not have talked to you as openly as I did without being convinced that your intentions were good. I owed that much to my father."

Sti wanted to set their concerns at ease. "Well do not be offended by our concerns. It seems that you are not the first to check our background. Matthew Harris did the same before he contacted us. I guess we should take it as a compliment that two independent checks have been done and we passed muster." This was said with a tone of humor and all chuckled.

It was Jill's turn. "Well, Juan and I are most comfortable with sharing information with the two of you. We know that a respect for the work of June and her parents accompanies your interest in June's demise. You too are interested in preserving the integrity of Paiute artifacts. It appears that you also are not about to compromise my father's wishes and role in this matter. It seems fortuitous. It would be difficult to share my father's interests, and what Juan is about to describe, with anyone except the two of you. I feel good about you, and I am glad you came along when you did."

There it was again. Jill dropped another hint of things to come.

"If I may, Jill?" Jill nodded and Juan continued. "What I want to share with you today is known only to Jill, me and one other person. This is an especially ideal situation since the information is too important to be held in confidence forever. I think what Jill was saying is that your interest in June's death has created an opportunity to bring certain information to light that will benefit both the Harris family and the many who are concerned about the integrity of the history of the Owens Valley Paiute and disposition of their antiquities both known and those as yet undiscovered. It is our sincere hope that you will exercise the greatest discretion in your use of what I am about to share."

The two guests nodded affirmation.

"Well, let me get to the point. For many years I worked with Henry Kubota in the matter of donations to the Eastern California Museum. During that time I came to have great respect for the people of the Owens Valley and their history. I too developed a keen interest in the disposition of Paiute antiquities. Although certainly not as knowledgeable and involved as Henry, my concerns have grown with time. And, yes, that picture that you both looked closely at is a photo of

Henry, Tom Littlebear and me. Tom was a dear friend to Henry, and I think Tom's death took much out of Henry's heart."

All four were now glancing over at the photo on the wall opposite Sti and Rob.

"Jill has given you considerable information regarding the friendship between Tom and Henry. I shall not revisit that. I want to backup several years, in the middle 1990's. It seems, and I only know this because Henry shared the story with me, that Jill intercepted a phone call at home that was intended for her father. The caller was June Harris and she left a telephone number. Only later did Jill realize the phone number was an Owens Valley area code, and then Jill recognized the Harris name. Although Jill had only met Matt Harris at UCLA lectures, she made the association and shared as much with Henry.

"Before returning the call to June, Henry and I talked and decided that a guarded approach was necessary. First, Henry would try to determine how his name came to June's attention. Second, he would listen, but volunteer no information that would reveal his longstanding relationship with Matt.

"I know the two of you never met June, but I had it on good authority from Henry that she was a very vivacious person who possessed a personality and conversation style that quickly drew others to like her. But, as Henry often said, once you got to know her you realized that there was a precocious and mischievous side to June. These latter qualities provided insight into June's boundless energy, commitment to her interests in her parents work, and willingness to go out on the edge when in pursuit of information."

These were qualities of June that Sti and Rob had discovered, but they had likened them to maverick qualities often found in independent personality types.

"How did June find Henry? Well, what would be complex to many was simple to June. Among the many volumes of information and artifacts contained June's mother's possessions was an old Rolodex file. One of the cards, apparently written in the proverbial Harris code, indicated that in an emergency June's mother was to call Henry Kubota. A telephone number was included. June knew the code and knew that it would not have been coded if it were not very important information. Also, by chance, June connected the name with the name of the donor of several Paiute artifacts at the Eastern California Museum.

"As it turned out, this chance discovery on June's part was, as you shall see, a blessing. Had June not made the contact, her information might have been lost forever. At worst, it could have fallen into the wrong hands.

"Between the time of June's initial phone call and Henry's death, Henry and June had several conversations by phone. To my knowledge, they never met in person. However, Henry knew that if June was anything like her father she kept a detailed journal. He asked June to avoid any journal references that included Henry's name or any references that could be linked to Henry. June agreed. During these years their conversations evolved into discussions about Henry's experiences during his night time excursions while at Manzanar, Tom Littlebear, Paiute artifacts at the museum in Independence, and especially the fieldwork of June's parents. Increasingly, Henry suspected that June knew far more than she was sharing...."

"That sounds familiar," said Rob.

Sti continued, "It seems to be a family trait. Do not tell all immediately. Let information evolve. It is almost as if the experiences of Harris family members have led them to be very guarded. Need to know information is not always volunteered. It seems to force its way into view."

"Henry was right. About two months before her disappearance, June shared with Henry that she had discovered two more Paiute "caches" as she called them. Neither had been touched. But the revelation was that on a subsequent visit, June clearly noted that the site had been tampered with since her previous visit. Immediately, she knew that someone was watching her and following her. Her voice belied the confidant and assured personality that was usually evident in their conversations. June Harris was worried. June told Henry that she had suspected for some time that she was being followed. She likened it to suspicions that she said her father had during his latter years of work in the valley.

"Only a few days later June called Henry to inform him that she was sending him a package. Would he please protect it? Furthermore, if something should happen to her, would Henry please hold on to the information in the package?

June insisted that the package not be given to her grandfather. When Henry asked why, June indicated that her reasons would be clear once Henry received the package and read the information in its contents."

Juan had the voice of a wonderful storyteller. He was organized, one could follow his train of thought easily, and he articulated the English language with precision. Sti and Rob very much enjoyed listening.

"Henry told June that he sensed that she was scared. June's response was that recent events suggested that others were competing with her to find Paiute artifacts. However, their interest was more in profits, and especially in the profits that would be generated by gold."

This comment was like a bolt of lightning to Rob and Sti. It showed in their nonverbal response.

"That was Henry's reaction. He was well aware that Matt had found some gold in some of his exploration of artifacts. But he assumed that the amounts were small and not indicative of a large cache of gold in some special location. The conversation ended awkwardly. Henry could tell June was scared, but for her part, June was not about to let her fear deter her from continuing her investigations. On the other hand, like her father, she was not about to let her information fall into the wrong hands. According to Henry, there was a forced pleasantness in June's closing comments, but her fear was still evident.

"Several days later a package addressed to Henry arrived at my office. To ensure his anonymity, Henry never gave his home address to Matt Harris, the museum or to June. Except for phone conversations with Matt and June, all other contacts were through this office.

"The package contained a long letter and a journal. Although Henry reviewed both several times, he kept me in the dark. His argument was that if he shared it with me I would be compelled to exercise my legal options. The contents only came to my attention after Henry passed away shortly thereafter. That was well after June's disappearance and well before your discovery of her body. In addition to me, only two other people have seen the contents of the package, Jill and my secretary." With that Juan called Ms. Rodriguez into his office. "You all know my secretary Rosalind Rodriguez." Rosalind was carrying a stack of items which she distributed to all four. "What you are receiving is a copy of the letter that accompanied the journal of which you also have a copy. I should mention Rosalind is one-half Paiute and was born and raised just outside Big Pine." This brought heads up. "She is familiar with the materials, and I trust her without question." Juan jokingly added, "I long ago forgave her for being a USC graduate."

The copies of the journal were of the finest quality and bound in the same manner as the original.

After a quick glance Sti spoke. "But, the dates of this journal are the same dates as a journal in Dr. Harris' possession. What gives?"

"The letter speaks to that issue, but it is long and will take some time to digest. Let me provide a short cut." Juan was speaking carefully. "This is, as June explains, a 'parallel journal.' To appease those who might pose a threat to obtain a journal she was keeping, June kept two journals current. The journal you have seen, which I have not, was the one to be sacrificed to appease any would forcefully acquire it. That is apparently why Jill sent it to her grandfather. This is the journal with the valuable information. You will recognize its value almost immediately and thereby understand why she worked so diligently to keep it sequestered."

It was quiet as Sti and Rob perused the two items.

"As you will see, there is much that is clearly decipherable in the journal. There is also much that is written in a code that was known only to June."

"And any other member of the Harris family," responded Rob.

"How's that," asked Jill.

Sti answered. "We have had access to June's other journals, some of her parents journals, and those of Matthew Harris. Matthew developed the code in his early fieldwork years. He taught it to his children and it was passed down to June. It is not overly complex, but enough so that it would take considerable time for the uninitiated to figure out what was being said. Thanks to Matthew, we are now able to translate much of the code as he knew it. Not always so for the work of Matt and June. Key information such as dates, locations, and selected artifacts appear to be encrypted in a very sophisticated code that we have not yet deciphered. But we keep working at it."

"Thank goodness, both Jill and I have been concerned about much of the journals content since we did not understand it. The letter explains much that is in the journal but there remain many coded details that stumped Henry, and subsequently Jill, Rosalind, and me."

Comments from Rob and Sti expressed that there was a good deal of information to be studied in the journal and letter. It would take some time, but it was doable.

"I do not think it necessary for us to prolong this meeting beyond reason. It may be best to reconvene once you have had an opportunity to digest the contents of this information. I would only add that Henry found the information very disturbing. He expressly forbade me sharing this information with the authorities. There is clearly not enough on the surface to suggest who is possibly responsible for June's death. However, should the information fall into the wrong hands, the results could be devastating to the legacy of the people of the Owens Valley Paiute. To the four of us, the information compiled in this Journal along with the letter promotes a much different meaning. Whether or not June's death was accidental, the evidence here provides no proof. However, the evidence does strongly suggest that she was in harms way. Only through the efforts of the four of us can we uncover additional evidence to corroborate June's fears and point the way towards the real perpetrators of crime in this matter. If June's death is related to complex circumstances associated with the Paiute artifacts, gold, the death of her parents, and the history of the Paiute, then it is up to of us to find sufficient evidence to move the proper authorities towards action and justice."

Jill's question spoke for all. "Are we walking a thin line here Juan?"

"Yes we are. But there is nothing on the surface of these documents that would suggest that the perpetrators of a crime could be identified. That is excepting, perhaps, Dr. Harris, for stealing and selling artifacts. But, as Henry so often observed, the good doctor is old and certainly all the good he has done far outweighs the onetime transgression many years ago. He does not deserve to be punished more. This could very well happen if we go public at this time. However, should this information assist us in identifying additional evidence that a crime or crimes have been committed by others, that evidence can then stand on its own and these two items need not enter the picture."

"So …" Sti was thinking. "Ours is a precarious situation. Should we continue to pursue this matter we must do so without tipping our hand too far and thereby bring about additional harm to one or more of us. I think your point is well taken. We need to spend time studying this information and its implications. Only then can we make reasonable decisions."

"Exactly! Also, although I have read this information and have had access to the expertise of my secretary regarding some of June's comments concerning the Paiute, I also know that the two of you bring to the table a perspective much different than mine, my secretary, and Jill. For now, I suspect the two of you would like to read, study, and discuss this information alone."

"Yes, yes." Rob reflected. "Once again there is a fork in our investigative trail. But what about potential liability?"

"An excellent question. For now, on this matter, I am the attorney for all three of you. Whatever we discuss is attorney-client privilege. If we maintain that mode on this matter, we can protect ourselves. We must be careful, regular meetings should help us determine next steps. At best, we can hope that June's fears cannot be substantiated. At the worst, we will discover something diabolical, and we will be forced to turn over all that we have to authorities. It must be clear to all of us that I will turn over to the authorities any information suggesting a crime has been committed. I will not jeopardize this office or your integrity. At some point it is very likely that the information we have or will collect must be made known."

There was considerable discussion to follow. But all knew that nothing more could be discussed in depth and to a purposeful end until Sti and Rob had a chance to study the documents before them.

Following some questions put to Juan regarding Henry's activities in donating artifacts and funds to the museum, the meeting came to a close with an agreement to meet again as needed. With that, the two guests were on their way; already sorting out the abundance of information that had fallen into their laps.

Chapter 27

June's Letter to Henry Kubota

Reading a photocopy

June Harris may have been a diligent journal keeper, but neither Sti nor Rob suspected that she would have the patience or time to write, in this case type, the long and detailed letter they were reviewing. Not only was it generated using a word processing program, but also it was a combination of formality and conversation. Both had studied the letter through many readings. June knew her life was threatened, and she was seeking to make sure that what was being said was presented as thoroughly and compellingly as possible.

June had few, if any close friends; she was too mature for many peers, never found a boyfriend who could hike at her pace, and preferred to spend an inordinate time alone in rugged and demanding environments. Nevertheless, she regarded Henry Kubota as her closest confidant. Matthew Harris was her grandfather and he was someone she adored. But history had created awkward circumstances, and what June shared in the letter and journal was not for her grandfather. In fact, it could pose a threat for Matthew and June wanted to protect him. Should anything happen to her, June was making sure that vital information regarding the research of her parents and her own would not go without attention. She may not have known how best to pursue the matter on her own, but she knew that Henry Kubota possessed both the compassion for the issues at hand and the knowledge about how best to deal with the circumstances. He was her only hope.

June Eaddie Harris
Lone Pine, CA

August 5

Dear Mr. Kubota:

I know that our phone conversation must have left you with many questions if not frustration. I apologize. The years that I have known you formally, if not in person, have convinced me that you are someone I can trust. After all, my parents, with good reason, trusted you. Your interests, experience, and actions suggest you are the only one I can share the enclosed information with. I hope some day we can meet and become closer friends, but I fear that may not happen.

Enclosed is a journal. It provides information on my activities over the past several years. What I am about to explain is covered in the journal. However, my coding system may make much of it unintelligible. Therefore, allow me to provide the basics.

As you already know, I have been trying to follow up on the work conducted by my parents. For some time I struggled to understand my Father's theories and methods. But there was always something missing. His final journal would have made it easier to figure out what he was up to. Its whereabouts remains a mystery. Through time and sometimes by accident I think I have put some pieces together. I do not mind telling you that the pieces scare me. I am convinced that my Father was a great researcher. His findings have contributed much to an understanding of the Paiute people and their trade routes across the Sierra. I am also convinced that he was caught in circumstances far beyond his skills to control. Dad had uncovered information; artifacts and gold that suggested the trade routes were more than they appeared. In doing so, he had stumbled into a very troubling situation that had earlier entrapped my grandfather. There were, and continue to be, a group of people who will do anything to access the archeological sites and finds associated with the Owens Valley Paiute. Although they profess an interest in the artifacts, the reality is that these people are most interested in the chunks of gold that my father and grandfather found at several sites.

I do not know these people, but I am certain of their intentions. I am also certain that they are watching and following me. They did this with my parents and my grandparents before them.

During the past two years I have managed to locate some of the sites studied by my parents. I have also found two that were not previously known. In both instances I found significant artifacts (pottery, leather products, and baskets). I also found chunks of gold. They were in leather pouches. I do not know much about the value of gold, but there were a couple of very large handfuls at each site. I was not surprised about this find. I knew that my father had similar discoveries at other sites. I was, however startled to find several weapons not of Paiute origin. These included rifles, pistols and knives along with baskets of ammunition. One site also had several items associated with mining—picks, shovels, and sledge hammers. They were very old, probably dating from the 1870's.

The real shock came when I returned several months later to inspect one of the sites more closely. Someone had been there since my previous visit. I grew up in a family of scientists. I know how to observe and investigate a site without tampering. My earlier journal notes provided all the evidence I needed to conclude that who ever had visited the site disrupted it enough that most people would suspect nothing. But it was obvious to me. Several pots, baskets, and pouches had been removed and very carefully replaced. Most pieces of gold had been removed, but enough remained to suggest nothing had changed. I knew otherwise.

Initially I was angry. Then slowly, I began to put things together. The only way someone could have visited this site was to have either stumbled across it, have prior knowledge of its existence, or to have followed me on my earlier visit. The more I thought about it, the more I have become convinced that I am being followed. Maybe not to the extent that my fears suggest, but enough to convince me that whoever it is has some knowledge about the artifacts and poses a threat to me and to the Paiute heritage. It is not a great leap to conclude that my Father and Mother had similar experiences. I am more and more convinced that their death was not accidental. For some time, someone has been eager to find these sites. I can not believe it is just because of the artifacts. They are valuable, but not enough to kill for. At least, that is my suspicion.

The gold, I believe, is at the root of my concerns. People will kill for gold. Many months ago I had occasion to see copies of articles regarding the 1872 earthquake at Lone Pine. Early editions of the Inyo Register, the only regular newspaper in the valley then and today, provided scant information about the earthquake. Although my initial interest was the reporting of the event, I discovered reference to the fact that local merchants were puzzled by the use of "chunks of gold" by local Indians seeking to purchase large quantities of supplies soon after the quake. At the time I remembered a gold necklace my father had made for me many years earlier. It featured what he liked to call a "chunk of gold." I made the connection. When I found the two sites with the comparatively large quantities of gold, I knew that the connection was far more than appeared on the surface.

You can see now why this whole thing has consumed me in recent years. Something is going on and I think it is larger than my parents could have imagined. I know there is trouble in it, but I can not back off. My instincts tell me that my parents were concerned for the future of Paiute history and heritage. Although their profession compelled them to seek, discover and study, they were concerned that others were doing the same but for greatly different reasons. The gold was more important to others. What might happen to Paiute artifacts was of little concern to those seeking the origin of the gold.

Finally, and this I share with a heavy heart, I know that sometime in the 1950's my grandfather was somehow involved in the removal of items from some Paiute sites. This is not something I stumbled across. The realization has evolved. Comments by my grandmother, conversations between my father and grandfather that I overheard when young, artifacts in the home of my grandparents, notes in my parents field journals, and scraps of information over time have contributed to this conclusion. When the realization began to gel several years ago I was distraught. How could my grandfather have done such a thing? What did he do with the items? Did he sell them? Eventually my research at the Eastern California Museum led me to reason that my grandfather had discovered sites; but not because he was searching for them. He was a geologist and he wandered the same areas my parents and other archeologists combed as part of their fieldwork. My own experiences as a young college student provided the motive for my grandfather's actions. Fieldwork is expensive in both time and resources. Selling a few artifacts can generate much needed money. But, it is also clear that my grandparents donated considerable numbers of artifacts to the museum in Independence and especially to the University of California at Berkeley.

You see why I cannot send this journal to my grandfather.

Except for the reality of some gaps in my work, the accompanying Journal contains information in support of the conclusions developed in this letter. I know that you knew my parents. I suspect that your relationship with them was much the same as it is with me. Should something happen, you are my only hope. I am confident you can make good use of the journal to help bring justice to a situation that I fear will rob the future of the great history of the people of the Owens Valley.

One more thing, this is a parallel journal. It is not a duplicate. For sometime I have kept two journals. One is in being shipped to my grandfather. It covers the same timeframe, but does not have critical information regarding locations of artifact sites, the logic of some of my conclusions, map information, and many other details that I would not want to fall into the hands of those who might be following me. The journal you have in your hand has always been kept most secret. I thought that the other journal, which has just enough information to suggest authenticity, would appease anyone who might break into my residence as someone did in search of my father's journal. If someone should seek to do harm to me, perhaps the other journal would buy me some time. The other journal also appeases my grandfather. As a scientist, he would always wonder what happened to my journal. He does not know this one exists, and to save him face and heartbreak, he does not need to know that I am aware of his early sales of artifacts. He has suffered much, and I have no intentions adding to this.

I hope you will put this information to good use. I doubt I shall see it again. If I am wrong, when we finally meet, perhaps I will have more to share. If not, the battle goes forth in your hands.

Sincerely,

June E. Harris

Chapter 28

The Code

The Harris Code through three generations

After what seemed like endless hours of playing with the Harris code, Sti and Rob slowly teased meaning out. Dr. Harris had provided insight into the code he and Eaddie had used. This helped early on in deciphering the code used by Matt and Kathryn. However, their method of coding, although based on that of Dr. Harris, evolved into much greater complexity. For her part, June had made the challenge of code breaking much more difficult. As the stakes got higher in her endeavors, it seemed that the code got more intricate.

* * * *

Rob and Sti found the process of decoding tedious, but it did provide information otherwise unavailable to them.

Using a code to record information is a practice as old as the written word. Over time, code methods have taken on uncountable forms. In the contemporary era, the computer has taken coding to new levels. But the reality remains; anyone can develop a code and use it for a desired purpose. Such was the case with the Harris family. Beginning with Mathew Harris who, like many researchers, sought to protect the originality of his work, developed a code that was little more than personally developed abbreviations and idiosyncratic wording. In time, with repeated use, Dr. Harris developed his own idiom, or language, to record data he deemed sensitive.

An example of his coding methods can be found in his journal recordings while working on volcanic activity evidence in the Poverty Hills area south of the town of Big Pine.

> AC-H-EB
> Rec: PH (Tin Cr X 395) ~ 4310'

Here the coded information is translated to mean that the entry was made on the 13th day of August, 1952. Using the European notation of the date, the day is entered (AC) followed by the month (H) and year (EB). The simple coding substitutes letters for numbers by using the number that corresponds to the appropriate letter in the 26 letter alphabet. "Rec" is an abbreviation for "Recorded at." This reference is followed by an abbreviation for Poverty Hills (PH) and the precise location in parentheses. In this instance, abbreviations again indicate the reference point as Tinemaha Creek where it crosses (X) US Highway 395 at about (~) an elevation of 4, 310 feet. In this instance, the location would be the old US 395, which remains passable with a combination of dirt and eroding asphalt conditions. The current route is east of the Poverty Hills, about two miles away.

Clearly, this code was not especially sophisticated. However, unless one was well acquainted with the area, it would not be easily translated.

For Matt Harris, the early years of his work reflected the influence of his father's code. Doubtless, both Matt and his sister, Megan, learned the basics of the Harris coding system. But of necessity, Matt had to enhance and complicate his father's code when he began to realize that his work regarding the Paiute cache sites, trade routes, and chunks of gold, aroused the interests of those who could do Matt and his wife harm. Also, Matt's work was far more rooted in hypotheses and theories than was his father's work. His father's code had to be modified greatly. Matt had to go beyond facts and locations to record competing observations, interpretations, and speculation. This was not easy because conjecture does not often lend itself to simple narrative.

The realization by Matt and Kathryn that the Paiute caches may have been used for purposes other than trade or hunting was certainly cause for caution when it came to writing research articles. When they subsequently realized their fieldwork on this issue was being monitored by unidentified others, the practice of coding began to reflect significant complexity. The following illustrates this complexity.

> E AA HH
> T—CPs: 13/7/8/3—EV.—→ strg sups (R,HG,F,amo,chks AU) ⃠consist w/ trd Rt Find. Lrg. Con Bskt (2) → trnsp + than usual sups.?g-on in bkcntry? W?W?W?W?BW?

Translated, this coded entry suggests the following: Date of recording was November 5, 1988. The entry focuses on theory (T) based observations and questions. The Paiute cache sites (CPs) 13, 7, 8, and 3 provide evidence (EV) that the supplies (sups) stored (strg) at the sites included rifles (R), hand guns (HG), flour sacks (F), ammunition (amo), and large chunks of gold (AU). Accroding to the entry observation, these are not (⃠) consistent with traditional (trd) trade route (Rt) findings (Find). Two large (Lrg) conical (Con) baskets (Bskt 2)for transporting (transp) all of this was also not usual for transporting normal trade items (+ than usual sups). Matt then asks himself questions. What is going on in the backcountry? He knows he must look at the What, Why, When, Where and By Whom of all of this.

Unlike her parents and grandparents, June was much more aware that there were others who would not stop at anything to get information about the location and content of the cache sites. She also knew, much earlier in the game, that these individuals, whoever they were, could do her harm as they had probably done to her parents. She modified the Harris code even more. Although her code is evident throughout her journals over several years, it is most sophisticated in her later writing.

June used normal narrative except where information was deemed sensitive. Locations, condition of cache sites, contents of these sites, and dates of visits are the usual subjects of her coding. The actual code is simple because it substitutes coded letters for actual letters. Coded numbers are substituted for actual numbers. The trick, however, is to note that there is a key incorporated in the code to indicate direction of the translation. For example, if a series of letters is preceded by 3> then the translator must note that each letter represents an actual letter that is three places after it in the 26 letter alphabet. A 2< would indicate actual letters two places before the coded letter. Letters near the front or end of the alphabet are accommodated by recycling. For example a letter 3 places after x is A because one recycles back to the beginning of the alphabet. For example, a journal entry from 1992:

U/G/IB: 3> pfqb txp zibxk. 2< pq jwo vcorgt.

Translated, this entry was written on July 21, 1992 and coded U/G/IB. No site reference is given, but this is not a problem because elsewhere in her journal she has indicated the dates of site visits. The narrative is short and to the point. The three groups of letters following 3> equate to "Site was clean." As an example, the setters s, i, t, e are each three places in the alphabet before m, f, g, b). The next two groups of letters equate to "was" and "clean." "No hum(an) tamper(ing)" is revealed in the groups of words following 2<. As is evident, sometimes she left the suffixes off or used abbreviations. For narrative, this code method is tedious, but efficient since it is only used for critical information.

Where an entry referenced location and items observed, the code could be very complex. The following example does this:

13(21&63&276)
Omega Tree SS V @ 12(14–42–184)
Loc:12(15Mtpo) = 365810/1183202 @~ 11200
C4: 5wb, 3cb, 3Fs, 6AU, 2r, 1hg, 1B, 7a.
C5: + more than just T. Clean

The key to this code is knowing that a number that precedes a number(s) in parentheses is used as an indicator of the divisor of the parenthetic numbers. For example, 13 means 1/3rd. So, 13(21&63&276) means the actual numbers are 1/3rd those shown or 21=7, 63=21 and 276=92. So the date of the entry was July 21, 1992. "Omega T SS V" is an abbreviation for Oak (Omega for Oak) Tree Stream (SS is symbol for stream) Canyon (V symbol for canyon). The site was visited on July 21, 1992, the day the entry was made.

The location (Loc) can be found on a 7.5 (1/2 of 15) minute topographic map at about (=) Longitude 36°58'10" and Latitude 118 °32'02" and at an elevation of about 11,200 feet.

"C4", corresponding to Chapter Four in a thesis, identifies the observations or findings of a study. The items identified are five water baskets, three conical baskets, three flower sacks, six chunks of gold, two rifles, one hand gun, one regular basket, and seven arrows.

"C5," represents the fifth chapter in a thesis where the writer presents conclusions and implications. Here June is indicating that what has been found is much more than just a transportation route site. But it is clean and has not been tampered with.

* * * *

Having deciphered enough of June's code to be able to identify possible cache sites was encouraging. Rob and Sti could now go to specific places that had been explored and studied by June.

On the matter of the other contents of her coded information, Sti and Rob sensed they were steadily learning more and more about the contents of the sites and June's interpretation of what she found. Quite possibly this information would prove valuable when the two went back to the site of June's death. However, as to information related to the High Route and the Muro Blanco, the two friends were not confident that they could decode location information in such detail as to lead them to specific places in these regions. For some reason, June made her coding methods even more mysterious when it came to these two locations.

CHAPTER 29

JUNE'S PARALLEL JOURNAL

The Pierce cabin, Big Bear Lake, California

Reading someone else's journal can make one uncomfortable. A journal is personal. It lays bare the thoughts of its author. When the journal is all that remains of the personality of someone deceased, reading it can give the reader a feeling of violation. It is as if the author is stripped of dignity and no longer enjoys the privacy of the mind. Reading becomes an invasion.

The journal of a scientist complicates the matter further. When it is written in part using a code, the task can be daunting and uncertain. June's journal, her last and most personal of possessions, was now the subject of the closest of scrutiny. Sti and Rob felt awkward as they read, reread, and studied June's parallel journal. The recognized numerous portions as being similar to information in the journal that June had sent to Matthew Harris. But the journal sent to Henry Kubota provided insight into a mind that was experiencing the exhilaration of the hunt while at the same time recognizing the position of the hunted.

June's notes recorded her discoveries; the Paiute "caches" as she called them. She detailed each site with drawings and notes that left nothing to speculation when studied later. Her unique code was evident in the maps and directions to the location of each site. Photocopies of articles, newspaper clippings, and notes from her parent's files were found at the back with accompanying commentary that reflected June's investigation and insights.

There was also extensive commentary and speculation regarding the purposes of the Paiute caches. Some exploratory thoughts were in the form of questions that needed to be answered. Theories were often the result of pieced together logic. In some cases it was almost as if June were adding up a list of "whereases" in order to make a case for one or more "therefores." In other instances her conclusions were very tenuous and lacking in solid supporting evidence. At times, her recorded thoughts were nothing more than pure speculation. But whatever the evidence, the journal made it clear that June Harris was on a mission and would not be derailed by circumstances. She was convinced that the Paiute caches and the artifacts contained therein were part of a story that addressed several hypotheses that had been developed in part by her father.

June had learned much; she also knew that there was much more to learn. Somewhere in the Sierra and in the canyons which descended the eastern slope were more answers. The Paiute were an old and patient people. The Owens Valley Paiute of the late 1800s were more than the history books suggested. All the evidence that her grandfather, parents and she had found provided a preamble to evidence as yet unfound. Only through continued fieldwork and careful analysis of evidence would June find the answer. She was committed to this end.

June's journal was also a story of tragedy. It recounted her hardships in life. It provided a window into the life of a young woman who was increasingly isolating herself from the outside world. June Harris was obsessed with seeking answers to a growing list of questions. The more she pursued the answers, the more she was sucked into an adventure that held both satisfaction and heartbreak. She believed in the Harris approach to research; you have to bridge the gap between theory and practice by immersing yourself in fieldwork. You must transport yourself mentally and physically into the environment being studied. Your subjects, their trappings, and their thoughts must become part of you. It was an extended empirical approach of observations, hypotheses, data collection, testing, studying, collating results, analyzing, synthesizing findings, and always reflecting. Fieldwork can be tedious and exasperating. At once one must see both the whole picture and each detail within. And always, reflect, reflect, reflect. This approach drove June almost to a state of distraction. She was exhausted.

Along the way June did find answers to her questions. She also found answers to questions she had not posed. Some of these answers must have hit her like a blind punch. Matt Harris and his wife were being watched, they knew it. As far back as the early 1920's, artifacts were being stolen from archeological sites in the valley. Someone or some group of people was engaged in systematic pursuit and plundering of Paiute artifacts, and especially the gold. June's own grandfather had sold Paiute artifacts to these people. And now June was under their watchful eye. The Harris family had always considered the deepest valley their home. They had all invested their life in its cultural, historical and physical qualities. And some had given their life for this effort.

June had doubts about her own future.

* * * *

Ensconced in Sti's family cabin at Big Bear Lake, they poured over the information. In front of them was a four by six foot kitchen table set with evidence including photocopies of letters, journals, and miscellaneous writings, maps, books, photos, other odds and ends stacked and scattered with minimal evidence of organization. As was the case when last they were at the Harris residence, a timeline covering a period from 1872 to the present was taped to the wall—a hundred and forty years covered in a four-foot long, one-foot tall chart. Next to it was posted a topographic map that featured the Sierra Nevada between Yosemite National Park in the north and Golden Trout Wilderness in the South. The flanks of the map included the Sierra foothills on the west and the Owens Valley on the East. Small "Post-its" with directional arrows and notes covered portions of the map.

It was quiet. The background noise consisted of the occasional crackle of burning wood in the fireplace and the subtle sound of the two laptop computers. Nearby a coffee maker kept a half-filled pot of coffee warm. On the table sat a small teapot, a bag of M & M Peanuts, and a half-empty package of Fig Newtons.

Outside the large bay window the temperature hovered at about 28 degrees and the snow continued to fall. Little could be seen that was not covered in white. It was a heavy spring snow; enough to ensure that the ski resorts would stay in operation a little longer.

Inside the temperature was warm and Rob and Sti sat reading and occasionally drinking from cups that were far from full and usually lukewarm. For several hours in the morning they had skied. The exercise had its intended effect. They were both relaxed and focused.

From time to time one of the two would speak. It was not a conversation per se, just the result of thinking out loud—the expression of an idea, sharing of information, or clarifying something. They had been studying June's parallel journal for two days and were at a point where it was about time to try and collate gleaned information with other sources of evidence. As usual, the two amateur detectives were approaching things in a slow, deliberate, and unorthodox method. Unlike the professional, they had time, they were unfettered in their thought processes by conventional wisdom, and they made no assumptions. There were no stupid questions. There were no ridiculous answers. Evidence and Information were taken at face value. It was studied and processed. It was compared with other information, and questioned. "What ifs" were considered? "I wonders" were contemplated. "What do you thinks" were discussed. At appropriate junctures notes were typed into a running log that could be printed out and added to a three-ring notebook that had grown in thickness over several months of use. Everything was in duplicate and each had a notebook set.

* * * *

The discussion had been lively for some time. At first it was a stream of information, but now it was settling down into an attempt to bring organization to disparate thoughts. As usual, Sti and Rob plodded through the evidence and tried to keep working towards convergence. They wanted to find a pattern in all the data that would allow them to see a story. Stories are useful; they make it easier to keep information sorted out and intelligible. A story is easier to remember than a loosely structured list of thoughts and information.

It appeared that although the journal covered just over two years in recorded information, June made reference to information and experiences that predated the journal. It was not always easy to make sense of some references, but the experiences Sti and Rob had reading and studying information at Matthew Harris's home made it possible to put enough pieces of the puzzle together to trace the thought patterns of some of June's theories.

The more the journal revealed the more convincing was the evidence that June had a unique analytical talent. Unlike her grandfather and father, June was able to see the forest through the trees. It was probably just as well that she was not narrowly trained as an anthropologist or geologist. Such training often results in establishing limitations to ones creativity and originality. But not so for June, she could see the big picture. Her journal was replete with very detailed information regarding artifacts, cache site locations, dates, specific observations and conclusions. But everything was viewed both deductively and inductively. In some instances logic prevailed. On other issues, June allowed her imagination to roam and conclusions seemed to hinge as much on concrete evidence as on conjecture and wonder. The more one studied her methods of analysis, the more it became clear that June Harris was a master of 'triangulation' analysis. She was able to employ the qualitative research methods that draw on multiple discrete pieces of evidence, compare the internal suggestions of such evidence, and then tease out common elements of said comparisons. Often the results tend to point the researcher towards conclusions.

June's journal revealed that she had drawn information from a wide range of resources. Among those were:

1. The journals of her grandparents and parents. It was evident that she was well aware that Matt's final journal was missing. Sti and Rob concluded that her awareness of the missing journal was motive for June to ensure that what could be her final journal would not go missing.
2. Miscellaneous notes and pieces of information that Sti and Rob remembered seeing in the Harris study.
3. Published articles, including some by Matt Harris, Matthew Harris, and others who had spent time studying aspects of the Sierra and/or Owens Valley.
4. Obscure and unpublished papers as well as selected doctoral dissertations connected directly or indirectly with the Eastern Sierra or Paiute Indians.
5. Notes of information gathered from sources at the Eastern California Museum.

6. *Inyo Register* articles dating back to the early years of settlers in the Owens Valley.
7. References to information contained in the small library at Laws Narrow Gauge Railroad Museum located just north of the town of Bishop.
8. Records in the possession of Inyo County.
9. The Paiute Shoshone Indian Cultural Center in Bishop.
10. Information and photos in the Los Angeles Department of Water and Power library. June's notes suggest that she was able to access material that others had not seen because she represented herself as just an interested college student doing a paper on the building of the aqueduct. One note said "I think they would not make this information available to anyone if they really knew what was in their possession." Apparently, bureaucracy begets ignorance and the DWP did not know that they were in possession of some incriminating evidence.
11. The Journal of Lillian Hamner. Lillian, as a teenager, was on the Sierra Club outing that made the trip from Horseshoe Lakes to Marion Lake via the route that was to later become part of the High Route. According to June, Lillian was no longer living. Her journal was in the possession of her aunt, Mrs. La Port who lived in the Bay area.
12. Contact with donors to the Eastern California Museum.
13. Caches of Paiute artifacts that June herself had found.
14. Attempts to contact several people familiar with the history of the Owens Valley.
15. Several books, online references, and articles regarding gold mining in the Eastern Sierra and the Great Basin.

The only thing missing reflected June's promise to Henry Kubota. He was nowhere mentioned. Also, as one would expect, critical information regarding cache locations, contents, and observations were encrypted in June's unique code.

It was an impressive list of resources. Clearly, June Harris had left no stone unturned. She was a dogged researcher. She had looked closely at resources, but she was not overly influenced by any one source. June maintained perspective. She seemed to sense that her answers were not of one suit. What she was looking for would result from the collation of evidence from several sources. So, confidently, exhaustingly and relentlessly June pursued information. It was a daunting task, and it left little doubt that June was consumed by her efforts. Little wonder that she appeared to not be living a normal life. There was not time in her life for friendships, extraneous adventures, or downtime. June Harris had been on a mission.

Anyone with interests similar to June's was bound to cross paths with her. If, as June believed, she was being watched and followed, whoever it was must have been well aware of June's interest in her father's research. They must have also sensed that June seemed possessed. Were they following June because she was interested in similar things or because June posed a threat? In either case, Sti and Rob concluded that June was probably correct in fearing that harm could come to her.

*   *   *   *

Piecing together evidence from June's journal along with other findings, Rob and Sti were able to structure a crude story line.

June Harris had always been an introvert, in part because she was raised in a family that surrounded her with adults. With no brothers or sisters, she was a part of the academic world of her parents. Vacation time was spent with her parents in the field. There were no kids her age among the friends of her parents and there were no cousins. June was bright, but her lack of significant relationships with kids her own age forced her to live a life that reflected academic endeavors, even as a young kid. Play for the sake of play was not part of her upbringing. She grew up being a scientist. Early on she learned the value of empirical approaches to study. It was a world of observation, hypothesis development, testing, and drawing conclusions from findings.

Because of this unique experience as a youngster, June Harris fell into her future. Raised on a diet of research, exploration, and analytical thinking, her destiny was not hers. It belonged to her bloodline. She simply fell into step behind the life of her parents and her grandparents. She was a Harris. She picked up the trail established by those who went before her.

Unfortunately, the trail proved rough. The farther down that trail June traveled, the rougher and more dangerous it got. Only late in her travels did June sense this danger, but then it was too late. Her life was committed to finding answers.

For June Harris, the questions were the same as those of her parents:

- What were the purposes of the Paiute caches?
- Why were there so many rifles, pistols and other white man's weapons in the caches?
- What items were the Paiute trading across the Sierra with their brothers on the West side?
- Was there more to the story than just trading?
- Were the Paiute caches also linked to events taking place in the Owens Valley, specifically those events involving conflict with the settlers?
- What was the significance and origin of the chunks of gold?
- Who was pilfering the Paiute caches? Was their interest the artifacts or the gold?

The final two points on this list were the critical ones. It appeared that June believed that there were two separate issues. On the one hand the Paiute caches were linked to a history that explained much about the behavior and endeavors of the Paiute in the last half of the 19th Century. The other, and possibly more critical issue, was the fact that someone or some group of people were surreptitiously stealing and purchasing artifacts found in the caches. It appeared on the surface that they were illegally collecting artifacts. But it did not take much evaluation of the situation to realize that their real interest was the gold. History suggests such interest is at the heart of events in Western Americana, and the lure remains today.

* * * *

June's insights into the question of where the gold came from were far from clear. On this point, June appeared to be more cautious than ever. Her cryptic notes were unlike any of the other information she had secreted away in her journal of coded documentation. As often happens, increased familiarity with the subject matter only confused the two friends more. Sti and Rob spent so much time trying to understand what June's journal was saying about the origins of the chunks of gold that they feared they were seeing things in her notes that were not there.

"I don't know. I just do not know what to make of these notes." Rob thought a moment more and then commented again. "I think we can agree that there are several sections of the journal that broach the issue of the source or sources of the gold, right?"

"Yeah."

"Do you see anything more here?"

Sti's pause before responding was long. "Looking at her entries, it looks like June spent considerable time studying the history of gold mining in the areas surrounding the Owens Valley. This coupled with her wealth of information regarding the geology of the region would suggest that she was trying to narrow down the possible origins of the gold."

"And she knew that it was not placer gold from the Western Sierra or the more traditional sources in the Northern and Western regions of the range. Therefore, it must have come from a source where the gold was actually embedded in the rock." Rob looked at Sti. "Reasonable?"

Sti nodded agreement and continued the line of thinking. "Yes, and if it was imbedded in the rock then it had to either come from a mine or be available on the surface without requiring any digging. But, I would not think it would be easily accessed on the surface. So.... . It must have come from a mine somewhere."

"And you are thinking that if it came from a mine then knowledge of the source would be known to more than just the Paiutes."

"Yep, the miners responsible for finding it. But, they would not part with that kind of gold. So, if the gold did originate from a mine, it is likely that the miners were killed. But what mine?"

Rob, thinking out loud, responded. "That, no doubt, was the question facing June. She had to have developed the same line of thinking. If that is true, then her efforts were focused on finding the potential mines."

"And that is why her comments in this area were increasingly cryptic. June knew that if the gold was the real motive of those plundering the Paiute caches, any information that could lead these thieves to the gold was more valuable than anything she had discovered. Even though she had disguised her research and findings by having a second journal, June had to know that on the chance the second journal fell into the wrong hands, the information about possible sources of the gold had to be even more cryptic than anything else she recorded." Sti hesitated; he was trying to extend this line of thinking. "And if she went to this great extent, then two things are evident. First, she was certain that her life was in danger. Whoever was trying to acquire information about the Paiute caches would do anything to get information. Such people would not be beyond killing for information about the source of the gold. And.... ."

Rob jumped in. "And second, I think I know where you are going. June would not be as concerned about encryption unless she both feared for her life and had a good idea about the source or possible sources, right?"

"Right! While she may have been concerned that she was being followed, she was also savvy enough to know that the number and quality of artifacts alone was not sufficient to motivate someone to kill her. However, if she had information regarding the source of the gold, then the stakes were much different."

Rob was thinking along similar lines, but he saw a parallel issue. "Does that mean that, if in fact June's father and mother were killed, it was due in part to their knowledge that the gold came from a possible source or sources? Could they have identified where the chunks came from? We don't have Matt's final journal. It could be that it contains information regarding this issue and that is why he hid it."

"True enough. But wait, you have been looking at the same information in June's parallel journal that I have studied. Are we missing anything? Are we not seeing the forest through the trees? Is information right in front of us and we just can not see it?"

"No, we have gone over this numerous times. But, in this case, the coding is just too complicated. Unlike other material in June's journals and the journals of her parents and grandfather, there are no common practices. On the issue of gold, June's code is again unique. We have no reference point."

"Well, let's try to summarize what we do have with this code. Is it safe to say that whenever June starts to talk about location, even remotely, she reverts to this special code?"

Rob agreed.

"So what we have in the place of specifics about possible locations of the source of the gold are words, ambiguous words, unintelligible words, acronyms. What we have on the Muro Blanco and High Route locations is even more difficult to decode because the apparent latitude and longitude data do not match known coordinates for those areas."

"Mmm, yeah. But, remember, some of the words are legitimate. Other words, if that is what they are, are not real. Some are nonsense syllables. Some are strings of letters. Sometimes the letters can be untangled to produce words, but even then the words do not always make any sense." Rob was grasping at ideas. "Somehow we need to find a way to translate these nonsense words or strings of letters if we are concerned about the gold. However, I think we should focus more on cache site locations."

Sti nodded assent.

"I also think we should try spending more time trying to decode information about the Muro Blanco and High Route because we will eventually go back there."

Sti nodded again as he listened intently.

"It seems that the coded information about these two locations may be more directly related to June's death than any other information."

"You know." Sti paused. "This sounds very time consuming, but I wonder if looking at the sources June mentioned would provide any answers. Between the two of us we have some of the books and articles she references. Perhaps looking at these could give us some direction."

"I don't know Sti. That is an awful lot of looking."

"I know. But, what other options do we have? Until summer when we can go back to the High Route, our research efforts are confined."

* * * *

The discussion went on into the late evening. In time it seemed that they kept revisiting the same information over and over. But the issue of the gold was never far from their thoughts. It seemed that even when they tried to focus on other elements such as the Muro Blanco, the High Route, location of caches, interviews conducted by June, and June's travels, their logic kept returning to June's investigation into the origin of the chunks of gold. The distraction was difficult to control.

When the long day of discussion ended, Rob and Sti had a better understanding of June's activities during the final two years of her life. With this information in hand they decided to take a trip to the Owens Valley and follow up on some of their findings and hypotheses.

CHAPTER 30

STI AND ROB WANDER THE CANYONS

Sawmill Canyon

The only way to describe the lower portion of Sawmill Canyon is steep and rugged. The canyon starts at 11,347 feet at a saddle in the ridgeline of the Eastern Sierra Crest. This is Sawmill Pass. The pass provides trail access over the crest and into the backcountry. At the pass the headwaters of Sawmill Creek originate.

On the western side of Sawmill Pass the drainage moves quickly down to Woods Creek, which in turn feeds first into the East Fork of the Kings River and then flows into the South Fork of the Kings River. About a 50 miles west of Sawmill Pass the Kings River flows into the Central Valley as one of the largest rivers feeding the valley. Evidence suggests this route across the Sierra was used extensively by the Paiute on the East and the Yokut on the West as a trading route.

On the eastern side of the pass, Sawmill Creek drops quickly over a distance of about one-mile to Sawmill Lake, which sits at 10,023 feet. Below Sawmill Lake the creek drops down to Mule Lake at 9,700 feet and then down to Sawmill Meadow at 8,700 feet. It is not a big creek but it runs hard year around. Below the lower end of the meadow are the remains of the old Blackrock Sawmill and flume that date from the late 1860's. At this point the canyon narrows to form one of the most precipitous gorges along the eastern slopes. From the pass to where the creek exits the gorge and flows onto the high alluvial slopes of the Owens Valley, the distance is about nine miles.

The terrain on both sides of the gorge is habitat for Mountain Sheep. Hunters have reduced these large animals, which at one time could be found from the northern end of the Sierra to Mount Whitney in the South, to isolated areas along the Sierra crest. To promote protection and growth in numbers, several canyons along the eastern slope have been identified as sanctuaries, and trails in those canyons have been closed. The ruggedness of Sawmill Canyon is a natural home for these sheep and the lucky and keen eye may spot them. Because the trail avoids the gorge proper, it has not been necessary to restrict access to the Sawmill Trail.

Because of the gorge, the trail over Sawmill Pass begins about a mile north of where the creek emerges from the gorge and into Owens Valley. It follows a circuitous route well north of the gorge, crosses over the precipitous ridge that follows the north side of the gorge, and drops down to meet Sawmill Creek above the gorge and just below the lower end of Sawmill Meadow. This diversion adds about a mile of hiking, thereby making the trip over the pass about 10 miles long. The first half of the hike, getting to the meadow, is exposed. There are no trees; it can be very hot and strenuous. From there to the pass the trail is typical East Side terrain that just keeps climbing. The meadow is small and narrow, but Sawmill Lake is beautiful and hosts several very good campsites.

* * * *

Rob and Sti were in Sawmill Canyon because Dr. Harris had provided information about the location of the cache site in the canyon. Also, they had made some headway with June's code and found that their translation of her journal entries relative to this site was fairly accurate. At least, what they interpreted to be the coordinates recorded in the journal pretty much coincided with the GPS readings they took when they reached the site. This gave them the sense that they were making headway in their effort to accurately translate June's journal code—especially the parallel journal code.

They scanned the site and surrounding area. Sti and Rob did not want to add their name to the growing list of those that had vandalized and desecrated this and other sites. Matthew Harris had been kind enough to give them very specific information regarding the exact location of the site. However, finding it was far from easy. The two friends had commented repeatedly during their search that they wondered what it would have been like if they had been given directions that only noted the general area. They could look for weeks and find nothing.

For several minutes the two just looked the site over from a distance. They did not need to talk. Each recognized that what they were looking at had a certain sacred quality. Paiute Indians had once deliberately established it as an observation and/or hunting site. The location was superb. One could scan the entire gorge from high on the southern side of the upper end of the gorge. Anyone passing through the gorge or along the opposite ridge could not remain unnoticed. At the same time, the observer would remain hidden. Also, if one were hunting Mountain Sheep, the site provided an excellent location for spotting movements of the sheep.

There were signs that small, very contained, fires had been used here. It was also evident that shrubs and a small tree had begun to grow in the site after its use many decades ago. As for the cave, it appeared first as an alcove. A large block of granite lay across several other blocks of rock forming a small opening. However, if one crawled a few feet into the alcove, the space widened considerably, revealing a cave that extended back about 10 feet.

It was late afternoon. The sun was already moving behind the crest of the Sierra and the site was in a deep shadow. As Sti and Rob looked around outside, they found nothing in the way of visible artifacts. Nor did they find any footprints. This was a relief. There was no evidence that anyone had been here in recent years.

Rob found his flashlight and poked his head into the opening of the cave. "Very deceptive. This seemingly small opening grows into a rather large area. Here, let me move inside. When you come in, bring a flashlight."

Sti crawled inside. "Wow, what a cozy place."

With concern in his voice, Rob responded. "Yeah, we want to be careful not to disturb anything, including these rodent nests."

Sti knew what Rob was referencing. Deer mice here could be carrying the Hantavirus disease. In places like this they made their nests and their droppings were the source of the virus which could infect humans.

They looked around, and their eyes grew accustomed to the dim environment. Again, they did not want to disturb anything. But it was not long before they both saw the same thing, an old flour sack like the one in June's package. It was shredded, covered with dust. Rob gently brushed some of the dust off, the unreadable writing was faded beyond recognition, and the cloth was no longer anything close to white, but what was left was recognizable to anyone who had seen June's sample.

As they moved their flashlights around, other items appeared. "Look at this," commented Rob. He was focusing his flashlight on several pottery shards. Even the uneducated could see that the pieces looked to be from the same piece of pottery. What ever it was, the pot had been very small.

In time they found several other items—a small piece of shredded basketry, some pieces of leather, the shafts of what could have been arrows, and a couple of pieces of obsidian. If there had been unbroken pots, useable baskets and weapons, they were long gone or were buried somewhere under the dust and dirt of the cave. However, cognizant of their very amateur status, Sti and Rob had no intention of disturbing anything anymore than they had to. They were here to look and get a sense of what Matt, Kathryn and June had been studying.

Getting a sense was important. It requires seeing, feeling, smelling, hearing and understanding. The two friends had backpacked together for years. They knew that one could describe in great detail the beauty of a scene along a trail, but to those listening who had never observed Nature along a hiking trail such a description was not equal to the sense experienced by describer. One had to see the scene first hand to understand. Only then could the listener share in the real mystery of the beauty. Photos, literary descriptions, drawings, and artifacts together were not a satisfactory substitute for being there. Only a first hand observation afforded access to the transcendental quality of an experience. Some have likened the experience to that of going into a great cathedral. Somehow, without being told, you sense you are in a very sacred and moving place. Sti, Rob and the many others who ply the trails and cross-country routes of the wilderness knew that one of the reasons they kept coming back was this spiritual quality.

Once you have absorbed the wilderness into your blood, you must have a regular fix. You must regularly refresh your memories and feelings and senses.

The Sawmill cave site was like any historical site to the visitor who recognizes that it is a privilege to be there. It had a quality that said 'others have passed this way and although they did so long ago, you can sense their presence and purpose, even now.' The Paiute and their ancestors traveled this canyon. And now, at this moment, Sti and Rob stood where the Paiute of some 150 years earlier stood. They could see what they saw. Feel what they felt. For this flickering moment in time the two shared the same space with history. They were at one with the Paiute of the 1800s. Like those who explore the past and walk in the footsteps of others, they could say 'As I leave, a piece of me remains here and a piece of this place comes with me.'

"This is what it must have been like to Matt and June." Sti spoke reflectively. "When you step on this site, enter this cave, you are transformed. For the moment you are back in time. No doubt, the more one does this the more one begins to understand those who were here before. On a small scale, this must be what it was like for Carter when he looked for the first time on the inside of King Tutankhamen's tomb and said 'I see wonderful things.'" Such an observation may seem out of place in a discussion among friends, but it was part of the relationship between Sti and Rob. They did not feel the need to talk continuously, but they did enjoy the occasional venture into philosophical discussion.

Rob too reflected. "If you think about it, June was not only seeing what her parents saw, she was actually growing closer to them by exploring where they explored. She could be one with them through time and space by standing where they stood, looking at what they looked at, and analyzing what they studied." This talking out loud ones thoughts was one way Rob and Sti ensured openness of ideas.

"So, June Harris becomes obsessed with the work of her parents because it was a way to connect with them." Sti's thoughts were racing ahead. "More than that, at some point her knowledge and comprehension about the things that her parents saw and studied became infectious. She began to think like her father, she began to hypothesize like him, and she began to rush towards where those thoughts took her. At that point she was on the same trail as her parents, moving where she did not know, but well aware that the journey was both exciting and treacherous."

"It is like the hunter who is so thrilled with the hunt that he is oblivious to the fact that he is increasingly venturing into harms way. At some point the hunter becomes the hunted. Except in June's case, and apparently in her father's case, they were aware that something was wrong. Others were present, and they did not share the sacredness of the calling."

"I agree," was Sti's response. "But there is another oddity. The entire Harris family, all three generations, was obsessed with exploring the unknown even when their lives were in danger. In fact, they were not really sure where their explorations would lead them. They seemed to follow the trail of evidence. The closer they got to truth, the greater the risks. At the critical juncture in their quest they did not pull in the reins. Instead, they took the next fateful step and it may have cost three of them their lives."

Sti and Rob never thought of themselves as philosophers, psychologists or detectives. But instinct, history, and experience were always a part of their thoughts. Chalk it up to two lives that had their fair share of adventure and exploration. You can not journey deep into the wilderness alone or with a partner without having your perspective on life changed. With each outing the fine-tuning takes place. This is especially true when backpacking cross-country. Leaving home with only what you carry on your back requires significant modification of lifestyle. Add to this the reality of leaving the established trail to venture where there are no directions, and the table is set for a feast of the senses. Ones visual and auditory senses in conjunction with ones sense of direction become heightened. Objective danger challenges decision-making and good decisions are wrapped up in judgment that marries the present with the past.

When they left the confines of the cave they were well aware that the hour was late and that they needed to think about returning to their camp near the meadow. However, without consulting each other Sti and Rob sought out good places to sit and observe the view down the canyon to the Owens Valley. That they should do this without talking and while fully aware that they needed to leave the area before it got dark may have been strange to an outsider, but it was all part of the experience for the two friends. Reflection! Life is about reflection. They needed to savor the experience of the site. They needed to come to grips with all the subtleties their senses had experienced in the past minutes. They would probably return tomorrow, spend more time poking around and taking pictures and notes, but they could never have the experience of the first time at the site again. It was time to gaze, sort through emotions, consider facts, and connect everything with their purpose for coming here. Tomorrow would have its own reactions; it was time to take care of today.

* * * *

Goodale Creek

Five days later Sti and Rob were occupying a campsite at the Goodale Creek campground. As is often the case at these small Bureau of Land Management campgrounds during the off season, they were the only campers in residence. It was a clear evening; Goodale Creek flowed noisily just a hundred yards to the north. Since returning to their car at the Sawmill Creek trailhead three days earlier, they had been exploring from sunup to sundown each day. Their itinerary had taken them to locations up and down the valley. Based on what they had learned from Dr. Harris, Matt's documents, and June's journal, they had explored several canyons as well as the locations where Dr. Harris and Eaddie had set up their fieldwork camp in the Poverty Hills. They ended their journey just up Goodale Creek at an old Paiute campsite. It was isolated and, like the one at Sawmill, it provided an excellent view of the area, but because of its accessibility it had been vandalized. Nevertheless, Sti and Rob began to see a pattern. The Paiute sites were strategically located. They allowed the occupant to easily survey the surroundings and they served as possible places to stay for those who might wish to remain out of sight while making their way across the crest of the Sierra. No doubt there were many such sites and, as Matt and June apparently knew, there were probably multiple sites in many of the canyons. Such an arrangement would facilitate trading as the Paiute moved up and down the canyons.

Eight days of wandering and exploring required some assessment of what was learned. With a small fire, a jar of Sierra Nevada Chileno Peppers, a six pack of Corona, and some other goodies, a long evening of discussion got underway. It was a quiet and warm evening.

The discussion initially focused on June's realization that her father's hypothesis about the extensive nature of the Native American trade routes was in fact a reality. Evidence abounded regarding the nature of this trade. The Paiute had access to several raw materials of interest to both the Yokuts and the Monache Indians. The evidence suggested further that the Paiute were actually the middlemen in matters of trade between the Yokuts on the western slopes of the Sierra and the Monache who occupied the North Fork of the San Joaquin River.

For their part, the Paiute had an abundance of salt, pine nuts and obsidian. The salt came from the Saline Valley, a valley in the Inyo Mountains just east of the Owens Valley. Pine nuts, of course, were a staple with the Paiute. The extensive history of volcanic activity in the Eastern Sierra made obsidian an abundant material. Obsidian was much in demand as it could be used to make a wide variety of cutting tools. Also in demand were the baskets made by the Paiute. The raw materials for making baskets were in great supply. This availability was enhanced by Paiute basket making skills that rivaled any other California Indian, except perhaps the Miwok Indians of the Yosemite area.

Of great interest to the Paiute were the acorns produced by trees that would later be named the Black Oak, Canyon Live Oak and the Inland Live Oak. A tree that ranges from Oregon to Southern California, the Black Oak produces an acorn that is about one and a half inches long. Harvested in the fall, the acorns could be ground in rock mortars to produce flour. Water would be added to leach out the bitter tannin before the meal was cooked. The Canyon Live Oak grows to massive proportions with a height of up to 100 feet and a trunk width of three feet. The Canyon Live Oak grows in shaded canyons up to an elevation of 6,500 feet. The Interior Live Oak is much smaller than the Black Oak or Canyon Live Oak and grows in the Sierra Foothills up to about 3,000 feet. Like the Black Oak, the Canyon Live Oak and Interior Live Oak produce an acorn that is edible once it has been properly prepared.

But Sti and Rob knew that Matt's theory was not an altogether new one. Anthropologists before him had shared similar conclusions. While it may be true that Matt held to the belief that trade was much more extensive than previously hypothesized, this alone did not suggest he had ventured into new anthropological territory. What did make his work unique was Matt's growing realization that the Owens Valley Paiute had established an extensive network of small, remote, and strategically placed camps in the canyons of the Eastern Sierra. These camps were small; they could be expected to provide shelter for more than a hand full of people at any given time. The critical piece of Matt's theory was that the sites, or camps, were being used to facilitate activity that went well beyond simple trade between tribes on opposite sides of the Sierra.

Matt and Kathryn had obviously spent a great deal of time hiking and exploring all the major canyons on the eastern slope. Matt's journals indicated that among the canyons that received the closest scrutiny were Taboose Creek, Sawmill Creek, Oak Creek, Independence Creek, and George Creek. In addition to the Sawmill Creek site that Sti and Rob had visited, Matt and Kathryn had apparently also found a site in Independence Creek Canyon as well as one in Oak Creek Canyon. As for Taboose Creek Canyon, they had apparently found multiple sites. However, to maintain the security of these sites, Matt and Kathryn did not identify their locations in their journals. And, of course, Matt's final journal which may have information about Taboose was not immediately accessible.

"No doubt," said Rob, "Matt's missing journal contains more specific information regarding locations."

"You may be right. At some point in time it would be good to see that journal, but for now we can only speculate."

Rob continued. "I think one of the intriguing aspects of Matt's theory is that some of the evidence we have seen, along with information from Matthew Harris, suggest that the sites may have been used for more than just trade. If you think about it, why would there be significant supplies of weapons and sacks of flour?"

Sti responded. "And we have talked already about the fact that Taboose, Sawmill, Independence and Oak Creek canyons all have one very distinctive quality—they provide quick access to the Sierra interior and canyons that facilitate travel across the Sierra to the foothills of the Central Valley. If you were involved in significant levels of trade, and if you wanted the easiest routes across the range, those would be the canyons of choice when traveling from the Central Owens Valley. But these conclusions are obvious. There has to be more to Matt's theory."

"Well, let's look at this differently. Remember the note in June's journal that the flour sacks she had found were probably from the 1860s because they matched several that she had seen in photographs at the Eastern California Museum?"

"Yeah!"

"We can reason that the Paiute were probably not trading flour across the Sierra."

Sti followed the line of thinking. "So, what you are really asking is why there were flour sacks in sites that supposedly focused on trade? We could go even further. From the evidence gathered by Matthew, Matt, and June, as well as our own observations, there was evidence of flour sacks suggesting a volume of flour in excess of what was needed to outfit the sites for those engaged in trade or hunting."

"Yes, and when we look at the situation that way, several other factors raise new questions. If there was something more than just trans-Sierra trade behind the existence of these sites, then perhaps the existence of hand guns, rifles, and chunks of gold take on another meaning."

Staring across the shadowed valley, Sti spoke. "Yes, the chunks of gold, the mystery of mysteries in all of this. That there would be gold is strange enough. That they should not be nuggets but rather chunks is very perplexing." There was a long pause. "Why would evidence suggest so much gold? Unless, of course, you are not trading with gold but purchasing something with gold."

The method of analysis being employed by Sti and Rob was old and proven. It amounted to nothing more than a belief that 'two heads are better than one.' By asking questions and hypothesizing answers they could probe an endless range of possibilities.

"And what would the Paiute purchase? Guns? Food? Information?" Rob too was thinking out loud.

"Maybe all of those."

"For what purpose?"

Sti, again conjecturing rather than providing an answer raised a question. “Survival; security, maybe. What if the stakes were high? What if they needed guns and food?”

“Such as you might need if you felt threatened by the influx of whites into your small paradise of the Owens Valley? I can see where you are going! The Owens Valley Indian Wars of 1861–1865.”

“Exactly! Except … how does stockpiling guns and food at several small camps scattered some distance from each other in various canyons help you? If you were a Paiute you would not fight a war from these camps.”

Rob volunteered another question. “Could it be possible that Matt had found answers to our questions?”

“How so?”

“Remember our first conversation with Matthew Harris about the so called ‘caches’?”

Sti nodded and raised eyebrows as if to say, ‘go on.’

“If I am not mistaken, Harris told us that on that last New Years he and Matt took a long walk and discussed Matt’s findings.”

“You are right, keep going.”

“During their discussion Matt told Harris that their finds of the previous summer paled in comparison to what they expected to find.”

“I think he said they were the ‘tip of the iceberg’.”

“Yes, that’s it. But you will remember that Matt also said that there were most likely more caches that were bigger and better. He also said, as we have discovered, that other people were aware that there were additional caches. What intrigues me the most is that Matt acknowledged to his dad that his, meaning Matt’s, ideas were always a little crazy. He was openly acknowledging that his theories were not close to the mainstream.”

"So, Matt was really telling his dad that there were many additional caches but that their purpose was nothing like what most people would think. Assuming Matt was correct, our theory is that the caches point to something far more than stopover places for trade or hunting. Is that what you are suggesting?"

Rob continued to pursue this line of thinking. "Yes, and if we consider some of the other information that has come our way, I'll bet we can find more credibility in Matt's theories."

"Certainly, June's activities tend to support Matt's findings. If I remember our discussion of her journal, she saw the caches as part of a bigger picture. She had determined that significant quantities of food related items had been transported over Taboose Pass. She also had found sites in the Muro Blanco where there was evidence of large amounts of flour having been transported to that location."

The discussion continued for some time along this line. But the fruits of this discussion provided no probable answers as to what the ultimate purpose of the cache sites was. Finally, the discussion came back to the one piece of evidence that confounded them most, and apparently all the Harris family members, the chunks of gold.

Sti expressed their frustration. "The gold! Somehow all of this is connected to the gold. We have talked about this countless times. The value of the artifacts that we have seen or are aware of is significant, but not enough to kill over. However, when we factor in the gold the potential for violent crime becomes significant."

Sti and Rob had purposefully tried to avoid the gold issue. They had tried to understand the issues without considering the gold. They found it was taking them nowhere. The chunks of gold appeared to be connected to all the other evidence.

Finally they began to focus on some 'what ifs.'

Quickly the discussion turned to Matthew Harris. "It wasn't the artifacts that Renaldo, Allison, Garsuch, Freeman and others who were involved in putting the squeeze on Harris were interested in, it was the gold."

Rob agreed. “Only the prospect that there was more gold could motivate people to squeeze Harris so hard. What does not make sense here is the killing of Matt, Kathryn and June if the objective was the gold. They had insight into the locations of more gold, if not the source of the gold. Why kill them? And yet, when it comes right down to it, the desire for the gold is the only good explanation for the possible murder of Matt, Kathryn and June.”

After a pause, Rob continued. “If we assume for the moment that the chunks of gold are at the heart of all of this, then we should look at every piece of evidence through a gold colored lens. Gold has to be factored into every analysis and interpretation of evidence.”

Sti tried to build on this assumption. “OK, if gold is the focus, then lets go back to the earliest information we have come across. We should start with the valley in the 1860s. We have the Paiutes who were upset with the settlers, the Indian wars, and Joaquin Jim. As far as the cache sites, Matt believed, and June’s findings seem to concur, that most of the sites are traceable to about the 1860s. We know the Paiute had the ‘gold chunks,’ and it is reasonable to believe that they knew where the chunks came from and how to get more. Even if we do not know the central purpose of the gold, we know that they realized its value. We know that because June had several photo copies of newspaper articles following the 1872 quake talked about how the Paiute used the chunks of gold to purchase flour and other supplies from valley merchants.”

“Which would suggest,” said Rob, “that they had the gold before the quake and out of necessity had to use the gold to purchase supplies. Did the quake precipitate this purchasing spree? Although there is no evidence to suggest the loss of life among the Paiute was significant in the valley, there was a reason why they needed the supplies and were willing to pay a high price.”

Sti’s turn. “Although we also know that the gold chunks were housed, stored, located, or passed through the cache sites, we have no knowledge of the gold in any other locations within the valley proper. Could it have been that the gold was kept at the cache sites because they were more secure than the small villages of the tribes in the valley?”

Rob was thinking about the information about Joaquin Jim that June had collected. He was a bit of an enigma for the Paiute, but June had photocopied many articles, book selections, and news items that talked about Joaquin's role in the Owens Valley Paiute history of the Indian Wars. "Given what we know about Joaquin Jim, I wonder if he had any connection with the gold." It was evident that Rob was probing his memory for some elusive ends regarding Joaquin. "I seem to remember that Joaquin was a bit of a fanatic. He helped to lead the Paiute in their revolt against the settlers in the valley. Although not a Paiute by birth, he seemed to be able the rally the Paiute to take up arms. At the conclusion of the wars in 1865, Joaquin disappeared. According to the press and some observers of the time, he was reputed to be alive and working to build support among the Paiute for another uprising. However, he was never again heard from. I wonder how this fits with the gold."

Both arrived at the same question at the same time. "What if Joaquin Jim and others were using the gold to finance their war efforts?" If they needed weapons to be on an equal battlefield with the settlers and soldiers, they either had to steal them or purchase them. Gold would go a long way towards meeting this need.

Rob put their logic into words. "If the Paiute had tried to obtain supplies and weapons through theft or some other violent act, they would alienate all settlers. However, the buying power of gold made it possible to acquire these items without generating the ire of all. Those selling would willingly accept the gold and say little to discourage such spending."

The evening was wearing on, but they continued to pursue the issue of the gold, Joaquin Jim, the wars, and events of the Owens Valley during the 1860s. They soon began to expand the time period to include the early 1870s because of the link between the gold and the 1872 quake at Lone Pine.

In the end, they painted an impressionist picture of the relationship between several factors. The picture was not clear, but it suggested a plausible explanation of things. If the Paiute had access to a large supply of gold, then the gold became their great equalizer.

If the Paiute had gold, they could be more assured of their ability to go on the offensive. However, purchasing the white man's weapons was not a simple matter. Not only did they need to have a source, they needed to position themselves to use these weapons. The Paiute knew that the settlers had access to soldiers who knew how to fight and had horses that allowed them to move quickly from one place to another. It was also reasonable to believe the Paiute knew that their numbers were small and they could easily be outnumbered in battle. Therefore, the gold had to be used to purchase weapons and to help the Paiute even the odds in battle.

Evidence in the cache sites indicated that hand guns and rifles were probably purchased. The evidence also indicated that large supplies of food had been purchased. Were the Paiute building a reserve of weapons and foodstuffs for a major confrontation?

Was the existence of the caches with their stockpile of guns and supplies an indication that the Paiute were taking their war into the canyons where they were at an advantage? Evidence suggested that the settlers and soldiers were reluctant to pursue the Paiute into the canyons. Certainly, the cache sites provided evidence that the Paiute had the advantage in the canyons.

However, the problem of this logic regarding the canyons was that it would be difficult to remain permanently in the canyons. The cache sites were meant to serve the needs of a handful of people, and year around residence in the canyons was not practical. In this sense, the canyons would be a dead end, especially in the winter. Why the emphasis on the caches in key canyons?

Sti and Rob began to conclude that the answer to the last question rested with the fact that the key canyons provided access over the Sierra Crest into areas where the settlers and soldiers would not follow. The major obstacles to this logic were the winters. The winters in the central Sierra could be brutal and could last five, six and seven months. Severe winters could last longer.

But, fanatics such as Joaquin Jim do things not consistent with the norm. Given the situation the Paiute found themselves in, were they willing to do the strange and bizarre in order to survive? Given that, Sti and Rob began to speculate on what could have been Joaquin Jim's relationship with what was happening.

"Joaquin knew, as I suppose the Paiute understood all too well, that the Sierra offered refuge. It was the one place the Paiute had the advantage. What if Joaquin had convinced the Paiute to stockpile guns and food in key locations of the Sierra? If you think about it, the key canyons led to passes and then to canyons that cut their way to the West Side of the sierra. The elevations of these canyons were much friendlier than the higher elevations that tend to dominate the central Sierra. Could this have been their destination?"

Sti was not convinced. "But for what purpose? Again, the winters were unreal."

"Perhaps the reason was the unreasonable. Maybe the idea was something like Hitler's redoubt. A place they could all go when the chips were down. Yeah, a place where they could retreat to after a battle; where they knew that they would not be followed."

Still not yet convinced, Sti played along with Rob's line of reason. "Like guerrilla warfare. Strike, retreat, and hide out. Then, when the time is right, strike again. Through a long summer they could do this effectively. But then what? What happens after winter comes along?"

"That is a problem. But assuming we could deal with that issue, would you discount this as a possible theory?" Rob did not wait for an answer. "In fact, what if we are not talking about all of the Paiute? What if it was a small band of followers? What if they followed Joaquin like people followed Jimmy Jones or that cult guy in Texas?"

"Ok, what if your suggestion is true. Are you suggesting they spent the winter in the heart of the Sierra?"

"Not at all. It could be that they would fight for a period of time and then go their separate ways in the winter, only to reconvene in the spring."

"Or, when winter set in, they could have gone down the canyons to the warmer climate of the western slope. They could have cut a deal with the Yokut. When summer returned and the passes were open, they could return to their activities raiding in the valley."

"Possible, but not plausible."

"There is another possibility, but do not take this to suggest I support your hypothesis." Sti was giving the 'what if' approach his best. "What if the purpose was to establish an arsenal and warehouse of supplies? I'm not sure where I am going with this idea. But just suppose that the purpose was to …" Sti was searching for ideas and words. "Wait out the settlers. If you were the Paiute you may not have seen the invasion of the settlers as an ongoing process. Perhaps you could believe that if you could buy time you could position yourself for some ultimate victory. If you could stockpile supplies and weapons over a period of time, you could wait and plan your revenge. This is also in keeping with the redoubt concept."

As their discussion went on the consideration of alternative hypotheses began to find a focus. The Paiute knew they could not fight the settlers and soldiers head on for any length of time. Joaquin provided a way to prepare for the future. He offered to create a hiding place or fortress where the Paiute could build for future encounters. To do this would take people. It would also require an ability to acquire the needed goods and weapons. Gold was the answer. The source remained unknown, but the possibilities were unlimited. California and Western Nevada territory were major gold mining environments and there were innumerable ways to have acquired the gold.

However, after all the discussion, Sti and Rob were confronted with problematic issues. How did the quake prompt significant expenditures of gold several years after the conclusion of the Indian Wars in the valley? Also, what happened to Joaquin Jim? If there was a stockpile, where was it? What happened to the stockpile?

The night grew late and the two friends knew that they could not pursue the discussion further. Nevertheless, they felt some headway was made. They were only amateurs, but they sensed that Matt and subsequently June had come to similar conclusions. They too had questions. They also knew that the gold was the key connection between the Paiute of the 1860s and the interest of contemporary treasurer hunters who were following them.

Rob and Sti were certain that future review of other evidence would involve more recent events of the Twentieth Century. But these discussions could wait until another day.

Chapter 31

June's Final Days

Tuttle Creek Campground,
Lone Pine, California in August

For June Harris, her final year was both an exhilarating and frightening. On the one hand her explorations and research had brought her close to resolving the conundrum suggested by the Paiute caches research of her father. On the other hand June was now more fearful than ever that her life was in danger. And yet, she felt a sense of satisfaction. For years she had carried the hurt and confusion precipitated by the mystery of her parents work and questionable death. But it was the hurt and the mystery that had been driving her actions for some time. Now, with her season as a wilderness National Park Ranger drawing to a close, she knew that many questions were about to be answered. What had once been a cloud of distended evidence regarding the Paiute, the caches, the gold chunks, the work of her grandfather, and the work and death of her parents was about to be viewed more clearly. So anxious was June to bring closure that the potential for harm seemed to be an acceptable risk.

* * * *

Tuttle Creek is a minimalist BLM campground some six miles outside Lone Pine, California. In August the daytime temperatures bounce around the

100-degree mark. So unbearable is the temperature that the campground is usually vacant and those who do camp there are seeking the isolation and quiet that the oppressive environment creates. There are a few trees, but the shade they provide is limited as the small shadows they cast move continuously from the west side in the morning to the east-side in the afternoon. Otherwise, the environment is high desert with sage, rock, and more sage. Several miles to the west are the sharp vertical lines of granite that shoot upwards from the desert to mark the eastern escarpment of the Sierra Nevada. Mount Langley, Loan Pine Peak, and of course, Mount Whitney dominate the skyline and their presence is always evident. To the east, the land slopes quickly towards the center of the Owens Valley as the slow and shallow remnants of the Owens River dissipate into the porous earth where the river enters the vast and dry Owens Lake. The only interruption to the rapid slope of the landscape are the Alabama Hills, an ancient and small range of hills so weather worn that their character is marked by a conglomeration of granite formations that have served as an ideal setting for many a Hollywood movie.

For anyone spending time in the campground, the days are long and activity is limited to the birds, lizards, and ants that seem to thrive in the environment. Sound is limited to the wind and the ever present rushing sounds of Tuttle Creek as it makes its way down the high desert slope, cuts its way through the Alabama Hills, and is siphoned off into the Los Angeles Aqueduct. The creek is small and the route down slope is quick, the angle is too steep to allow for a winding course. What little water remains in the creek after it passes the aqueduct disappears before the creek would pour into what remains of the lower Owens River. All of this aside, the campground can be a very peaceful and relaxing place for the traveler. If one does not mind the heat, hours can be spent relaxing, reading, studying, and thinking. The mornings and evenings are exceptionally pleasant and quiet in the summer. For June Harris, it was a final stopping place before she returned to the backcountry. It was an opportunity to take stock of her experiences of the past several months and to organize her thoughts for the weeks to come.

June had come to Lone Pine this morning. Yesterday morning she left her camp along Lake Marjorie Creek, hiked south over Pinchot Pass in the morning and then Kearsarge Pass in the afternoon. She reached the trailhead in the small parking lot at Onion Valley in late afternoon. There she got a ride with a forest service employee down to Independence where she spent the night. Arriving early this morning, June visited the National Forest Service facilities at the south end of town. There she retrieved some of her personal things from a friend who works for the service. She took time to renew acquaintance with several people in the headquarters. She also took time to eat a good meal at a local restaurant on U.S. 395 in the center of town. Then it was off to the post office where she picked up some mail. There was nothing important.

It was at the post office that she completed the primary purpose of her trip. June mailed a letter and package to her grandfather. The letter had been difficult to write, but the harder task was the telephone conversation with her grandfather later in the morning. June also mailed a letter and her parallel journal to Henry Kubota. The purpose was to guarantee safekeeping of the journal during the weeks or months to come. Mailing the journal had been a difficult decision, but June knew that she could not take any chances that the journal would fall into the wrong hands. Perhaps she was being excessively cautious, but June's memory of her father's death had long ago forced her into a very cautionary mode.

After a stop at Jensen's Buyrite Market to obtain some supplies, including a bottle of Sierra Nevada Chileno Peppers, which she would eat later in the day and evening, June returned to the Forest Service office. She provided the office with some information on data that she had gathered from hikers and packers during the past month. The Lone Pine Forest Service issues wilderness permits to backpackers entering the Sierra Backcountry through any of the backcountry access trail heads along the southern part of the valley. From Olancha Pass in the south to Taboose Pass in the north, the service has a quota system to insure that on a given day the number of backpackers entering the Sierra backcountry is not excessive. It is a way to control both crowds and damage to the delicate backcountry habitat. However, once backpackers enter the backcountry, their habits are not known. As part of her regular duties, June kept data regarding backpacker movements along the John Muir Trail. She also checked with backpackers to make sure they had the proper wilderness permits. The data she gathered on this latter matter was very useful to the Forest Service and its efforts to monitor backcountry travel.

In mid afternoon, one of the Forest Service officials headed up to the Horseshoe Meadows area and dropped June off at Tuttle Creek. Tomorrow that same employee would pick June up in the early morning and take her to Lone Pine where she would get a ride north on U.S. 395 to Taboose Creek. There were always Forest Service employees traveling back and forth between their offices in Bishop and those in Lone Pine. Hitching a ride was never a problem. Often she knew the driver and enjoyed talking over old times. Although the NPS and the Forest Service were different entities within the federal government, in the Sierra their working relationship was a good one. Each agency had responsibilities that buttressed the other. Working together was critical to effective management of resources and control of human impact on wilderness environments. Although very independent, June enjoyed interacting with those who shared her enjoyment of the wilderness of the Sierra. She found Forest Service employees very engaging and she found that over the years she had learned a great deal about the Owens Valley and the Eastern Sierra from her discussions with them, especially those who had long careers in the National Forests of the Sierra. On several occasions June had been steered towards a valuable resource as a result of a casual discussion with a Forest Service old timer.

As she thought about it, June had found that many public and private employees of the valley had unique pieces of knowledge that proved useful. Highway Patrol officers and Inyo County Sheriff Deputies had an intimate knowledge of the Owens Valley byways. Bureau of Land Management employees were especially knowledgeable about the too many to count nooks and crannies of the Valley. Like most very rural areas, the Owens Valley attracts a wide range of personalities. Among them are those who are seeking to avoid much, if any, contact with the established world. These latter types have personalities that thrive in isolated, in some instances, hidden places. They also wander the environments they inhabit. BLM officers, Sheriff Deputies and wildlife enforcement officers know about this reclusive class of people. They work with them when they can, enforce regulations with them only when they have to, and above all, keep tabs on them. Neither side wants confrontation, so a symbiotic relationship has developed between the law and the self proclaimed outcasts.

The old word for these reclusive personalities was, and for some still is, 'hippie.' Although the word was used commonly by people in the valley, June and others knew that in fact most of these people just wanted to be left alone. Some had been miners in younger years. Others worked odd jobs when they needed money. Some were squatters. And some were very accomplished people who at some point in their life left it all for a more remote life style. Oh, there were the few who created problems, but for the most part they were just independent but friendly types who found luxury living on the margin. June had befriended some, and she counted a few as good friends. They enjoyed the wilds as did June. They might talk negatively about the 'establishment,' but they also wanted someone to ensure the preservation of much of the open and wild spaces in the valley. June had also found in these loners a source of information regarding much of the valley that was not visible to the casual observer. She also found in them a kindred spirit.

June realized that although she was herself a bit of an outcast who enjoyed solitude, she also enjoyed the company of people who respected the valley and knew something about the unique qualities of the valley. This included Department of Water and Power employees. Although June had at one time found the DWP to be a distasteful part of the valley history, she eventually realized that most of the employees were from families who had lived in the valley for many decades. They may work for the DWP, but they loved and respected the valley. Also, for some, their jobs took them to some of the most remote areas of the valley. June had found a couple of DWP field employees to be a wealth of knowledge about the geology, history, and special places in the valley.

Similarly, June had found the Paiute Indians of the valley to be a fascinating people. This was their valley. In discussions with some older Paiutes, June had found that they could trace their heritage back for many decades. On a couple of occasions she had been given a tour of some historical and hidden sites where the Paiute had camped during years long past. June smiled to herself when she recalled the 'History Week Project' of one young Paiute student whose project had focused on the hunting camps of the Paiute in the 1800's. The two had had a long conversation and June was struck by both the familiarity of the young girl with the history and culture of her people and the determination of the student to focus on preserving heritage. June remembered how she tried to encourage the young student to stay on the path she was following. June felt somehow guilty that she had never followed up with her. Perhaps when this is all over she would make an effort to find the young student.

Like all of these people, June too loved the Owens Valley. She felt that she was destined to be here. But, like some of the valley residents, she also loved the Sierra and could not imagine loving a mountain range anywhere else the same way. June had thought many times that the Eastern Sierra seemed to have it all. That all of her family—grandfather, grandmother, father and mother—had also loved this environment was not surprising. Over the years June had met many people who had similar feelings. These were people who did not mind sharing the Eastern Sierra with the tourist. They were also people who took serious issue with those who did not respect the qualities of the environment. Theirs was a possessive attitude. They may debate hotly issues related to tourism, water use, land use, and environmentalism, but when all was said and done, they were united in their love for the world they lived in. They would have it no other way.

Inevitably though, June's thoughts came to that juncture so dreaded by any good line of thinking. Despite all of this, the Eastern Sierra and the Owens Valley were not without their antagonists. Somewhere in all good things are those elements of decay. For June, her father and her grandfather, the experiences were the same. Someone of great greed had and was continuing to discard all that was good in favor of personal wealth and power. Although June did not personally know the perpetrator or perpetrators of this evil, she had a good fix on their affiliations. She also knew that they would do anything to reach their goals. This included murder.

* * * *

June's earlier thoughts about the valley and Sierra had given way to more focus on preparations for her return to the backcountry. She had sorted through her gear, and set aside those items she would leave with her friends in Lone Pine until her return several weeks hence. But now, as the heat of the day dissipated with the journey of the sun behind the crest of the Sierra, June began to think again about the purpose of her upcoming journey.

Reflecting for what seemed like the hundredth time, June reviewed what had happened during recent years.

Years earlier, while helping her grandparents clean up after the Berkeley Hills fire, she had began to take an interest in the research legacy left by her parents. Unbeknownst to her grandparents, she had made copies of several documents, maps, and her father's journals, all but the last one, which was missing. In the months that followed, her interest in Matt's theories consumed all her free time. Eventually it became a calling. Since then, her life had been increasingly focused on finding answers to her parents' research questions and to her own questions.

For several years, June experienced only frustration as she tried to make sense of pieces of evidence gathered and recorded by her parents. As she thought back, there were times when she thought her father's ideas were so off base that it was embarrassing. But then, several years later and after many months of combing Taboose Creek canyon she found the breakthrough evidence. It was the discovery, in the thick undergrowth of the canyon, of a cache that had not been touched since the last Paiutes departed its roomy, though not large, interior cave. The site contained items consistent with the findings recorded in her father's journals. Several rifles, numerous pottery bowls, and several large canonical baskets were neatly stored on a rock shelf. In one basket were several empty flour sacks. This had startled June because it was exactly like the one she had seen among her parents possessions stored at her grandparents' home. Another item was equally stunning. Chunks of gold, twelve of them were found in a canvas pouch in one of the bowls. The fact that they were similar to the one on the necklace given to her by her father was not lost on June. Clearly, the chunks of gold were a key to understanding these cache sites.

June did not remove anything from the Taboose site. The three times she had returned to the site provided no indication that anyone else had visited the site. As far as she knew, everything remained in order. But the Taboose site was a breakthrough. The experience there had convinced her that there were more caches and that her father's theories about the existence of other sites were correct. The discovery sometime later of a second Taboose site at a much higher elevation provided further confirmation. The second site, although it housed several weapons and a conical basket, revealed no gold, pots or other items. But it provided clear evidence that there was probably a chain of sites in several canyons. This realization led June to extend her investigation across Taboose Pass and into the Sierra interior.

Initially, she had found nothing on the west side of the pass. So, in the off seasons, June focused her research on other canyons of the eastern slope of the Sierra. As she thought back over her adventures, June speculated that there was not a significant canyon between George Creek and Big Pine Creek that she did not comb on multiple occasions. She doubted that there was anyone who had investigated these canyons more closely than she had. And yet, despite all of this exploration, she had discovered only three other sites. The one in Oak Creek canyon had clearly been visited before. There were some potsherds and leather items; however, there was no evidence that anything had been taken. A second site in

Sawmill Creek canyon, above Sawmill Lake, had been damaged by an avalanche/landslide. There were no discernable artifacts in the site. However, it was the second site in the canyon. An earlier site had been discovered during the 1940's by her grandparents. June had visited the other site below Sawmill Meadow several times. As with the Taboose sites, the two sites in Sawmill Canyon suggested they were part of a string of sites.

But June had not confined her study to field exercises. In the winter months she had investigated every available resource in the Owens Valley—Law's Museum, Eastern California Museum, Paiute Cultural Center, and public records in Inyo County. In each of these sources June had found information about Paiute artifacts discovered in various places throughout the valley. In addition, an unexpected resource was suggested by an employee of the DWP. This suggestion took June to Los Angeles where the DWP had several artifacts, which allegedly had been found during the construction of the aqueduct.

Through persistent inquiry, June had learned that most of the items were donated by the son of a former DWP employee, George Kennicott. Several months later, June heard from her original DWP resource that Kennicott's grandson was spending time in the Owens Valley trying to follow-up on the origins of the artifacts found by his grandfather. Only later would June learn that the grandson was also inquiring about the work of her father.

June's research at the Eastern California Museum was especially fruitful. Because of her position with the NPS, June gained the confidence of several curators at the museum who gave her access to limitless information about Paiute artifacts and anthropological studies in the valley. It was here that she first encountered the name of Henry Kubota. Henry's donations, although few, played on June's mind for some time before she realized that the most puzzling issue about his donations was the fact that the artifacts were old but relatively undamaged. These were undoubtedly artifacts that could only have been found sequestered in a location protected from the weather. Since they were not stolen from homes or other places, June concluded that Henry Kubota must have found these artifacts in one of the cache caves. The clincher came when one of the items matched a description of a bowl found at the Sawmill site by her grandparents. When June tried to locate the whereabouts of Henry Kubota, the museum had no information about his residence or if he was even alive. Then, just by chance she stumbled across her mother's Rolodex file and found the name Henry Kubota (in coded form of course) and a phone number.

In time, June realized that what she thought was paranoia on the part of her father regarding the possibility that someone or some persons were shadowing Matt and Kathryn was in fact a reality. As she delved ever more deeply into the journals and other writings of her parents, June became all too aware of the possibility that the death of her parents was not an accident. The more she began to read between the lines of data and evidence recorded in the work of her parents, the more June realized that they were very concerned that someone was raiding cache sites, taking the contents and selling them. But, more than anything else, June, like her parents before her, was increasingly aware that the real motive of these raiders was the desire to locate the source of the gold found in the sites. Gold, she knew, caused people to commit murder.

An independent spirit, who liked to spend time alone thinking, June eventually realized that her father's last journal had not been stolen. If it had, the contents would have eventually been decoded, and more site locations would be located and raided. June conjectured that the journal would have provided sufficient information to lead others to the sites she had discovered in Taboose Creek and Oak Creek. Since those sites had not been raided, June could only surmise that her father had hidden the final journal. Its whereabouts may be unknown, but at least the information it contained would not fall into the wrong hands. June also conjectured that her father was not so stupid as to ensure its loss for all time. No doubt the journal was hidden and would come to light in due time.

* * * *

As the evening wore on, June began to realize that she was increasingly becoming anxious about her impending trips.

June realized the turning point in her adventure came when she made contact with Henry Kubota. Cautious and nervous at first, June soon came to realize that she and Henry shared several common bonds. They had both visited the lower Sawmill Creek site, Henry had known her father, and Henry wanted to support her efforts. Henry filled in a lot of answers to questions. Yes, there was a final journal of her father and it was safe. Although Henry knew the whereabouts of the journal, he said it would be too dangerous at the present to retrieve it. He did, however, indicate that there were two pieces of information June might want to pursue.

First, Henry indicated that he had come across documented, but unpublished, anthropology information suggesting the Paiute had spent considerable time at campsites in the upper end of the Muro Blanco. Matt had intended to spend more time investigating these sites because he was convinced that they were more than just the normal seasonal campsites. Second, Henry had learned about a curious incident that had occurred on a Sierra Club outing in 1935 in the area now recognized as part of the Sierra High Route. He suggested contacting the Sierra Club as well as the grandniece of Lillian Hamner, Mrs. La Port.

Visiting Mrs. La Port had turned out to be a major break. The contents of Lillian's 1935 journal were so intriguing that June had made several trips to the region of the High Route visited by the Sierra Club in 1935. The visit to the Sierra Club headquarters had confirmed the suspicions generated by June's reading of Lillian's journal. Something had happened in the Marion Peak area and along the Muro Blanco that was connected to the Paiute caches. During three visits to the areas June had discovered some small Paiute artifacts—decayed leather items, arrowheads, some pottery shards, and most interestingly an old flour sack. The flour sack matched those traceable to the 1860's and 1870's. From June's perspective, the Paiute of those years had spent considerable time in this region and for purposes that went well beyond just participating in the usual trade. Her father had been right about the importance of the caches for trading purposes. However, unless his final journal indicated otherwise, she could not be certain whether or not her father realized that there was more happening than just trade.

And then there was John. Perhaps the most significant piece of information to come June's way involved comments made by an elderly Paiute she encountered in George Creek. It was a warm fall day when June was returning from a two-day trip into the upper end of George Creek. She had encountered significant evidence of mining in the upper reaches of the canyon, but, as in past visits to the canyon, she found no evidence of a cache site. Near the outlet to the canyon, which is shaded by large oak trees, June was surprised to see the elderly Paiute sitting quietly observing her.

June remembered that his smile was very disarming, and yet she quickly sensed that he was friend and not foe. Although his Americanized name, John Littlebear Bowers, meant nothing to June at the time, she later learned about his heritage from Henry Kubota. What did stand engraved in June's memory was the substance of a very friendly conversation with John. She remembered it as if it was only yesterday.

After her surprise and a mumbled "Hello," John Littlebear had commented "Hi! You are the one they call the 'wanderer,' aren't you?"

"The 'wanderer?' Who calls me that?"

"Oh, you did not know? The people in the valley call you by that name. Well, not all the people, but those who are familiar with the canyons you seem to explore over and over."

"Well, who are these people?" June was fearful that the John was referring to those she suspected had been following her from time to time.

"You know. You have talked to some of them. They are those who tend to live alone, like hermits. Some are of my people. Some are what you call 'hippies.' Like me they have watched you for several years as you have explored the canyons in strange ways."

"Strange ways?"

"Yes, like your father and grandfather before you."

The comment startled June; it took her seconds to recover. "Well, you seem to know me and my family. Who may I ask are you?"

"Oh, I beg your pardon. They call me John Littlebear. You can call me that too."

"Well, John Littlebear, have you been watching me also?"

"Oh, yes, many times. I saw you go into this canyon yesterday. I was going to leave it at that. But then I decided I would wait until you came out. I thought it was time for us to meet. I have wanted to meet the one who wanders because I think we are like each other."

"How's that?"

"I do not wander as well as I used to. And I was never very good at wandering these difficult canyons. But, like you, I find the heritage of my people to be most interesting, and I find that the more I wander in their faded footsteps, the more I see their fading history. It is, as you would say, a labor of love."

June: "A passion."

John Littlebear: "Yes, a passion. Oh, yes, a passion. But it is also like your passion because it carries with it dangers."

"What do you know of my passion? What is the danger?" June's interest moved from conversation to a serious demeanor. Clearly, John Littlebear was more than just a wandering Paiute interested in his people's history.

"When one is obsessed, it draws attention. Such was the case with your grandfather the geologist. But it was even more so with your father and mother, the anthropologists. Like them, you seek to understand the trading habits of the Paiute. And, like them, you walk in harm's way. The more you discover, the more you pose a threat."

June remembered being stunned. She was startled. Who was this Littlebear? What was he inferring? Where did he get this information? But June did not get a chance to ask those questions.

"I can see you are confused. I have forgotten my manners. Let me backup and tell you a story."

John Littlebear went on to explain that his uncle had once encountered a man named Kubota who lived in Manzanar, the great camp, during the war. Kubota had also been a wanderer who investigated the canyons. In the process, he found Paiute artifacts. Together, the uncle and Kubota formed a bond that would ensure that the artifacts would be protected. Today, many of those artifacts are in the museum in Independence. June commented that she had seen the artifacts and that she knew who Kubota was.

John also said that June's father was also a protector of the Paiute heritage. But he was more than that. He was obsessed with exploration. He sought to understand the Paiute trade routes. John said that Matt's journey was not a smooth one. He discovered more than just artifacts.

"You mean the rifles?" asked June.

John's response was quick and firm. "No! The gold!"

The bold and firm statement overwhelmed June. John Littlebear was much more than just a valley wanderer. Where was this conversation going? Seldom the one to be speechless, June found herself searching for words.

It was also late in the day, and June knew that she could not talk to John for much longer because it would be dark. With no moon it would be hard to navigate her way back to her campsite several miles away. It was an awkward situation, but John clearly had something to say and June did not want to discourage him.

"Why don't we make our way to my camp where we can have a fire, food, and time to talk. I have some food. Unless you have a problem, we could talk through the night."

"No, that is not a good idea. Your campsite is some distance and is being watched and that is what I wanted to tell you."

While the conversation went on, John Littlebear began to build a small fire. Slowly and methodically, he cleared an area of twigs and leafs, arranged a small circle of rocks, and arranged the fuel. June sensed that this night of conversation was more than just the result of happenstance. Something inside told her that John Littlebear had intended this situation all along.

"I have suspected for some time that I was being watched. Do you know who it is?"

"This is what I wanted to tell you. There are at least two of them. One is an Anglo. The other is, I think, Mexican or maybe of another Native American tribe or maybe even a mix of Mexican and Indian. I don't know, I just think this."

"But I have never seen them."

"They are very clever. They watch from great distances. I think they even watch from a helicopter. Sometimes, they go where you went after you have returned. I think sometimes they find the places you find artifacts, and then they take them. But I have not seen them do this. Others in the valley have seen them take some artifacts, but nothing very important. But that is not the important thing I wanted to say."

"You seem to know a lot Mr. Littlebear."

"I don't know a lot; but I know you are in danger. This I know because you are from the Harris family. It is a family burden that you carry. They could be watching now. A fire through the night would draw too much attention. This fire is far from your camp and is small. It will not draw attention. We can sit here until this fire dies down and it gets cold; then I must go."

"You have said danger twice. What kind of danger?"

"The kind of danger your father was in. The kind of danger that comes from knowing too much. The kind of danger that goes with the gold."

June kept quiet. She knew John had approached her to tell her this information. She decided to keep quiet and just listen.

"I do not know everything. But some elders in my tribe have spoken about the gold. The gold your father found and the gold you no doubt have found is part of a great evil. The closer your father got to the truth about this evil, the closer he got to the gold. That is what those who watched him and you want. They want the gold."

"Do you know where the truth is?" June used this question rather than a blunt question about the location of the gold. John was smart enough to see her discreteness.

"No. I do not think any of my people really know where the truth is exactly. But they do know it is over the mountain you call Taboose."

"Over the pass? That is a lot of territory on the other side."

"Oh, yes, but I can be more specific. Long ago my people fought wars with the settlers in the valley. But they could not resist the flow of the white river. And so a few of my people thought they could build a place and hide until they had the weapons and support of other tribes to bring a big and final war to the settlers. They would wipe the settlers out, and the valley would be theirs again. So they went over the mountain to build their hiding place."

June could not help responding. "But the winters over the mountain are vicious. It is not possible to build traditional Paiute dwellings and survive."

"This they knew. But stories tell of a different kind of dwelling in the ground. A big one that could be lived in by many people. A cave that opened at two ends. One opening high in the mountains and the other below and in a valley"

Again, June was taken aback. "How do you know this? I have not heard it from any Paiute with whom I have talked. I have found nothing in my fathers work about what you have said."

With a deliberate tone, John Littlebear responded. "Oh, I did not hear it from one source. And I do not think any Paiute here in the valley would tell you this, even if they knew. You are not Paiute, and they do not know you well. What I have told you is from my thinking about the many stories I have heard during my lifetime. I pieced the information together over the years, and the picture began to emerge. Somewhere over the pass is a much larger place where my ancestors stored supplies, arms, and gold. But they never got a chance to use it. Why? That I do not know."

June and John continued to talk. It grew late and cold. Though warm in the day, the nights in the fall could be freezing, and they needed to bring their discussion to a close. John shared little else with June. She wanted to meet with him again, but he refused saying that it was not a good idea for her or for him. They separated and she made her way back to her camp after several hours. She never heard from or saw John Littlebear again. But she sensed that he was always watching whenever she returned to the Owens Valley.

Days later June talked by phone with Henry Kubota. He knew who John was. He had known John's uncle as a close and personal friend. During their discussions, Henry and June concluded that John was conveying a message for June on the part of others. The message clearly suggested that the answers to the questions that had plagued June for some time could be found somewhere in the High Route and the Muro Blanco.

In response, June had explored these areas very thoroughly and now knew that John Littlebear's suggestion was accurate. Something had happened in this region involving the Paiute during the second half of the 1800's. What happened exactly was not known, but it warranted continued investigation. Once again, June was planning to return to the High Route.

* * * *

A backcountry ranger for the Forest Service had dropped June off three miles up the difficult dirt road to the Taboose Pass trailhead. Another two miles and she would be at the trailhead. It was early in the day and June was confident she could be at her creek-side camp on the other side of the pass by sundown.

The ride north from Lone Pine had been uneventful but talkative. The driver, Caulder, was an old friend. Although from different agencies, the two shared a common love for solitude in the backcountry. They talked at length about places they had been and experiences that made them laugh. June participated in the discussion, but on reflection she had no doubt that Caulder sensed that June was distracted by other, deeper thoughts. As they were parting only minutes earlier, Caulder gave June a hug and commented intuitively "Be careful June!" Nothing more need be said. Caulder sensed June knew it was an awkward situation. For June's part, she knew that Caulder was of similar ilk, and would say no more. They parted quietly.

* * * *

June had been setting a quick pace for three hours now. She was well up the Taboose Creek canyon trail. All along the same thoughts were going through her head.

Three weeks earlier June had camped at Marion Lake. The next day she was exploring the High Route in an area west of Red Point, which was at an altitude of about 11,200 feet. As she was doing so June found a piece of leather protruding from under some decomposed granite. When she unearthed the leather it turned out to be a Paiute moccasin. In fact it was a cross between a moccasin and a shoe and was probably not more than 50 to 75 years of age. June was initially ecstatic with the find. Could this be evidence to substantiate the claim of Lillian Hamner that the packers on the 1935 Sierra Club outing did indeed spot Indians?

But her surprise was short lived. After taking off her daypack and sitting down to study the artifact, she spotted several shoe prints from a modern tennis shoe. June was startled and quickly looked around as if she sensed someone might be watching. But she also knew that the print was probably a day or two, or maybe even several days old. Certainly they had been left since the last big rain several weeks prior. But the fact that it was a tennis shoe print was the confusing part. June had hiked enough trails in the Sierra to know that occasionally there were backpackers wearing tennis shoes. She had come to know a wide variety of prints found along the commonly traveled trails. However, she could not ever recall finding backpackers wearing tennis shoes in the deep backcountry where there were no trails. Rugged trails, slippery surfaces, creeks and streams without crossings, soggy turf, ice and snowfields, and seriously cold weather at the higher altitudes precluded footwear other than the best made hiking boots. No, these footprints were out of place.

June followed the prints, which showed up intermittently, down and across the slope to an area of large granite slabs where she lost track of the prints. This was very difficult terrain to wander, let alone search for something. After looking around for some time she was about to head back towards Marion Lake when she found a small pile of artifacts. Among the items were several horseshoes, old leather straps and buckles like one found on pack animals, some old and weathered pieces of oil canvas as were used in tents that preceded the modern nylon variety. There were some pieces of undistinguishable and severely weathered and shredded cloth, probably from clothing.

Still feeling as though someone must be near, June looked around and did not touch the pile of artifacts. She circled around the area in search of more footprints. She found none. But what she did find very puzzling was a strange, narrow, several feet long, indentation in the combination of decomposed granite and turf that bordered one side of the granite slabs. A second indentation several feet away paralleled the first. It was difficult to tell what the indentations suggested. Maybe someone had drug something through here. Perhaps they were just lines drawn with a stick. She could not imagine what could have made such marks in this remote and high altitude environment.

June was tempted to pick up the items she had found, but she hesitated. Something told her that all was not as it should be. Again she looked around. Nothing! There was nothing to indicate who had been here. Still, June did not touch the artifacts. In time, she determined that she would leave them for another visit. She sat down and made some notes in her journal. Despite the shoeprints, which were recent, the other items suggested a much older timeframe. Above all else, they suggested the Paiute had been to this remote spot at least as recently as some 60 years ago. Without disturbing the pile of items that were weighted down by several small pieces of granite, June began to record what she saw in her journal. As she was doing so something she previously thought was undistinguishable struck a visual nerve. She knelt closer and probed a piece of cloth with her knife. She did not want to believe what she saw, but there was no doubt. June was looking at an indistinct piece of cloth that had once been part of a flour sack, circa 1860's or 1870's. For a few minutes she just stared. Then she found herself breathing deep to make up for the loss of oxygen she was experiencing. At these high altitudes, even for those conditioned, if one stopped breathing because they were mesmerized or distracted, they soon found themselves gasping for air. A few deep breaths and June was recovered, but her mind was racing. She had stumbled onto something big. She wasn't sure what to make of it all. In trying to do so her mind jumped around as it searched options. What she quickly surmised was that she had found what she was looking for. Again, she was not at all sure what she had found, but she had no doubt it would prove important.

Deep within her thoughts, June also knew that she was not alone in her discovery. Others had been here recently. Thinking back on her experiences, those of her parents, personal suspicions, and the comments of John Littlebear, June knew that there was trouble ahead. On the surface her thoughts were of elation and excitement. She was close, so close to the answers to questions that had haunted her for years. But, try as she may she could not escape the raw and ominous thoughts that were increasingly eating at her excitement. Suddenly she became awash in fear, crouched down and sought to identify a place to find some sort of cover from unknown harm. But as she sat crouched in a wide but shallow cleft between two large pieces of granite that had eons ago been one solid piece, she felt helpless. June's mind raced with thoughts. In the pit of her stomach primal fear was wrestling with the logic of her head.

After a few moments June took a deep breath and sighed. She stood. For the moment, she had conquered her fear. Logic had prevailed. She sat on the edge of the slab and scribbled several notations in her journal. As usual, these were cryptic notations, but she had done so often enough that it was easy to code in the information. Coded or not, recording was habit. The consummate scientist side of her family had instilled this practice in her. First observations, impressions and thoughts could never be retrieved. The next best thing was a carefully recorded note that she could refer to later. "Or someone else," was a fleeting thought.

It was growing late when June had completed her entries. She was unprepared to spend the night at this altitude and she had to be back to her base camp near Bench Lake by tomorrow. She must make her way back to Marion Lake where she could again record more thoughts in the journal and her duplicate journal. After noting GPS coordinates in the journal, June began to contour east towards the lake. Always taking stock of everything around her, June knew it would be at least two hours before she got to her camp, by then it would be dark.

* * * *

It was now four weeks later. After squaring things away at her base camp, June planned to return to the site where she had encountered the artifacts. It would probably not be for several days. But she needed to do it soon. The weather patterns were changing. Fall at the high altitudes was already creeping in. If she did not return soon, she could find the area buried in an early Fall snow.

Just the thought of returning made the adrenaline flow. The excitement and anticipation of returning had worked on her mind for days now. But what she would bring to the site on revisit was much more than what she brought to her thoughts during her initial visit. The time since had provided ample opportunity to study evidence, consider hypotheses, and cross reference what she saw with photos, notes, and other evidence in her possession back at base camp and in Lone Pine. June's expectation was that several days in the area would unlock doors to evidence and answers. She could not wait.

Just as these thoughts of excitement rushed through her system, so did the blood of fear. June was aware that she might be walking into her own demise. She was certain that her parents' deaths were the result of similar circumstances involving Paiute artifacts. And, like her father, June sensed the uncertainty of her future and had taken steps to secure her journals and other evidence.

For the true adventurer, walking the line between life and death is always a reality. Without this reality, there would not be exploration. A willingness to walk this line was what separated those willing to venture into the unknown from those who only dreamed of such adventure. June knew there was danger. That she could lose her life, however, was not sufficient thought to deter her from stepping into the unknown. Long ago she came to grips with the fact that her destiny lay somewhere in the environs of the Eastern Sierra. Knowing this, she could only go forward. There was no going back.

With these thoughts on her mind, June was not impressed with the increasing intensity of the wind and the buildup of cumulus clouds over the Sierra. The weather was changing. Within days, especially at the higher elevations, the season could change from Summer, to Fall, to Winter within hours. But June had seen this all before. She had learned to accept what Nature presented. Experience and wise judgment had allowed her to survive Nature's wrath in the past. She could do so again.

The thought that other humans could alter these odds did not enter June's mind.

Chapter 32

Putting the Pieces Together

Somewhere south of the Owens Valley along U.S. Highway 395

June's duplicate journal was a treasure trove of information. It was evident to Sti and Rob that some of the coded information contained in the journal was meant to remain hidden to all except those willing to spend considerable time in the decoding effort. June had not wanted some things to fall into the hands of just anyone. Even her father would have initially had trouble deciphering some of the code. But Matt, like Sti and Rob, was very familiar with the Eastern Sierra and would have made much shorter work of it than an outsider.

The two friends and backpackers had spent considerable time studying the journal before they had a handle on its value. Several detailed areas of the journal remained as yet undeciphered, but Sti and Rob now felt that they had enough background experience with June's travels and theories that breaking the coded messages of the remaining portions of the journal would happen in the days to come. No doubt, some of the details of the yet to be decoded portions of the journal would be critical to their understanding of June Harris during her final summer in the Sierra backcountry.

Drawing on some of the information in the duplicate journal, Sti and Rob had set off to explore some of June's haunts during the final two or three years of her life. After spending more than a week probing some of the references in the duplicate journal, they had spent the previous evening debriefing at the Goodale Creek Campground. Now, as they made the long drive south towards Sti's home in Orange County, they continued to wrestle with their findings.

The process of discussing their findings and conclusions and theories was a delicate one. As with any effort to understand, it is important not to read into evidence meaning that is not really there. As one with a scientific bent to his career, Rob wanted to take a very analytical approach to any discussion. For him it was a matter of linear thinking. On the other hand, Sti tended towards an open systems approach. He did not discount the value of the more closed analytical approach; rather, he liked to consider a more eclectic approach.

As usual, Rob was driving. The midweek traffic was light and they were making good time, albeit with a couple of stops that took far more time than needed because Rob liked to talk. "It is a given, we have to go back to the area where we found June's body. I think we also have to explore the Muro Blanco. Although she did not reveal any specific knowledge of the role of the Muro Blanco in her research, the often repeated references to it suggest she found the canyon tied in with what was happening in the High Route area."

"I concur," was Sti's response. "But don't you think that the real focus has to be the area where we found her body? After all, it seems that the whole reason for the duplicate journal and the sending of that journal to Henry was attributable to the fear she had about her return to the High Route." There was a pause. Rob did not respond because he knew Sti was not done. "We have gone over this several times, but I think we both know that June was drawn back to the High Route because there was something there that provided answers to her questions and those of her father."

Rob chimed in. "Yes, the artifacts she had found earlier were clear evidence that the Paiute of late had been in the High Route area. However, the flour sack she found is not conclusive evidence. While I will grant you that the sack was dateable to the 1800's, its presence on the High Route does not imply real significance. Going back to our discussion last evening, I think that it is a real possibility that the Paiute were stockpiling weapons and supplies for some future event.

However, the High Route just does not make sense. The much lower elevation and accessibility of the Muro Blanco seems more practical for such purposes."

"Hey, you do not need to convince me. The High Route area is not a place to be in the winter, let alone the spring and fall. I do not care what kind of buildings or shelters you build up there; it is not a place to store things or to live. But, again, that was the focus of June's attention and it was enough of a focus that she feared for her own life in returning to the location. It was a fear that appeared to hold true. I am not sure June had any idea about what she would find, but she was drawn to that area between Marion Lake and Windy Ridge because it held answers. Answers, I'm becoming more convinced, that cost her life."

"Let's back up a bit." Rob was organizing his thoughts and paused before going on. "We both agree that June had assembled a body of evidence that pointed to Joaquin Jim and the effort to establish a remote and safe place to accumulate weapons and supplies for a future effort to expel the settlers from the Owens Valley. Agree?"

"Agreed!"

"The evidence suggests that the Paiute, at least a select or small body of Owens Valley Paiute, transported these items up several canyons."

"I agree, and I also agree that some items such as gold, rifles and hand guns, and food supplies were left in some of the cache sites. I do not agree that the cache sites were really all that important. They seem, and I think June would have agreed, to be just stops in route to the place where they were gathering all these things."

"And how do you account for the existence of cache sites in canyons that really provided no easy access to the Muro Blanco or the High Route area?"

"Diversion places, maybe. Maybe places to hide and fight small battles when needed. Or, perhaps they were meant to be temporary camps. If we are talking about a few Paiute, we could conclude that these cache sites allowed them to move about the Eastern Sierra without having to camp in vulnerable places at the lover levels. They may also have been just a way to keep the settlers and soldiers confused so that they could not focus on the most important transportation route."

"You mean the Taboose Pass route." Rob was confirming, not questioning.

"Yes!"

"Then we come back to the stockpiling idea. Joaquin and the Paiute were creating or stockpiling a redoubt. It would be a place they could escape to when things got bad. To do this they would need guns and food supplies."

"And many other things—blankets, storage containers, bowls, baskets, leather, cloth, and fuel."

"And to acquire most of what they needed, except the pottery and baskets, they needed purchasing power which they traditionally lacked. Thus, the purpose of the gold."

"That, of course, is the biggest unanswered question."

Rob commented with a smile. "Ah, yes, the gold source. Clearly, unless it is in one of the sections of her journal that we have not yet been able to decode, I do not think June had any ideas about the origin of the gold. But we both agree that it was the gold that probably is at the root of this whole mystery of June's death."

"Again, I agree. June knew that the death of her father and mother was probably linked to a desire to find the gold on the part of others. She also knew that her own fate was linked to the gold. Her brief journal entries about John Littlebear make it clear that her life was in danger. Like her parents, June was onto something that threatened those who were interested in the gold more than they were interested in the artifacts."

"We have seen one of those chunks of gold. Wouldn't you, if you were of that type, be interested in where the gold came from? Or, in the least, you would be interested in where you could find more of the chunks."

Sti was reflective in his response. "I suppose so. But I have a hard time putting myself in the shoes of a criminal. My love of history and historical evidence is such that I see more value in the artifacts of the Paiute than I do in the gold."

"That's what's wrong with you social scientists. Your social frame of reference does not allow you to understand the warped mind of the criminal. Your sense of value is affective rather than effective. You cannot understand the mind of the criminal or for that matter the linear mind of the scientist." Rob's comment was a dig and not in any way intended to be an important part of the conversation. They both laughed. Whenever they had the chance the two friends would not pass up an opportunity to take a shot at the profession or orientation of the other.

"Touché'," commented Sti. "But it does not make sense that someone wanting the gold, or even the artifacts, would dispose of the lives of Matt, Kathryn or June unless they already knew about the gold. If I wanted to know about the whereabouts of the gold, wouldn't I follow these three in hopes that they would lead me to the gold? I might kill them after they had led me to the gold, but not before."

"Unless, of course, you threatened to expose these people who were following or threatening you." Rob kept thinking along similar lines. "Unless ... Well, let's assume for the minute that you already had many pieces of a puzzle put together. You waited until Matt, and later June, put some of the other critical pieces together, and then you kill them before they can put the final pieces together. That allows you to complete the puzzle without competition."

Sti added. "Or, there were competing criminal elements. Each vying to get to the gold and willing to do whatever was necessary to keep the other party from getting to it first. So, you kill Matt, Kathryn and June as a way to keep the other side from the benefit of the work of these three non-criminals."

Rob offered another alternative. "It could be that June's murder was not committed by the same people that murdered Matt and his wife. Or it could be that they are murdered for different reasons. Perhaps Matt and Kathryn are killed because they would not play someone else's game. Their fate could be the result of a threat that was actually carried out. June's death, on the other hand, could be because she stumbled onto something and thereby posed a threat. I think we both would agree that June knew that others were watching her, and that she feared for her life. I think we would also agree that June really did not know who posed the threat or why."

Sti added, "except for the gold. She had to know the gold was the issue. Someone wanted the gold."

"But I don't think June was about to find a gold mine. I may be wrong, but the High Route and Muro Blanco areas are not where one would find a gold mine. I could understand her posing a threat to someone who had an illegal gold mine in a National Park. I just can't see that explanation. Can you?"

"No! This whole case has been outside the ordinary. So, I agree with a caveat. The gold is tied into this whole affair. Whoever it was that killed June, they must have seen her as a threat to their efforts to find or access the Paiute gold. I doubt it was a mine, but it could have been a gold stockpile or information that would lead to the source of the gold. Boy, I hope we are not going out on a limb with these conjectures."

"I don't think so. Everything we have just discussed is compatible with the information in June's journal."

They sat there as the miles went by. From time to time there was vigorous discourse filled with theories and ideas. Equal lengths of time and miles were filled with quiet as each pondered possibilities. For the observer this may have seemed to be a pointless exercise—conjecture, theory, hypotheses, and what ifs. For Sti and Rob it was the usual pattern. It was a methodology employed many times in their travels together. Backpacking, off-road exploring, wandering and roaming, day hikes, poking around wilderness environments and exploring unknown places, such adventure requires communication that considers all possibilities. Such communication is not the result of indecision or fear or confusion. It is the result of minds that seek understanding. What one observes may be clear on the surface. But the unknown, the uninhabited wilderness, often holds secrets not at first seen. If those involved are willing to pose competing points of view and engage in subsequent debate, there is a greater chance for more complete understanding.

Rob broke the silence. "We know that June had narrowed her focus to the High Route and Muro Blanco. This focus centered not on the issue of trade but rather on the issue of building a redoubt that included weapons, supplies and gold. We know she believed that Joaquin Jim was involved. We also know that she believed that the Paiute had a source of gold that was financing this operation. And finally, we know that she was returning to the High Route in a state of fear for her life."

Sti attempted to continue this line of thinking. "June feared for her life because of three factors—the death of her parents under similar circumstances, what Littlebear had said and because she had known for some time that she was being followed. Don't you also think that what may have concerned June the most was her previous experience on the High Route when she found the artifacts, shoe prints, and strange lines on the ground? Could it be that something in the journal that we have not yet deciphered holds the key? If I recall, there are a couple pages of information in the journal that were entered by June after she returned from the High Route and before she mailed the journal to Kubota. I have to believe that June spent considerable time pondering her experience on the High Route and speculating on what she saw."

"You know…." Rob was trying to tie pieces of information together. "You know, as we were studying the journal before we left, June had made some notations about the Sierra Club outing of 1935. I think she made a notation that she had found a shoe, I think the wording was 'moccasin/shoe' that would have been worn by a Paiute in the 1920's and 1930's. This was found along with other artifacts including straps that would be used by packers in the 1930's. As I recall, she did not speculate on the importance of these items. She just listed them. It seems odd that she would not comment more on the Paiute shoe. What did it suggest? She did not say. Could it be that later she sat down and analyzed what she had experienced, what she had found, on the High Route? Or are we making more out of this than the evidence and journal suggest?"

"I think you may be on to something. What if the notes recorded on the High Route are minimal? What if they are just notes that were to be used later? Perhaps, once she had returned to her base camp, she had the chance to sit down and reflect on her experience and analyze her notes. Could it be that on consideration of the evidence June developed some conclusions that startled her? Maybe it was in this time of reflective and analytical thinking that June realized something that changed her level of concern or understanding of the evidence."

Rob sensed where Sti was going with his thoughts. "And this new understanding changed her approach to finding answers. Or, and this may be a better way to say it, her new understanding increased what was at stake. June Harris had stumbled onto something that so scared her that she went to great lengths to put things in place should she not return from another trip to the High Route that she knew she had to make."

"So, she does everything to make sure that if she does not return, those who kill her cannot access what she knows. You know, you may have pegged it. The final portion of the parallel journal that we have not yet decoded could very well provide some critical information or clues. The journal begins to change to reflect the degree of concern developing in response to her High Route experience. I wonder if June also put things in place to insure that if she was the victim of foul play, there would be a greater chance that the perpetrators would be caught."

It is funny how pursuit of a line of thinking triggers other thoughts. It is like playing charades. You are being bombarded with stimulation in the form of symbols and you must make sense out of it all. In trying to do so things jump into your mind unexpectedly. Suddenly disparate pieces come together. Sometimes, just as quickly, thoughts that occur to you disappear and you try desperately to retrieve them before they are lost forever. But always, you are trying to make sense of the symbols. Somebody is trying desperately to tell you something. You are trying just as desperately to hear what they are saying. When this happens, your mind races through information and ideas come to you. Some ideas are easily cast aside. Other ideas are possibilities, but are not exactly what you hear. And then, sometimes the light goes on, and you understand the symbols even though you do not really realize how it is that this understanding came about. When this happens, there is excitement, elation, and a sense of accomplishment.

"I've got it. I think…."

"Got what?" asked Sti.

"The final piece of the code. You said 'degree.' It just might…." There was a long pause.

"Rob! Give me a break. Spit it out!"

"The coded longitude and latitude."

"OK."

"Remember the coding of the coordinates when she referenced the High Route late in the journal?"

"Yeah, yeah. I remember. The coding changed and we could not figure it out because the data looked incorrect when we compared it to topographic map coordinates."

"No! We were not completely wrong in our interpretation of the coordinates. It was a matter of degrees."

"Go on."

"What if she knew that what she had found was so compelling that her usual method of coding the coordinates would not due? So, for matters involving the High Route, she changed her coding format. In the place where she would normally code in the list of artifacts found, she coded in her longitude and latitude data. She simply added or subtracted degrees equal to 16. It makes sense. In the Sierra true north is about 16 degrees from magnetic north. Anyone who knows this makes adjustments when using a topographic map and a compass. She knew that those she feared probably would not make sense of this. What do you think?"

"Give me a break. You have been thinking hard. You rang the bell again. You can record information about a place, but such information is of little value to someone else unless that someone knows where to go to find meaning to the information. Really, what June was saying to anyone who might get a hold of her Journal was 'You do not know what I know. You only know part of the information. You do not know the critical piece because you only think you know how to translate my code. As long as that is the case, you can not win this game. And what I know begins at a certain location. And you will not find it.' I think we had best focus our attention on decoding the last portion of the journal. It may take some time, but we cannot go back to the High Route until we have done that."

* * * *

Later

The last portion of June's Journal contained two key topics. Their investigation to date indicated that significant attention was focused on the importance of the High Route. Clearly, June's death in this area and the research she put into investigation of the area made translation of the journal code a priority. Sti and Rob also knew that interpreting this portion of the Journal would reveal additional information about the link between the High Route and the Muro Blanco. Of this they were certain. But if they were certain about what they expected to find regarding the High Route and the Muro Blanco, they were equally uncertain about what they would find regarding the other key topic, the origin of the gold chunks.

Since their first reading of the parallel journal, the two friends had become convinced that June invested considerable time in trying to locate the source of the gold. As yet, they had no inkling about how to decode this portion of the journal. Suffice it to say that they really did not know whether the information contained in this part of the journal was conclusive. However, they sensed that the unique quality of the coding, and their inability to interpret it, suggested its importance.

On the drive south along U. S. 395, Sti and Rob wrestled with their interpretation of June's notes regarding the High Route and the Muro Blanco. They were destined to return to this area and they were eager to conclude their translation of this portion of the journal. Regarding the gold, it was a subject they left alone. They knew that if they allowed themselves to start discussing the possible origins of the gold, they would only experience frustration and anxiety.

It was an interesting dilemma. They knew that they would eventually have to spend considerable time trying to understand June's notes regarding the possible origins of the gold. They also knew that when they did tackle this task, it would consume them. It seemed that gold had a way of changing people. Even though Sti and Rob were not looking to benefit from knowing the origin of the gold, the gold somehow cast a spell on their endeavors. It was a little like Robert W. Service's poem about Sam Magee, "... but the land of gold seemed to hold him like a spell." People do strange things in pursuit of gold. They will endure the harshest of conditions. They will risk their life. They will go to the ends of the Earth. They will betray friends. They will kill.

Sti and Rob knew that the Paiute gold was at the heart of their search for answers to questions about June's death. All things led to the conclusion that June's death was tied to the gold. It was equally reasonable to assume that the death of June's parents and the threats to her grandfather were also somehow attributable to the gold. They could only hope that they would be fortunate enough to find this connection. Only then could they and Juan Batista sell the authorities on the idea that three deaths were not accidents.

CHAPTER 33

RETURN TO THE HIGH ROUTE

Approaching the discovery site again

Revisiting the site of June's death was a necessity, but nonetheless a welcome outing. Where else does one go but back to the beginning when a puzzle is a mystery. For Sti and Rob the evidence kept suggesting that the solution to understanding June's death was somehow associated with the site of the crime. They knew that June had returned to the High Route completely aware that her life was in jeopardy. Moreover, they thought they knew, from a decoding of her parallel journal, the coordinates of June's search area location when she was last on the High Route. They had spent considerable time trying to understand all the notes in June's journal regarding her past experiences on the High Route and her plans to return. But the final part of the journal had proved very difficult to decipher. Clearly, June had not wanted just anyone to figure it out unless they were willing to commit considerable time to doing so. In the end, Sti and Rob sensed that June had intended that whoever was to try and translate her encrypted message would have to do so only after developing a thorough understanding of the High Route as June had known it. Thus, the two experienced backpackers, and amateur investigators, had to return to the scene of the crime.

They were really not sure what they were looking for. They would go back to the spot where they found June's body. They would search the area for artifacts. They would also try to wander the entire area north of Cirque Crest between Windy Ridge to the West and Marion Lake to the East. This is the portion of the High Route they thought most likely to be associated with whatever it was they were looking for. Also, this is the area where the 1935 Sierra Club outing lost the mule. The link between these two elements was unknown, but Rob and Sti sensed they would somehow find the link. Based on what they thought were the coordinates, they would return to the place that June had allegedly found several artifacts including Paiute footwear and articles from the 1935 Sierra Club outing. From that point on they could only hope that their search would reveal information that would unlock the final portions of June's journal.

The High Route, like much of the alpine Sierra, is not an easy area to wander. If the weather is not cooperative it could be impossible. They could only hope for good weather. It was also a very rugged region of the Sierra. The ruggedness can easily mask reality. One could literally be standing next to something important and not notice it. The idea that their search would turn up anything was a long, but necessary shot.

In addition, the trip would include exploration of the Muro Blanco. June's journal included considerable information about her search of this remote canyon.

Like the High Route, the Muro Blanco is rugged, remote, and not easily understood. Although much lower in elevation, the Muro Blanco, cut by the westward flow of the South Fork of the Kings River, is a challenge for even the most experienced backpacker. So rugged is it that there is no trail through this long canyon. Those who venture into the canyon do so knowing that the going will be slow, tedious, and exhausting. One does not easily wander through the Muro Blanco. If it is a normal summer, the water in the river is running hard and full. Crossing the river back and forth is not easy. So travel on one side is usually the norm. This limits the traveler's options and ensures that all attention will be on route finding. The canyon is long and there are few places to make camp. For those passing through it is a bushwhack at best if you remain low in the canyon. If you go higher, where the upward slope of the canyon floor meets the canyon walls, the going is almost impossible and you are constantly forced lower. The idea that you will have time to look around and investigate the nooks and crannies of the canyon is not reasonable. Sti and Rob had been down the Muro Blanco before. At the conclusion, they said never again. But, one never knows. In the case of the Muro Blanco, they had even less of an idea about what they were looking for than they did about the High Route.

One quality of the Muro Blanco is that it was a logical route for Indians moving across the Sierra. Perhaps there remains evidence of their passing. It has been said that very late in the summer, or in a summer following a very poor snowfall in the winter, the passing is much easier because the river is so low in volume that one can actually use the river as a route. Although plausible, Sti and Rob knew that this was not likely to be the case for most summers, even if one went down the Muro Blanco late in the summer.

No matter the reason, Sti and Rob always looked forward to a trip into the backcountry of what John Muir called the Range of Light. But, unlike the homicide detective who can jump in a car and make a journey back to the scene of a crime in short order, a return to the High Route required some planning and an adequate block of time, preferably in the mid to late summer.

The trip could be done in five days, three days to hike in and two long days back to the trailhead. However, on this occasion it would not be a rush trip. The mixture of the fun of backpacking and investigation resulted in a trip that would take nine days.

There was, however, one major difference between this outing and the many others the two had taken together over the years. Planning for the trip took on a certain air of paranoia. Sti and Rob began to feel that if Matt, Matt's wife Kathryn, and June had been the victims of foul play at the hands of those also interested in the Paiute cashes, then at some point those responsible would become aware that there were two new players. Sti and Rob were not interested in raising the suspicion or ire of those capable of murder. To insure that the odds were more in their favor, the two took certain precautions while preparing for the trip.

Gambling that there was greater safety in numbers, Sti and Rob decided to invite two additional people to accompany them on the trip. Both Phil, Sti's cousin, and Ron, Sti's brother, had been on previous trips with them. The only challenge here was to convince Phil and Ron to join the trip on short notice.

However, the expected challenge proved to be nonexistent. Both were eager to participate.

There were other advantages to having Phil and Ron along. If it was necessary to search for anything, eight eyes were far better than four. Also, Phil was a prolific photographer. If you needed something photographed, Phil was your man. He would capture it from many angles. Ron provided the advantage of having someone else exceptionally familiar with the region. He and Sti grew up backpacking. The art of investigating is really the art of knowing what questions to ask. Ron's experience, and neutrality on matters surrounding the Harris family, would provide an uncluttered perspective on things.

However, Sti and Rob had no intentions of telling Phil and Ron about the total purpose of the trip until the trip had started. This would not be a problem because Sti was always the one who planned and set up the trips.

A second precaution involved obtaining the permit on the day before they set off from the trailhead. If anyone wanted to really monitor who was nosing around the Marion Peak area of the High Route or the Muro Blanco, knowing who was taking out backpacking permits would be a good way to do that. Sti and Rob had no doubts that the Forest Service did not give out this information. However, corrupt people find ways to acquire needed information, and the Forest Service was not immune to their influence. So, they would take out the permit and provide as little information about the projected route.

Another precaution was to have their wives relocate while they were gone. They would stay at Rob's place in Colorado. They were not happy about all of this, but they were assured there was no problem. Surely, the four were not about to do anything stupid. At least that was the plan.

Sti and Rob also typed a very detailed itinerary of their planned trip (this was a first). They would leave it with their wives and with Antonio Juan Batista. A highlighted map accompanied the written description. They purposefully did not tell Matthew Harris.

As for the trailhead, they did not intend to leave their vehicle unattended there. Rob had a friend in Bishop. They left their vehicles in Bishop and Rob's friend took the four to the trailhead.

Finally, and this was something Sti and Rob had never done, they took a cell phone with them. The uncertainty of what to expect, and the need to alleviate any concern on the part of their wives necessitated this action. The cell phone would not work in most situations. But it would work from a peak or ridge that had a line of sight with the Owens Valley. Also, they took two powerful and compact binoculars, also a first.

* * * *

The hike in was uneventful. As usual, the first day was a grind, but the weather was very cooperative. The clouds tended to keep it cooler. One could only hope that the clouds were not a sign of impending change for the worse in the weather.

The second day they made only a cursory exploration of the Muro Blanco. If they found nothing along the High Route, they could easily return to more closely investigate the Muro Blanco on their return trip. The canyon runs for many miles. However, they probed only about a two-mile segment to a point just below and north east of Arrow Peak. This was an exhausting day, and they discovered nothing. But this was not an unexpected outcome. The real goal was two days of hiking away. The straight-line distance on a topographic map was only about three miles. But trails in the Sierra are not straight. They follow contours. The route was many miles with considerable altitude gain over terrain that was mostly cross-country.

* * * *

On the third day Rob, Sti, Ron and Phil crossed through Cartridge Pass. This was very familiar territory to Sti, Ron and Rob. But the pass was a special reminder to Rob and Sti. They had entered the High Route from this point and exited it by reversing their entrance four days latter, after finding June's body.

Rob was thinking that he hoped they had not made an error in judgment by bringing Phil and Ron along. It was in the evening of the first day that they told Phil and Ron that the purpose of the trip was much more than just a return to the place where they located June's skeletal remains. It was about trying to find evidence that would provide some insight into the reasons for her death. With that introduction, they told Phil and Ron the details of their investigation to this point. Ron's response was "Alright!" Phil was more subdued in his response. An attorney, Phil was thinking of the implications rather than the purpose. Nevertheless, here they were, about to reach Marion Lake. Tomorrow they would be back where it all began. What would they find? Perhaps they would find nothing. Perhaps they would find more than they bargained for. Oh well, too late now.

* * * *

They approached carefully and quietly. It was not hard to find. Although they had brought photos and their GPS unit, these were not necessary. The route was just as they remembered it. As if on a solemn mission, there was reverence in their approach. And then they were there.

Phil and Ron were given a description of how the body was first noticed, the position of the body, and the location of several items. Included was a description of the ice axe and how it was positioned when they found it.

When the Park Service and Sheriff's department investigated the site they picked up every visible artifact that was not a native element. In the time since they had been here, however, the rain, wind and snow had exposed some new items. There was not much. Sti and Rob looked closely at these items. They found the same kinds of things they had before—a mixture of artifacts from contemporary cloth and rubber to older items from earlier in the twentieth century such as old style canvas. They also found a sizeable piece of leather. It was not the thick and rugged type of leather associated with more recently made things but old animal leather like that perhaps used by Native Americans. But one could really not be certain. It could just as easily be leather from the tack of a packer. Together these were not significant items.

Rob got out his GPS unit and triangulated the location of June's body with their translation of the coordinates noted in June's journal. If their translation was correct, the location of June's discovery of several items on her next to last trip to the High Route was about a mile and a half north and west of where they were. This was an approximation; there was plenty of room for error. It was not clear whether June had used a GPS to identify the coordinates or had estimated the coordinates using a topographic map. However, despite this uncertainty, Rob and Sti sensed that somewhere, not to far from where they were standing, were answers to the mystery.

Sti and Rob decided to hold off trying to verify the accuracy of June's parallel journal coordinates. Instead, they decided to expand the search area around June's body a little. They would fan-out. Search the immediate area in an ever expanding ring.

"What are we looking for?" asked Ron.

"Anything that is man made or not natural to the area. Anything! Anything you were not expecting to find."

After looking around for about an hour, they stopped and had something to eat. Conversation gravitated to June Harris and speculations about her demise. Now that they had seen the actual site along with the photos Sti and Rob had taken during their previous trip, Ron and Phil had a better understanding of the mystery. The High Route certainly did not qualify as a place where murder was likely. Not only was it remote, but the area where they were searching was vast. It was also a very difficult place to search. There was absolutely nothing that could make it easy.

Later they wandered some more. The weather was changing and it looked like they could have rain. This was not a good sign. One would not want to be caught here if it rained hard or if the rain turned to snow. If the latter turn of events took place, it would also be very cold. It would be just like it was when June Harris came here for the last time.

Suddenly Phil and Rob yelled. They had found something.

Rob and Phil had been walking and talking while scanning the ground for anything that caught their eye. Then Phil saw it, the corner of a piece of cloth. It was more than that; it was the corner of two pieces of cloth sewn together. It was the remnant of a sack. It wasn't much, just a corner piece. But it was quickly evident to Rob. It was the kind of cloth sack that he and Sti had seen before in June's collection of items at the Harris residence. At one time it had held flour or grain. When Sti and Ron arrived, Rob probed it with his hiking stick. Indeed, it was very weathered and buried superficially. When they pulled it from the ground, a piece of leather strap was revealed. Ron pulled out the twelve-inch remains of a halter, the kind one would use with a horse or perhaps with a pack mule. Sti and Rob were thinking the same thing. Could this be what was left of the mule that had run off in 1935?

The discovery caused the four to search some more. They did not find any additional items, but did mark the spot where they found the flour sack and piece of leather. Visually they sited along a line connecting this location with that of June's body. Did the line suggest anything? Initially it appeared that it lined up well with what Sti and Rob believed were the coordinates noted in June's journal. This was a good sign, but Rob and Sti wanted to approach this search deliberately and with caution. They did not have time to go back over an area. They would work steadily in the direction they thought held more information, but they would do so without haste. So they continued to search.

The discovery of the two remnants spurred the four to search hard. However, the temperature was dropping quickly and the cloud cover suggested they needed to retreat back to their campsite at Marion Lake. They marked the spots where they discontinued their search. Then they made their way back towards their camp several miles away.

That evening the four backpackers discussed any number of things regarding June—the High Route, the artifacts they had found, and what they should do the next day. The general consensus was that they would start early and pick up where they had ended the day's search. They would work their way over to June's journal coordinates. Along the way they would keep their eyes open for anything. If June had gone back to the coordinates on her last visit, then the line between these coordinates and the location of the body could be important for finding evidence.

As it got late they realized that although it was cold and drizzly, it probably would not rain. They turned in about 9.00 p.m.

Two hours later they were awakened by the sound of a helicopter. It was obviously a large one and it was moving from West to East at an altitude that could not be too far above their location. The discussion between the two tents noted that all four had heard the chopper and there was general wonder about its destination. A quick glance outside by Ron revealed nothing. There was only the fading sound. Like the sound of the chopper, the conversation quickly faded and they were all soon asleep.

* * * *

The fifth day was very overcast, excessively cold and drizzly. It was classic alpine weather in the higher Sierra. It was a day to make sure that one consumed considerable carbohydrates before venturing very far. It was also a day to be prepared for any kind of weather. All four had spent considerable time in such conditions, so it was not a deterrent to their efforts. Steadily, but not hastily, they made their way back over the rugged terrain to the location of the previous day's activities. There was not much discussion, just an occasional comment or suggestion about what they should or should not do. The more they gained altitude, the lower the cloud ceiling. The peaks to their left and ahead were all lost in the low clouds. There was a cold breeze, the air was damp, and all the surfaces about them were damp. One had to be careful not to slip on wet rocks and alpine tufts of grass.

It had been agreed the night before that they would expand their area of search. They would spend the day looking for any new artifacts or evidence that may be connected with June Harris. Weather permitting; they would spend the entire day in the area. For no other reason than a hunch they would focus their attention on working down slope from where June's body was discovered and in the direction of the line suggested by the previous day's finds and June's coordinates. From the perspective of logic, anything up-slope was very exposed. It was not the kind of environment conducive to any sort of extended stay. However the terrain down-slope harbored greater variety and the possibility of greater interest. Of course, such logic only sounded good. The reality was that the area was so rugged that applying restraint to expectations was the best way to approach things.

Meandering and looking is a silent activity. To those disposed to this type of activity, it is of necessity a solitary endeavor. For four backpackers who sought the solitude of the backcountry, this portion of the High Route had much to offer. To some it might appear to be a place where the granite, raw, tundra like atmosphere is relentless and sterile. To Sti, Phil, Rob and Ron, it was quite the opposite. None really knew what he was looking for, but the feeling was of no concern. To an outsider, they would look to be wandering, searching, and occasionally stopping to stare at something. But above all, they would look to be content. Their actions were deliberate, coordinated, and unhurried. They were wandering with purpose.

They had been at it about twenty minutes when Ron raised his voice to draw Phil's attention.

"Find anything?" Phil noticed that Ron was in a crouching position, poking at the ground.

Ron's response was uncertain. "Maybe. Take a look."

As the others gathered, Ron made his point. "This looks like part of a tennis shoe print. It is not from our boots, and I don't think it was here yesterday. I have checked down that way," he was pointing down slope, "and I think whoever it was walked up this way and then back that way." Pointing to clarify what he was saying, he pointed up hill. "They walked up that way, how far I don't know, and then they walked back down, retracing their path." He made a special point to finish by stating his conclusions. "I followed these prints uphill a good distance to where we were walking yesterday. I do not believe these prints were here then. At least they were not here when we left." With that statement, all four began to look in all directions. Their reaction was instinctive. Was someone watching them now?

As the four began to wander around looking for more evidence, Rob glanced uphill and began to follow the direction Ron had pointed out. After several minutes, he returned. "You are right Ron. Up there about 200 yards is a tennis shoe print over the top of one of our boot prints from yesterday."

The attention of all four was riveted on the prints as well as on the situation. Ron's discovery was like a slap in the face. They instantly went from nondescript wanderers to being a captive audience. In a matter of seconds their outing ceased to be a game. They all knew their situation had been changed. Someone was here or had been here. Their presence had upped the ante in the game. Suddenly they found themselves conscious of all about, and they looked in all directions as if such searching would clear things up. None said a word. They listened and searched near and far. Each was seeking answers to the same questions. Whose prints are these? What are they doing here? How long ago were these prints made? Where did they come from and where did they go?

Then, without extended conversation they began to follow the prints down slope. They would follow the direction suggested by the toe of a single print, searching for the next imprint. This was difficult because the area was not all sand or soil. Much of the area showed no signs of any footprints. Occasionally one would find a print and summons the others and they would continue on until the trail ran out. Then they would search for the next sign of a print. And so it went for a couple of hours. It was tedious work. The wandered from side to side, retraced their prints, and searched again. They would locate a print or a partial print—sometimes only a small portion of a print—and then nothing for 10 or 15 minutes. Whoever it was that left the prints had tried to stay on the rock and away from the soil or decomposed granite. But this could not be done consistently, and prints were left behind to be discovered by the four.

Individually, and as a group, they began to see that the terrain was changing. It was undulating. It was not rolling; it became more an undulating of ridges of broken granite slabs separated by troughs of decomposed granite and/or wet tundra-like turf. The entire area was like a labyrinth of shallow gullies, fractured and polished granite slabs. To those unfamiliar with this terrain, it could be likened to a huge parking lot that ran for miles in all directions. The lot would have small cars, trucks, cargo trucks, and huge semi rigs. No matter where one stood, one could not really see all the vehicles, nor could one see the spaces between vehicles. To search the parking lot, one had to walk between all the vehicles.

Rob, Ron, Phil and Sti were searching a very rugged terrain. The view in any direction could be deceptive. As so often happened in the Sierra, two people could be twenty-five yards apart and have no idea of the whereabouts of the other person. Like a deep bunker at Saint Andrews golf course in Scotland, it was just deep enough to prevent you from seeing over the edge. This was disconcerting. All of this made for very slow going.

While all were searching, they were nagged by questions about whose prints they were following. They were also anxious about the fact that they had no knowledge about what lay ahead. The unknown is always unsettling.

And then the prints just disappeared.

At one point, all four got on top of what appeared to be an exceptionally large slab of granite near them, and turned and sighted up slope towards where June's body had been. They sought to see the line that included the route they had followed in tracking the prints. They sought to note where it was they had found the artifacts from the day before. It appeared to the four that it was all in a relative straight line. They turned down slope and tried to estimate where June's coordinates fit into this linear route finding. It appeared that the route to the coordinates was a continuation of the linear route they had been following earlier.

The four friends and backpackers paused long enough to allow the implications of their situation to raise questions. But such thinking did not change things. They knew which direction they had to go. However, their reflection also suggested caution and they proceeded cognizant that they must remain alert while at the same time continuing to search their way along.

* * * *

It took some time, and their route turned out to be less linear than anticipated. Dodging the rigors posed by the terrain enforced a circuitous route on them. With responsibility for monitoring his GPS and determining direction of travel, Rob got all four to the place he and Sti believed were the coordinates noted in June's journal. At least he said that they were within a 100 feet of the location.

Ron, Phil, Sti and Rob began the task of looking around. As before, they had no ideas about what it was they were looking for exactly. However, they had no doubt that whatever it was they sought, it would only reveal itself if they looked.

There was nothing. They kept looking. Rob rechecked his GPS unit. They were in the area where they should be if they had correctly decoded June's coordinate data. They wandered and searched more. Still, they had found nothing.

Although certain of their location, Sti and Rob began to question whether they had accurately decoded June's information. Perhaps the coordinates were meant to throw someone off so that they would not find her actual location. This was a possibility, except for one factor. The line between where they were and where June's body and the artifacts were located appeared to be accurate and reasonable. The four were now taking a break as they discussed their options when Rob spoke.

"What if we extend this linear route farther down slope and searched along the way?" It was now about noon. The weather seemed to be cooperating. They probably had about four more hours of search time before they had to return to Marion Lake. Rob's idea was logical, and the timing reasonable.

As Rob and Phil stood on the highest point of their current location and tried to site across the landscape, what appeared logical in concept soon appeared questionable in fact. This was not a steady slope. In fact, the slope that they had been following for some time and distance had really lost little elevation. What remained ahead appeared the same in that regard. However, what appeared ahead of them was anything but an easy hike. In fact, the closer they looked the more they realized that it was very broken terrain. Large granite slabs and blocks dominated the immediate horizon. Where they were standing was relatively flat. Where they were headed looked to have no flat spots. They would be making their way through a maze of broken rock and talus. The going was about to become much more difficult.

After some discussion about how best to proceed, they got underway. It was quickly evident that making forward progress was a route finding nightmare. Deep depressions between large slabs and broken rock made looking ahead difficult. Maintaining a straight line of travel was next to impossible without reference points. They stopped after about 50 yards of travel. To move forward with confidence they needed to ensure their linear route.

"Ron and I will go back to the high slab where we sited up hill and build a trail duck." A trail duck is made by stacking three or four good size rocks on top of each other to create a marker visible from a distance. The name 'trail duck' is suggested by the fact that from a distance the stacked rocks can take on the appearance of a sitting duck. "If we make it large enough it will serve to enhance our ability to determine a straight line between where we are and the location of the duck and where we know June's body to have been." Sti and Rob agreed and waited. A half-hour later, the four continued to move forward.

Not only was the route finding challenging, but also searching the ground at the same time was very difficult. Something, an artifact of almost any kind, could be in plain sight and be missed. What compounded this search even more was the fact that they could not really fan out. Passage routes were often narrowed or impossible, thus forcing them in a different direction until they could find a way around and back on their line of travel. To the extent possible, they tried to search the landscape all along the way, but it was not easy. Their progress was slow.

They had gone about a third of a mile when one of them found a wrapper from a piece of gum. The tin foil wrapper does not easily decay and it caught Phil's eye. It could have been blown to this location. That is what they wanted to believe. Still, it could have just as easy have been dropped by someone. If that were the case, it had to have been recently. Had it been here weeks, months or years? It was not likely to have come from June. In any event, it was on their hypothetical line of travel. In that sense it was confirmatory. Somehow this small silver wrapper was telling them to continue.

The landscape was fascinating. It would be easy to get lost in this alpine maze if it were not for the peaks as references and the ability to mount high points and spot other references. But even to these seasoned backpackers, forward progress in a relative straight line was difficult and very time consuming. It was a process of walking, searching, and constant checking the line of travel. Circling to the left, and then to the right, retracing footsteps, checking around a corner and returning, and hand and foot ascending and descending were the norm for this route. It was tedious progress.

Soon each was thinking the same thing. How far is far enough? How far should they go before admitting they were heading in the wrong direction and decide to turn around.

Then three of the group realized Ron had stopped. "This is strange," said Ron.

The others turned and moved in Ron's direction.

Phil responded first. "Something has happened here."

Soon all four were starring at the signs of an altered landscape. All now saw the tell-tail signs of impressions in the tundra-like soil where stones had been removed. In the Sierra alpine environment the broken talus and boulders become set in the tundra-like soil over time. The tufts of grass grow up and around these rocks. Each year's growth eventually dies and adds another layer of spongy matting to the soil, and the result is a gradual grasping of the rock by the surrounding soil. When at a later date the rock is pried, and usually not easily, out of the ground, it leaves an impression that often takes many years to disappear.

"Someone has removed sizeable rocks from here sometime in recent years. Tough to say how many years, but they have taken the rocks that were here to another location," said Ron.

As the four looked around, they found other evidence. Also, they noticed that any rocks that would normally be lying around on top of the large slabs or among broken talus and decomposed granite had also been removed. Sti voiced what they all were thinking. "You do not go to all that work to remove rocks to another location unless you are building a fire ring or something else. I doubt it was a fire ring since there is no wood up here to burn, unless of course you bring it here from far below. Maybe it was something else. Let's keep looking."

Shortly, all four began to notice that they were entering an isolated area where the ground had been made relatively flat by the placement of thousands of flat and small rocks—pieces of granite about six to twelve inches in diameter. As they stood looking at what was before them, it was clear that the area in which they were standing was probably an anomaly in the surrounding area. It was a spot with a large flat slab of granite surrounded by decomposed granite and tundra. Through the use of the rocks brought to the location and carefully placed, someone had been able to create a large, relatively flat surface that was very much out of character with its surroundings.

"What the ...," Rob was starting a reactive sentence when they all glanced in the direction he was looking and saw the same thing. Fuel drums, several of them, were lined up side by side along one side of the flattened area. They were old khaki colored five-gallon military-like fuel containers. And then they began to notice several other items. There were some old hoses, a couple of empty plastic milk bottle containers, and two large sledgehammers.

Standing near the center of the flattened area Phil was staring at the ground. He was probably thinking something similar to the thoughts of the others when he said, "This is a helicopter landing site. Look around; there is plenty of room for a helicopter to land. If you knew where you were going, and if you had good weather, you could drop right into this spot."

"Even if it was dark you could do it with the assistance of this box of flares," commented Rob as he pointed to a case near him.

Sti was crouching down, looking at the rocks below and running his fingers across several of them. "You can see where the metal of the helicopter landing gear has scraped against these rocks as it settled down." Nothing more was said as the other three ambled over. Then another comment by Sti, "Someone went to a great effort to build this spot. It has been here some time, although rocks have been added from time to time. I wonder …"

"You wonder about this spot and that helicopter we heard last night," said Rob. "Was it coming or going? I seem to recall it was headed east. I think the weather was too unsettled to have tried to fly into this spot last night."

Now they all began to circle the site looking for more information. They found it in the form of trash, some plastic engine oil containers, and several large earth colored plastic tarps folded and stacked with a large rock to hold them down. They also found a large piece of white plastic strips 3 feet in width. "A landing cross commented Rob. You place this in a large cross pattern at the center of this flat area to serve as a reference point for the pilot landing a helicopter."

After some time as they wandered around, Phil spoke. "You do not go to this trouble unless there is something else nearby. I think we need to photograph this and then search in a wider area."

* * * *

It had not taken them long to find the 'something' they were looking for. Trash and other items led the way. All four were standing looking at a site that was both startling and exciting. They were looking at a very large depression in the landscape. The depression sloped down about 50 yards to what appeared to be the entrance to a cave or mine. The initial opening was large but went back only 40 or 50 feet. It really looked like a big amphitheater. It had sort of a Hollywood Bowl look to it.

"Holy cow, will you look at that," mumbled one of the four.

Was this what they were searching for? They looked around. Mining implements, some sealed boxes of who knew what, and a couple of old backpacks were stacked on a rock bench. A small portable Coleman stove sat on a rock shelf with two accompanying lanterns beside it. There were a number of cooking and eating items in the area along with a can of white gas. All of this and most of the other items were covered by camouflage tarps that blended with the granite.

All four poked around. Each uncovered several items which were brought to the attention of the others.

After looking around a while, they decided to stop and have some lunch and talk about things. While they did so Sti climbed through the large slabs and boulders that made up the landscape above and in front of the amphitheater. After exploring a while he returned. "Amazing! Unless you knew exactly where this spot was or you just stumbled across it, you would never know it was here. It is truly hidden."

Rob raised the logical question. "But is it a cave? Is it a mine? Or was someone just beginning to dig?"

"It could have been either of those—a cave or mine." Ron lived in the Lake Tahoe area and had spent considerable time hiking and climbing about the mining areas on the western slope of the northern Sierra Nevada where the gold rush had greatly altered much of the landscape some 150 years earlier. "What is important is what has happened. It looks to me like this may have been a mine or cave that collapsed. It is hard to say when. All of this debris and the effects of weather over time make it difficult to know. So, I don't know if the people who came here with the helicopter were miners trying to reopen a mine after a cave in or if they were trying to reopen a cave following a cave in. You can tell by the work that has been done that who ever it was tried to clear out the debris of the cave in. In fact, I would be willing to speculate that the actual original opening was closer to us and the ceiling collapsed. Whoever have been working at this has been doing so for some time. There is no evidence of blasting. There is evidence that much debris was cleared away over a long period of time. I suspect that the large helicopter landing area was created in large part from much of the debris."

* * * *

Later that afternoon they found what they suspected had always been there. The discovered a large box filled with Paiute artifacts. There were arrowheads, knives, pottery bowls, small and large baskets, what looked to be weathered pieces of clothing, and several shredded moccasins. There was also a pair of more recent footwear that matched the description of the moccasin type shoe described in June's journal. On the one hand the pair looked like shoes on the bottom but the uppers were clearly reminiscent of moccasins. There were numerous pottery shards, undeterminable instruments, and numerous small identifiable items. If these items made their way up here on their own, then the evidence was clear that the Paiute had been here off and on for many years or even decades. By any standard this was a prime collection of Native American artifacts. Of special interest were the many conical baskets that would have been used to transport a considerable supply of food, weapons, and other items from the Owens Valley to this remote and hostile location.

The box also contained numerous items that must have originated from the 1935 Sierra Club outing. These latter items included leather straps, rope, splintered pack outfit box, a halter, and very weathered pieces of canvas. Also among these items were several old flour sacks. Whoever had put these in the box must have thought they went with the items from 1935. However, to Sti and Rob, these were clearly flour sacks brought into the area by the Paiute. It was almost ironical. Flour sacks, like the trail of crumbs left by Hansel and Gretel, seemed to mark the trail throughout the investigations conducted by June and also by Sti and Rob.

A large piece of plastic coated nylon tarp covered with camouflage was lifted to reveal a pile of very old rifles, handguns, knives and ammunition. All were very rusted and no longer useable except as collector items. All total, there must have been forty or fifty firearms. Their age suggested that the Paiute must have been responsible for bringing these weapons here.

It was a fascinating scene. Here they were deep in the most remote reaches of the Sierra Nevada. It was a place where the modern backpacker passed through and did not stay for long. This was the most unwelcome place for a prolonged stay, and yet, they were starring at evidence that suggested the Paiute had been here in significant numbers and with the intentions of spending considerable time.

But what had happened? What had happened to the Paiute? Who where these people who had come in here with the helicopter? What were they doing here? It looked like they had come recently but surely they were not here legally. This was National Park land and the park service did not look on kindly towards any alteration of the landscape. Yet, this area was so remote that it would be almost impossible to monitor the area if someone was flying in and out of here during the night.

After considerable time probing and poking around, they realized the day was growing short. Phil and Rob had taken copious photographs of almost everything. They had studied their map and using the GPS unit noted the exact coordinates, as precisely as possible, on a 7.5 minute series topographic map.

To the extent possible, Sti had made notes about what they found. They took nothing. Instead, they inventoried every item they found in the area. They noted its location and the number of items where there were multiples.

Using a fifty-foot piece of nylon cord, the four even tried to take measurements of the location. Included were measurements of the depression and the cave/mine opening. Distances between key items were measured. Also, very careful measurements of the landing site were made. They all knew that although it could be that none of them would return after reporting their findings, the National Park Service authorities would no doubt attempt to investigate by helicopter.

It was about 5 P.M. when they began to think about heading back to camp. Even with the light of a gibbous moon, they did not want to be making their way back in the dark. Although they had brought sufficient clothing and supplies that they could have easily spent the night bivouacked in these environs, it was not something they had really expected to do. That is not expected until Sti raised the question.

"You know, this place is really protected. It looks like it will be a clear, no storm weather night. We could easily stay here. Using these plastic tarps and some of the other items we could have a very comfortable stay. We could even have a small fire using some of the two by fours and four by fours stacked by the landing site. There is even a stove to heat water. Perhaps staying here will give us some additional time to explore."

The discussion on this matter went on for a short time. Of concern was the potential that those with the helicopter could return. However, they all tended to agree that the helicopter people probably left because the four were wandering the area and that was what they had heard from their tents. It is not likely the helicopter will return until the four friends left the area. Finally it was decided that Sti and Ron would stay and Rob and Phil would hike back to camp. Early the next morning, Sti and Ron would make their way back to camp and all four would start the trip out upon their return. Upon agreement, the four split into two parties, and went on about their tasks.

*   *   *   *

It was late, about 8:00 P.M. Sti and Ron had eaten and had made preparations for the night. With no sleeping bags, they had to plan to sit up most of the night, and wrap some of the plastic and other items around them to be comfortable during a night that would get down to freezing. They avoided lighting any of the lanterns they had found. They would avoid lighting a fire until as late as possible. If not needed, they would not build one. The sky was clear and there was not a sound. Unlike earlier in the afternoon when the wind was blowing as it often does, now there was nothing. It was the silence of the high altitude Sierra where on a few nights each summer the weather was very moderate. Everything was ready for the night. Ron was making some last minute preparations while Sti wandered near the edge of what must have been the opening to the mine or cave.

As he climbed about the moon-lit boulders that formed the debris, Sti was moving slowly and quietly while lost in thought as he reflected on the day's experience. Sitting down to look up the draw to where Ron was sitting, Sti listened to the sound of silence. But the background sound was not silence. Somewhere below him was a sound unmistakable to anyone who has spent a night in the Sierra backcountry. It was the sound of water running gently but rapidly over rocks. Sti sat dead still and listened. Then he looked around and stuck his head into several openings between rocks. Like most rock slides, the pile of rocks was thick and on the surface looked to be impenetrable. But sometimes, like a stack of rocks or marbles, the spaces between weave a route that, under certain circumstances, could carry faint sounds, wind, or even smells to someone well removed from their origins below. Trying to not breath and concentrate on listening, Sti was as still as possible as he put his ear in one crack and then another.

Several times he heard the sound. It was definitely the sound of trickling water. "Ron, come here quickly."

Ron looked up. "What is it?"

"Come here and listen. Tell me what you think you hear."

Ron made his way over and climbed carefully up the talus to where Sti was. There was no exchange of words. Ron copied Sti's actions and bent low to listen. It was dead silent, and both tried to control their breathing at this high altitude so as not to create any noise. "What do you hear?" Sti asked anxiously.

"Water! Water is running down hill somewhere deep inside. It is definitely water. It is not very close, but I swear I hear it."

"It is a cave or mine then," said Sti. "Probably a cave. Perhaps a cave formed by water."

"And it is big enough that the sound of water is echoing. That is why we hear it," was Ron's assessment.

After listening a little while longer, Sti got up and scrambled to the highest point above the cave in area. As he looked around it was clear. They were in a small basin. Even in the moon light, this was evident. The entire area they were in sloped up towards Marion Peak and Cirque Crest. But the immediate area for several hundred yards suggested this was a depression within a sloping landscape. This looked to be the lowest point in the basin. All water in this area drained eventually to this point. Did it then go down through this cave? He looked at Ron.

Ron was smiling. "This is a cave that drains water to some other location at a much lower level. I suspect that at one time you could walk into this cave. It must have been large."

"Large enough to house many people and supplies and to be protected from the elements?"

"Perhaps. Perhaps not. But large enough to store things in."

"That's it! This is where the Paiute were headed. This was their fortress or hideout. Or, at least it is part of their effort to stockpile and prepare to wait out an extended conflict."

For both, their thoughts were racing in various directions. It was now growing very late. But their excitement and wild conjectures left little time to think about anything else. With the idea of a large cave now driving their visions, they began a discussion that would eventually end long into the night. The issue of a bivouac became secondary. Their discovery had just opened the window to a large number of possible scenarios. They could not wait to share their finding with the others.

* * * *

Ron and Sti tried to make good time as they headed back to Marion Lake the next morning. However, as agreed, they worked their way back towards the place where June's body had been found. Along the way they repeatedly sited back towards the cave and took occasional photos in that direction. Having started at the crack of dawn, they were able to be at Marion Lake by 10:00 A.M. Rob and Phil had broken camp and all that remained was for Sti and Ron to pack their items before heading back towards Cartridge Pass.

But on arrival, the news that Sti and Ron had to share took precedence. The result was an exciting flurry of speculation. All four knew that as they hiked in silence away from Marion Lake, over the pass and down to the South Fork of the Kings River, they would be lost in reflection about the meaning and importance of what they had seen and heard.

* * * *

As they had planned, the four spent the afternoon and evening probing the Muro Blanco again. It was hard to concentrate on the task because their minds kept telling them that the real story was at the cave on the High Route. But they explored anyway. Outside of evidence of old Paiute camps, which June's journal had already made known to them, they found nothing in the Muro Blanco.

That evening their discussion returned to the cave, or mine, or whatever it was. The same questions and conjectures resurfaced over and over. But the dominate questions were two—what was the purpose of the cave for the Paiute and what were these modern day helicopter explorers doing at the cave?

Sometimes discussions run out of time. Those participating in the discussion find that they are plowing the same old ground. When that happens, usually the discussion is brought to a close. If not, the discussion often decays into silliness and nonsense. But the search for meaning and answers is not always lost when frivolity takes over. Sometimes, after the seriousness is replaced by the absurd or unrealistic, in a discussion, one begins to actually think outside the proverbial box. When this happens, ideas sometimes come to the surface, which are initially dismissed as ridiculous. But with time and reflection these ridiculous ideas become more viable. Such was the case with the discussion this evening.

Thinking back on it at a later date, the four could not remember who exactly raised the question. It is quite possible that it was not as much a question as it was a statement of the ridiculous. What they did agree on was the delayed reaction to the comment. They could not actually remember the precise phrasing. They did, however, remember that Phil had later commented, "Maybe the tunnel to the Muro Blanco is not really such a wild idea."

Could it be possible that the cave that they discovered above actually drained in a southerly direction and into the Muro Blanco? The idea seemed wild beyond belief. But the more they thought about it the more it became in intriguing question. Perhaps, if the two places were connected by a cave, June's focus on both the Muro Blanco and the High Route had some merit.

The entire next day was spent trying to explore the northern side of the canyon. They were looking for evidence of water entering the Kings River from a cave. They aligned their maps to get a fix on where such a cave could be located. They searched for streams that deposited water from the north side. They followed these streams and creeks in search of any evidence that suggested a possible underground source. They found noting. But then, searching here was even more difficult than along the High Route. The dense foliage and ruggedness of the canyon made such exploration exhausting and frustrating. Finally they called it quits.

The following day they made their way up and over Taboose Pass. They had stopped to visit the backcountry ranger who was stationed at June's old site along Lake Marjorie Creek. A note on the information board indicated the ranger would be back the following day. So they moved on towards Taboose Pass to the west.

Chapter 34

Bishop and Discovery

Whiskey Creek Restaurant, Bishop, California

The long hike out had deposited the four at the trailhead for Taboose Pass. It was another five miles down a long and rugged dusty road to U.S. Highway 395. They were exhausted. It was about a half-hour before dark. With the side trip to the backcountry ranger's camp, they had hiked some 20 miles today. First they had to gain some 2000 feet to the pass. Then they descended 6000 feet to the trailhead. The descent was a killer. The first part was a couple of miles of broken stones and talus that was constantly unstable. Then they had to compete with the scorching heat of the valley. Finally, they finished the last mile hiking in the sand. They were glad to get to the trailhead, but this was as far as they were going to go for the day. Retrieving water from the creek, they settled in for a hot night at 5000 feet in the Owens Valley.

The next morning they made the long hike to Highway 395. As luck would have it, not one person drove up or down the dusty road during the five-mile hike. Thus, they got no chance to hitch a ride. However, at the intersection of Taboose Creek road and U.S. 395, they did manage to hitch a ride north to the town of Bishop where they had left the car. After thanking Rob's friend for allowing them to park the car at his place, they checked into the El Rancho Hotel at the south end of town. The four made the obligatory phone calls to family, cleaned up, and then decided to walk to the center of town (about one half mile) for a meal at the most popular restaurant in town, Whiskey Creek.

Seated outside on the Whiskey Creek patio, all four enjoyed the cooling effects of the misters. It was about 100-degrees in downtown Bishop. This was just the usual summer day in Bishop. They were also on their second round of a local beer that Sti and Rob had come to love, Double Nut Brown Ale, brewed in Mammoth Lakes. There was nothing better. Soon they would go into the restaurant and have their first real meal in over a week.

It was Thursday; the city was quiet and not too busy with tourists. Tomorrow the crowds would come and by Saturday night Main Street Bishop (really U.S. 395) would be packed with cars and people like a scene out of American Graffiti. But for now it was quiet, only a few tourists, and the chairs were soft and comfortable as the four sat and watched people.

After their meal, the four would make their way up the road to the White Mountain station of the U.S. Forest Service to report their findings. Bureaucracy being what it was, they decided to eat first. It could be a long afternoon of questions and explanations.

Delivering a third round of beer, the waitress, making conversation asked "Where you boys been?" She knew they were not usual tourists. From her perspective the four were probably backpackers or hang gliders.

Rob, the group's renowned conversationalist with anyone, responded. "Oh we have been in the backcountry for about a week."

"Missed the big crash did you?" she commented.

"What crash?" three asked in an almost uniform tone.

"The helicopter crash up by the Poverty Hills. Article and photos about it in yesterday's Inyo Register." She took their change and moved on.

While the three looked at each other and recalled the helicopter sound they that had heard along with the landing pad that they had seen, Ron got up to go get a copy of the paper.

On return Ron distributed four copies of the newspaper. "Here, we do not have to fight over the paper."

On the front page was a picture of the mangled remains of what was clearly a large helicopter. The headlines told the story, 'Three Men Die in Mysterious Crash.' The article went on to describe how the helicopter, flying late at night in very poor weather had crashed while south-east bound on the extreme western side of the valley. Although the cause of the accident was not known, employees of the Birch Creek Mine west of the Poverty Hills indicated that the helicopter had no lights, sounded like it was experiencing trouble, and then just crashed.

When they got to the scene, the employees found the chopper ablaze with no sign of life. They were able to use portable extinguishers to douse most of the blaze. But it was quickly evident that there were three dead bodies inside the helicopter. The pilot was unknown, as was one of the passengers. The third victim was Richard Renaldo, a one-time resident of Bishop who most recently was living in Southern California. The Renaldo family had at one time been very active in Bishop politics and Richard's father had been a key figure in the earlier days of the Tungsten Mine in Pine Creek.

Sti mumbled "What the …!" as he stared at Rob.

The two then explained to Ron and Phil who Renaldo was and his connection with the Harris family soap opera.

But the story did not end there, the article also commented on the large number of Native American artifacts that were found in and about the crash site. A local representative of the Paiute-Shoshone Cultural Center noted that the articles were very old. Further comments indicated that there had been no known thefts of such artifacts in recent years and the origins of these items were not known.

They read the article thoroughly. But no new startling information, beyond their initial surprise, emerged. For their part, Sti and Rob were stunned. This outing was just one revelation after another. Pieces of the puzzle were literally appearing out of nowhere. They also knew two additional things. First, this afternoon's report to the Forest service would undoubtedly include the county sheriff.

Second, the questions surrounding the deaths of June and her parents were to soon take on more urgency once the authorities were informed about what could be found on the High Route.

The next several days were going to be interesting. They all knew that a good meal, and precautionary telephone calls home were in order. They would not be leaving Bishop as soon as they thought.

Following their meal Sti and Rob called Juan Batista who counseled them on preparation for their visit with the Forest Service and county authorities.

CHAPTER 35

A FINAL MEETING WITH MATTHEW HARRIS

The Harris Residence,
on a warm day with
a clear view of San Francisco Bay

Sti and Rob were staying in San Francisco for several days. They had brought their wives. It was a journey with two purposes. On the one hand, they owed a trip to their wives. On the other, they needed to have a final meeting with Matthew Harris. The two wives had acquiesced to the idea of setting aside an afternoon so that Sti and Rob could meet with Matthew. It had been a month since they returned from their four-person trip to the scene of June's Death.

When Matthew received their call he was clearly anxious to learn the results of their trip. He had not known that they were returning to where his granddaughter's body was found. That they had gone there did not surprise him; he knew that it was probably something they would do. That they wanted to meet with him to share their findings was a surprise. He knew that his new-found friends would not be journeying to the Bay area unless they had important information to share. He also knew the meeting was important because Rob had dictated the date and time of their meeting to Matthew. He also knew it was important because he was aware that his sister's husband, Richard Renaldo, had perished in the helicopter crash in the Poverty Hills.

* * * *

When Sti and Rob arrived they were surprised to find that Matthew was not the only one to be on the receiving end of their comments. Matthew welcomed them into the living room where they encountered another guest, Matthew's sister Susan Renaldo. Although they had never met Susan, Sti and Rob recognized her from the family pictures. Before Harris finished introducing her, Sti and Rob were shaking her hand. They expressing greetings and condolences.

Matthew was nervous. "I invited Susan here when I heard her husband had been killed in a helicopter crash in the Owens Valley. I figured it was time that I mend some very old fences. I have no other family and it is time to bury my pride."

"I hope the two of you do not mind," commented Susan. "I know that we have only had a one sided communication. But after the death of my husband, I realized that I did not really understand what was happening. So I was bold and called Matthew. We had a very pleasant conversation and he filled me in on how the two of you were trying to help him out."

"And later, after Rob called me to set up this meeting, I decided to invite Susan for several days. I can no longer hide anything, and I figured this would be as good a time as any to put all the cards on the table. I hope you do not mind."

Speaking for both, Sti responded. "Of course not; we are only too happy to bring all of this to an end." Of course, Sti was also thinking that the good Dr. Harris, true to his character, could have informed them in advance of his sister's contact and participation in today's meeting. But then, he and Rob had come to expect the unexpected with the Harris family.

Rob added, "Of course you will find that there are a few loose ends that probably will never be known, but I think what we will share is conclusive and compelling. Hopefully, we can bring some closure to this in a way that serves the needs of both of you."

"That's good! That's excellent!" Matthew was clearly eager and excited.

Sti and Rob sensed that this was not the moody, down cast, and cautious Matthew Harris they had interacted with on previous occasions. Matthew seemed up beat. He was glad to have them present. He was also very pleased that his estranged sister was with them.

"First, I cannot forget my manners. Let me get you something to drink. Susan has made some snacks and I have something for you to drink that I know you will like. I fondly remember June's visits when she would bring a jug of Double Nut Brown Ale she would acquire before heading south…."

Another oddity. With Matthew Harris you just never knew what was going to happen next. Sti and Rob showed surprise.

"Oh, I know that look on the part of both of you. Did I say something wrong?"

"No! No!" Sti laughed. "We do not know how you acquired the beer, but it is an excellent choice."

"It is also another odd event in all of this. You see," Rob was moving into his casual conversation mode where he was never at a loss for words, "It is like another connection between the two of us and June. Whenever we are in the Bishop or Mammoth area we seek out the Double Nut Brown Ale. Sti even takes a jug of the brew home with him if he can."

They all laughed. Then Matthew encouraged them to take a seat while he went for the snacks and drinks.

With Matthew out of the room Susan spoke with some trepidation. "I do hope that this does not make the two of you uncomfortable. Really, I do not want to appear to be putting my nose where it does not belong."

"Susan, this is not a problem for us. Sti and I are only too willing to share with you our findings."

Sti commented agreement. "Yes! But I suppose we should begin by expressing how sorry we are for the death of your husband. It was indeed a tragedy. I only hope that our comments are not too painful for you. Rob and I are not professional investigators. We are just two friends who happened to be involved in all of this because of happenstance and our experience and interest in the Eastern Sierra. We have nothing to hide and really hope to end this whole thing with our meeting today. In fact, we are rather glad that we are not paid employees on this matter. It has allowed us to take a more casual approach to looking into multiple tragedies. Were Matthew paying us, I suppose our approach would have been much different."

Rob recognized that Sti was sliding into his lecture approach to things. So he sought to rescue Susan. There would be time later for the didactic approach. "Susan, it is our pleasure to share our observations with you and Matthew. All that we have to share involves the Harris family and you, after all, are really a member of that family and we have nothing but respect for all members of the family."

Matthew had returned. "Sit down, please sit. Here, don't sit on the sofa. These two reclining chairs are much more comfortable." After placing a tray of food and drinks on the coffee table, he opened the door to the patio to let in the cooler air. It was a warm day in the hills, but the bay provided its traditional cooling breeze.

The two guests savored the beer. It was unexpected, but welcome, refreshment. "You know Dr. Harris, whatever we say here today may not always be to your liking. But I assure you, you have excellent taste in beer. Just drinking this has a transforming quality. I can almost see myself sitting beside a campfire at Horton Creek Campground outside of Bishop. I am sipping Double Nut Brown Ale and eating Sierra Nevada Cheleno Peppers. It would be warm, peaceful and the only background noise would be the trickle of Horton Creek. It just does not get any better."

"Give me a break" Rob chuckled.

"You, Rob, as usual are correct. I have forgotten my etiquette. We are here for a purpose. I just find it easy to allow my thoughts to drift."

"Well, I hope we do not have to put up with too much of your drifting thoughts." Rob comment was just another barb in the long running exchange of barbs between the two. "You will forgive us. Age and retirement has allowed erosion of our ability to take all things seriously."

In reality, this kind of exchange had often put others at ease. It allowed others to see Sti and Rob as the good friends they were. In the right setting, it took the edge off a tense or concerned situation. It was their way of managing a difficult situation.

Matthew spoke assurance. "Well, I think I have met with the two of you enough to understand what you are saying. I only wish that I had been able to take a more humorous approach to life at an earlier age. Perhaps I would not be the grumpy person I am today."

"Oh, go on," said Susan. "You are not by nature a grumpy person. I just think events of past years have worn on you."

Speaking apologetically, Matthew responded. "Well, I don't know. I think I have provided heartache to undeserving people. I only hope that I can change that for whatever future is left."

* * * *

After several more minutes of idle conversation, all knew it was time to turn to the task at hand.

"Well, Sti and I have some information to share that will probably take some time. No doubt, you will also have some questions. We need to take care of this business because there are two wives across the Bay who expect us back for a late dinner. We have stood them up before when we were not paying attention to the time. I do not think they would take kindly to us standing them up again. The two of us agreed that Sti would take the honors of starting this conversation." Rob turned to Sti.

Sti and Rob had not expected Susan to be present. They did not expect anyone but Matthew. Without conferring, they both knew it would be necessary to edit some information from their report. There would be no reference to Matthew's earlier experiences in selling artifacts. That was water under the bridge and there would be nothing gained by rehashing that piece in Susan's presence. Both knew that the relationship between these two siblings was already difficult. No need to make the relationship more strained.

"I think the best way to approach this is to back up to the 1800's and consider some history in the Owens Valley."

Sti then shared that the wars between the Paiute and the settlers and soldiers in the 1860's was a history of on and off battles. Sometimes there was peace. At other times hostilities erupted into war. Although the Paiute prevailed from time to time, they knew that over the long haul they could not succeed in repelling the settlers from the valley. After experiencing the devastation to warriors, family and home, the majority of the Paiute were willing to sue for peace to preserve what was left. But it was too late. The soldiers were gathering the Paiute and transporting them south towards Fort Tejon that is located at what is now Tejon Pass on Interstate 5, north and east of Los Angeles.

One Indian, Joaquin Jim, who was not a Paiute, would not concede to peace or removal by the soldiers. He sought to rally a small group of Paiute to continue to carry on the battle in an unconventional way. Joaquin Jim was a rebel, an outlaw Indian as far as the soldiers and settlers were concerned.

In and of itself, Joaquin's actions were not much different than the many other small bands of Native American's who sought to refuse to settle for peace along with the majority of their tribe. In 1863, 200 Paiute fought the soldiers at Big Pine Creek, and then used the creek canyon to withdraw into the upper elevations of the Sierra Crest where the soldiers could not follow. Learning from this experience, Joaquin developed a plan to create cache sites in all the major canyons. These sites would allow the Indians to have access to food and weapons in almost any canyon. They could strike at the settlers and soldiers and quickly make their escape up the canyons and over the passes into the backcountry.

The realization that escape was one of the purposes of the caches was deduced by Matt and his wife. The evidence from the early discoveries by DWP personnel, Matthew and Eaddie, and others supported this hypothesis. But Matt and Kathryn knew that if this was indeed one of the purposes of the sites, there had to be many more sites. Each canyon flanking the eastern slope of the Sierra above the valley was a candidate for one or more sites. Matt and Kathryn found additional sites. But it was June who was most successful at finding sites. She was the consummate wanderer and explorer. And, like her parents, June soon came to the conclusion that the sites served other causes that went well beyond just meeting the needs of Paiute warriors escaping from battle. What this cause or causes were, Matt and Kathryn had only an inkling. June, on the other hand, began to put together a puzzle that suggested a purpose beyond wild imagination.

In her quest to understand the cache sites, June discovered, after reading W.A. Chalfant's *The Story of Inyo*, that the caches were more than just supply depots along trade routes. She also realized that her father knew this to be true as well. But unlike Matt, June was not an anthropologist. This in a way freed her from the conventions of research. She began to realize that some things were better understood by study in unconventional ways. So, she read everything and anything she could get her hand on, even unreliable sources.

June's journals, notes, and maps are filled with references and resources consulted in her quest to unlock the secrets of the caches. And, like her parents before her, June's journals are encrypted. Translating the notes is not an easy task, but it does require some knowledge of the Eastern Sierra and the note taking methods of the Harris family.

In time, June's hypotheses pointed to cache site activity that went well beyond the needs of escaping warriors and trans-Sierra trading between the Paiute and tribes west of the Sierra. The exact purpose was perplexing to Matt and Kathryn. When June inherited the investigation, the perplexing nature of the sites was subjected to her unique way of looking at things and she began to broaden her scope of investigation. Eventually this search took her west of the Sierra Crest and into the heart of the backcountry.

All along, Matt, Kathryn and then June realized the real issue was the gold that had been found in some of the cache sites. This was an elusive piece until June found a brief article in an edition of the Inyo Register in April, 1872. The article mentioned that several Paiute, following the Lone Pine Quake of March 2, 1872, began to purchase food from merchants and farmers throughout the valley. The source of payment—chunks of gold. But why were they purchasing so much? June discovered that in fact the Paiute were purchasing large amounts of flour. She, like her parents, found flour sacks in abundance at the cache sites.

But there was a more significant piece of evidence. Also referencing Chalfant's 1922 history of the valley, June found that soldiers in the late 1860's discovered that two merchants in Auora, a small town on the Eastern shore of the old Owens Lake, were selling large quantities of rifles and handguns to the Paiute. On searching other records, June noted reference to gold being used to purchase the weapons. This made sense. The Paiute did not have anything else to use as purchasing power.

For June, her parents, Matthew and Sti and Rob, the source of the gold remained unknown. But Sti posited speculative information. "All we have is a shred of information in June's journals about the possibility that the gold came from the infamous, and whereabouts unknown, Lost Cement Mine north of Mammoth Lakes and west of U.S. 395." Sti stressed that this was only conjecture, and there was no evidence beyond what June noted. What Sti and Rob did not share was that after arduous work over many hours and days, the two came to the conclusion that some of June's encrypted notes suggested latitude and longitude coordinates that focused on the Pumice Flats area between Mammoth Mountain and June Mountain. Speculation had long focused on this area as the location for the infamous "Lost Cement Mine." Allegedly the site of the mining here commenced in 1858 by a "band of roaming placer miners." Why was the mine site lost? Conflict with local Indians forced the miners to abandon the mine. There is much conjecture that in fact the miners were killed. The existence of the Lost Cement Mine has never been confirmed.

Sti added to the conversation. "You must keep in mind that this issue of the origin of the gold chunks is, on our part, highly speculative. Although the preponderance of the evidence points to the Lost Cement Mine, June's notes contain references to other possible sites such as the Lost Breyfogle Mine and the Lost Gunsight Mine, both in the Panamint Mountains to the south and east of the Owens Valley.

Matthew Harris expressed confusion. He had read June's journals. Sti saw this confusion. "I know Dr. Harris, the information I have just shared with you is not in the journals you have. But bear with us. All will be clearer in a little while."

Rob took over and began to talk about the 1872 earthquake. He noted that later in the discussion the quake would be more important. For now, remember that the quake was severe and impacted the environment well beyond the immediate locale of Lone Pine. Rob illustrated this by noting that John Muir experienced the severity of the quake in Yosemite Valley some 200 plus miles to the north. Also, it is important to note that the gold chunks, in the hands of the Paiute, appeared publicly following the quake.

Rob shared that there was another piece of information that would be important later. With this said, he shared the information from Lillian's diary of the 1935 Sierra Club outing into the area that is now the High Route. Sti produced a map and Rob described the route of the Sierra Club outing. Like the chunks of gold issue, the Sierra Club outing would be more important later in the discussion.

The two then shared with Susan and Matthew a sequence of events involving George Kennicott and subsequently several other of Kennicott's friends. Kennicott had discovered multiple cache sites during the first three decades of the Twentieth Century while working for the L.A. DWP. He did find some gold. He likely became obsessed with finding more gold. Eventually he came to believe that there was a source of gold in one or more canyons. Later still he came to believe that the Paiute had a source or stockpile of gold in the Sierra backcountry. June had stumbled on Kennicott's name at the Eastern California Museum and later when she went to Los Angeles to visit the DWP headquarters in LA. Later, when talking to various self-appointed historians of the valley, she came to realize that Kennicott waged a quiet but forceful campaign to find the gold.

Rob noted that George Kennicott's approach to finding the gold was less than effective, in part because of Kennicott's methods and also because of his personality. "He did not know how to finesse things. Kennicott was a hands-on man. There are stories of how he would get frustrated with his workers and decide to do the job himself. This apparently happened because he was not a good communicator and did a poor job of giving directions. He kept information to himself and shared little with others. This desire to do things himself caused problems with his efforts to keep quiet his search for the gold. Those who knew him were well aware that his constant ramblings in the canyons of the Eastern Sierra slopes had a purpose. But because Kennicott was so secretive about his adventures, he also deprived himself of the opportunity for input from others. Kennicott was also not a researcher; he just wandered indiscriminately. Whatever he found was strictly by chance."

"Later in life, whether from guilt or some other motive, George Kennicott donated several Paiute artifacts he had found to the DWP museum at their Los Angeles headquarters. Eventually some of these artifacts made their way to the Eastern California Museum in Lone Pine. First Matt and then June followed up on this connection and in time viewed the artifacts located at the DWP headquarters. Both came to realize that Kennicott had invaded several cache sites. Some of these sites were eventually located by Matt and his daughter. It is quite possible that some of the sites Kennicott found have yet to be found by anyone conducting legitimate research."

"As Kennicott got older, his son, Edward, took up the cause. Along with friends, the younger Kennicott, began to press the search. He even hired packers to take him and friends into the backcountry in search of the gold. For several years he followed several leads, but all to no avail."

"Then, during one of his trips, Edward Kennicott learned from a packer that the packer had a friend who had been on the 1935 Sierra Club outing. During the outing a mule was lost in an area between Marion Lake and Windy Ridge on what we today would call a section of the Sierra High Route. The packer alleged that during the search for the mule, two Indians were spotted. When they tried to find the Indians, they disappeared in very rugged terrain. To Kennicott this was strange. He found the packer who was elderly and not able to provide any details except to confirm that they had seen Indians. Convinced that the two Indians must have been Paiutes, Kennicott set out to explore the area. Whatever happened as a result of Edward's search is not clear. However, it is evident that Edward's focus on the High Route area was a portent of things to come. As we shall see, the Kennicott connection with the High Route did not end with Edward."

Sti picked up the dialogue at this point. "June had learned about the Paiutes in the High Route area theory when, as a ranger for the National Park Service, she heard stories about the Sierra Club outing. No one since had ever taken stock into this area. On reading the *Sierra Club Base Camp, 1935*, a sort of scrapbook and compellation of vignettes about the outing, June discovered reference to Lillian Hamner who had kept a diary of the experience."

Sti continued. "June tracked down members of the Hamner family and eventually talked to Lillian's niece, a Mrs. Laport. June was able to read the diary. She also visited the Sierra Club headquarters and went through their collection of artifacts from the trip. She recognized among the items some leather products that were Paiute in origin. The Sierra Club curator did not realize that the items were Paiute. He just thought they were leather items related to the mule that ran away. Apparently June did not enlighten the curator. She kept the information to herself, but did note her discovery in her journal."

Rob interjected a point. "I too visited the Sierra Club collection. Had I not known that some of the artifacts were probably of Paiute origin, I would have drawn the same conclusion as that of the curator."

Sti went on. "From what we now know, it appears that, in fact, there very well could have been Paiute in the High Route area in 1935. If that is true it is likely that these Paiute were part of a small band living outside the conventions of the larger tribal groups living in the Owens Valley at that time. Whether they were descendents of those who accompanied Joaquin Jim, or whether they were part of a band that sought to live separately from their Paiute brothers in the valley is not known. We may never know. What is apparent is that the presence of the Paiute on the High Route in 1935 is a link between the events of the 1860's and 70's and the events surrounding the work and perhaps deaths of Matt, Kathryn and June."

Susan and Matthew displayed looks of incredulity. Sti and Rob knew what was going through their minds. The story they were hearing sounded like a novel. But the reality of the truth overwhelmed them. No doubt each harbored many questions to be asked. But they would not ask them. Each knew that most would probably be answered as Sti and Rob continued. So they sat with rapt attention, nodding occasionally, and reflecting their reactions on their faces.

Rob continued. "The more June probed all the leads she found, the more convinced she was that the Paiute were doing more than just trading across the Sierra when they created the caches and ventured into the region of the High Route."

"With each piece of the puzzle that was added to her knowledge, June seemed to be energized to do even more exploring. She visited every known cache site on multiple occasions. She also discovered several more sites. Her expertise was unrivaled. But all of this exploration and acquisition of knowledge came to the attention of others. June realized that she was being shadowed."

Rob went on to point out that during the last several years of her life June's journals reflect an increasing concern for the future of Paiute artifacts as well as the future of her safety. "For June this was a dilemma. She was well aware that increased research would only stimulate more exploration on her part. Exploration was visible and would only draw increased attention. Also, the more she researched and explored the more answers she found. June knew that all of this increased her liability. She also knew that more research and exploration required continued and more sensitive documentation in her journals. June had to deal with her safety and the security of her journal entries. Her response to this dilemma was to enhance the way she coded information into her journals.

"Susan, this may all sound strange to you, but I assure you Dr. Harris understands." Harris nodded and mumbled agreement. "Diligent field researchers write everything down. And, like most in their line of work, they worry about others who would infringe on or even steal their information. So, they develop personal codes. The codes allow their information to be encrypted. Interestingly, coding often allows information to be entered in a more abbreviated form. So, you see, this is a common practice. Only in June's case she was increasing the complexity of her code with the acquisition of increasingly sensitive information.

"I know Sti agrees; June's coding became very complex and in some instances we never did actually manage to translate everything. Our methods, of course, lack code breaking expertise. However, in describing how we went about trying to understand June's journals I would describe it as a process similar to solving a crossword puzzle. Translating some information allowed us to guess at the meaning of related entries."

"What Rob is really saying," Sti continued, "is that we were able to decode pieces and then, because of our familiarity with the Eastern Sierra and our access to other resources, we were able to speculate with some degree of accuracy, on the pieces in between. I think it worked. It was frustrating at times and there are still some pieces that we can only conjecture about. I think you can sense when this is the case as we go through our discussion today."

Rob continued to take Susan and Matthew through the history of events by turning their attention to Henry Kubota. He did so without violating Henry's desire for anonymity. "Sometime in the 1990's June made contact with an elderly gentleman of Japanese American descent, who shall remain nameless."

Matthew Harris looked concerned and Rob responded. "Dr. Harris, we can not share the name with you and I can assure you that the name is of no consequence to you or Susan. You will have to trust us on this matter. It is something we will not discuss further than the information provided here.

"Although June never met him, they talked several times by phone and letter. Often they communicated through an attorney." Rob went on to describe Henry's experiences while living at Manzanar, and the donation of Paiute artifacts after the war without referencing his name. He also explained that Henry had been an acquaintance of Matt's. Henry was a man with great integrity. He was deeply concerned about the welfare of the Paiute heritage. He had also been concerned about the welfare of Matt and Kathryn. Henry's investigations indicated that Matt's life was in danger because his research threatened a group of people who were looking for the Paiute gold. They were already searching in the High Route area and in the Muro Blanco. These same people had, sometime before and after World War II, found some of the cache sites. They had absconded with some of the artifacts. They did not want Matt to find out what they were doing and then blow the whistle.

Sti and Rob, without using the names of their subjects, went on to explain that they had never clearly understood the source of Henry Kubota's knowledge about Matt, Kathryn and later June. However, there was good reason to believe that through his good friend Tom Littlebear, (again an anonymous reference) and later Tom's nephew John, Henry had eyes and ears in the valley that went well beyond the normal sources of information when it came to matters involving the disposition of Paiute artifacts, research related to Paiute culture, and especially the search for the Paiute chunks of gold.

Sti and Rob also noted that another mystery was whether or not Matt and Kathryn knew the actual identification of the younger Kennicott. It is not clear whether Henry even knew the actual names. But there was no doubt that Matt, Kathryn, and June knew that someone or some small group of people were pushing hard to find more artifacts. They also knew that the gold was probably a major objective of their search.

As carefully as possible, Rob explained that he and Sti had visited the anonymous Henry's daughter. They explained that Henry's daughter provided information about the relationship between Henry and June. During the course of this part of their report, Sti and Rob were careful not to tell Susan or Matthew about Henry's donations of large sums of money to the museum. Nor did they explain the whereabouts of Matt's final journal. This was a matter to be dealt with later. Perhaps it could be dealt with through the auspices of the new Manzanar National Historical Monument officials. This was also a matter best left in the hands of Batista. It would be a legal issue for sure.

Sti explained that June eventually met a Paiute who had been observing her ramblings for some time. Again, Sti used an anonymous reference for John Littlebear. "June found this individual to be a very mild mannered person whose tendency is to always spend time reflecting before talking. He is very bright and mature beyond years. His knowledge of the valley history and especially the history of his people is extensive. His knowledge of what June was up to startled her initially. He also warned her that she was being watched and needed to be very careful. Based on this experience, and June's increasing awareness that others were actually following her in her explorations, June made some important decisions to protect her knowledge. She began to keep what we have come to call a 'parallel journal.' In this duplicate or parallel journal she recorded much of the information in her regular journal plus very sensitive information she did not want in the hands of others. It was June's theory that should something happen and her regular journal fell into the wrong hands, sensitive information would not be available to these others. Also, since they would find themselves with a journal that did not reveal any sensitive information, they could do little harm. The key for June was to keep the duplicate journal with the sensitive information secluded in such a way that it could not fall into hostile possession."

Matthew Harris could not contain his concern. He felt pained that June had not sent the duplicate journal to him for safe keeping. "But why not send me the journal along with her other items? I don't understand." Sti and Rob did not respond immediately. They let Matthew think about his own question. "Oh, now that I think about it, I understand. June did not want me to be in harm's way. If these people who were following her should try to break into my house again they might find this duplicate journal."

Sti and Rob knew that Harris had answered only half of his own question. Although they were not going to reveal as much to Susan, they also knew that Harris would eventually realize that the real reason June had not sent the duplicate journal to her grandfather was because she was knowledgeable about how her grandfather had many years earlier sold artifacts to representatives of the Kennicott clan. June had been smart enough to know that those who were following her were probably related or affiliated with the Kennicott family and if they had to they would again go to Harris.

After a few moments, Sti continued. "Yes, Dr. Harris, your granddaughter was protecting you. But we will come back to this matter of the duplicate journal in a moment. What is important to remember is that during this time that June was developing the duplicate journal she was posted near Bench Lake in the Kings Canyon National Park. June had relatively easy access to Taboose canyon, Muro Blanco and the High Route area. Over time she came to know these areas better than anyone ever has. More and more she focused her attention on these areas. The duplicate journal began to accumulate key pieces of information about her findings and projections."

Sti and Rob explained that under the conditions of confidentiality they had been given a photocopy of June's duplicate journal. Only after a difficult time decoding much of the journal did the picture begin to become clear to them. In her explorations, June had discovered evidence that someone else was exploring the High Route area. Sti and Rob went on to explain June's second to last trip to the High Route.

It then became evident in their tone and parsimonious explanation that Sti and Rob were starting to describe what happened to June during her final month or two. They explained that she had made several trips to the High Route over many years. However, a month or two before her death she explored the High Route as she had not done before. It was on this outing that she found signs that confirmed that the Paiute had been in the area in the Twentieth Century. She also found artifacts that suggested others were interested in the area and their interests were not in the interest or welfare of Paiute heritage. Sti explained that June found a Paiute moccasin. This prompted her to continue her exploration with close attention to anything that shed light on what she had found. Her continued search in the area of the High Route eventually brought her to a flat rock where several other artifacts were part of a pile of items. This was the turning point in June's exploration. She knew that she had stumbled onto something. How big it was she did not know. But she also soon realized that what she had discovered had put her into a delicate position. Should others know of her discovery her life could be in great danger.

Sti proceeded cautiously. "Later, when June found a collection of items while searching the High Route, including the other half of a pair of Paiute moccasins or shoes, she knew something was wrong. However, it was not until a day or two later, after she had returned to her Bench Lake camp, that she realized that in her haste she may not have accurately recorded all of her findings. This was evident in her journal."

Sti went on to describe what he and Rob had found in the parallel journal. June also realized that there had to be additional evidence. June realized the significance of signs suggesting someone had been more recently in the area where she had found the artifacts. At the time fear had taken hold of her, but she could not get out of her head the memory of the artifacts grouped together in a way suggesting someone had deliberately collected and weighted the items down with a small rock as if they intended to return for them. More importantly, June realized that the two lines she had noticed could only have come from one source, a helicopter. She realized that she had seen those lines before when a chopper on an emergency rescue in the backcountry set down in sand, grass, or on rock it left parallel lines when it took off. She had to return to the area and explore at greater length. To do this she would clearly be putting her life in jeopardy. As she began to plan a return trip, June took precautions to ensure that if something happened to her, what she knew would not fall into the wrong hands. Fearing for her grandfather's welfare and mindful that someone had once broken into the house and ransacked Matt's materials, June chose to send the regular journal to her grandfather and the duplicate, more sensitive journal, to someone she knew would guarantee its safe keeping. Someone who was also out of harms way.

There was a long pause. The atmosphere in the Harris residence was dead silent. Susan would not speak. She knew that all of this was like a flood of bittersweet information for Matthew. For his part, Matthew simply nodded understanding and repeated several times "I see."

Carefully breaking the silence, Rob picked up the story. "When Sti and I returned to the High Route along with Sti's brother Ron and his cousin Phil, we had the benefit of June's duplicate journal information."

Rob and Sti together explained the events of their return to the High Route. They explained how they returned to the location where they had found June's body. They went on to describe the journey that led to their discovery of the cave and the nearby helicopter-landing site.

Rob did not want to leave any questions about the condition of what they found on the High Route. "The weather we encountered was wet and cold. We spent two days searching down slope from the site of June's death. It was only by chance that we eventually found the cave site. What we found was the entrance to a large cave. At the time we did not know whether it was a cave or a mine. However, from prolonged observation and recent information from a Park Service geologist, we now know that at one time there was probably a cave entrance. It was probably a small entrance. Later, reading Rob Moor's book, *Exploring the Highest Sierra*, we learned that there are certain geological phenomena in several regions of the Sierra that make the presence of what are called by geologists 'pendant caves' a reality. I know Dr. Harris that you are probably familiar with such conditions and with such cave sites as Boyden, and many others in the Kings Canyon, Mineral King, and Sequoia areas. Apparently the one in the High Route area is an anomaly, but one on a grand scale.

"The cave we found appears to be one that was also found at some distant time in the past by the Owens Valley Paiute. How long they had known about the site is not clear. However, the evidence we and others found suggest that the Paiute were using the cave during the 1860's and 1870's. Conjecture on the part of Park Service geologists is that the cave entrance was once very small and over some time the Paiute had tried to enlarge it. This activity may in fact have weakened the roof of the entrance. When the Lone Pine quake of 1872 hit, the quake effect was to collapse much of the entrance into rock rubble of great extent."

Sti continued. "Based on June's documentation, preliminary findings by Park Service officials, and our meager speculation, the High Route cave site had a complementary entrance, probably somewhere in the Muro Blanco. Since there is no evidence of such an entrance, we can only speculate that it lies buried below tons of talus deposited by the 1872 quake or events since.

"However, regardless, it appears that the Paiute, probably under the leadership of Joaquin Jim, established a repository of goods, weapons, and quite possibly gold in the cave. In essence, the cave was intended by these Paiute to be a shelter or haven where they could go and survive for considerable time in the face of hostilities. June's word for this cave was 'redoubt.' It was a fortress."

"Clearly, others had found the site well before June came wandering into the area in search of it. Exactly how and when we do not know. We do know, however, and this was noted earlier, Edward Kennicott explored the area. We also know, or at least we think we know, that the Paiute continued in this area into the Twentieth Century and were here in 1935. It remains a mystery whether they were ever successful in reentering the cave after the 1872 quake. From the looks of the rubble it is doubtful."

Rob interjected the necessary reference. "I am sure your thoughts at this time are the same as ours have been. No doubt those interested in the cave were really interested in the possibility of finding gold there. It is likely, although we shall never know, that June realized this as well."

And then the moment came where Sti and Rob had to speculate on the cause of June's death.

Sti started the explanation. "After putting everything in place, June headed to the High Route area she had visited a couple of weeks earlier. As she was doing so, the weather was changing rapidly. The barometer was dropping. A major storm was closing in. June had been in similar situations many times. One wonders why she left with a storm approaching. The only answer is that it was late in the year and should an early storm drop a significant amount of snow access to the High Route would have to wait until the next summer. June was caught between the excitement of the moment and the reality of objective danger. She was prepared. But she could not know what lay ahead."

Rob took over. "When she arrived at the site of her previous visit she probably began to search where she had left off. Her parallel journal indicates that she intended to return to the coordinates of this site. Given her past practice, she would go from there. It would appear that she was prepared to camp in the area. She had everything with her and had left nothing at Marion Lake. At some point in time, and probably when it was snowing and blowing hard, June stumbled across the cave and helicopter-landing pad. Who knows whether the helicopter was present. If there was a helicopter, then there were probably at least two or three of them. If there was no helicopter, and if the weather was not good, it is quite possible that June did not immediately encounter anyone. If the site was like we found it, the area was strewn with material and June would not likely detect that there was a tent or some small living quarters in a draw sheltered from the wind. Throughout her exploration June had been collecting pieces of evidence that she had placed in a small pack. Although startled at what she saw, June probably decided to collect some pieces of evidence. She took off her pack, and began collecting items. At some point in time someone sitting out the storm realized June's presence. Seeing June he or they confronted or went after her. Who knows what happened? At some point June probably fled for her life. Somewhere along the very long and arduous route between the cave and where she finally expired, several things could have happened. She could have dropped her ice axe which was picked up and used against her. Or, she could have been injured in some other way. There could have been a physical struggle. All of this we will probably never know. Finally, whether it was exposure or whether she was hit with the ice axe, June died trying to save her own life. In any event, having suddenly discovered the cave site after hiking, June was probably only in her shorts and light jacket she was wearing at the time. Fleeing under duress, she left her pack and other possessions behind. The weather was declining rapidly and at that elevation, she could not have survived long in such light dress. This would have been especially true if she was wounded. There are all kinds of possible explanations about what really happened. We will probably never know the truth."

Sti explained that at the time of their visit he, Rob, Phil and Ron had not noticed that one of the weathered packs at the cave site was really June's. Only later did they learn that June must have fled the cave site without any of her possessions other than the windbreaker she was wearing, maybe a small collecting sack, and probably the ice axe.

It was Rob's turn now. "As you know, it was only after we had returned to Bishop that we learned about the helicopter crash that killed your husband Susan. Apparently the pilot remains unknown. But we recently heard that the third victim was the great grandson of George Kennicott. However, among the many Paiute artifacts thrown from the helicopter, when it crashed, was a large Paiute basket that contained many of June's possessions—a down parka, wind pants, sleeping bag and pad, and a tent. In addition, there were other personal items and pieces of her clothing. To our knowledge, there was no note book or journal among these items. Given June's concern, it could well be that she had decided to take no notes. There were several blank pages remaining in the duplicate journal, which was the last one used before she took her final trip. Sti and I believe that June went to her death alone. We believe she may have been hit with the ice axe. But we also believe, given her strength as a hiker and conditioning, that she had managed to avoid the perpetrators at least for some period of time. It is likely that she may not have been hit and just had an accident. We will never know. But the records from several sources suggest it was whiteout weather at the time. It was bitter cold. Dressed as she was, June could not have survived. Without her gear, she was doomed to die of exposure."

Sti and Rob paused. Matthew Harris looked sad and just nodded. Susan patted his knee. The issue of murder had not been resolved. The issue of possible conflict that could have precipitated June's death had been resolved.

"Susan, your husband's role in all of this is not certain." Sti was speaking. "However, it appears that for some time he had been an associate of the youngest Kennicott. Both Kennicott and your husband had relatives who had earlier been involved in locating Paiute artifacts and stealing them and selling them. Given indications from those knowledgeable about the helicopter in which they were killed, the flights into the backcountry had been going on for years, usually under the cover of night. While it is probably true that your husband was not a passenger on all of these flights. It is apparent he was deeply involved in an effort to dig out the cave in debris that had blocked the entrance to the cave."

Susan had cried much in the last month. She was beyond tears now. She just sat, sad, confused, and resigned to complications beyond here understanding.

"It also appears that Rob and I were being watched. Perhaps we were lucky in part because there were four in our party. In any event, when it was evident we were going back to the High Route, your husband and the others were concerned that we would find the remains of June's belongings if we found the cave. They flew in and removed these and much of the Paiute artifacts as well as any other items they thought could be subsequently used to identify them."

Rob again. "We spent considerable time talking with representatives of the Inyo Sheriff's department, the National Forest Service, FAA, and the National Park Service. In subsequent conversations with the Park Service geologist, we have learned several things. Apparently the cave site was most likely large and accessible in the 1800's, but the Lone Pine quake of 1872 caused a massive cave in. It is most likely that the cave carried water from the High Route area; and it is also possible it carried that water as far as the Muro Blanco. However, we will probably never know because the evidence indicates that the quake damage in the region was very extensive. It is not likely, even if the debris were removed, that the cave could be explored. There is reason to believe that for the Paiute, the cave in the 1860's was much more navigable and perhaps the Paiute saw it as providing a redoubt that was accessible at both the high elevation and at the lower elevation of the Muro Blanco. Entrance from the Muro Blanco, if it existed, would have made for easy access compared with the High Route area."

"It is likely that your husband and the others, and maybe others before them, considered the cave to be the origin or storage place of the gold. Perhaps they felt that if they could remove the debris for several yards they could access the cave and the gold. According to the geologist, this is not likely. The internal damage is extensive, probably extending throughout much of the length of the cave. Water can still run through it, but passage of humans is not likely. Also, it is not likely that the cave was the source of the gold. It probably came from another location and was stored in the cave." Sti thought for a few seconds. "Susan, we doubt that your husband ever made any real money out of this adventure. It would appear that earlier generations of Kennicott and Renaldo found what little gold there was in the caches they discovered. But we can take some satisfaction in the fact that they did not discover all of the sites. June discovered several that were not subsequently visited by others. That information is in her duplicate journal. For our part, we have destroyed our photocopy of the journal. We did however turn over the site location information to three people—a curator at the Eastern Sierra Museum, an Eastern Sierra anthropologist from UCLA named Batista, and an anthropologist from Cal Berkeley who is part of the Krober Institute. Each knows of the other being informed and all three were asked to work together in exploring and analyzing the sites. A source of funding to support this research has been confirmed by an anonymous donor."

Looking at Matthew Harris, Rob commented. "Dr. Harris, your granddaughter was the consummate explorer. Like many that have gone before her, she was focused, thorough in her research, and completely ethical. She wanted nothing for herself. Her purpose was to find out first who killed her parents. Second, she wanted to know the real purpose of the cache sites. She found the answer to the second question. We do not ever think she knew who actually murdered her parents, or, for that mater, June herself. It now appears that the helicopter crash brings an end to the chain of greed that perpetrated the killings and the destruction of priceless Paiute artifacts. We can, however, hope that the long line of thorough and compelling research conducted first by you and Eaddie, then by Matt and Kathryn, and finally by June, will go forward in the hands of three noted and contemporary scholars."

Finally, a closing comment by Sti. "As for the gold, which seemed to foster much of the tragedy experienced by both of you, it is not likely that we will ever know the actual source. If there is a stockpile, we do not think it will be located. June's research and travels were, if nothing else, exhaustive. It is hard to imagine that anyone else will ever spend as much time in as thorough a way exploring the Sierra East escarpment canyons of the Owens Valley. June was one of a kind. But, after all, she was a Harris, and the Harris scientist is among the best. You, Dr. Harris, can be very proud of your granddaughter."

As an after thought, Rob addressed the duplicate journal. "As for the journal that June sent to the man from Manzanar, we think it best that it is in the hands of an excellent attorney. As noted before, we have destroyed our photocopy. We can assure you, the attorney will make it available to the three researchers. However, there is other sensitive information in the journal. It is not information about either of you, but there is information about people you do not know. Left in the hands of the attorney we have every reason to believe this information will be sequestered and will not result in problems."

That was it. Sti and Rob sat quietly. For several seconds no one spoke. Then Matthew knew that it was his turn.

* * * *

An hour later, as Sti and Rob were driving back toward the city, they felt comfortable with the outcome. Matthew Harris was no longer dogged by guilt. He could now take pride in the accomplishments of his offspring and granddaughter. He would always live with the haunting memory of his own transgressions. But now he could hold on to the knowledge that his granddaughter had really acted in the best interest of the Paiute Indians. Her actions brought an end to a long history of Paiute artifact abuse. Dr. Matthew Harris was an elderly man with only a few years ahead of him. Hopefully he can enjoy them without the haunting past.

They also knew that research in the Owens Valley would continue. Jill Kubota and Juan Antonio Batista would see to that. Three researchers were about to be the recipients of support that would move their research beyond current limitations. One recipient, Batista's niece, would receive support without ever knowing that it originated from her uncle's best friend. As for the Eastern Sierra Museum, it was assured of ongoing support that would take its work well into the future. And the Krober Institute, with the financial support it was about to receive, the institute would be positioned to play a major role in promoting the history, heritage, and culture of the Owens Valley Paiute.

It was a good life. The two did not talk much about their experience as they made their way to the rendezvous with their wives. They had years ahead to reflect on all of this. No doubt they would check in on things periodically in their quiet and subtle ways.

But as they drove west across the San Francisco—Oakland Bay Bridge, Sti mumbled with a note of humor. "You know Rob, in another life I could get into this investigative line of work."

Rob comment was the usual sarcasm that the situation demanded. "Well you might get into it, but at the pace you work in solving problems, if this experience is any indication, you won't get rich. As a result, in another life, you may not find retirement to be so exciting."

They both laughed and drove on towards the setting of the sun behind the skyline of San Francisco.

CHAPTER 36

TWO LETTERS

On the same day,
at the residences of Sti and Rob

It was probably just coincidence that both letters arrived on the same day at the home of each. But like so much related to the Harris case, strange occurrences were not unexpected. Several weeks after meeting with Matthew Harris and his sister Susan Renaldo, both Sti and Rob received two letters. One letter was from Jill Kubota. Her letter sought to bring closure and it was precisely what they would have expected from Jill—a kind, informative, and intriguing communication. The letter from Matthew Harris was far more than a thank you. It revealed shocking information that Matthew had not shared with either Sti or Rob. In this instance, they understood why, and they were not upset.

* * * *

Dear Dr. Pierce and Mr. James:

Let me begin by thanking you both for your friendship. In an age when it is difficult to judge the merits of others, the two of you are refreshing personalities.

Before going too far, I must confess that it always seems awkward to have investigated someone's background before meeting him or her. And yet, in the case of both of you, everything the background check revealed was true. You are both people of integrity. It is easy to see why you get along with others and with each other.

Also, I thank you for the letter summarizing your 'investigation' of matters related to the death of June Harris. I use the word investigation, even if the two of you avoid it, because in fact that is what you did. I also understand why you did not use the word. Your approach was always above board and completely ethical. I am not surprised that in the end you managed to resolve the issues without creating conflict with anyone. That is a credit to your skill as well as your personality.

I am confident all will work out satisfactorily from this point forward. Your suggestions for distribution of information regarding the cache sites found by June have been implemented. Also funds been channeled to support the work of the three people the four of us agreed upon. Both Juan Antonio and I were pleased with your suggestion to anonymously support the work of his niece. In her own right, and at the exclusion of any knowledge about the interests of her uncle, she has worked hard to be an effective researcher. The Krober Institute will do much to promote education regarding the Paiute. And, of course, the Eastern Sierra Museum will be able to expand its work on the history, heritage, and culture of the Paiute.

In the end, I think we are well positioned to ensure that the work of my father, Matt, Kathryn, and June is continued. Many thanks and much appreciation goes to what you have done. As you requested, your names will also remain anonymous as we move forward in supporting the agreed to projects.

As for Matt's last journal, well you need to know that with the help of John Littlebear, Juan Antonio was able to retrieve the journal without creating any problems. Juan Antonio's research suggested that a legal approach to retrieval would take many years, and in the end the journal could fall into the wrong hands. For now, the journal is sealed in special wrapping and is in my safety deposit box. In my will there are specific instructions that should something happen to me, the journal is to be given to the two of you. In the event that neither of you is alive, it is to be forwarded to the then current curator of Paiute artifacts at the Eastern Sierra Museum as well as to the Krober Institute. I have taken the liberty to make those arrangements on the assumption that such arrangements are acceptable to the both of you. I am confident you will agree with these arrangements.

You both have my respect and confidence. If ever I can be of assistance, please contact me. I am sure we will talk again. Until then, go in peace.

Respectfully,

Jill Kubota

*　*　*　*

The letter from Matthew was equally informative, but much shorter.

Dear Sti and Rob;

Again, thanks for all that you have done to make my life better.

Susan and I have been making significant progress in renewing our sibling relationship. I was so wrong to have shut her out all those years. I have the two of you to thank for making restoration possible.

I must confess, however, there is another reason for writing. I was not able to share something with you when you were here. It is something I did not want Susan to hear at the time. In due course, I of course will tell her. I fear she has experienced enough tragedy and to pile on another item would be too much.

One of my reasons for contacting you when I did was that I had just been informed by my doctors that I was suffering from a rare and ultimately fatal disease. I won't go into details because they are not necessary. Let's just say I hope to live at least another year or two. I hope in that time that I can heal some of the wounds between Susan and me.

I know you are probably wondering why I never told you about my health. But I think you will agree that in this instance, unlike some of the other instances where I did not tell you everything, my illness really was not important. Also, and this was important, I did not want you acting in haste because you thought you needed closure before I died.

I have friends and I now have family. Your friendship I count among my best. I thank you again and reiterate my commitment to providing whatever services I can give upon your request.

Your friend sincerely,

Matthew Harris, Ph.D.

* * * *

As they read the two letters in the confines of their separate homes a thousand miles apart, Sti and Rob had independent, but similar thoughts. The Harris case was ever perplexing. At every stage along the way, there was a mystery. Just when they thought they understood something, a new conundrum emerged. And now, when everything seemed to be at closure, there was a nagging thought. 'Somewhere out there is another piece of the puzzle.' There is a journal. Without consulting each other Sti and Rob each knew the other was having the same quizzical reaction. 'Is this case really closed?'

978-0-595-42874-8
0-595-42874-6

www.ingramcontent.com/pod-product-compliance
Ingram Content Group UK Ltd.
Pitfield, Milton Keynes, MK11 3LW, UK
UKHW041949190726
13854UKWH00004B/1866

9 780595 428748